SUICIDE NOTES TO KURT COBAIN

(a memoir of sorts)

By

Gunner A. Bush

Edited by Kayla Bush

DEDICATED TO
MY FAMILY

And the memory of Darrell "Scottie" Harris, the world is quieter now that you are gone, but we all miss you.

PART I FEAR AND LOATHING

"It was all a dream…"

- Biggie Smalls

Certain names have been changed to protect the guilty and innocent and myself from the guilty and innocent.

CHAPTER 1

I was on assignment for *Rolling Stone Magazine* when I stepped in bubblegum. A fresh, pink piece that only seconds before was in the disease-ridden mouth of a malicious adolescent. I glanced around to find the prepubescent savage, but it could have been anyone. Luckily, the culprit gave it away by singing.

"Too much bubblegum, my shoe got stuck!"

Standing in front of me was a filthy child, likely sickened from something—at the very least, a small cold that I would catch if I touched this spewed candy with my bare hands. Children are vectors for diseases. That's not ageism, it's a fact; I was once a child myself. This girl sang the line again, out of tune. I didn't have time for this. I pulled out my special water bottle and took a hard, deep drink of the clear stuff, figuring it had to be five o'clock somewhere.

This child's mother was behind her, taking a pic for the Gram. She was a cunt. I have a sixth sense about these types of things. I turned her child around so she wouldn't walk into her own death on Independence Avenue, and proceeded to continue dragging my loafer across the sidewalk.

That's exactly where we were as a country, back on the first day of October in 2016. Not to get all philosophical, but a democracy gets the leader it deserves, and the hoi polloi was made up of people out for them. Sure, I get it—we all want instant gratification without putting in the work. We don't even want the escalator to success; no, we demand the microwave version that comes with a large fry and bigger soda. If we were in ancient Rome, Nero would be getting ready to fiddle. Personally, at the time, I blamed the Kardashians, but this started long before those inflatables came to be. The self-proclaimed greatest country on the planet was heading toward a lost cause. That's what happens when enough bad guys rise to the top of capitalist democracy.

When propaganda is the true maker of kings—combined with a mass plan to under-educate the youth—children are raised to believe that everyone deserves a trophy, and they want to be famous for no fucking reason with no talent. Narcissism is the name of the disease, and it's not the missing healthcare missing the diagnoses. It's been here for generations. Since the 80s, a guy like Trump could prosper on greed. So instead of creating a utopian society where humanity is jointly focused on getting better and smarter so we can figure out how to get robots to do everything while we live in peace and harmony, we are still fighting imaginary lines over things like the right to own an AK Chopper or determining the rights of unborn babies, which was decided in the goddamn 70s!

Yep, 2016 feels like a score ago now. We were still trying to climb out of the freaking Alan Greenspan debacle, and the two political choices felt staged. It was as if both had been planted by the other to screw up so they could win. They were laughable: a TV game show host who made his money in construction (but would get jumped if he went to a construction site), pitted against a former first lady married to a philanderer president.

The entire country was ready to get voting over with; but instead, we were less than 40 days out and dragging the election like a piece of bubblegum stuck to the bottom of our shoe.

I didn't have the fucking time for it.

As I was saying, I was on assignment right then for *Rolling Stone Magazine.* My shirt was sticking to my back from the humidity, and I was sweating. Global warming or sumshit. I did the forward moonwalk enough to rid myself of the gum, and I moved along while singing:

"Too much bubblegum, YOUR shoe got stuck."

Damnit, now the song was stuck in my head!

I was on my way to a rendezvous for information that might be detrimental to one of the two presidential candidates—either the former first lady, or the yuppie construction worker. I didn't know which yet, and the race between these two so far had made mudslinging look clean. It had been filthy with sleaze, and it was only the first of October. The final weeks were preparing to be the ugliest America had seen this century. Each day brought a news cycle and a chance to stain whichever candidate's reputation. The bar was being moved lower daily. Just when we collectively thought we were in the basement, we heard a knock on the floor below.

I wasn't quite sure on the legal aspects, but I did figure I was tiptoeing on the right side of Johnny Law. Ignorance of the law is no excuse, but this was a thin line and ignorance is bliss. Not that I cared if it was against the law. Getting dirt on another political candidate is an intrinsic part of America; we wouldn't protect the Kennedy's any longer. Gary Hart had shown the way.

Besides, I grew up Catholic, so my whole basis of life as a child was do whatever you want, and then go be sorry for your sins while saying the assigned riddles.

So, I was getting the dirt either way.

This had to be my big break; I had been hired by *Rolling Stone* to work through November, but hadn't yet been published. And it's not from lack of trying! I had been submitting my pieces weekly, but my editor Terry was never satisfied or very helpful. My last piece had been great, in my personal opinion, but was rejected without a word. It was on the new rhetoric I was hearing across the country:

"Donald Trump is going to save America!"

It was a simple catchphrase, but I was hearing it from sea to shining sea. I was also coming into contact with a new political person: cricket eaters who were known to the pollsters as a new wave of the silent majority. They were mostly white folk, disenfranchised by something, but the propaganda was primarily responsible for their tendency to project this sentiment. Most had never voted or cared about politics, but they weren't fucking silent. These newly found good-old-boys and girls wouldn't shut up about Trump and were all parrots for this new terminology. It was alarming and Orwellian, if that's not the same thing.

Donald Trump will save the country, and nobody ever gave me a how or a why. I noticed the trend, but nobody else did. The pollsters, who I still hadn't met, were clueless, and the media was a joke, still thinking that making fun of Trump wasn't giving him free airtime. Trump was getting more looks every day than OJ got for the high-speed chase. I put my heart and soul into the 1,423 words that I turned in. Terry didn't print the piece, though, and I had to settle for my weekly pay. I had to get published before November, and this leak was my best chance. I was desperate, so if I had to do some shady shit, so be it.

The sky was blue with curly white clouds spinning by, and the area finally opened up so the foot traffic could disperse outwards. The freshly-paved sidewalk would have been great to rip—I wish I had my board. Skating wasn't allowed, but I'd been blowing loud all morning and I was ready to skate. I jumped up onto the long railing, put my hands up, and pretended to skate. As I made my way across the opening, I noticed a black man with an ear piece. He gave me a big head nod, and kept walking. I paused. He made eye contact with another man with a camera. Neither one of them looked like tourists. They were both secret service or perhaps undercover. They both acknowledged me; I was certain of that. I turned back to look at the black guy with the earpiece. He returned my gaze.

They were onto me—it was a sting!

I stopped walking. It was about to go down like a new-age Watergate, and I was in the middle of it. I halted completely to watch this man, and when I did, he turned from me and walked away. Maybe he wasn't here for me at all. He never looked back at me again, and the man with the camera was gone too. I questioned my life choices, pondering once again if I could be arrested for collecting dirt on a presidential candidate. The feds wouldn't be trying to entrap me when this whole ordeal fell into my lap. I still didn't even know who the dirt was on! I was contacted anonymously from an email: DeeperThroat2016@gmail.com. I figured DeeperThroat@gmail.com must have been taken.

I took a deep breath, bending down to pretend to tie my shoe before taking another long, hard drink out of my special water bottle. Then I pulled out and ate a mini-sized Snickers; after all, chocolate and peanut butter will mask the smell of any booze. The men were gone, but they had been watching me. My paranoia was always real.

I needed to remember what the emails had said exactly. It was two emails: the first felt very spammy, almost like a mass email blast sent out to a ton of press contacts to get a bite. That was my gut feeling, so I didn't respond. Then I drank a few, and changed my mind. I took the bait and replied. Perhaps I shouldn't have.

The response I got in return was swift. Despite it mentioning my name a few times, it still felt spammy. It went on to say if I was interested in being the one who broke this election's October Surprise, I could meet them at the hot dog stand west of the Monument at 1 P.M. on Saturday.

She told me her name was Morgan. She claimed to work for the Clinton campaign team, and stated that what she had would change the course of the election. So, I confirmed that I would be there. It was cloak-and-dagger stuff, and I didn't know who the dirt was on. I could speculate, but either way, this person was leaking it to me. I couldn't be arrested for that.

Meeting at the hot dog stand in a very public place wasn't the same as the shadows of a basement parking garage. My watch read 13:02, and my mind was sprinting with every paranoid thought imaginable.

"Gunner! Hey, Gunner!"

I could see a young lady standing just beyond the hot dog stand. She was yelling at me like I was a cat she was beckoning for. I turned to my left, and then slowly walked closer. She was one of the hottest women I had ever seen in the District. She was motioning at me with one finger, and in that moment, I just knew it had to be a sting or a prank. I turned around quickly to make sure that her six-foot-nine boyfriend, also named Gunner, wasn't looming behind me.

The woman had long, blonde hair, cutting green eyes, and a symmetrical face with a nose pinned on cute as a button. Her figure was similar to a coke bottle with more dimensions; thick in all the right places like a good bowl of chili. My nerves kicked in. I could hear myself stutter in my head before I even said a word. Her good looks were that distracting, and there was no denying that she was talking to me now.

"You're Gunner Bush from *Rolling Stone Magazine*, right?" She said loud enough for any wire or microphone nearby to pick up. It was a trap. I began to panic, but didn't have time to react.

She started to reach into her bra to pull out the wired microphone, so I blurted out, "No! I'm Hunter Bush, not Gunner—you must be looking for my twin brother!"

She looked at me like I had just smacked her. She was obviously digging into her shirt now, adjusting her cleavage right in front of me. She was wearing a wire! Removing her right hand from her bra area, she straightened herself on the outside and showed me what looked like a green and white USB drive. It had been hidden wherever women put things in their bra. I didn't know, and I watched her do it. I was just relieved it wasn't a wire.

"Huh, your twin?" she finally replied, curling her face up in the cutest way and adding, "You're joking, right?"

"Ye-s, y-e-s, I am," I stuttered, and then asked her, "So you are deeper throat, huh?"

"Yes, that was the email I picked. I don't even know why I used that, it was sophomoric, but I was hoping it would get your attention. I didn't want to come off too brash, you know." She was talking fast in a Valley girl-type of voice that I didn't understand. After a moment's pause, she dropped her voice a bit, got closer to me, and grabbed my tie.

"I know you're Gunner Bush with the *Rolling Stone*, though, because I looked you up. I found your picture online."

"Okay, well, what can I help you with?" I asked her as I grabbed back my tie. I was trying to act like I didn't like this beautiful woman rubbing my tie and saying my name in a soft, sexy voice.

"Well, Gunny, this is going to change the entire election."

She paused and stared me right in the eye. She wanted me to understand what she was saying.

"What is?" I asked in response, letting her know how confused I was with a grimace on my face.

"This," she handed me the jump drive, "is going to sink Trump's battleship."

As I took the evidence, I felt like I was going to be arrested again.

"What is this? I don't know you!"

"I told you, it's going to change the election," she said, seemingly upset that I didn't know exactly what was on the USB. She was beyond beautiful, and that was messing with my judgment.

"You work with the Hillary camp? I assumed you had some dirt on her." I stared at the USB, flipping it around as if I was tracking an ant crawling around on it.

"Yes, I work for Senator Clinton, and I am the person who found this in the Trump files."

"Okay..."

"I want it noted in *Rolling Stone Magazine* as such, so you guys get the video first. You can break it a day before this is going to come out, and then you can do a great article for me— it's a win for everyone." It felt rehearsed.

"What are the Trump files?"

She loosened her shoulders a bit, and the tension flew out of her. It wasn't until that moment that I realized it wasn't a sting. I reached into my pants to put the USB into my tighty-whities. She made a face at me like I shouldn't put it into my pants.

"You just had it in your bra, why can't I secure it?"

"I'm out on my run and don't have any pockets in this," she gestured toward her jogging outfit while looking at me like I was a moron. I felt like one. I might have been one, but I wasn't going to let her be condescending to me.

"You said this is from the Trump Files, but what are the Trump files?"

"It's a database of all things Trump. It has like... videos, audio recordings from interviews, old footage, quotes from newspapers from back in the 80s, and just all this stuff on Trump. We would like, go through it looking for anything bad he might have said, or whatever."

"Gotcha. And you do this as a Clinton staffer?" I asked, now wondering what her real angle was here.

"Yes, I do, and I'm the one who found this recording. I'm giving it to you, and I want you to make sure that everyone knows I'm the one who found this. I want the credit. I was the one who gave it to Sarah and Richard, but they didn't tell Senator Clinton that I found it. Instead, they're taking all the credit for something I did. This is Senator Clinton's October Surprise—it will change the course of the election and history. She will finally shatter the glass ceiling!"

"Why do you care who gets the credit?"

"Because it's not right. I'm the one who found it, not Sarah or Richard. I deserve the credit." She was hiding something, and she wasn't exactly good at lying.

"Why does it matter? Trump is down over five points. Why does this change the race?"

I had hundreds of more questions on the tip of my tongue and even more running through my brain.

She raised her head and told me proudly, "Trump will be down fifteen points when this hits. This is a game-changer."

She was still avoiding my main question. I used my stern voice and asked her, "So, this will change the polls ten points? Now, a ten-point swing is pretty big, maybe even huge. But why do you care who gets the credit?"

"Listen, in the USB, I have a contract that states the main video and audio has to be played after my logo, and my watermark is on it, too. So that's there, and..." The end of her sentence hung out in dead air, and she was staring past me.

"And?"

"And...well, there's an article I want you to publish for me in there, too. It's about how I'm the one who found this, and how I knew it would change the election," she was starting to daydream, watching herself receive the Nobel Peace Prize or sumshit. She was full of herself, that was for sure.

"Okay—wait, you have your own watermark? No—I mean, answer my other question. Why do you care who gets credit? Tell me now, or everything is off!"

She reached for my tie again. "Well, Gunny, after Senator Clinton shatters the glass ceiling and wins, she'll be in the Oval Office. And, of course, she will be looking to name someone press secretary. And...shouldn't that be me?"

Ah-ha! She was an opportunist like me.

"Well, I need to literally run, but all my contact info is in there, and I already have your number. 502 area code, right?"

"It's the 502 remix," I sang out, quoting a Nappy Roots song she didn't know or care about. "Okay, you got my number, call me. Gotta check this out first," I yelled, pointing at my junk and quickly regretting that choice.

She just smiled and took off running.

There was no way to predict what might be on the jump drive, but whatever it was, it would have to be devastating to derail the Trump train. I had seen the massive power of the Trumpies over the summer while on the road, and it was a base that wasn't easily swayed. Hillary was up now, but it felt like she was clinging for dear life.

Trump's campaign was threatening a major October Surprise. The political world in 2016 wasn't the one that Bernstein and Woodward had covered. Times weren't changing—they had already changed.

CHAPTER 2

"Hollywood Access"

The tourists were still clamoring for selfies when I turned to leave, but it didn't bother me anymore. I left the monument area in search of a safe haven to view the contents of the mysterious USB. I found a bench, and quickly learned that my laptop was dead. I had the charger, but nowhere to plug it in. A local place like Starbucks would be too risky, and I felt the same way about my own place. I wasn't paranoid, per say—I just didn't trust my Russian roommates, who perpetually made me feel like my room was bugged. My roommates were always really quiet when I was home, so even if my room wasn't bugged, they might be able to hear into my room. They were annoying and not spies, as roommates often are; but they pissed me off when they always whispered in Russian around me. Although they weren't the worst roommates I had ever had and I could have put my headphones on, I was also worried that they had root access to my laptop. Maybe I was paranoid. Regardless, I didn't want to risk it, so I headed in the direction of the Hill and my boy Eddie's crib.

I was dressed how I always dressed when going to an appointment in the District: creased khaki pants, black DCs that looked enough like dress shoes to pass, a matching belt, and a blue button-up dress shirt along with a Republican red tie that was tied in a Windsor knot. My hair was parted to the right, framing my black coke-bottle lens nerd glasses. It was a "do as the Romans" approach—strategic and conservative. I wanted to look as clean-cut as I could, and I figured that a white guy's best shot at surviving in the District was to look as Republican as possible. And sure—the District is more Democrat than any city in the entire country, but Republicans run the place like the mafia. That's how war criminals like Bush and Cheaney could survive two terms. I wasn't a Republican by any stretch of the imagination. I might have been a hick from the Ville, but I wasn't stupid. I also wasn't one of those converted Democrats with a brand-new ticket on the Trump train, either. I understood things like the Southern Strategy, and I most definitely didn't subscribe to the tail of the fox.

I hated the GOP, but my own personal hatred built up only half of my excitement. Sure, I wanted to see the party burn. But if the information on this USB was as big as Morgan said it was, I would be published in the magazine—or, at the very least, on the website for *Rolling Stone*.

I had been living in the District since May when I wasn't on the campaign road, and that gave me ample time to learn the nooks and crannies of the city. I knew the public transport—and, of course, the birds and bikes that could be rented if sober enough. Riding one was quicker than walking, and I could make my way through the alleys and side streets to get to Eddie's crib.

Eddie was one of the first dudes I met in the District, and like most of the locals, he was a transplant. He was a local

DJ who played most of the larger clubs in the city, and he was great on the wheels of steel. His spot was just beyond the Hill before Georgetown. I just called the area Bricktown since every house was brick, and I didn't know all the little names of the towns in the District, although the locals wouldn't shut up about them. I wasn't going to learn them.

Eddie had a red brick house in the middle of the block surrounded by brick houses. I walked up, and I could see into his place through the glass door. Eddie's spot was a bachelor pad on steroids. It had a DJ booth, dance floor, and even poles. It was decked out with other things straight out of a movie: a pool table, a hot tub, and even a working traffic light. Everything was over the top, like a dance club. It had been the official after hours spot all summer, so anytime I was in the District, I stopped by.

A short, round, morbidly obese man opened the glass door and nodded at me. I had met him a few times before, but I couldn't remember his name. It was either Allen or Albert—perhaps Fat Albert.

"Thanks for letting me in. Is Eddie around?"

The aroma of the place was like a skunk smoking a Newport, and there was still smoke hanging in the air. Fat Albert mumbled sumshit, but I could see Eddie was cutting in the DJ booth. On the left were two ugly white barracudas with a hooker or drug addict vibe, and they were likely both. They were dressed alike with the same body shape, adorned in matching bleached blonde hair and oversized bobble heads. They had to be sisters—bobblehead sisters—and they were at least Eddie's age at 35, but looked closer to 55. Maybe they were 40, it was impossible to tell. I faked a smile and kept it moving, making my way to the booth.

Eddie had his speakers up to the max, and I couldn't hear my own thoughts. He was spinning an old school Biggie

Smalls and Method Man, which was a classic from another time that nobody in the room was educated enough to really enjoy. I walked up the steps to his booth, and he dapped me up.

"Gunner A. Bush, my man! What's been up, young-blood?"

He had one ear free and one covered by a headphone.

I dapped him up, and then I asked if I could use his other laptop to check out something on a jump drive.

"A jump drive, huh? What's on it?" He asked back. I watched his mind go back into the other ear, listening to the music in the one headphone.

"Just something for work. Nothing major."

"Yeah, I mean, I guess. It's not music, is it? You know how Trent Reznor would leave USBs outside the offices of—"

"—Pretty Hate Machine." I cut him off. I knew the story and had to remind him, "I work for *Rolling Stone Magazine*, of course I know that story. That isn't what this is. My laptop is dead, and it's just a real quick work thing."

"Yeah, well, what if it's a hacker's USB with a virus that takes over your computer, and you have to pay a ransom to some weird Bitcoin account to free it or they steal all your nudes and post them?!"

"Yeah, well it's not. Can I use it or nah? I have to charge mine, and the charger is at home."

Eddie shrugged and handed me one of his three laptops. It was open, so I took it and moved slowly down the steps to a big square pleather chair that was oversized—even for America's fat ass standards.

"When are you going to put some of my mixtapes into *Rolling Stone*? I got the best mixes on the entire East Coast!" He said, now speaking into the microphone.

"Soon!" I yelled over the music.

I inserted the USB, and it popped up on the desktop. It only had one folder in it, titled "Top Secret." I had to laugh to myself and roll my eyes before I finally opened it.

Inside the folder was the contract that Morgan had told me about. It even listed her full name, Morgan REDACTED. It had another .doc file with her name on it again, and tons of bullshit written on it about how wonderful Morgan was, how she graduated from George Mason and was pre-law at Georgetown before joining the Hillary campaign and taking a semester off. It also talked about how she found the video, and how she knew it would change the course of the election and history. It went on to sing her praises: saying she was a great person and "a star in the making" (her words), and she was the top of her class in high school, like anyone cared, but it didn't say she was top of her class in college so I assumed she wasn't. It was the article that she wanted me to publish on her in *Rolling Stone* after the election to secure her place as press secretary.

Then there was a video in the file. It was titled "Morgan's Secret Video," and I clicked it without having a clue what to expect. It had a six-second intro that stated her full name again, and was followed by a makeshift logo that she had designed badly in MS Paint.

I hit play, but I couldn't hear it. The sound wasn't working on the laptop, and Eddie's music wasn't helping. I could smell something loud that the barracudas had lit, and they were now dancing, or attempting to. It was a distraction, so I stood up.

"Hey Eddie, can I use your headphones?"

Eddie couldn't hear me. He had headphones over both

ears while trying to mix some Hozier song with ChonkyFire by Outkast and failing tremendously. I walked up, grabbed a pair of headphones next to Eddie, and then went and sat back down. I plugged the headphones in, and then started the video over. Morgan's logo came up again, and then it was just a video of a bus with Trump talking. Trump came off the bus, and he was with Billy Bush, and some other lady I couldn't place. I only knew who Billy Bush was because I had been asked several times if I was related to the asshat.

Then it ended. That was it. I must have missed something so I started it over, but as soon as I did, my phone started to vibrate, and it was from a private number so I hit ignore and tried to watch the video. As soon as the logo showed up, my phone rang again. And again, it was from a private number. I picked it up.

"Hello, yeah, I usually don't answer private calls but go ahead and tell me I won some sort of award with a prize!"

"Hey, hello, Gunner, is that you?" It was a lady's voice, but I didn't recognize it.

"Maybe it is Gunner, but not if you're trying to collect a debt!" I said, trying to confuse them and confess.

"Hey it's me, Morgan, uh, from the thing. We just met, remember? I emailed you from Deeper Throat," she said the last two words out loud for the first time, I could tell by how she said it, she didn't like it. She thought it was a play on words that fit perfectly, but now she was hearing it out loud and realizing it didn't quite fit.

"Ah yes, Deeper Throat, just what I needed! So how are you, Morgan?" I said to her, I stood up and started to walk away from the music, making my way into the kitchen.

"So, what do you think of the video? It's a game changer, right?" She was confident now. The deeper throat jokes were childish, but so was I.

"Yeah, the bus video…do you think it's really a 10-point swinger?" I asked her as seriously as I could.

"The bus video? Did you not hear what he said? What Trump said?" her voice was raised now, and I could tell she was mad and upset over my take.

"Naw, not really. Something about tic tacs or bubble-gum, I have no clue," I said back to her, swinging open the fridge to see if I was lucky enough to score a beer someone got too drunk to drink. Empty. The fridge didn't even have condiments in it.

"You need to go back and listen to what he said," Morgan said in a serious tone. She clearly knew I wasn't about to go watch it, because she immediately followed it by saying, "He said…."

And she repeated it verbatim to me. I listened, but I didn't know what to think.

"Grab them by the pussy?" I asked her, a little confused about the context of Trump saying this.

"All of it is right there!" she said dramatically.

"So, this is the October Surprise?" I asked her, trying to not sound like I believed it was a dud that she thought was a grand finale. "I mean, Julie Awning is hyping up some big October Surprise too. What if the one they have is more powerful?"

That shut her up, but I wanted her to talk now. She was quiet. Thinking. I could hear it in the silence.

"Do you know what they have?" Morgan asked me as if I knew and I would tell her, a person who had just leaked something to me.

"I don't," I told her, and I didn't.

I flung the swinging door to leave the kitchen, and I could see Eddie looking at me right when I did. He had a big smile on his face like he knew the numbers for the Pick 3 midday, so I started to walk towards him. Morgan was on the phone, and I could hear Trump's voice coming over the speakers that also had "Panda" by Desiigner playing.

"Grab her by the pussy, grab her by the pussy, pussy, grab her by the pussy, pussy!" And it didn't sound bad at all. Eddie could really work the 1s and 2s.

I realized that he was playing the audio from the USB video, and Morgan was still on the phone. I ran towards Eddie yelling at him, "Hey, that's mine!"

"Grab her by the pussy, grab her, pussy, pussy grab her by the pussy!" It was the best blend Eddie had ever done. And as I walked towards him, he was adding in other parts: "When you're a star, they let you do it!" He was really cutting it up like a record now with some software program, *Grab her by the pussy! Grab her by the pussy! Grab her by the pussy!*

The two bobblehead bitches were dancing, while Fat Albert was trying to groove and snapping his fingers off beat.

"Where are you? Who is that?!" Morgan yelled through the phone. She could hear it, too.

"Hey Ed, that's my stuff, you can't mess with that!" I yelled at Eddie while Morgan yelled at me.

"And it's MY computer!" Eddie said back over the microphone in front of him. He was right, but it was my video and USB.

"Where are you?! That is my leak! My leak, MINE!" Morgan was screaming into the phone, but I couldn't do anything about it now.

"Eddie, please bro, stop!" I said before finally ripping the USB from his laptop.

"Hey, you could destroy my whole hard drive like that!" Eddie yelled. To be fair, he did have some grounds to be angry, as ripping out a USB without properly ejecting can cause your computer to do something crazy. It didn't matter, though. Eddie had already copied the video onto his own hard drive, and the music was still playing. He just smiled again as I looked at him. I shook my head and went back to my phone conversation.

"Morgan, are you there? Yeah, I am here at a top-secret *Rolling Stone* meeting and we are discussing this video. And obviously, we're also discussing the great article that we want to publish about you. The higher ups here all agree this could be a game changer!"

"So, you *do* think it will be a game changer?" she asked meekly. I could hear her blushing through the phone.

"Of course we do."

I walked back into the kitchen so she wouldn't hear the brand-new "Panda" remix that a large portion of D.C. might at Eddie's next DJing gig.

"I thought maybe you were being sarcastic earlier, but you're a hard guy to read, Gunny," Morgan said with some assurance. Getting called Gunny usually made me cringe, but she was attractive enough to get away with it.

"I can't write what you wrote exactly, you know? I gotta change it up, and rewrite it myself," I told her to let her know I was still on her team. There was zero chance of an article on her finding this video. I did want more info on the Trump files, though. "Can you tell me a bit more about the Trump files?"

"I did tell you. It's just these old clips, videos, and

photos, like Trump with this pedophile named Epstein. I guess that was going to be a big breaking point for us, too. It was Rich who had found out who the guy Epstein was, and like, how he was this giant pervert who Trump was like best friends with back in the 90s. I guess he had his own fuck island, or something. There were a ton of photos of these two together, and flight records of Trump flying to this private island. We had a pitch all ready to go to the press when Hillary saw it and almost fainted, or something. I wasn't there when she saw the pictures, but it didn't take long for us to find out about pictures of Bill with this same guy. Calling a spade a spade when your husband is a spade just doesn't do anything."

"Right," I said. I had heard the stories of this island before. "So, give us a few days to process everything, and then I'll give you a ring back. Can you text me your number, since you called me from a private number?"

"Of course, we all have to have private numbers. I can text you right now!"

"Okay, we'll start putting everything together!"

"We need to release it before the 25th. That's when Sarah and Rich are going to put it out, so we need to before them!" She was giddy. I assured her that we would, and hung up.

I left the kitchen and returned to the DJ booth. The two broads were dancing, and it was as ugly as ever. The sauce had run out and there was no way I could watch these two barracudas try to be sexy, so I let Eddie know I was leaving. I had never been drunk enough for that.

As I did, one of the fishes offered me the J, so I took it. It was half gone and smelt like flaming strawberries. Up close, I could see the age in her hands. Her face was plastered in makeup and the bacteria Clostridium botulinum. Her teeth were yellowing, and it was clear to me that life had taken its toll on this woman.

"I loved that remix of 'Panda' with Donald on it," she informed me as I inhaled.

"Oh, did you like the remix that Eddie did with my top-secret files?" I said loud enough so Eddie would hear me. He was on the couch, and lit like a match. Not even 5 PM yet, and he was drunk and high enough to watch the barracudas get on his pole and work. That was a nightmare I couldn't imagine, but he was anxious for it.

"I love me some Donald Trump," She said to me as she pulled a long skinny smoke out of her purse.

"Oh, you like Trump? Are you voting for him?"

"Yeah, I am. All us girls at the agency have to go vote, and Billy said he's driving. He said he would come get us bright and early on that day in December or November, or whatever," she informed me as she started smoking. Eddie stood up and they started hugging.

"Rii-iight," I said, truly interested in why she was going to vote for Trump. I asked her, "Have you ever voted before?"

"No, I wasn't never signed up to vote, Billy did that for us girls, too. He got us memberships to vote and all that. When I was a little girl, I went to vote a bunch, though. I still remember that these guys would come around our neighborhood, and pick up hobos and old hags like my mom, and if they were on the voter's registrations, they would give 'em a bottle of liquor. Since my momma was a wino, she would have me and my brother outside on that day because she knew they would come around. She called it 'Free Bottle Day.' That's the only time she would watch me and my brother when we was outside. Otherwise, she wouldn't give a damn if we was hopscotching in the freeway, ya'kno? She didn't want the van to miss her, and once they picked her up, they would even give her a pen with the name of the person they wanted her to vote for on it. Ya'kno, so she wouldn't forget who to vote for, and mom could remember stuff like that, she wasn't on no dope. She'd go vote and when she got out, they'd have her a dark bottle of something in glass. Mom always saved the glass ones. My brother and I didn't mind, 'cause they always had toys for us. Can't wait to vote this year for Trump and get my free glass bottle. I love me some Jack, and for free, shit!"

She was ranting, and I was taking it all in. I didn't have the heart to tell her that she wouldn't get a free bottle like her mom did. She might if the guy at her escort agency, Billy or whoever, got her one. She wasn't done yet, though.

"I don't even need a ride to go vote for Donald, I would walk there in the snow. I love him, and if Hillary Clinton wins, our lives will be ruined. Donald Trump is the only one who can save America!"

Ding, ding, ding, and there it was again. And she was as serious as a malignant tumor.

I wanted to ask her a thousand questions, but Eddie cut me off in a real deep voice even for him. "Hey playboy, maybe you can go ahead and leave."

He was upset. He thought I was gaming on his chick, but in reality, I wanted to hear why she was voting for Trump. Why did she think he might save America, rather than say, Jeb Bush or perhaps Mickey Mouse? I didn't want to mess up Eddie's game with the barracuda, though, so I bounced. I had one stop to make before I could go back to my own spot—I was headed to the mansion.

CHAPTER 3

"Turtle Food"

The sun was gone, and with it, the warm weather. A chill ran through my body as I stepped outside; I bent over, reached under the couch on the porch, and pulled out the skateboard I had left. I jumped on it and headed towards the mansion. The rush hour traffic wouldn't be as bad on a Saturday, but it would still be thick. I kicked and pushed and avoided stopping. The sidewalks in the District are just good enough to get by skating on. Morgan was still texting me after the initial text with her number, and it was constant now - maybe she liked me or sumshit.

I had one more stop to go before I could go home. I kicked and pushed on my board and started to get a strong feeling about the election. Trump's chances still felt like a wing and prayer type of horse that might hit at the Downs. This October Surprise wouldn't move the needle that much, and Hillary wasn't stepping on his neck to get the victory. She was trying, but perhaps she didn't know how, or maybe Trump wasn't the type of guy you could step on his neck to kill. He still had a path to victory if he could swing the swing voters and get a low voter turnout.

I'd been on the road all summer following both camps, and when I wasn't following them, I was here in the District where politics is magnetized tenfold. Trump was getting out his new message, and it was getting heard and repeated. He wasn't running for a political position as a public servant; he was running because he was here to save America. It was a much bigger deal to his voters. Hillary was still running on the fact that she wasn't Trump, and she wasn't even a Democratic extension of Barry.

I made my way back to the Hill, slowing down as I approached a white wall about 3-feet high. I hopped onto my board, pulled down a metal fire escape ladder, and climbed up one level. This was one of the most secure premises in the District, but somehow they didn't know about a 3-foot wall from another building and a fire escape ladder. I knew the area from delivering envelopes full of advertising information for *Rolling Stone*.

Some of my deliveries felt cryptic, they weren't, but it felt like espionage stuff. I would play into it a bit, even more so when I found this back entrance. I was sharing squares with some greenies and found how to enter the building. Terry always had me take "babok" over to this part of the Hill, and it felt like money through the envelope. One time she showed me what it was, and it was layouts for print advertising. Same shit I had seen at the CJ. Terry loved that I contacted so many people and always looked for a story. I met all types and always used the side and backdoors when I could.

After climbing the ladder, I was on a side roof that the greenies would use to smoke when they realized that being an intern of any sort, paid or unpaid, was enough to start smoking. I crossed a small ledge, turned, and entered another roof area. It was for the stressed staffers or senators, and it even had a couple of old chairs. They'd left the door to this part open a smidge since before Reagan lost his mind.

I pushed it open, walking in like I owned the building. It was dark, and I had to wait until my eyes adjusted. As they did, I pulled out my magic water bottle again, and it hit it - and tried reading the signs. A light at the end of the hall was on, which was odd this late on a Saturday, but I kept going. Maybe somebody left it on and left for home on Friday. As I got closer, though, I spotted an oversize woman walking back and forth holding a poster board in another room. She had on an ugly flower print dress, and her gray hair was up. She was startled to see me, so I stopped.

I started to undo my backpack.

"I have a delivery for the Senate Majority," I said very politely, which surprised even myself. She did a double-take, noticing my skateboard as I pulled out a brown paper bag.

"Oh, you scared me, sweetie, " she said as she put her hand over her chest as if to clutch her pearls or sumshit.

"I can take that for you to his office. I am one of his secretaries. I am here getting the Halloween stuff set up. The Senator gives me special permission to come in and set up the stuff for the holidays. I am the only one, though." She really thought I cared. "We don't do all the holidays like we did when I started working here. We used to do Valentine's Day and Flag Day, but he wasn't much of a romantic, so we canceled that one pretty quickly, and I think we just altogether stopped celebrating Flag Day as a nation. It's sad, really; I don't remember when it was, probably when Clinton was in office."

She was opening up to me as if I had known her all my life, and I could give a fuck.

"Did you sign in?" She had asked me that already, but I wasn't paying attention.

"Huh? Yeah, of course, I have to give it directly to Senator Mc-Connell. It was a direct or-der from the person who paid for thi-s." I never stutter unless I am really lying, but I've been working on it like Pinocchio naked in front of a mirror.

She was trying to figure me out.

"Well, Senator McConnell is never here on Saturdays unless it's required for legislation, so unless you want to come back on Monday, I will need to take it. Did it really say that in the delivery instructions? That it had to be hand-delivered to him? Can I see the directions?"

She pushed her glasses up her nose, waiting for me to hand her the delivery slip I didn't have.

"No, I don't - I guess someone got into his cookies or Christmas snacks because I am only supposed to put the package in his office."

"Cookies, huh? I bet it was Janice. She ate a piece of my birthday cake, and I told Mitch. I bet she is trying to get back on his good side by sending him cookies. Who is your package from?"

She stared at the paper bag.

"M'am, this is from a third party who wished to mail this anonymously. It is a federal offense to mess with the mail!"

She wasn't one to break the law. She made a snide face.

"Oh, I know! You didn't say it was sent anonymously, mister!"

She was deflecting.

"I didn't even know you could do that." She added, and I

didn't either. I was trying to be on my way, though.

"Well, I can show you where his office is, and you can set it outside since I don't have a key."

As I followed her, she started back onto her story, like I was training in.

"It was probably Janice. You know the Senator, Mitch, said I could call him Mitch, he came and sang happy birthday to me, and I got the first piece of cake even before him, and Mr. Mc-Mitch got the second piece. Janice came in later after we had cut a lot of pieces, and I was going to take it home with me since it was ice cream cake and I love ice cream cake, and it was my cake and MY BIRTHDAY! Well, Janice just thought she could help herself to my cake, do you believe the nerve on her, and she got into the fridge, opened my box of cake, and she took a slice. I ate that cake every night for two weeks, but it would have been longer if Janice didn't get her hungry little fingers into my food!"

She was ranting and also mad with insanity. Any person that was happy Mitch McConnell showed up for her birthday needed medication. I followed her through the hallways listening to her drivel until finally, we arrived at his office.

"You can set it on the side of that desk there; that is Suzanne's desk."

She turned her head like I was about to pull my penis out and start peeing.

"If I set it there, then you are going to dig through it once I am gone to see if Janice sent it, and I am assuring you, this package isn't from Janice."

I pulled out my phone and held onto the paper bag tight.

"It isn't Janice? I thought you said you couldn't tell me."

Now she thought she was Sherlock Holmes.

"I can't, but I do have to run soon, so I need you to promise me you won't look into this bag," I was toying with her now. I turned around and pulled the contents of the bag out, and she was starting to poke her nose.

I snapped a picture of it with the nameplate from the door that read, Senate Majority Mitch McConnell.

"I promise - hey, what do you have in there?"

"I just need to get a quick pic for confirmation."

She had snuck in closer and was more nimble than I thought. She snatched at the bag, pulled it hard to see what it was.

"Hey!" I yelled but stopped as she began realizing what was in the bag.

She screamed, "What in the lord's name is this, Turtle food?"

"Who are you with? What service? Who hired you!"

"I am with Fedup taxpayers of the Blew Grass State!"

She was trying to box me in.

"Are you the guy who has been mailing Mr. McConnell, Mitch, the turtle food once a week?"

I wasn't, but that was hilarious to hear. Betting is a part of life back in the Ville, and I was winning one right now. She grabbed the turtle food bag. She tugged, and I pulled, and the bag ripped in midair. Pellets of turtle food shot everywhere.

This old crank was heated. She was older and a big woman too, and if she did grab me or fall on top of me, she might break a hip, and we might not both survive that. She began screaming, flaying her arms out like a 1920s football player about to make a tackle.

"Security!"

I wasn't caught, but I was in trouble. I had to bounce but needed another picture of the pellets all over the floor, so I faked left and bounced back to the right.

She moved towards her right, and I snapped a photo. Then, I shot down the hallway like a dart. She was too old, too slow, and too fat. I turned and watched her slip- that was the actual photo I needed. My conscience kicked it, and I could only think that this old hag would die, so instead of snapping a picture, I walked back towards her to help her up, but she bounced up like a coiled snake and started screaming for security.

I turned and ran. I would need to move or be arrested. I was lost and didn't know where the smoke door was. Then I heard walkie-talkies. Security. I opened the first open door I could find and found myself in a waiting area. I locked the door behind me and rushed towards the window. It was only one story, and I knew it was my only choice. But I couldn't get it open—damn child safety locks. I could see a security guard below, and he could see me. I turned and bolted.

The hallway was empty, so I sprinted in hopes of finding a door to escape. I saw an exit sign and turned down a flight of stairs, hitting them three at a time. I had to get to the courtyard before security. As I bounced out the door, I put my board down - and started to kick. If I didn't gain momentum, I was toast.

I was chased by government security inside the senate office building, who wanted to take me down harder than tower seven.

And I guess, maybe, I should start over a little bit and tell you who I am and why I am here, and of course why it all matters, since I was holding a piece of intel on the USB in my pocket that could sink the hopes of one Presidential candidate, granting the keys to the white house to another. The leader of the free world was on the line, and I was about to be a key player. And let me assure you, there is no way Mitch McConnell's security was going to catch me.

CHAPTER 4

I was 23. My frontal lobe was still a pile of mush. I wasn't an anarchist, but I am pretty sure Bob Dylan was at 23, and he was one of the people my mom told me to aspire to be. Obviously, I hated authority and wanted to burn it down, but I didn't have a clue where to start. I shouldn't have even sniffed the job at *Rolling Stone*, and not just because I was drinking a little more than prime Mickey Mantle; my political knowledge was paper-thin - Wikipedia top-paragraph level- or maybe just unawareness.

I was working in the industry, if you want to call it that, at my local paper in the Ville. My position at the Courier-Journal wasn't exactly setting the world on fire. Mainly, I was writing obits and horoscopes. I had college loans hanging over my head like an ax to a bride of King Henry VIII, and barely any income coming in; I was lucky enough to need a second job.

So, I picked up extra paychecks working for Smith and Smith, a private investigator's office down on 7th street. The cash cow for Mr. Smith wasn't really in PI work but rather bail bonds, as through a legal loophole they could issue them, but most people that need a bail bond need one at 3 am on a Sunday, so they needed someone to man the window to sign paperwork and collect the cash. Mr. Smith's old man, Mr.

Smith, had kicked the bucket a few years back, but the name wasn't changed. That would have been another bill, and they already didn't want to fix a hose connected to the AC so I had to empty a bucket with water in it if I wanted to run the air.

Now Mr. Smith did some PI work, but I didn't have much to do with it. He was an old head; he'd been in the business since "the good old days," whatever in the hell that meant. Now and again, he'd send me out on a wild goose chase, but it mostly was just to grab him a coffee.

Journalism was a dying entity. I learned this the minute the ink on my diploma dried. It was like being handed the family buggy whip business just as Henry Ford rolled out his Model T. The masses didn't care because they wanted the news now. And now news meant blogs by Karen and Twitter feeds and memes. That was the future. Either way, I had a degree in Journalism, not foresight.

The *Rolling Stone* job landed in my lap like a friendly cat. I was looking for something new, and using my new tactic of applying for fucking everything. If it was a job for a writer, I would apply twice.I didn't know it was *Rolling Stone* right off the bat though. When I read the posting for the job, it was interesting, but I was going to apply no matter what. According to my own statistics, 70% of all job postings online are scams.

**A national print magazine is looking for someone to cover an event in the Louisville area. This is a political event, and we are looking for someone who has a history of working in politics.*

Please apply with a resume, links to work, and references.

--

It felt like a scam. It wasn't a national magazine, it was some asshole in his bedroom trying to convince people to send him money. I still applied because that was my philosophy at the time, and if they wanted money out of me, good luck. Can't get blood out of a turnip.

I emailed the standard bullshit, cover letter, resume, and links to pieces I had written for online magazines. Mostly on how the best underground music scene in the country is in the Ville and a longer piece about a band from Germantown, The Villebillies, and how they should have blown up but never did. I hit send and hoped for the best. And what I mean by hoping for the best is I went right to the next listing and applied for that job. The job I was looking for was a winning lottery ticket, and I didn't even play the numbers.

I got an instant reply, which is typical for most scams. It was a stock answered reply probably from an automatic bot. It had a link at the bottom that I could click for more questions. I clicked it, which was a risk, never click a link in an email, and filled out all the questions the best I could.

Within 24 hours, I had another reply from an email that looked like an automatic reply again. It wasn't formatted very well, and it said that a "National print magazine was looking for someone to cover a May 4th event at the Seelbach Hotel." The event was for a Republican front runner in the Presidential race, Donald Trump.

I replied and said I could do it. No problem. I lied in the email, just a bit, a white Christmas lie, and I said I was a political junkie, and maybe a bigger lie after that was when I stated I worked for the CJ, and I would be at the event taking pictures. Now I never said I was going to be at this event taking pictures for the CJ, I just put the two things in the same run-on sentence. I wasn't going, but if I did go, I would snap a photo of the dude from that TV show about businesses. I liked the song by Mac Miller.

I started to ask around the CJ, and nobody knew Trump

was coming to town. Not the political staffers, the editors, nobody. There were a few things on a google search, but I didn't investigate that thoroughly because it was April. And April in the Ville only means one thing: The Derby is coming. The annual horse race, known as the running of the roses, is really both decadent and depraved.

The Blew Grass State is known for horse racing and bourbon, and when those two get a chance to interact, it turns into a month-long party. The tap water turns to bourbon, and the locals drink it by the gallon. It's the biggest, best, longest celebration for anything that minuscule in time.

It is the quintessential partying for nothing. A two-week party for a two-minute horse race. It's part of the culture and heritage of the city, and if you can't find a reason to drink during this period while inside the state lines of Kentucky, check your GPS because you likely stumbled into Indiana.

So, I was partying to get ready for the upcoming partying. I wasn't expecting an email back, I wasn't even thinking about it. I had applied to hundreds of jobs and rarely got a response. Somedays I would spend my entire time at work applying. So when I got what looked like another stock, spam, bot email back, stating they would be contacting me about the event in the future, it piqued my interest to look into the event again. Plus it said it would pay a rack, which had my attention more than anything.

Again I asked the guys at the CJ - they hadn't heard of an upcoming event involving Trump. And the date, May 4th, was three days before the running of the roses.

Finally, by chance, at a back door, hole in the wall in the Highlands, the truth was revealed to me. It was from my old buddy, Shitty, and he informed me the event was a scam. Not the job posting, but the entire event at the Seelbach. It was a promoter scam or ticket scheme. Essentially, it was grifters who would set up an event, sell tickets, then cancel at the last minute. The tickets are no refund so once the event was canceled, it was all profit. He didn't know if it was Trump's people doing it, but he said he knew it was some two-bit cons.

And any info coming from my boy, Shitty, was gospel. Despite his nickname, Shitty was a man who knew things in the Ville. After Shitty and I poured a few more brews down our gullet, I went back to my spot and decided to send an email while very intoxicated.

Hello Job Posting of Fake Job,

Here is a tidbit of information: The Donald Trump event at the Seelbach isn't going to happen. Trump isn't coming to Seelbach, period. You would have a better chance of getting Donnie Wahlberg. So, if you are a national print magazine, and you didn't know that this event was a con being put on by 2 two-bit bandits, then maybe you guys need to re-evaluate my resume and see that I am not just a journalist, I am also a private investigator. Maybe your national print magazine should take a chance on someone like me who has connections to find things out for you guys!!

Otherwise, don't waste people's time! Time is money and money is time!

Sincerely,

Gunner A. Bush

I barely remember writing it, yet of course, I hit send. The outgoing email time stamp read 5:43 am, and that should tell you everything you need to know. What a fool I was, and when I woke up, I had a response.

My brain was still hazy, so I didn't know what I was reading at first. It felt like a dream, and I couldn't remember sending the drunk email out. I was reading it on my phone, and it was so confusing that I got up and went to read it on my laptop. The email was from Terry at *Rolling Stone* Magazine. Yep.

Rolling.

Fucking.

Stone.

I was as hungover as New Year's Day, but my mind was putting together that the national print magazine was *Rolling Stone magazine. I had never dreamed of working for it because I am a realist and even that dream was out of my league.*

Hello Gunner,

Thank you for the information, and we are always looking to hire people like yourself who can find things out! We actually are hiring for another position, and we would love to consider you for this new position that has just opened up.

We are looking for someone who can help us with setting up interviews, gaining contacts, and things of that nature. It wouldn't be in music or entertainment but of course politics. We need someone who can fact-check and help to set up interviews. This would be ideal for a political junkie who understands how to contact and connect with people inside the political realm.

If you think this is something you can help us with please let me know, and we can move on to the next step.

Terry
RollingStone.com

I had to make sure Rolling Stone dot com was actually still connected with the magazine that I grew up reading so I typed in, www.RollingStone.com and made sure. It came right up, and then I double-checked the email again. Then I went and found a magazine in my closet, and made sure it read the same domain name. It did.

HOLY SHIT! ROLLING STONE.

It wasn't a scam, it was legit. I wanted to reply, but I couldn't. I didn't have a clue as to where to start. I didn't want to mess this up, and I really didn't even care if it was unpaid, naive I know, but I was back then. I was even willing to lie even more to get this job. I needed this job, and what would a little lie hurt? What would a big lie hurt?

Politics and setting up interviews? How hard could that be? Sure, my political knowledge was limited, but I wasn't an idiot. I was way off the spectrum of being any type of political junkie. I had taken a government class in high school and again in college. I knew most of the Presidents, and how many senators there are, but I didn't know things such as who Michael Dukakis picked as his running mate back in 1988. By my calculations, half of America didn't know.

So of course I wrote back after a few minutes of deep contemplation with an email riddled with lies, and none of them were as white as Santa's beard. I quoted both John F. Kennedy and Hunter S. Thompson. And again, I didn't get an immediate response. I had plans to get drunk and finish out Derby week strong. Low expectations.

I DID get an email back, and Terry at *Rolling Stone* was interested in hiring me. He was looking for someone to set up connections inside political camps of people running for President like Jeb Bush, Donald Trump, Ted Cruz, Bernie Sanders, and Hillary Clinton. He wanted someone like myself who was a journalist and a public investigator. Even though I just worked for a public investigator, I wasn't going to change the narrative. He loved that I was a PI, but he also loved my spunky attitude, whatever that meant. I just hoped I could keep it up. At the end of the email, it asked if I could start to try to contact Trump's children, including his son-in-law, and asked about names in the Hillary camp I had never heard of. The very last line asked when I could start.

I almost fell out of my chair. I responded immediately and told him, immediately. I also added in some new quotes from Tim Crouse and a long quote from *Fear and Loathing,* letting Terry know I knew my political journalism books.

I immediately started to taste the job. Something I had never had before became something I badly wanted. I would have walked on hot coals for this position, and I didn't even know what the pay was. If *Rolling Stone* needed me to make contacts inside the camps of Clinton and Trump, I would not stop until I had made contact with every person in both political camps.

So before I even got a response back from Terry, I started to google who in the hell Trump's kids were. Then Terry wrote me back. He wanted me to fly out to the District. It started to feel spammy again. I was just waiting for him to tell me about some odd fee I would have to pay, but it never came. What did come was an offer to buy me a ticket and talk to me about a full-time position. I would be moving to the District, would need to bring enough clothes for two weeks, and had to be prepared to follow the different campaigns on the road. I told him I was ready to leave right away. He wanted me to reach out to two other political camps besides Trump's: Hillary Clinton, and Ted Cruz.

This opportunity was once in a lifetime. I had to jump at it no matter the pay, where I would be staying, or what I would be doing. I didn't even think to ask for a contract or inquire about a 401k or anything. I just emailed him back saying I'd take it, and I was ready. This was Rolling Fucking Stone, the cream of the crop as far as journalism is concerned.

Immediately, I started trying to find ways to contact those two camps. I had already been googling Trump's children, so I reached out to Trump's camp first. It was like shooting fish in a barrel, but I wasn't getting the prime meat yet. Every makeshift Trump website I emailed, I got a response from, and it was never just one. Each email had five email offsprings, but nobody wanted to connect me with the big man himself. I got responses from every email it seemed. Long-winded ones from people who created Facebook pages, so I thought they might be part of the team. I wrote down the info on a legal pad. Most of them weren't even part of Trump's team at all, they just ran websites because they badly wanted Trump to win.

It was the same with Trump's kids or people in relationships with them. All the Twitter handles and Facebook page owners wrote back quickly. I do need to add that I said I was with *Rolling Stone,* which likely played a role. A lot of emails from the kids' handlers felt desperate, but I was the one who reached out to them. I wrote at the top of my notes his kids really wanted to show their old man how much they were campaigning for him.

The kids were easier to contact, but it wasn't phone numbers. It was personal contacts all through apps. Either KIK or Snapchat or WHATSAPP or some other weird shit that people only use to send money for hookers and blow. They were secure though, so I could see why they used them. I didn't reach out to the underage Trump kid, but both his daughters, his son-in-law, who for some reason Terry wanted me to reach out ot, and his other two boys, all replied within 12 hours. I had seventy-nine emails or phone numbers directly contacting campaign staffers, event staffers, and more inside Trump's camp. They were all ready, so I sent them to Terry so he would know I was too.I had direct phone numbers for everyone besides Donald Senior by 5 pm. It was astonishing.

I tried my luck with Hillary's camp, but it was air-tight. Her web presence was simple, a dated website that exchanged

Hillary 2008 with 2016. Her websites had contact forms and phone numbers leading to dead ends. Mrs. Clinton was a former First Lady, she had been inside politics for over 50 years and was untouchable for people like me. It was the complete opposite. A *Rolling Stone* editor would need to contact them.

Terry sent over another email, asking if he could book me a flight. It also had some other formalities for the hiring process- there was a link to fill out private info. The website said it was secure, and I could see it was the backend of Rolling-Stone dot com.I hit submit and didn't think about it because if *Rolling Stone* wanted to hack my identity, well, good luck paying off my student debt. I got another email then that told me the pay. I almost jumped out of my pants. It was $1,700.00 bucks a week, double what I made working two jobs. And it also came with a room to live in the District full-time until November. I didn't call and quit my jobs just yet though. When the plane ticket confirmation came in, I called them to take off. I let them both know there was a good chance I was peacing-out.

And then I started to pack. I didn't care that I was leaving Saturday morning, and the Derby was that afternoon. I didn't care about the parade, the boat race, the Oaks, the Derby, none of it. I was ready to leave the Ville, and interview for *Rolling Stone.*

I started prepping by watching job interview techniques online. I called my mother, who was at the damn Pegasus parade and told her the news. Her response, "Yes, it is April, but it isn't April Fool's day anymore!"

She didn't believe me, and I don't blame her.

"Well, sweetie your little friend, Sawyer, is going to be upset. Are you really leaving on Derby Saturday?"

She was right, but Sawyer would have to take a backseat

for *Rolling* Fucking *Stone* magazine. I could hear her telling my aunt, "Gunner got a job working for the Rolling Stoned!"

When I hung up, I glanced at my left hand and saw the scar. It had been almost 8 years since Sawyer and I made the pact. The scar was right through the middle of my pal, and it had hurt when we made the cut. It had scabbed up for 10 weeks afterward.

Sawyer was my best friend. Well, he had been in high school anyway, and we had made a blood pact to always attend the Kentucky Derby together. Every fucking year until one of us died. We cut our hands and shook on it. We were both fifteen, standing in the middle of the infield at Churchill Downs, and were both drunk for the first time in our lives.

It was bombastic and pretentious and dumb, but at the time we both were. Sawyer and I had grown apart since high school and grown up since we made the oath. It was something teenage guys do after they get drunk in the infield of the Derby. Sawyer would have to understand why I was going to break it.

CHAPTER 5

"Sawyer Barnes..."

I met Sawyer Barnes on the second day of my sopho-more year at Atherton High School. He was in a new district since his parents had split and was in my homeroom, math, and gym classes. He was an overgrown child with the post-puberty body of a man but the pre-puberty brain of a child. He was already 6 feet tall with a mustache and didn't have a nickel of common sense. He was hilarious, mostly because he understood his own ugly and didn't know anyone at school, so he didn't care about the high school social games. It didn't take long for us to become friends, especially when we started to realize we both hated the same shit. Hating the same shit as adolescents can lead to a lifetime bond, and that's how it was for us. We both hated to run so we'd cut laps together in gym, we both hated the same people, teachers, both hated authority, and knew anyone who abided by the law all the time was a sucker.

We were punks and losers and whatevs, and the im-aginary hierarchy of high school didn't apply to us because we weren't invited. We weren't winning any awards. We were just trying to do our time. The five days a week, seven hours a day for twelve years that the government required of us, and if we could do it together while reading Mad Magazines and pulling pranks, so much the better. Then we found booze together. Our first love and for no good reason. Maybe because we weren't the losers anymore, now we were the boozers. We became tighter than a double knot. We eventually become blood brothers, cutting open our palms and shaking them while drunk for the first time in the infield of Churchill Downs during the running of the roses. We kept the pact alive for seven years. It had turned into a weekend full of non-stop boozing. We would start on Friday and continue in the infield Saturday afternoon at Churchill Downs.

After high school, Sawyer entered the private sector. He did some jobs here and there but finally stumbled upon a bimbo who could stand him for more than two nights, and they got married. Marriage came with new responsibilities and that meant a better job. That new position came from her family in St. Louis, so he was living in Missouri working on two and a half kids and a picket fence house. Derby was the one weekend he got to let it all hang out. He looked forward to the Derby like kids do Christmas. Our blood pact meant a lot to him, but this was my big break in life. No more sweeping the floors trying to make an impression at CJ, no more chasing down insurance fraud cases, or selling cash bonds in the early mornings.

On Derby eve, he busted in like Kramer, standing with a suitcase, paper bag, and backpack, all probably filled with booze, and yelled out, "Honey, I'm home!"

I didn't respond, but he did.

"You ready to get white girl wasted?!"

And he shut the door laughing hard at his own joke.

Sawyer was now a tall man at 6'3, the chubby baby fat was gone, so he looked physically in shape. He wasn't, and I knew he wasn't because he ate like an alligator at a steakhouse and never worked out, but genetics are funny. And to add to the humor, his acne was gone, but his hair was receding. He was going with a comb-over anytime he didn't have a hat on, but it didn't matter to the ladies, they loved his square chin. Ladies always love a man with a perpendicular jaw line, and Sawyer had one fit for the cover of a US Army brochure. Hard, square chin, dark eyebrows, no facial hair, and sharp blue eyes.

But he stood in front of me looking ridiculous. He never did learn how to dress and was wearing an oversized blue dress shirt that looked like he stole it from an inmate, jeans with holes in them, and a little rascal's hat like he wanted to be a bookie. Before I even said hello I had to ask, "Why do you have holes in your jeans?"

He dropped his backpack and suitcase on my couch and carried the brown paper bag into my kitchen before answering in a mocking tone, "Why do you have holes in your jeans!"

"It's the new style, and not just because that fag* Con-Ye either!"

**The use of the word faggot is to remember people like Kanye West which is not fine, not someone who is homosexual.*

"Yeah, dude, okay, but you buy the jeans like that, people don't rip holes in their old pair of jeans and say it's the new style!"

He didn't want to hear it though. He moved into my kitchen and began unloading his bags of booze into my fridge.

"Gunner, Gunner, Gunner, you old El Camino asshole! I ain't seen you since Thanksgiving, but let me tell you this, you ain't got no sense of style, and you don't have a beer in your hand, why aren't you drinking?"

He handed me a beer.

"Why do you call me that? El Camino? What's that from?"

"You don't remember the song?" And he started to dance a bit and he sang out.

El Camino, El Camino, El Camino
The front looks like a car, the back looks like a truck
Ellll Camino, Ellll Camino, E-lll Camino
The front is where you drive, the back is where you ----

"That's not even a real song, and I would never drive an El Camino, I just said that because Kermit's step-dad had one."

"Whatever, El Camino Bush, you always wanted to drive one. That's your favorite car, and you know it!"

"So let's get the shots going and the party crackin'. It feels like I walked into a morgue. Turn the Cubs game on and get your shot glasses out!"

"Last year was the drunkest we have ever been. Drunkest I've ever been in my life probably," I reminded him, but I was dreading what I really had to say.

"Drunkest you have been in your life …..so far!" He corrected, chugging his beer.

"Either way, you need another beer, drink that one pussy, and I was thinking pizza, more beers, and shots, and I mean more beer like we don't drink anything but beer all weekend! We don't even take in oxygen, just beer, and the shots, we need one every fifteen minutes, starting as soon as I open up a bottle, right now."

He went to get his bag in the kitchen for more beer. I

sat down on the couch, listening to him singing the El Camino song again, adding in verses about how it was my favorite car.

He walked back into the living room and belched.

"What? What is it Gun? I know something is up with you, are you on some sort of antibiotic for weird anal warts and you can't drink alcohol for up to six months?"

He took a swig of his beer as he grinned at his joke.

"Yep, I caught anal warts, and now I am on antibiotics that take six months to work, and I can't booze while taking them. How did you know? Did we both get them from your wife?"

"My wife, your wife, whatevs. Get the Cubs game on!" He searched for the remote.

We had a mutual love for the lovable losers. We would skip class in high school, go to his dad's apartment in Jefferson-ville, and watch WGN day games while drinking his old man's booze. The glory days.

"Well, something is up, I can feel it like a disturbance in the force. Drink that beer, and come look," he said, pulling up his bag

The suitcase was filled to the brim with Jell-O shots.

"Two hundred and fifty of them bad boys, and look, we can shove them down our pants or wherever to get them into the Downs tomorrow."

When I didn't grab a shot, and he saw I wasn't chugging my beer, I knew I had to tell them. Basically, I just told them, this is *Rolling Stone*. A blood pact we made when we were fif-teen wasn't real. It was kids' stuff - it's not like we were kings or lords or that it really mattered at the end of the day.

I explained this wasn't even my dream job; it was bigger

than that. It was every writer's dream. I brought up how he had moved to the Lou for a job and a wife, trying to play into empathy or sympathy or something he could relate to. He was an understanding guy, he would get it.

But when I looked at his face, I could tell he didn't.

"Bullshit! *Rolling Stone* wants you? You?!"

"What the fuck does that mean? You think I've just been sweeping the floor at the CJ? I am a damn good reporter, and I pretty much got this gig because I found out about a Trump event not happening that freaking *Rolling Stone* didn't even know about!"

"So you're breaking our pact, our lifetime agreement, I mean fuck, you have to fly out tomorrow morning? The whole goddamn world is trying to get into the Ville, and *Rolling Stone* wants you to fly out of the Ville. Sounds suspect to me."

He grabbed a Jell-O shot and tossed me one.

"Tomorrow morning? Derby morning, I honestly don't even think flights fly out of the Ville on Derby, seriously! It's incoming only, like until after the race, seriously, they fly in all those east coast yuppies on private jets."

He leaned back, took the shot, and cracked a beer.

"Yeah, I have a flight direct to the District. I leave at 11am, I know it's our annual, but this is more important," I told him as sternly as I could.

"I mean, the blood pact is what it is like you said, we ain't dukes or kings or warlocks or wizards so it's not real, I mean as far as we know it's not real."

He was accepting it as he was realizing it.

"This was going to make eight years, eight fucking years man, almost to a freaking decade, and hey, look, aren't you

SUICIDE NOTES TO KURT COBAIN

going to feel sick tomorrow? You could get sick tomorrow and fly out on Sunday or Monday. Do you have a fever? Your cheeks look red, and you are a little pale!"

He was ranting.

"I get it, man, grab you a beer though, we can still do pizza and drinks tonight, right?"

"We are for sure doing that!"

"Doesn't it seem odd that *Rolling Stone* is having you fly out of the Ville on Derby Saturday though?" he asked while pulling out more shots..

"I mean the Derby is great, but it's a two-minute event. That's it. That two minutes, the whole world is watching the Ville. Then it's over, and sure, musicians are here for the race, but I am not covering music. I am doing politics."

"You? Politics?" He asked before chugging the beer I brought him.

"I mean, I am going to get into covering music at some point, I hope, but yeah, I am starting on the road, covering the campaigns of Trump, Clinton, Bush, some ugly dude from Texas, Tom Cruise, or something, Ted maybe?"

"You don't know enough about politics to be a writer for *Rolling Stone*. You don't even know Lyin' Ted Cruz," Sawyer said as he put his feet up on my coffee table.

"Oh, that's the guy that Trump called his wife ugly?" I had seen the headlines.

"Yeah, and she is ugly, but how are you working at *Rolling Stone*? Are you sure you aren't getting punk'd?"

"I'm not getting punk'd. They bought me the plane ticket. I thi-ink they saw the po-tent-ial in who I am as a writer." I was lying to him because I didn't know who I was as a writer.

"Either way that's lame, and it's only going to be two campaigns you need to watch, Trump and Crooked Hillary, but really just Trump!" he said, pulling out his phone.

"Yeah, I mean, I think *Rolling Stone*, Terry, the guy who I am interviewing with, just said Tom Cruise and other Bush boy as a formality. I think I will be covering those two camps only."

Sawyer wasn't paying attention.

"Let me show you something." He handed me his phone. There was a picture of Kurt Cobain with a quote under him.

"In the end, I believe my generation will surprise everyone. We already know that both political parties are playing both sides from the middle and we'll elect a true outsider when we fully mature. I wouldn't be surprised if it's not a business tycoon who can't be bought and who does what's right for the people. Someone like Donald Trump as crazy as that sounds." - Kurt Cobain 1993

"Kurt Cobain never said that shit," I said, handing him back the phone. I didn't know if Kurt Cobain had ever said it, but it felt like propaganda to me.

"How do you know? Were you there?" he snapped, snatching his phone, looking at me like I was an idiot.

"Was I there? No, I wasn't fucking there - what's next, you got a quote from Tupac endorsing that toupee-wearing mother -" I didn't finish the sentence.

"Trump is the only one who can save this country, man, you wait and see!"

I shook my head, it had become a reality. Sawyer was a Trumpie. Red hat. A brainwashed enemy! Trumpies were a new phenomenon; even without any political knowledge, I knew what they were. Trumpies were Faux News watchers, who didn't subscribe to reality. More than that, they were a new group of people sprung from the offspring of the disenfranchised and silent majority, and they were full of undereducated loudmouths and cricket eaters.

I had seen some of the signs on Sawyer's social media, but I wasn't convinced until he showed me the bullshit Cobain quote. It was only May, and I still had time to convince him otherwise. So I brought up our old arch-nemesis.

"I don't think Kurt said that, but let's just both agree to vote out Addison in the fall."

"Addison Mitch McConnell! That's a man we can both hate. Haven't you been paying attention? Trump wants to drain the swamp of the guys like the Turtle. Old Allison will be gone in the first 100 days of a Trump presidency. Ya know, my old man wants to move across the river just to vote against the Turtle."

"I never understood why your old man lives in Indiana. The best thing in Indiana is the Colgate Clock and it faces towards the Ville!" I said and we both chugged our beers.

"The old turtle motherfucker!"

"He does look like a turtle - remember when he shit his pants?!" I said. We both did hate the dude who represented us Kentuckians in the Senate.

"Addison shit his pants!" Sawyer yelled, handing me a shot.

"Mitch McConnell pooped his pants." I said in a deep voice as if it was breaking news.

"Addison lives in the District. You will probably see that motherfucker. I bet you $500 you won't hand him a bag of turtle food if you see him!" Sawyer said, raising his shot.

"I am only there until November; I might not see him."

"You will see that weasel, $500!" He put up a jelly shot so we could cheer over the bet.

"Bet, " I said, laughing before downing shot number two.

It was only shot number two, but it was shot number one at ruining everything. The night, the morning, the flight, the job. Everything that had anything to do with *Rolling Stone* magazine. I wasn't thinking. We hit Bardstown Road like pirates in town for one night and one night only. It was Derby Eve, so the entire city was lit like a match. At one point, I saw cops in uniform leaving a liquor store with a brown paper bag. Sawyer and I proceeded to get to the level of destroyed, two sheets to the wind, and that's one of the only memories I have of the entire night. A vague glimpse of losing my guts behind a redneck bar somewhere off Dixie Highway, but have no full memories.

It was dumb and dangerous. I was given a once-in-a-lifetime opportunity, and I tried my best to fuck it up. I woke up on Derby morning somehow in my own bed. I wasn't hungover but still drunk. It was ten to nine, and I felt like a kid on his birthday. When I went out to the kitchen, Sawyer was in his underwear with two ladies both in their underwear, and they were all about to bong a beer.

Of course, I decided to bong one after they had, and right after I did it, Sawyer asked me, "So you aren't going to DC, or are you?"

"Shit!' I had forgotten all about it. I ran into my room, threw together the last part of my duffel bag, and brushed my teeth while dressing. Toothpaste shot down my black pants, but I didn't have time to do more than just rub it off. It smeared, I grimaced, and I started to order an Uber.

I came back out and the two ladies were dressed and saying goodbye. The taller one, both were brunettes, leaned in and kissed Sawyer. They left.

"You are really leaving huh?"

"Dude, who the fuck were the girls and why were they naked, no, naked is fine, why did they leave?"

"You don't remember them two? We met them last night at the bar off Dixie Highway. You were pretty wasted."

"Yeah, no, yeah, but why didn't you wake me up?" My brain wasn't working yet. I noticed a deck of cards scattered across my living room floor, "Were you guys playing strip poker?"

He didn't respond.

"What about your wife?"

He held up his hand and pointed to his empty ring finger. It took me a minute to get it, but I didn't have time to get into it with him.

"Yeah, so I am pretty sure she is cheating on me, but dude, you shouldn't have fallen asleep, Gun!"

"Look, I gotta go, I have a flight to the District so can you lock up here?"

"Yeah, I can lock up. They are going to Waffle House to get me some grub, and coming back. I think that one likes me, but I don't know yet." He rubbed his oversized belly. At least he had pants on now.

"Are you an idiot? That chick you just kissed, you wondered if she likes you? She kissed you, on your lips!"

Sawyer dapped me up, showing me the scar on his

hand. I looked at mine. And then I left. I didn't have time to think about it.

"Can't believe you are breaking the pact, we could get cursed!" I heard him yell through the door.

I arrived at the airport at 10:35 and had to sprint to my gate. I was the very last person on the flight. I was seated in the last row, center seat. I smelt like a sink at a bar at closing time. It was the quickest flight of my life, since I fell asleep. I woke up as the plane was taxiing into the gate, and my pants were wet and warm. I had pissed myself.

Since I was riding in the bitch seat, the red-headed, short dude next to me knew I had pissed myself, and so did the wrench of a wicked old hag on the aisle seat. She let me know about it as soon as I woke up too. And she let the stewardess know too.

"He urinated himself!"

The stewardess came in for a closer observation. I was embarrassed, but I used it as an advantage to get up and get my shit first. I ran to the exit instead of the bathroom. I didn't change clothes though; airport restrooms are where the seasonal flu starts every year.

And that's how I arrived in the District before my interview with *Rolling Stone*. Hungover and smelling like piss.

CHAPTER 6

"The Mansion"

Addison "Mitch" McConnell's security team wasn't going to catch me on my board. I floated down the boulevard part of the street and then took the long way to the overpass that would lead me back to my digs at the mansion I was staying at in Georgetown.

I moved to the District the same day I showed up and learned the ins and outs of the city, the shortcuts, and the backdoors that led into the back alleys. I'd met the riff-raff while setting up meetings with the lords of the city that ran the country. The meat of the District wasn't the political scene. The Hill controlled the national narrative, but it wasn't who the city was. The character of the city was in the night-clubs and the graffiti that was taken down at light speed. I loved living in the Capitol, and it wasn't because of the political scene. I hated most of the brown noses who got into politics - I would let it be known by my graffiti in the bathroom stalls when I was inside any of the political offices. It all felt pseudo. My attitude was rudimentary, but I've always been immature for my age.

Now at this time, I was holding a USB that could change the fate of the free world. It was bouncing around, free to fall out of my pocket at any time as I floated down the ramps of the overpass. I rolled down the last ramp, did an ollie, and popped my board up on the curb. I was mostly just cruising along so I picked up my board and cut through a house renovation that took me into the alley that led to the backdoor of the mansion.

The mansion was a six-bedroom, five-bath, red brick house in Georgetown that I had been staying in. I had two roommates, Olga and Dirk, but I rarely saw them, and if I did, it was fine. It wasn't like having roommates in an apartment or a dorm since the three of us each had a master room that was bigger than my whole place back in the Ville. Besides, they barely spoke to me; I didn't have a clue if they worked for *Rolling Stone*. I didn't have any staff meetings for the magazine.

Olga was beautiful; I was pretty sure Dirk was screwing her. They were both a few years younger than me and Russian. Terry was also Russian. It's not that I had a problem with Russians, it's just I thought I had Terry pegged. The hiring manager and editor at a magazine like *Rolling Stone* would be a middle-aged white dude with messy hair, who wore shirts from obscure bands, had a quick wit, played a little guitar on the weekends, and stored an unhealthy amount of music facts in his amygdala. But that wasn't Terry.

Terry was a fifty-year-old woman from Russia. She had a tough demeanor about the way she presented herself - it was standoffish - and almost crude. She wasn't cocky but rather very to the point. She was a business-woman. Fierce. That's how she climbed the ranks at a huge corporation like *Rolling Stone.*

To sum her up, she didn't take any shit.

I met her in the mansion on Derby Saturday back in May. I was licking my wounds and smelt like it. Terry was sitting with her back to the wall, smoking, drinking Diet Coke in the kitchen.

I had taken an Uber to the place and still didn't know what I was in for. Dirk had let me inside, but he wasn't much for conversation. He said five words tops, and "no" was three of them.

Terry was direct so I didn't ask a ton of questions. She gave me a ton of info right off the bat. She stood up to meet me and sized me up. She was in heels or something close, I don't know women's shoes, but she was about as tall as me. As she shook my hand, I smelled myself. I wasn't prepared for the interview and was mentally kicking myself in the ass.

"Mis-ter Gun-ner Bush so happy to welcome you here to our team. So have a seat, do you want some coffee?"

"Yeah, is that it? I can get it," I said, turning to grab a cup off the wall pouring myself a cup. She sat back down, so I followed suit. I was trying to shake off the hangover. She had a leather bag on her side and pulled out a few things, setting them on the table in front of us.

"Thank you for coming to work for us at *Rolling Stone*. I am a freelance employee, which means that I pay you, I hire you. You work for me. Your work will be credited in *Rolling Stone* if it is published – this is a basic economics deal, right? Do you understand?"

"Uh, huh, yes, yes," I told her, but I didn't. My head wasn't working. It felt like a temp service, but I didn't ask. I wanted to hurl, but she was starting the interview off as if I had the job!

Her English wasn't great, but it was better than my Russian would have been. She opened a white envelope and pulled out a key.

"Dis key open the back and front doors."

Then she flipped the same envelope over and handed it to me.

"Dis is the Wifi password."

"Okay, okay, great," I was nodding at her, but I was staying back a bit hoping she wouldn't smell me. And still trying to process if I had landed the job.

"Please, not have guests into this house. It is not a rule, if you do, it is okay, we are only asking that you not have guests in the house." She stopped talking and looked at me.

"Are you okay? You not sick, huh?" She was worried now that I was sitting back so far, so I stopped slouching.

"No, yes, no," my brain still wasn't working, so I continued quickly, "I ate something on the plane and it made my stomach upset." I rubbed my belly and moved back again so she wouldn't smell me.

"I understand," she said, and I could see her face had a ton of wrinkles. Her smile didn't match her face either. It was a fake smile that she had learned like a bird taught to mimic voices. She handed me another key.

"Dis open your bedroom. It has a bath inside. The door to your room has a nightstand outside with a red and gold lamp on it. I will pay you weekly there. So I will put the money into the nightstand."

She again looked at me like she wanted an answer.

"Right, so I got the job?" I asked. She wasn't looking at me though, she was digging into her leather bag again. She pulled out another white envelope. It was thicker.

"Yes, of course, you gots thee job!" she exclaimed, slamming her hand down onto the table and flashing the fake smile at me again. The envelope was full of money.

"This is for week number one, and you will get that same amount every week. It will be on the nightstand outside your room every Friday. Friday is payday, no?"

She was looking at me for confirmation, so I said, "Yes,"

while I flipped it open and saw it was full of crisp hundreds.

"These envelopes have the contacts we want you to make. Starting right away, please," she said as she flipped open a manila folder. It was detailed reports on a ton of people. It had pictures, phone numbers, emails, and some even had both work and home addresses.

"Okay, you have the contact information already here listed, so you want me to contact them through email or phone?"

I could tell she didn't like when I asked questions.

"These pictures and names are good, maybe the email works, maybe not. Maybe the phone number works, maybe not. You will find out." She dropped her smoke into the soda can.

"Okay, and I am going to set up interviews or?" I was already confused on the job, and it wasn't because of my rank odor or hangover.

"No, you set up an appointment with them for *Rolling Stone*," she said, very condescendingly, as if I didn't know what I had signed up for.

It wasn't the job I had signed up for, so I asked her, "What about the writing?"

"Yes, the writing, you will submit at least 500 words each week. Maybe we print it, maybe we don't. It goes through a committee; it is not one person." She told me sharply.

"Okay, five hundred words weekly...And when should it be turned in by?"

She was staring at me as if I was a monkey at a typewriter not quoting the Bible yet.

"Friday, I should turn it in before I get paid on Friday,

right?" I answered my own question.

She nodded at me and continued, "You need to reach out to all of these people for us, and it will be all sorts of people, not just politicians, maybe, maybe not. This is for lots of different things. Interviews or maybe fact check a story another person said. It doesn't matter. You set up the meetings, okay?"

"Right, contacting people isn't a problem."

And that would become my real job over the summer. Despite submitting an article every single week, I was never published. Not yet anyway, and I know the payday on getting an article published has to be lottery big. I had tried everything, deep pieces, funny pieces, damn-near plagiarized shit from Hunter S., a short piece with exactly 500 words, a long piece that was 3,500. I had tried everything and still hadn't been published yet.

But now I had the goods.

Before she left, she pulled out a credit card and told me it was a company card and she wanted me to start booking. The card didn't have a name on it, it was just numbers, and she showed me a company name to put in.

"Start booking? Start booking what?" I thought it was a language barrier now.

"You can use dis card to start booking your trip like Timothy Crouse and Hunter S. Thompson, who you quoted in your email applying for the position."

She said it very matter-of-factly again, but with her smile on it felt like she was reading a script.

"We will get your official company credit card with your name on it soon but for now you use this one."

"Right."

In the first folder in front of me was the list of stops for Trump and Hillary.

Anxiety was creeping in, and it was like I had missed a whole meeting or phone call.

"Okay, so I just book the flights and hotels?" I asked, but she didn't respond. She was flipping through another envelope.

"So, 500 words to you by Friday, and I am writing each week from the campaign trail?" It was the dumbest question I had asked yet.

"Yes," she said, and I was starting to wonder.

"I bet it pays more to get in the magazine than it does the website doesn't it?" I asked, but I was really just thinking out loud. I had no idea how hard it would be to get published.

She looked at me like she didn't know what I was talking about. As if my question had hurt her brain. "I will pay you $1,700.00 a week. Is that not okay?"

"Yeah, no, yeah." I did it again. "That's great, but what if I get something published in the magazine? Do you pay me more, like a bonus on top of that?"

"Okay, we will pay you a bonus if you make it into the magazine." She said, but she looked confused, and she was still upset. And I still felt as if I had missed an important email.

"Yeah, I am just making sure. The last thing I want to do is try to recreate freaking Crouse, I mean, Hunter S. had his own style, but I want to mingle with the people, not the candidates. It's a new approach. I have heard the horror stories about how the writers in the box back in '04 had to smuggle in smokes, and I know how the press is demonized by some of these candidates, so I can't say I will be right in the middle of the pack. I want to write the real stories!"

I was trying to sound as smart and passionate about the position as I could. It was all bullshit though. I was as hungover as Jesus on Passover, and nervous, excited, hungry, and amped up on the dark roast I was sipping.

She didn't reply; she just nodded at me and began flipping through the names and pictures of senators she wanted me to set up meetings with. It started to feel like I was staring at top-secret government files. She wanted me to reach out to them immediately to make contact. That's how sophisticated everything was, and I knew I had signed on to the right team.

Sen. Steve Daines (R-Mont.), Sen. John REDACTED (R-N.D.), Sen. Ron REDACTED (R-Wis.), Sen. John REDACTED (R-La.), Sen. Jerry REDACTED (R-Kan.), Sen. John REDACTED (R-S.D.), and Rep. Kay REDACTED (R-Texas). And also, REDACTED, REDACTED, REDACTED.

"You will have your email set up, GunnerBush @ Rolling Stone dot com. We will forward you the login information. Please only use it to contact people. We can see all of them, and we can trace your emails."

"You're tracing my emails?"

"Yes, on that account, so please only use it for business. Do not mix your personal life into things," she told me and I could see she was all business. She was projecting, letting me know I needed to be all business too.

"Every morning at eight am you will get an email from me. I want you to respond every day on the daily events by five pm or so. It could be important, or it could be nothing. We will see each day, okay?"

She was starting to sound like a foster mom talking to a new foster.

"You share the house with Olga and Dirk. You have met Dirk, Olga comes later. They are like niece and nephew to me. Dirk will show you into your room. It is upstairs. You look sick, Gunner Bush, pale in the face, you need to get some rest and then get to work. You work for me now, okay?"

She said the last part quickly, but I caught it. It didn't seem like a slip of the language. If she kept paying me envelopes full of cash, I would continue to work for her.

"Here is my contact, it is my name on WHATSAPP, because of the nature of the business, you will talk to me via WHATSAPP and WHATSAPP only."

"I don't even have a WHATSAPP, or at least not one that I can log into, I think I had one when it first came out, but then everybody moved to Snap so I just kinda followed along not that I am a follo-"

"No, it's fine, we have created one for you using your new email. Here is your password and log in." She handed me another slit of paper.

"What's that mean, the nature of the business?"

"It means I am available 24 hours a day, 7 days a week, as is much of the industry, so we can't have people calling our house lines at all hours, some of us have newborn babies, and that is how you will contact me, okay?"

Of course I understood. I had noticed it when contacting the Trump camp. The apps were all the rage.

"You have done very well with making contacts, using your outreach. We have set up a meeting with Junior Trump and Trump's son-in-law in July at Trump Tower. It is very good work by you, Gun-ner Bush." She smiled again, but this time it was genuine. She was happy about this.

She stood up, so I did too, and she said, "You do look very sick, Gunner A. Bush, please get some rest, but not too much, then work. Work! Okay?"

And then she left.

No contract. No paperwork. No background check. That was it. Seventeen crisp hundred dollar bills straight out of the ATM into my possession. A company credit card to plan my own tour across the country and a room in a fucking mansion. It was the Life of Riley, and it didn't feel real. I had the job, I had my first payment, and I was to start immediately.

Everything felt fresh back then, in May – like the dopamine rush from hitting the lottery.

Dirk showed me my room, and I went to work mapping out how I would follow the two campaigns. Terry was adamant that I met the staffers on the campaign trail. They would become the people in the White House to know. So I used Google Maps, and I plotted my stops.

I picked modest hotels and humbling seat positions on cheap flights. I didn't want to be the one guy in the company booking first-class trips. It was a test, and I knew it. I passed with flying colors because I never heard from anyone about any of my purchases. Stay off the radar. I had learned some things at CJ.

So that's what I did all summer. I followed Hillary and Trump's campaign across the lower 48 and turned in one article a week. Terry would send me names of different people I had to contact, and I would go get them. She would have the money on the nightstand outside my bedroom, even if I wasn't in town. I never even really saw Terry, we always just contacted back and forth through WHATSAPP. Olga and Dirk never stole the money, and for all I knew, they might have put it there.

It felt like a dream. If I didn't have access to the email address, GunnerBush@Rolling Stone, I wouldn't have believed it. Imposter syndrome to the max. My name had never been published in the magazine. Not once. Besides the email, I had nothing that showed I worked for *Rolling Stone*.

It was $1,700 every week, except for the July 4th payment which was double, and a note that read, Merry July 4th.

It was like getting paid to eat candy, but now I was determined to get published. I was eager, and not just for the payday, which I could only imagine was astronomical. I wanted it so I had a bigger shot at working for the magazine after November, or could at least have it on my resume moving forward. I had been trying since May to get published, and it was already October. Only now that I had the flash drive did I feel like I had the pieces to put together what felt like a Pulitzer for the magazine.

CHAPTER 7

"Loveland, Colorado"

Trump had a campaign rally in the ski resort town of Loveland, so I flew into Denver and had to overpay for a yellow cab. It was sunset, and the sky was dancing with pink color hanging over the mountains. Since the legalization, the Mile High State had a reputation with right-wing media for being full of homeless addicts, but that was far from the truth. Most people's lives hadn't changed at all, and homelessness is a problem everywhere. I wasn't in Loveland to deal with either.

The Hillary October surprise fell into my lap, but I was vigorously working on getting my paws on the Trump surprise that Julie Awning kept swearing was up to his sleeve. I was heading to the Mile High State regardless, but now I had a meeting with my guy in the Trump campaign, and he had made it a point to let me know he really wanted to talk with me. Dude D was the man in the camp, and if anyone had the dirt, it was him. David was his real name, but after our initial email, which came back when I first started at the magazine, he made sure we only contacted each other via WHATSAPP. His username was DudeDeplorable –I shortened it to Dude D and it stuck.

I had officially met Dude D in person at the Good Old

Boys convention in August at Believeland when I fell off the wagon. I wasn't ever fully on the wagon, just avoiding the hard liquor before five pm. I thought I could walk the line. It was impossible to avoid the harder stuff while both covering the GOP and being in Northern Ohio. I went full Hunter S., and it was surely because Terry wasn't giving me any tips on what would get me published. So for the betterment of my own mental health, I was able to skip most of the boring parts of the convention, especially when Trump's kids spoke. I had set up an interview with Terry and the heathen kids back in July at Trump Tower, I was hoping it would lead to a huge payday, but I never heard anything more about it. When I inquired, Terry told me the meeting was about adoptions. She was happy for me to set it up. She didn't say anything, but I could tell. So instead of hearing the speeches, I hit the local scene and explored the Mistake on the Lake. I watched the Browns lose, went to the Rock and Roll Hall of Fame, and found the other side, the pubs, and the cabarets. All while boozing like a fish in a keg. It was part of being a journalist to hit up the local watering holes and drink with the locals. I was lucky to keep my pants on, and at one point, I ended up at a place called Crazy Horse. I got hammered like a hung changeup, celebrating nothing and everything on a Tuesday night in August. A few of the ladies that worked at the Crazy Horse heard I was staying at the hotel headquarters for the Good Old Boys, so naturally, they wanted to come to see the digs and perhaps score some sort of payment from any horny Republican they could. I believe in free enterprise, so I obliged. They had tried before, but hotel security wouldn't let them in if they tried on their own. The Good Old Boys always had the tightest security at their hotels during conventions – they had since watching the Chicago scare back in '68. I had the golden ticket inside, so we all took a cab. Upon entering the hotel lobby, I met Dude D for the first time in person.

Up until this point, Dude D had just been an email, as

I had to him, but now we were face to face. He was a lanky dude with string bean arms and the walk of a man with a bad back. He was in his 30s but looked younger than me. He didn't seem like much, but he was. He had been with the Good Old Boys since '08 working the state of North Carolina for McCain, and he had kept climbing the ladder doing the jobs nobody wanted to do. He was also one of the few insiders that really wanted Trump to win the nomination. He would do whatever he could for Trump, and he got giddy talking about the guy. It was odd to watch a grown man turn into a fangirl for another grown man, almost like when a young boy gets infatuated with Ewoks or Spiderman. Those types of feelings are usually gone by puberty, but here was a grown-ass man acting this way about Trump of all people. He was working harder for Trump than he did for Romney or McCain. Not that he didn't work hard for them, he always told me. Dude D was able to get me out of the press area for the entire convention too. The press row for Trump events was like standing in the lion's den as entertainment for Trumpies. They would yell, spit, and throw sodas at us, almost getting into fisticuffs with someone before the night was over nearly every time. It was barbaric. A madhouse.

Now, I was going to meet Dude D again, this time hoping he would deliver the goods. A nice fat piece of skullduggery to seal my fate and get me published into the magazine. I was plastered by the time I ran into Dude D in the lobby. It wasn't my fault I was boozing so hard; Terry should have put me on a tighter leash or sumshit. And don't forget life on the road is hard. I needed the extra shots.

The lobby was full when I arrived in Loveland. I stepped in, feeling like I was in the wrong place. It was as if I had made a wrong turn and ended up at a Klan meeting the night before a cross burning. Red hats galore, all of them on the heads of white folk. The hotel, a chain, knew what was up too because they had every flat screen in the place tuned to Faux News. It was happy hour or sumshit. Everyone in the lobby was drinking and trying the different types of cheese and crackers that were sitting out. Dude D had offered to get me from the airport, and I was happy I had declined. I got wasted on the jet and didn't want to deal with him.

He didn't let that happen though, he approached me while I was in line to check in to the hotel.

He was dressed in a suit as was much of the room, meanwhile, I was in sweatpants and a long-sleeve Ron Jon shirt with giant Sony headphones around my neck. When he approached, I acted like I was super surprised to see him, though I knew he was coming. He told me to join him at the bar after I got my bags upstairs. I stared around the room, noticing a lot of the folks were old school Republican types – typical Good Old Boys. Most of them. The type that voted straight R in the voting booth no matter if their own sisters were running Democrat. Like that adage, Democrats fall in love, and Republicans fall in line. It wasn't the same crowd that was at Trump rallies.

The last thing I wanted to do was dance with Dude D around a bunch of Trumpies, but there was no way around it. I was drunk from the flight but needed another drink to deal with him. I didn't want to act like I was stressing over the October Surprise because if he thought I was trying to get it, he might not give it. Also, the Cubs were on, and I wanted to catch a few innings, even if that meant changing the channel on one of the hotel TVs.

I didn't even change my clothes, all that "When in Rome" shit is only good when you care to impress people, and I didn't give a flying. I hit the lobby in search of my favorite beer, a free one, and then lurked around trying to find a TV remote. I didn't see Dude D, so I decided to mingle with the red hats a bit. I stood around a black baby grand that played chopsticks or some other tune every 11 minutes and tuned into the propaganda on the flat screen. I did my best to grab beers from different bartenders each time, as I didn't know the limit. I tipped well enough for it to not matter, but I still didn't want to cause a scene by grabbing ten free brews at happy hour.

The flat screens were tuned into Faux, which was a propaganda piano for the new strategy put in place by Trump's new campaign manager, who resembled a homeless person with less style. It was a simple strategy, not much of a change from Trump's former strategies. It was a 3 point plan, attack, attack, attack, and with Faux News, the bullshit could spew out 24 hours a day, 7 days a week. They didn't even need talking heads anymore, they could just run clips of Hillary shooting herself in the foot. She had called Americans, "Deplorable," and "Basement Dwellers." And according to the station, her Benghazi incident had turned into a scandal the size of Watergate. They kept the talking heads who were the best in the business at spreading propaganda, telling their audiences lies, and adding, "of course you already know this," because "you are smart." So the viewers felt smart even if their IQs were next to a donkey. The masses were just uneducated enough to take it in and say, "yeah I did know that" and feel powerful.

Most importantly for Trump, the Crooked Hillary nickname had stuck like bubblegum, and here I was, standing in a whole lobby full of these types of believers.

I drank my free brew, watching an oddly round man pick at free food like a fly. He saw me looking so he stopped, then pointed at the flat screen with his fork and said to nobody and everybody, "Can we please lock that cunt up."

Then he laughed at himself to show he really was talking to himself, but he turned slightly to look at me and some other ass hat who was next to me nibbling on cheese like a squirrel. The squirrel man laughed, and they both looked at me for some sort of acknowledgment that I also thought Hillary Clinton should be arrested for nothing.

So I tipped my beer up and said with dramatic flair, "She won't be, buttery males!"

"Butt-ery males?" And "Huh?" was the reaction from the two clowns, and as the round man turned I could see he was wearing a red hat and a Trump University shirt.

He asked me, "What do you say?"

"Butt Er E Males?" The squirrel man said again.

"What? No," I grimaced, "Buttery Males? That's kinda weird," I said back, acting like I just didn't say that and they made it completely up, "I said, BUT HER EMAILS."

"Oh, right…"

They both nodded and felt like they had thought something crazy. I asked the man in the University shirt, "Are you an alumni?"

He looked down at his own shirt to see what I was pointing at, and nodded yes but said, "Naw, man, I didn't even go to college."

I nodded at him and so did the squirrel man. He was still nibbling, but he stopped and asked, "Well, where'd you get the shirt?"

"Shit, my wife got it at Goodwill. She almost didn't buy it because it was made in China, and I told her we are done with buying shit from China. Everything we own is made in America," he said. "You boys want another beer?"

"Yeah," I yelled quickly and loudly. I had just hit that bartender up and would have had to find a new one to get another brew.

The squirrelly man brought out a whiney voice and yelled, "I'm good. I have one."

I chugged my beer fast since I was holding two and needed to make room. I slammed the last bit down my throat and placed it on top of the grand piano. "Thanks, bud, I appreciate it. The names, Gunner." I said in my dad's voice.

"Gunner, huh, nice to meet you, I'm Rusty," he reached to shake my hand, but I was full of beer bottles so he just put both his hands up and pretended to dap himself up before laughing and taking a drink from his brew.

"Double fisting!" he said and I did the fake laugh thing.

A whiney voice shot into my left ear, and I thought it was an alarm. It was loud and shrieking, and it said, "My name is Thomas!"

He might have been half squirrel with his voice. His whole demeanor screamed married virgin with his dirty New Balances and sloppy dress shirt. He had hair around his ears but was bald as an eagle on top. He was taller than me but hunched over picking through the food on the buffet as if it was his personal plate. Taking a bite, then putting it back onto the tray.

"That's just how I roll, I mean, look, I was a trucker for 26 years. I have been around the globe, you know what I mean? All over the West and Midwest, and that's American jobs. So my wife and our kids know, you know, if you buy something, you buy American."

"Except for the Trump University shirt," I said to him, tipping my beer together to make a chime and they both laughed.

"I always buy American too. Always."

"It's kinda funny, you know? That's why I would never buy any of Trump's ties, because I wanted to buy American and he had them made in China." It was the booze talking, but I wanted to stir it up.

They both laughed again. Irony hits the hardest.

Silence crept in since we didn't know each other, so I went to the common denominator. "You probably didn't wear a lot of ties on the road though, right Rus? Well, shit, what about that hat? I can't wear the MAGA hat because it was made in China. The damn Democrats and their stinking unions made that shit happen!"

Rusty became upset, thinking I was condescending to him. Thomas's whiney voice hit like a doorbell in my eardrum as he said, "Yeah if you take it off and look there is a tag that says where it was made. If it was made in Mexico, Trump pays them extra to rip them off. I guess it costs too much to have them do that in China though." He said matter of factly, so we both nodded to agree with them.

Rusty got the itch though and ripped his hat off to see where it was made.

"Goooo-dda-mn it," he yelled, moving his head back like he just lost his last scratch-off.

"Is it Mexican?" I asked but didn't get a response.

"See that's why we need the goddamn wall!" Thomas added.

Rusty turned his upside-down hat so I could look in – I saw the made-in-China tag. We collectively shook our heads in agreement. I almost started laughing but was able to turn it into a fake cry.

"Man, everything in my whole goddamn house is made

in this fucking country, and here I am wearing two things made in China. I swear to fucksake," he said with his hat still off.

Thomas was standing closer to me now, his voice ringing out of my right ear this time, "Do you have an American flag hanging outside your house?"

"Well, hell yeah I do!" Rusty told him as if he was stupid for asking, and then he looked at me so I could confirm I did too, but I shook my head.

"I don't own a place, I rent." I now grabbed some cheese off of a tray I was hoping Thomas hadn't touched. Rusty nodded back at me.

Thomas squeaked out, "You can't find an American flag that's made in America anymore. I looked for three whole months, online and everywhere. You can't do it; it's likely your flag was made in China or Vietnam or Mexico or somewhere else, but not America, so that's another thing, it's not in your house though."

"Well, shit, I ain't gonna buy a flag and hang it outside my house if it ain't made in the US of A!" I chimed in to say.

Rusty didn't get it because he thought Thomas was calling him out, he wasn't, he was just a fact guy, likely a banker or some sort of numbers or stats guy like an accountant, just wanting to share the info.

"Yeah, so only three things you own are made in China. That's not bad. I still got a pair of Nike's that my old lady bought me, and I drive a Toyota, but it was made in the states of course."

"Yeah, it's just the three things, just this Trump hat, which I kinda wish was made in Mexico now, maybe, hell, and this Trump University shirt, and I guess my American Flag.

Goddamn, that's some bullshit, that's why Trump's gotta win. He is the only one that can stop this shit, I swear it!"

"I'll drink to that," I said, but I just wanted one of these two knuckleheads to finish their beer so they would offer to get another one. The bartenders were on to me.

"Hell yeah!" Rusty said, and Thomas put his beer up.

Dude D approached us, holding two glasses of something dark and hard with one extended towards me. I slammed the rest of my beer, placed it on the piano, and took it from him, saying, "David, just the guy I wanted to see! Can we talk about that private thing? Can you boys excuse us? And Thomas if you get us another round of brews, grab me one. We will be over here talking."

I put my arm on Dude D's shoulder and moved him away from the piano and two Trumpies. My throat was parched, and I needed a hard drink. It was the moment I had been waiting for. Dude D was about to give me the October Surprise.

Rusty rolled his bald head up at me and said, "We got you bubba," and then he turned to Thomas and said, "You hear about this Comet Pizza Place?"

I walked away with Dude D, who was both excited and confused.

"What is up, Gunner Bush!" he said awkwardly as if he was my boss and was about to ask if I could stay and work a double.

"Cheers buddy!"

I moved the straw in my cup and put it on the other end of the piano, tipped his glass, and took half the cup in a swig. It tasted like heaven going down. We moved to a quieter part of the lobby with no chairs or people. More importantly, the corner featured the lone flat screen that wasn't tuned to Faux. I had changed the channel myself earlier to ESPN. Since the Cubs game wasn't on, I figured I could get an update on the ticker, so I positioned Dude D right where I could see the score updates over his shoulder. It was an old trick my old man used to do to my mom.

"So," I said, waiting for my present.

"I just wanted to talk to you, and you know, I'm glad you made it out and whatnot."

"Anything man, we can talk about anything. I owe you, you really helped me this summer, getting in contact with people, and those other dudes from the Green Party in Cleveland. So man, yeah, anything you need to talk about is fine with me. What is it? Are you getting married? I don't see a ring on your finger, did you propose, David?"

His face got a little red, and he ducked a bit not to show it, "No, I'm not married or getting married."

He grew quiet from the embarrassment or sumshit, so I had to start talking. "It's hard to see a Truman over Dewey moment right here, one month out, I mean, it could happen. Trump is down in every poll this side of heaven, and I mean unless Julie Awning really has the goods, ya know? Who knows what Hillary has; maybe it's nothing big, just Trump saying sumshit on a hot mic or whatever."

I let it linger in the air and took a sip. I can go on rants when I'm nervous, and I wanted to shut up and let him talk. His whole demeanor changed, and he was the one nervous now.

"I wanted to talk to you about talking to women."

"Huh? Yeah, no, of course, but what do you mean?" I tipped his glass with mine. I raised mine to my mouth, and so did he. I quickly added, "take a big one!" I finished mine. He threw some down his own gullet. It hit him hard, crept into his blood, and eased his nerves a bit.

"I can't talk to women." He said it softly, and then he looked away like he had just told me he killed my dog.

I could only raise my eyebrow in confusion and ask, "What do you mean? You can't talk to women? All the bartenders are women, and you got me a drink. Why don't we walk over to her there, you order us some drinks from that nice-looking female bartender."

"Remember in Cleveland?"

He didn't say anything afterward, so I ran through my brain and tried to remember Cleveland. Nothing came up, so I just nodded. It was highly likely that even if I was put under hypnosis, I wouldn't be able to remember parts of Cleveland. I could only hope what Dude D was about to say didn't involve me losing my pants or having sex with a hotel maid. I nodded harder, but he didn't get my signals so I asked, "We talked about a lot of things in Cleveland."

"Remember, you were with those three women, you had three women, they were half-naked, beautiful, and you told me you would take me out and help me find a lady."

"The ladies from Crazy Horse? Yeah, I mean, we should go out and find you a nice lady, but not from a place like Crazy Horse. I mean, nothing against the exotic type, I love 'em but that's not a type that a guy like you would want, you know? Let's go talk to the bartender, and we can order a few more drinks."

The bartender nearest to us was a beautiful blonde bombshell with a smile that lit up a room.

"Two more old fashions, please." I smiled at him to let

him know he was doing great talking to a female.

We got our drinks and moved back to our corner. By now, I am just waiting for him to throw the news into my lap. Of course, he doesn't so I put my glass up again, and we do a quick toast.

"So?" he says.

"Yeah, man, I can take you to the club anytime you want to go – do you want to get an Uber and go now?"

He laughed. It was the first time I had ever heard this dude laugh, and I smiled at him again. I felt like a used car salesman trying to land one.

He put his head down, pushed his glasses up, and said, "No, not that, I want to talk to women like you do. Get to know somebody. Remember in Cleveland, what you said?"

"We talked about a lot of things, buddy." Again, even with hypnosis.

"You said you could get me a girlfriend in less than a week, remember?"

I did vaguely remember saying it, and if I didn't, it sounds like something I would say, especially in the company of three beautiful women. I could visualize the three broads, barely dressed and all over me because they thought I was on my way to inheriting a small fortune. Perhaps I was the mark the whole time. Either way, Dude D must have thought I was some sort of Hugh Hefner. I wasn't, I was just a key to get those ladies into the lobby. Seven minutes after meeting Dude D, I lost them and never saw them again.

"I am sure the ladies love you, David, no freaking doubt about it!'

He looked like he might cry or throw up. I started to

panic and looked around for help.

"I'm a virgin, man, a virgin. I am 37 years old and a virgin," he cried, putting put his head down to let the waterworks flow. It was bad timing –I finally saw the Cubs score across the screen. They won.

"Yes!" I exclaimed, without thinking about the 37-year-old virgin before me. I didn't know what to say to save that, so I blurted, "Well, at least you're not 40!"

It was cringe-worthy –not the sympathy he was looking for. I wasn't trying to be a jerk, I was just waiting on him to hand me the goods. I didn't want to hear about his nonexistent sex life.

Then, it finally hit me; Dude D didn't have the October Surprise. It was a gut feeling – I had an innate trait to see through bullshit. If he had it, he would tell me, but he didn't have it.

So I asked him straight up, "This is what you wanted to talk with me about that was so important, isn't it?"

He looked at me like I was wearing headlights. I tried clarifying, "You wanted help picking up chicks, huh?"

He nodded. I felt my stomach crash into my knees. It was the feeling of bitter disappointment, but I was open from all the booze and never a pessimist. Dude D needed my help, and despite him not helping me here, he had all summer. I needed to be there for him.

"I can teach you some icebreakers, pick-up lines, and things of that nature," I told him as I chugged the rest of my drink, the ice crashing into my nose.

He put his head up, excited that I was going to help.

"We can't just rely on textbook examples, though. We

need real-world practice. There has to be a club in the area, and with us staying here at this hotel, it really ups our chances of bringing some entertainment home. I know from experience, in Cleveland, remember?"

I was drunk, and he didn't know what in the world I was talking about. I barely did.

"Listen, David, you just gotta be yourself with the ladies, it's not about pick-up lines or icebreakers. Just be yourself."

He looked at me like I had begun speaking Greek. "Who else would I be?"

"Right, well, that's a good point," I said, taking another drink of the hard stuff and chasing it with the beer.

He leaned in close to me and said, "You know all that Dewey-Truman talk earlier, I think it might happen!"

"Really and why is that?" I wasn't entirely paying attention, I was on my phone trying to find a nearby place for us to go.

"Well, look, and this is top, top-level secret, but our own internal polling from phone banking people is showing that people really hate Hillary. It is unprecedented the level of hate for this woman. The middle of the roaders aren't saying who they are for unless we say we are with Trump or something, and then, man, they open up about how much they hate her!" He said the last part as he leaned back and took a big hit from his cup.

"That's interesting to hear," I said, but I knew this. It was interesting coming from him, a person inside the campaign. I was only half paying attention because of the booze and I was on my phone reading about an adult club that had been around since the early 1900s.

"Yeah, honestly, I think the polling is off because of this," he said very confidently.

"So, what do you think?"

His body was moving a little more now. The booze was spreading through his blood, and I knew I would start to get the good info now. I sat back and prepared to receive all the info he was about to give me. But that was all he had. Their internal polling numbers were showing Trump was up by more than the national polls were showing – people didn't want to admit they were voting for Trump. I already knew that.

"I found the perfect place for us," I said as I watched his eyes dance with a dazzle of excitement. I ordered an Uber. It would be a night to remember. I never got any more out of him, that I remember anyhow. He'd been a helper all summer, and despite his love for the enemy, I knew I had to show him a great night. I did.

CHAPTER 8

"The Debate, The Lou, October 9th 2016"

The Hollywood Access tape leaked, and it hit every major news show within the hour. It was as hot as lava—so hot it was even shown on the International Space Station. And I had missed my big break by one day. While eating freshly-legal edibles in the Mile High State, I pushed back sending the tape to Terry. It was a decision that cost me everything. Morgan was beyond pissed, but not at me. She was convinced that her team was releasing it on the 25th, and it wasn't even the 10th! The leakers couldn't be trusted; and so, it was leaked by someone else. That's how Morgan explained it to me, and I had to let her know that I would still try to do a piece on her for the magazine. I wanted to see her again, and giving her some glory was a solid reason.

Behind the scenes, wheels were cranking and gears were turning. Each side was carefully moving chess pieces around after the Clinton blow. Dude D informed me that no matter what the Good Old Boys said to the press, they weren't going to cut Trump off. Trump would still have the funding and the resources, so they would keep it moving at the status quo. The tape could only sway the swing voters, despite the usual anti-Trumpers coming out of the woodwork to kick the man whenever he was down.

Publicly, the Good Old Boys turned on Trump like rats on a sinking ship. They were still rats, though. The media pulled out their forks to begin prodding Trump, and started to tune tracks from fat opera singers. They all claimed that the fat lady was singing, and her chorus was clear: Trump was finished.

The lip service from guys like Paul Ryan and other cricket-eaters with sticks up their asses was extreme. It was like they had been ordered to apologize for hitting a dinger into a window that broke. After that tape, they were still going to fund the bastard!

All the big dogs—as far as funding—were sticking with him too. The evangelicals would stick by their man, and Mike Pence made sure of that. Pence was the one who got the word out that Trump was now saved, whatever in the fuck that meant, and this was an old video from before. There was no logic involved; but there never is with Pence. The guy wasn't going to move an eyelash or even make a single comment unless it was pro-Trump. Mother wouldn't allow that—not if he fucked up their lone chance to lick the floors of the White House. There was an old, unconfirmed rumor that Pence had done a White House tour back when Ronnie Reagan, the actor, was in office. The story goes that he licked the bathroom floors then, but that wasn't the same thing. So, Pence was going to hold steady, even if Trump shot someone on 5th Avenue. If he still had the Christians and the funding, it was status quo.

Trump didn't take it sitting down, either. He's a counter-puncher who usually fires first, but he's always prepared to miss because growing up, he couldn't land a sucker punch. He knows his own weakness and prepares accordingly. His counterpunch came via Julian Assange and Wikileaks. It was hacked emails from Hillary's campaign chairman, John Podesta.

The emails were really much ado, with one highlight: an email from Donna Brazile of CNN, who leaked Hillary questions ahead of time for the CNN town hall. It was peanuts compared to the Access Hollywood tape, which had both Pence and Trump googling how to pray. Trump immediately entered the role of the victim. The establishment was out to get him. The deep state didn't want Trump to save America.

If it wasn't for being located in a legalized state, I would have been super pissed myself. I had just missed the biggest chance to break something in my career. Something of that caliber might never come again. I should have freaking leaked it myself! And it had crossed my mind, but I didn't know the legality of it. It might have been a major payday, but it might have also meant jail time—or worse. There are powerful people on both sides. The legal edibles helped, but I was soon on a plane flying in the middle seat to Missouri.

I arrived in the Show-Me-State as this was all making the rounds. My phone had been destroyed on a side quest, but there was a brand new one waiting for me when I checked into the hotel. Terry had ordered it for me and had it delivered. I really did have the best job in the world, working for a company that truly cared about its employees.

The Lou in Missouri had been circled on my calendar, both for the debate and because it was Sawyer's new city. Dude D had squeezed me an extra pass, so I could take Sawyer to the debate as my cameraman. When he hit up my phone, I told him to fall through, and we could pregame before the debate at the only socially-acceptable place to day drink in a hotel: the indoor pool. When he showed up just before 2:00, he was carrying two 24-packs like they were briefcases and he had an appointment at a frat house. He also had a handle of the hard stuff in his pants. We had a cold one cracked before we left for the pool and got annihilated.

Sawyer even scared off a mom and her children when he let out, "Guess I'm gonna jump into the pool and piss now!" And I don't blame her; Sawyer shouldn't have just outright said it.

Either way, the beer went down like water at a well in Israel. We even ordered room service and a bottle of bubbly to top it off. By the time 6:00 PM rolled around and we caught an Uber to get to the debate, we were gone. We couldn't leave the rest of the beer there. Sawyer's bright idea was to pile them into the duffel bag for his camera, but I told him the Secret Service was going to go through the bag; so instead, we just loaded the beers up in our pockets and down our pants. Then, Sawyer made us some mixed drinks using the small, plastic mouth rinsing cups from the bathroom. He made four of them because the cups were so tiny—at least, that was our excuse. On the way out of the hotel, we wobbled through the lobby trying to not lose our pants full of beer.

Sawyer hopped into the shotgun of the Uber, and immediately asked the driver, "Do you want one of these drinks?"

The driver was a young man, and he declined. Good for him, too—the cost of a DUI is outrageous.

"Are you guys going to the presidential debates?" the kid asked us with a smirk like a narc on his face.

I chugged my drink before crushing it down so he would know I wasn't breaking the law. He pulled out of the parking lot, and my phone went off. It was Dude D, and he had been blowing me up like I stole his last fork. Calling. Texting. He was telling me to hurry up and get to the university, or I would miss it. I sent him a text and said I would be there in five minutes as we pulled onto the ramp of I64.

I leaned up to the driver from the backseat while he merged into traffic. I asked him, "How much longer?"

He glanced back at me like he had forgotten I was there before replying, "Ten, twelve, fifteen tops."

I had enough time to drink a cold one, so I pulled one out and popped it open. The driver was a young white guy with an overdrawn chin that caused an underbite. He was dressed up like he was going to Sunday school, and although I couldn't see his shoes, I just knew they were uncomfortable. If I drove an Uber, I would wear pajamas. Slides with socks and pajamas, and never, ever uncomfortable shoes.

"You sure are doing a lot of drinking for two guys going to the debates," he said in a high-pitched, whiny tone.

"It's a requirement from the government," I lied to him as Sawyer cracked a beer and stared at the kid.

"What?" he responded.

Sawyer repeated what I said to him, but slowly sounded out the big words. "It's a re-choir-ment from the gov-ern-ment."

I nodded in agreement. "Yeah, so every year the Portland Fest—that's Portland in Louisville, not Portland, Oregon—has two guys go to the debate drunk. Then after the debate, they go answer questions for focus groups. It's how the Koch brothers and Murdoch are able to manipulate the hillbillies year after year!"

Sawyer chugged his beer until it was almost gone, took a breath, then finished it. He burped before turning around with a puzzled look. "What?!"

"I'm just messing with you. We didn't get picked at

Portland Fest this year. Nah, we're with *Rolling Stone*, the magazine."

"You actually have tickets to go inside the debate, though?" the overdressed driver asked me, and I showed him my press pass.

He didn't know what to believe, though, since we were pulling out brews from our pockets and slamming them down our throats like alcoholic magicians.

Then Sawyer asks him, "Tell me, Kyle. You ain't one of those gay, liberal cuckolds, are ya?"

He was drunk and intimidating, but Kyle didn't care. He must have had an older brother.

Sawyer just continued. "It drives me crazy," and I could hear the four hours of boozing spilling out as he went on, "these libtards are making all this fuss about the Access Hollywood tape."

Sawyer took another large sip of his beer. We were both silent, so he took it as a chance to continue. "It's just locker room banter, if you will." He tried to sound like an English aristocrat, but his drunken attempt came out more trashy, South Jersey Shore-ish.

"Trump said that they let him do it because he's a star. He's famous. He said, 'they let me do it.' He isn't groping women that don't want to be groped by him. They want him to grope him!"

Finally, I put down my phone, stuck my head up to the front, and said, "You wouldn't defend your own brother this hard!"

Kyle laughed softly, and I could tell it hurt Sawyer. Every joke has a little bit of truth to it, though.

"That's just because Gun, he is a liberal fuck," Sawyer told Kyle with a slurred laugh before adding, "My brother doesn't have any luck with chicks, though, so no chick would let him grab them anywhere!" He started laughing again.

"That right there, about your brother? *That* is locker room banter!" I told him.

Sawyer laughed, too, but he was a Trumper now, full throttle. He was openly supporting the conman and it didn't feel right. Not that Trump needed Sawyer's vote; no, Trump hadn't lost his army just yet, despite the Hollywood Access tape. Most Americans had heard worse in their own living room, and that was while pausing the action horror movie. All of us have heard perverted stuff before, and if we hear it and it crosses the line, most of us turn into Billy Bush and just stand there. We aren't the priest in the box listening and assigning riddles. It's not our job. And if it's our boss or manager saying it, we often just stay silent. 85% of the country has access to free internet which comes with access to free adult porn, among other things. So, although the talk on the Access Hollywood tape was disgusting, it wasn't new to most Americans. It was rhetoric that we assumed Trump would say when the cameras were off—he just happened to get caught on a hot mic.

Of course, the mainstream guys can't come out and admit it so easily, considering a lot of them have daughters and wives. Some of these wives are women who are playing the part of aristocrats and "godly" women. They can't blow all those precious years spent lying just to benefit Trump. Especially if the polls are correct, these guys are trying to be lifers; and if unhitching from the Trump train helps them later, they will certainly do it now. The voters, however, like Sawyer, didn't care. Most of them cuss themselves more than Johnny Knoxville being lit on fire. And they aren't lit on fire when they cuss—instead, they are just losing the little league game they are coaching. That's why it was status quo for the Trump base.

"We can just walk from here," I told Kyle through the drone of traffic. The car wasn't moving, but people were walking by us.

Sawyer and I both stumbled out of the car like clowns with our shoelaces tied together. I found my balance and called Dude D. Street vendors were out selling Trump merch, and the vibe outside was closer to a WWE event rather than a presidential debate. A can fell from my waist down my pants, and I couldn't get it out without shaking my leg as if I was doing a solid Elvis impression. While I did the leg shimmy, Sawyer was double fisting his last mixed drink and an open beer.

I could see Dude D, so I put my hands up to show how happy I was to see him. I was grateful he was hooking me up with an inside scoop on a story. He pointed with his other hand towards Sawyer and asked me, "Who is this?"

He was obviously a bit concerned, as Sawyer was chugging his beer like we were tailgating.

"Oh, this is my brother. He is the one doing the photography for the magazine tonight."

Sawyer came back and nodded at Dude D, but didn't shake his hand. Dude D turned around toward the building and banged on double doors that only opened from the inside. One of them swung open, and we entered into the romantic side of the arena. It was dark, and the man who opened the doors was holding his phone flashlight so we could see. As soon as we were inside and the door closed behind us, Sawyer cracked a freaking beer.

"*Step*brother," I clarified to Dude D, and the guy with the flashlight shook his head back and forth. I rolled my eyes when they both looked back at me to let them know that I wasn't amused, either. Then I smacked Sawyer on the chest to let him know he was out of line.

"I have to run to get a few things. Victor here, Vic," Dude D pointed at the upper-thirty-year-old guy with the flashlight, "will show you where to go. Follow him."

And he bounced off like a rabbit speeds away from hunters.

We started to follow this guy Victor, who was wearing a conservative red tie and dress pants. We followed him the opposite way that Dude D went, and then we turned left. As we followed along, I could see people through breaks in the wall. The people on the other side were dressed to the T. It looked like prom—or, perhaps, a freaking presidential debate.

I was wearing a wrinkled polo with dirty khakis, no belt, and my hair a train wreck. As we turned to walk upstairs, I noticed Sawyer was wearing freaking jeans paired with a sloppy shirt he must have copped at a St. Louis Blues game.

"Pshh," I shout-whispered to Sawyer so he would look at me. He did, and I motioned for him to tuck his shirt into his pants. He just shrugged at me and shook his head like I had done something wrong. He was holding his beer like we were at a Nascar event, and Vic had us walking at such a swift pace that Sawyer hadn't been able to take a drink. So, once we finally reached the top of the stairs, Sawyer stopped to take a big swig.

That's when I remembered we forgot the camera.

Vic looked back at us to make sure we were still with him, and I nodded at him while Sawyer chugged. Vic turned around and opened a door into a hallway that had people in it.

I again made the noise to Sawyer, "Pshh, we forgot the camera." He didn't hear me though.

"This way, gentlemen," Vic beckoned to us, and we followed him as he went right.

Sawyer started to realize we weren't in Kansas anymore, so he began hiding his beer a bit as we walked by people. We both had on dirty old New Balances—something I noticed as we walked by a man in a tuxedo! Saying we were underdressed was like saying the Pharaohs built small tombstones. Sawyer looked like the lost drummer from a shitty metal band, and I wasn't much better off.

The men were adorned in sports coats at minimum. Women were in full gowns. If people did see us, they swiveled their heads once more to catch another glimpse. Sawyer stopped again to take a drink, and I slowed down.

"Come on, dude!"

Vic kept up the breakneck pace.

"Just finish it and throw it out," I urged Sawyer, pointing at the trashcan and then walk-running awkwardly to catch up to Vic.

Sawyer didn't run, but he caught up. He pulled another beer from back pocket, and cracked it open.

"Dude!" I said in another whisper shout.

"What? I'm 21, I can legally drink." He was slurring his words.

He put his mouth over the top of the beer to drink the head coming out. We followed Vic into another closed-off section. We went through a door that led to a stairwell, but didn't go down the stairs. Instead, we walked out a door on the other side into another main hallway with people.

After entering the room, Sawyer yelled, "Jesus Chrysler, are we walking fast enough?"

I shook my head, and then pulled my last beer out of my own pocket. I was going to need it. It didn't matter if people were staring at us now. I just chugged like it was the last call, and then Vic led us into a side door.

My eyes had to adjust to the press lights that assaulted our vision. I squinted, and Sawyer burped. The room was full of press, with microphones and cameras all over. Victor turned to a security guard at the door—who was likely concerned about us—and informed him, "*Rolling Stone* magazine writers."

The guard smiled; I could see that he was armed. Either Secret Service or hired by them to guard that door. He winked at Vic as our guide left us. We had just started to rub elbows with the other media guys when, like the idiot he is, Sawyer said, "Man, I forgot the camera!"

He had a lack of common sense. The whole room heard him, and a press dude with a stale haircut and ugly elbows turned and loudly said, "You remembered the beer, though!"

When the burst of laughter cleared, Sawyer wanted to rock this dude. He stepped toward the guy, but I jumped in front of him. Thinking on my feet, I warned, "He's a liberal elite with a cocker spaniel at home. You don't want to fight that guy!"

I pushed Sawyer back against the corner wall, adding, "We aren't in the infield, calm down!" I wanted him to know we weren't at a Germantown picnic—this was a goddamn presidential debate!

This wasn't a typical presidential debate, though. The circus was alive, and if Trump remained in politics beyond 2016, we were heading back toward fisticuffs for sure. Shit, if he won, who knows, maybe dueling would be back on the menu. Trump himself would never duel anyone, but he would pick one guy in the sea of many who were ready to die for him. He would have his pick from the flyover folks. Even Sawyer would be ready to heed the call! Despicable.

Right on cue, I noticed Trump was already in the room. He was at the front, and I had missed his entrance. He was sitting down at a large table, waiting to talk. Then I realized he was waiting on everyone to shut up—that was just Sawyer and myself.

Four women were with Trump, two seated on either side of him, and I had never seen them before. I was very far back, but I could see that Trump was wearing his oversized red tie that resembled a young man's first attempt at a Windsor knot. Slithering through the crowd to get a better view, I moved my skinny butt through the press, trying not to get in anyone's way. Then, of course, Sawyer followed me through the crowd like an idiot. He knew he was too big to follow me —at least, I thought he knew, and assumed that he would stay back. Although I snuck past everyone smoothly, he followed directly behind me like an oversized linebacker, muttering, "scuse me," as he maneuvered through the crowd.

We were cutting in front of cameras and reporters who had been positioned for hours. Trump still wasn't talking, and it felt like he was waiting on Sawyer to stop his obliviousness. I smacked him in the chest lightly, put my pointer finger to my mouth and whispered, "Shhh!"

I pointed at Trump, and Sawyer saw him for the first time. At that moment, his eyes bulged out of his head; his jaw dropped as he quietly yelled, "TRUMP!" He was like a four-year-old seeing Spiderman in the Macy's Thanksgiving Day Parade. He stood up on his tiptoes and stretched his neck for a better view. Trump was talking now.

"These four very courageous women," Trump began, with the four women who flanked him looking like Bambi in headlights. As he continued talking, I could see his lips curling like a fish taking a drink, but his speech was hard to hear. I was still too far back. His facial reactions didn't ever match what he was saying. Up close, the Trump-viewing experience was strange. It always felt like watching a certifiable guy going all-in like he had a full house—except he really had eight and two.

As I moved forward, I started to figure out what was going on. It was the good old-fashioned double-down.

Yes, Trump was doubling down. If the media and these "elites" wanted to call him out for what he said on the *Access Hollywood* tape, then he was going to remind the world what the Clintons had done. These were four women who had accused the former president of sexual misconduct.

And the world hadn't forgotten what Clinton had done in the oval office. Hell, Monica Lewinsky had gotten famous from it! The lizardman himself, Newt Gringrich, had made sure the entire world heard about what Monica did, almost as if Newt didn't have worse skeletons hiding in his closet. Most Americans knew about the Kennedy Breweries and the infidelities of former presidents. Those, however, were mostly consensual.

Trump wasn't going to take anything lying down. The media had been reporting on the *Access Hollywood* tape non-stop since it leaked, but now they would have to report on this. It was going to be huge. *HUGE*. I could hear that orange motherfucker say it in his head. Trump didn't go around spreading lies that he was a Christian, or even a good person. Sure, he lied if he was asked; but he wasn't in the same boat as other politicians. He didn't preach about following the preacher, because it didn't matter. His base knew how he was, and they liked him more for it.

This speech wasn't about that, though. This was all about continuing the attack—spreading the word that the Clintons were the crooked elitists ruining the country. They were the one-percenters who attended the Bilderberg Meetings and screwed over the working class. Trump was the savior. He was the good old boy; a hard worker who once got caught on tape talking about grabbing pussy. The Clintons were the real enemies.

He was Hollywoodin' the politicians, hoodwinking the hillbillies, and conning the people. It was a fucking dagger to the heart to start the debates.

A below-the-belt punch at the weigh in.

It was brutal and unfair and inside the one part of the country that still had rules. All is fair in love, war, and politics —especially if the other person started it.

The rules weren't mandated, and this punch wasn't going to get him disqualified. It was going to show his base that he didn't care. He wasn't playing by anyone else's rules because he would lose. Instead, he was making up his own rules like a spoiled white kid on the plantation, playing a game with the slave children. If Hillary thought he was hitting low before, she was now learning that Trump could always go lower. He was an artist, and this was his preferred medium.

And then it was over. Quick as a lizard's tongue grabbing a house fly out of the air. I didn't even know what I had seen, and I had been there in person to see it. It felt like a pep rally mixed with an infomercial. It was a pre-debate fucking of the whole establishment. Trump and the ladies left, and Sawyer and I stood there holding our beers trying to figure it out.

"Trump's a goddamn genius, man," Sawyer finally breathed, pulling out what had to be his last brew. He didn't open it, though; he just looked right at me and said, "I didn't know we would be that close to him, man. I wanted to ask him to take a picture with me."

"Yeah, but you forgot the camera," I said jokingly, but he didn't laugh.

"I got a few on my phone."

And as he started to show me the photos he got—the best being a selfie he tried to take with Trump distantly behind him—Dude D came in through the same door Trump had exited from.

"I kept telling you that Trump had something up his sleeve for their assholes!" Dude D wasn't walking towards us, but skipping.

Sawyer asked him, "Those are the women that Bill Clinton raped back in Alabama when he was Governor?"

"You mean Arkansas! And he is going to bring them out at the start of the debate, like right when they have to shake hands. BOOM! Right into Hillary's face." Dude D was straight giddy; he had the excitement of a monkey drinking stolen rum.

"Old Billy Boy was a pervert back in the day," Sawyer replied, and they both laughed.

Dude D took us to our seats, and Sawyer and him were discussing Trump the entire walk. My head was starting to hurt, and I felt like I might get sick. Right as we got into our seats, Sawyer turned to me and said, "I gotta drain the main vein!" loud enough for the TV-viewing audience at home to hear.

He left me there, with my head spinning and my vision blurry.

As Sawyer staggered in the direction of the restroom, I slouched back in my chair. I put my left arm across my body, my right arm on the arm rest, and rested my head. Before he returned and the debates even started, I was dead asleep.

CHAPTER 9

There's a waffle house in heaven—I'm sure of it. The extra grease on the food absorbed the booze in our belly like a sponge. It wasn't heaven on Earth, but it was close. After we grubbed, we got a cup of joe due to a sliver of undeniable common knowledge: the waitresses in diners make the best pot. And this one didn't let us down. We had both missed the entire debate. While I was sawing logs in the building, Sawyer went outside to smoke; but without a ticket, he couldn't get back in. He stood outside doing who knows what until I woke up.

I finally rose from my slumber with slobber on my chin to the sound of clapping, and just like that, people were exiting the debate. The affair was over, and I was just hoping I hadn't snored. Sawyer had texted me, "Where are you @ Beavis?"

He didn't even know he was setting himself up. I replied appropriately, "Where are YOU at, Butthead?"

He just wrote back, "LOL."

After playing a tedious game of calling and finding Sawyer, the two of us hailed a cab to go eat. Since I had missed the debate, I was asking anyone I could who they thought won. Of course, Trumpies felt that Trump had won. The lefties thought

Hillary got the victory, and the people who still couldn't decide who to vote for also couldn't decide who had won the debate. No gain for Hillary, and no loss for Trump. The status quo was maintained—and the race was far from over. There were still two thirds of the month left, leaving apt time for some old-fashioned mudslinging to commence. It wasn't an option anymore of who would come out clean; the entire country was about to get filthy.

After we ate and drank enough coffee to cause a heart attack, we slid into another cab and returned to Sawyer's spot. I asked him about Cammie, but his response was vague: "We've been going through it, she's out of town right now," and some more pass-over words. He still didn't have his ring on.

I had only met Cammie three times, and to me, she seemed like a controlling bitch. Each time we'd crossed paths, it was by accident, as Sawyer wasn't even allowed to see me. He wasn't allowed to see anyone. Cammie kept him locked up —ball and chain for real. Nobody saw Sawyer after he got married. He didn't even have a wedding because Cammie and Sawyer's mom notoriously don't get along. I wasn't a fan of her, so I was relieved she wasn't there when we arrived. It was obvious that Sawyer missed her, though.

It was equally obvious that Cammie had decorated the place from walls to windows. Towels hanging up in the bathroom that you aren't allowed to use; pillows on the couch that you also can't touch. It had a real adult, Pinterest-chick's-apartment style to it. The only outliers were an old recliner that was probably Sawyer's, as well as two whiskey barrels turned into chairs that I remembered from his old spot before he got hitched.

He had a bar in his living room where most people had a dining set. He showed me a bottle his brother got from North Korea. After downing a shot, we were disappointed to discover

SUICIDE NOTES TO KURT COBAIN

that it tasted like watered-down brandy. Outside of that, he didn't have much else to drink inside his own home bar. There were a few half-full bottles of scotch that looked aged and well, but not very fun.

There was a knock at the door; Sawyer handed me a beer from the small fridge and went to answer it. I sat on the old whiskey barrel chair, kicked my feet, and spun around in circles. I stopped twirling when I saw an old, dirty white dude. He said hello or something to me. He stunk like cigarettes and rot.

Sawyer turned to me and asked, "Can you give us a minute here, Gunny?" Then he told the stinky dude, "Step into my office."

It was obvious that it was a purchase of something harder than chronic, but Sawyer was trying to sell it off as something else. Either way, I left the kitchen area—no questions asked.

I sat on the recliner in the living room, and two minutes later, the old stinky dude came out of the kitchen. He had on a red Marlboro jacket and a pair of threes. His hair was messy, long, and greasy. He smiled at me and said, "Alright, be seeing ya," in a really awkward tone, and then he left.

Sawyer appeared a second later.

"What was that about?"

"Nothing, dad. Jesus Chrysler... I'm just getting a little something to help me stay awake, you know?"

"You got like an eight ball or something, huh?" I asked him, but I knew. I hadn't seen the booger candy since college. I didn't do it then, and don't want to do it now.

So, we did a few shots of the old ass scotch he had, piled in beers in between, and then headed off to a bar called Colorado Bob's Ship of Fools. By the time we arrived hopped up on the old scotch buzz, we were ready to drink like Jim Morrison in his twenties. The place wasn't very crowded, and Sawyer was familiar with a few of the locals. He didn't see anyone he liked or that could help him, so we ordered some hard shots to get our blood flowing.

Just two shots later, I was ready to leave. The place was great, but the mood was off. So, I told Sawyer, "Look, I took off these days after the debate so we could hang out. When you said for me to come, I mean, I'm sorry you and Cammie ain't doing well—I've told you I never liked her. That doesn't matter, though. What matters is that I'm off work these next few days. What kinda trouble can we get into?"

Sawyer just smiled, shook his head, and said, "Yeah, fuck that bitch. You wanna go to the casino?"

Of course I did.

We left the bar to find another cab. The sky was dark and clear, but a vicious wind was hitting us with cold air that felt like a coastal breeze. Luckily, we found a cab. We jumped in without hesitation and tried to warm up.

The casino was across the Mississippi in East St. Louis: an infamous area known for murder and crime. We rode in on Jackie Joyner Kersee until we reached the exit without any lights. The driver knew the back way, and we traveled under the elevated roads of the massive highway system. Then, out of nowhere, like a desert oasis, the sky was on fire with the dazzling flash of neon lights. We were on the backside of a massive casino hotel.

When we pulled up to the front, we were struck by a kaleidoscope of colors and a Foley kit full of noises. The entrance was grand, and we walked in like two men with a purpose. Our chests were high and our minds happy. We were about to get as many free drinks out of the casino as we could using comp drink tickets. The average person can't hold their booze, so the casino offers free drinks. The reason is simple: they want to keep people playing and drunk. That's why a casino never closes. 24 hours a day, 7 days a week, 365 days a year. With this in mind, comping drinks at a casino while barely gambling was our intent.

Upon entering the building, we instantly discovered that the place was swollen with all sorts of people. The women weren't as beautiful as they are in Vegas, but I also didn't see any old people in diapers playing penny slots. It wasn't Vegas, but it luckily wasn't Reno either. The eight ball came out of the corner pocket in the very first bathroom we saw. First time for everything, I figured—and I was sloppy drunk already.

As soon as we walked out of the bathroom, my eyes were drawn thin and into my head as the blood flew to my heart. Everything was sharp, present, and louder. I felt stronger, higher, sharper; I was alight with a false bravado of confidence from a white girl. We then entered into the two stages of black.

Blackjack and blacking out.

Blackjack is a simple game of 21. It's player versus the dealer, so Sawyer and I could sit right next to each other and order drinks from waitresses eager to get a big tip. The casino lights and other eyeballs make the game a little difficult, but Sawyer and I were lit and ready. We didn't care who was watching. We were both fairly good at the game, counting percentages rather than counting cards. We buckled our seatbelts and prepared to win some big money.

It wasn't our night, though—our losses were a clear omen that we should have left the place entirely. On the very first hand, I drew 19 right out of the box and Sawyer hit on 14 and got a 6. He cooled on 20, and the bald-headed dealer snickered like a fat lady stealing Christmas cookies. His ugly ass had blackjack. We should have gotten up from the table, but we were drunk and high, so we doubled down.

I had drawn 19, but I had a flash in my mind that the next card was a two of spades. I could sense it like a Jedi sniffing out trouble. I told the dealer to hit me, and he gave me a look like I had just told him Jesus was back. I said it again. "Hit me!"

He did, and it wasn't my two. It was a jack. I busted. Sawyer had an eight of spades showing.

"There's a two close," I told Sawyer with the confidence of a prince.

The dealer snapped right at me. "No table talk! You can be removed, banned, and fined!"

"Table talk? I'm not card counting, I just have a feeling that the next card is a two of spades. Who could count like that?"

I turned to Sawyer and told him, "I can feel it. It's like a Jedi instinct or some shit, the two spades flashed in my head. That's why I hit. Do you think I would normally hit on 19?"

I flipped over my cards so Sawyer could see them.

The dealer looked at me like I should have been an in-patient somewhere. Sawyer flipped over his other card; it was a jack of hearts.

"Sir," he said back to me.

"We have played two fucking hands, who can count cards that quick? I just have a feeling."

I shrugged, but Sawyer looked right at him and said, "Hit me!"

The dealer shook his head and pulled off the top card of the deck.

Another jack.

"What are the fucking odds?" I gasped.

Sawyer was mad as a wasp.

We both stood up. We weren't going to let this Oscar-Meyer-wiener-looking dude take our money all night just because we were on a cold streak.

"You had a Jedi instinct? What the fuck was that, Gun?"

Sawyer was right, and I admitted defeat. So, we hit the bar to regroup and figure out our next plan. We were cold, so we decided to split up. One of us had bad luck and was holding the other one down. We would link up again later.

I walked up some magnificent stairs, and then crossed into a hallway that had six tables with men playing poker. My heartbeat was so rampant I could feel it in my shirt, and I noticed an older black dude watching the poker action. He was looking for someone to chat with, so I stood near him. It wasn't world series level or anything—just some local guys playing to win a nice jackpot of a quarter million, or sumshit.

I still had the false confidence from the yayo. I could see the game being played in front of me in several different layers, and I understood each one. I turned to this older black man, and started to tell him what I saw. I tried to sound as elegant as a professor on a Ted Talk.

"It's America's game, poker. It really is—screw America's pastime of baseball. Men don't want to run and slide and pitch and then run some more. No, most Americans hate to run. I hated to run the very first time I had to run in gym class. Hell, I didn't even run then," I laughed to myself and nodded at the man. He was a little bit concerned, and I was using my hands a lot like a guilty con pleading innocence in front of a judge. The old man nodded back so I continued my rant.

"And that's not the only reason it's America's game. It's modern-day chess. Nobody wants to play chess anymore. Every single video game ever invented is better than chess. Castling and then the queen is the best piece on the board. No man wants his king to only have one move, might as well make the king a pawn. No, no, no! It all makes sense; poker is a chance for these people to have some combat and win some money. For Money Games© is the official gaming system of capitalism. So, of course, that's how Americans want to win or lose their money. We aren't a country that has developed its citizens into thinking people. We are instinctual, Neanderthal —we're cavemen for crying out loud, and poker is a game you gotta feel in your gut. It's a feeling. It's knowing when to hold them and knowing when to fold them. Fucking Kenny Rogers, shit! It's the game of the Wild West; Wyatt Earp and Doc Holiday didn't sit down and play Chess or Uno or Spades. We are still in the fucking Wild, Wild West. America has more guns than people, and this right here, poker, it is America's game! America's pastime, it's not baseball. And look, I love baseball. I'm one of the few remaining lovers of the sport of baseball in my age group. Think about it: fifty or seventy years ago, all people had was their baseball. But times have changed, people don't want to watch baseball anymore and there are two or three games a night. And kids don't want to be baseball players. No, kids want to be gamers and influencers because kids are lazy, but they want the easy money—and that's the American way, too. And I should know, I was just a fucking kid. Shit, I still identify as a kid. Poker is America's game. What American wouldn't want that job: a professional poker player. Show up here to work, the people would kill for that job, likely the last...."

I paused. I was speaking with vindication like JFK coming back from the dead. I turned to make sure the man was feeling what I was saying, but he was gone. Then I turned the other way to make sure, and I was alone. I had been talking to myself. I scanned the area quickly and left before I was escorted away.

I sped away towards a bar; at this point, I was out of comp tickets, so I had to pay cash. I wandered around looking for Sawyer when I suddenly spotted a roulette table that had my name on it.

Roulette isn't a game that people flock to at the casino. The dictionary states that the game involves a high degree of chance and unpredictability, which puts people off. It's not America's game of poker and it's not blackjack. It's similar to the slot machines in that roulette takes no skill to win. All it takes is luck—the good, old-fashioned kind of luck that makes a man buy scratch-off after scratch-off. This table was hidden off the path of the mainliners, tucked away in a far corner of the casino. It was shy, almost like it didn't want to be found. Even the lighting was off a bit in this corner, flickering and dull in comparison to the bright, loud building. The table was empty, besides one skinny man with a neck brace on.

Usually, there are no chairs or stools at the roulette tables. The casino has a reason and it helps them, I'm sure, but I don't know what it is. This guy with a neck brace had a stool, and there was another one right behind him, so walked over to grab it. He moved up a bit, but not enough, so I was forced to nudge his seat forward. Once I had pulled my own stool across the floor—which screeched for the last few inches—I sat down and got my first close look at the dealer. I noticed two things: he had red hair, and he didn't seem to be in a good mood at all.

In contrast, the man beside me was a mutant-like dude who looked like he was on a prank show, tricking people with his weird neck brace. He was rocking a polo with sweatpants and he had big, wiry silver glasses. He was over 40 but under 50, had a five o'clock that was stretching on two or three days, and he nodded at me when I approached. It was a funny type of nod; he stretched out his neck at an awkward angle because of the brace.

"What's up, my name's Gunner," I said in a cocky tone, like he should know it already.

The dealer dropped his eyes to the right and then back at me before saying, "Place your bets."

"Hey Gunner, I'm James!" The neck brace guy declared, once again doing the weird head nod.

"So, what's hitting here tonight, Jim?" I said as a joke, but he dropped his eyes down and pulled his head straight back. Then he looked at the dealer with an odd face—strange even for this strange-looking dude.

I turned to look at the dealer, who was looking back at James whispering something to him. My eyes flickered between the two.

"W-wh-y-y?" James whined. His voice was like a child who had just painted his bedspread with chocolate.

"Why? Because I want to win! So, look, I'll just play around where you played," I replied with a smirk. I was joking once again, but as James exchanged a look with the dealer, I could sense fear. It was my gut speaking to me, and not some Jedi sense I didn't have.

James had laid his chips in a certain area, so I did the same. He had one on my favorite number, 23, so I laid one next to him.

"Maybe it's my good luck number, so I'm bringing good luck to your chip," I told him as I tapped the top of his chip with mine, and he did the funny head nod again.

"Yeah, 24 and 23 have both been hitting a lot tonight."

His eyes darted around a bit, and the dealer sighed slightly. Something was up. I peered over at him and he played it off, but I knew it. I was higher and drunker than a skid row hooker, but I still had a sense.

The dealer waved his hand over the table to let us know that all our bets should be in. Next, he took the small white ball, placed it into a crevasse in the wheel in front of him, and flicked it like he was snapping with his middle finger and thumb around the numbers as they all spun. Suddenly, a ball shot out of the crevasse. It bounced up high, down again, and up, and then one more time before it landed on 22.

The dealer jolted his shoulders, almost as if saying, "I did it!" It wasn't a big tell, but I caught it.

James had his chips on 22. The dealer took my chips, and then paid James with a large amount of chips. He had thirty-five dollars for every one James put down, and it looked like he had about thirty bucks on each.

James looked right at me as the dealer was paying him, and the dealer stared at him. Then they made eye contact and smiled. They were friends—or in on it! I could feel it in my bones. So, I followed suit, and hoped it wasn't the blow. I put my chips right on top of the three numbers that James did: 22, 23, and 24. He played black, so I did too.

Then I told him, "I'm only bringing in my good Irish luck!"

And he nodded at me. Sure enough 24 hits. It was a black number. We both won.

James smiled while bobbing his head, and the dealer paid us out. Repeat. James put his chips down on the same three spots. I placed my chips on top of his own, stating, "If It ain't broke," and James laughed a bit.

24 again. Black. We both got paid out again, and then James didn't put any tokens down. I did—the same three numbers. The dealer threw the ball. I looked at James, who was acting like he was fidgeting with his phone. Instead, it was an old school joint that flipped up.

The metal ball stopped on red seven. I lost. A middle-aged couple scurried over from the bathroom area behind us; the guy wanted to try to win since he had seen us win a few times while he was waiting on his chick.

James only put one chip on the table, despite having placed maybe 5 or 10 on his numbers before. He put one chip on the number 1. I did the same, and placed a single chip on 23. It came up 11, and we all three lost.

The guy and the lady wanted to try one more time, and by that point, another guy had walked up.

James again only played one chip on the 1. So, I put one chip on the 1. The dealer waved again, and then flicked the ball. It bounced up and then right into the 11. James didn't play again for two throws; during that time, I put one chip on 23 and one on 7. It came up 1 this time.

The guy who had been at the table a minute ago walked over as James put a five-dollar chip on the 1, and I did too. I figured I better find my own strategy, though, so I began placing chips on a few other numbers.

We all lost again. The guy's girl came back, and they both left.

As the other players left the table, James returned to his old spots—tried and true. Right in a row, like he had future information: 22, 23, and 24. I did the same. I looked at the dealer, and he was looking at James.

"Let's see what happens," I said with a shrug.

The dealer waved his hand in a half-assed way across the table, and then threw the ball. It bounced, up and down while rolling more this time, like it had been doing when it hit, and it landed on red 19. We both lost, but not by much. The dealer had just missed his throw.

As soon as the dealer took our chips, James went right back to those three numbers and black. I did the same. The dealer didn't even wave his hand this time, he just flicked the ball. It bounced up, and then rolled along the side again, and fell right into red 23. James shook his head back and forth, but he didn't make a noise.

I did a fist pump, letting it be known to the casino.

James looked right at me and in a voice of authority, he demanded, "Act like you've been in the endzone before, kid!"

The dealer was giving me eyes too. James didn't play the next hand, and he acted like he was on his phone again. I didn't want to play, either.

The dealer asked, "Are you going to make a bet, sir?"

"Yeah," I said nodding, and then I put my one chip on the 23. He waved his hand across the whole table, and rolled the ball. It landed on 7.

James then put one five-dollar chip on the 1, and that was it for the next 6 spins. Then, on the 7th, James went right back to his routine. The same three numbers and black. I followed suit, placing two chips on each. The dealer waved his hand, and before he flicked the ball, I heard Sawyer's voice boom toward me.

"Gun, you over here playing roulette like a fool? Nobody ever wins at roulette!"

He was double fisting. I reached out to take one of his

drinks from him; he pulled the one for me back while he took a sip out of the other drink. Then, he gave me the drink he had just taken a sip from.

"Let me get in here! Can I get in? I got a few more chips, hold up!" Sawyer said to the dealer, hurriedly pulling just four chips out of his pocket. He placed them at the top, and the dealer nodded at him with a look of annoyance creeping into his expression. Then he flicked it, and just like the balls before, it bounced up once, and rolled. It landed on Black 24. We hit again.

"Boom!" I yelled right as Sawyer said, "Fuck!" followed by, "You hit, Gun? Damn!"

"I'm trying to tell you, you were the bad luck," I said.

James was only playing one chip, and the numbers were all over the place. Everyone was losing, and Sawyer was out of chips. I told Sawyer I would catch up with him in a bit, and as soon as he left, James was back at it. The same three numbers and black. I did the same; sure enough, it landed on 23.

"Boom!" I said, but not as loud as before.

I sat at the table, playing and witnessing a host of people come up and leave losers. I would only play one five-dollar token somewhere on the board when James didn't play those three numbers. Six or seven other people approached and tried a few rolls, but nobody won. Nobody found a win besides me and James, and we only won on those three numbers. It was some sort of scheme they had going on, and I couldn't figure out what it was. Magnets, maybe.

Clearly, the casino couldn't figure it out, either; or they didn't know. We were off in the cut with bad lighting. I had heard of roulette dealers' on riverboats being able to drop a ball close to numbers, but this was pretty incredible. That's one of the reasons the riverboats don't go out anymore—it wasn't magnets, but it was just as sophisticated of a sting. It was all in how the dealer threw the ball and spun the wheel. This dealer could spot it, and James had cleaned up. These two would likely meet up later at a diner and split the dough.

The pile in front of James wasn't big, but it was still bigger than mine. Whenever he won, he would quickly grab a bunch of chips and stuff them into a fanny pack. He was cleaning up.

At this point, I was hungover from the slew of day drinking. My head was throbbing, my legs were Jell-O, and my brain was barely working. I wanted to go to sleep, but I didn't want to miss out on my chance to win. There were no clocks or windows inside the casino, so I didn't have a clue as to what time it was. Eventually, I hailed down a waitress and asked her for some Tylenol, but she said she couldn't give me any because it was illegal. Instead, I could go to the first aid spot; but there was no way I was leaving just then.

I wasn't 100% sure that James and the dealer were working together, but as long as it was going this way, I was staying. I had never won at a casino before. Ever. We did the routine one more time, and it hit on black 24. I clenched my hands and fell back a bit. The dealer paid me, I looked at my phone, and then back up, and James was gone. He didn't say bye; I didn't even know he was gone. I felt like Batman had just vanished, and I was looking for him. I tried the next roll, and missed.

So, I pulled all my chips from the table, flicked two chips at the dealer, and then told the people standing around the table, "Make sure you tip your dealer!"

I felt like I had hit the jackpot. I got the window to cash out, and I felt like the biggest baller in the world. There was a nice looking 35-year-old white lady with an ugly upper lip behind the bars. She smiled and sounded like an infomercial as she said, "Looks like you were a real winner today." I nodded, and she began counting my pile.

"Three thousand, one hundred and five dollars," she concluded.

"That's it? It feels like there should be a lot more."

She didn't respond, instead turning to face another man who was behind her. He put his glasses on his nose and stepped over with a dominant energy, addressing me through the bars.

"Is there a problem with the count, sir?"

"No, no problem at all. I was just contemplating how fast and good this lady here was at, uh, counting my chips up. She's great," I stated. I could sense this old dude was the type of manager who writes up every little dispute, and I didn't want this lady to get in trouble because I assumed I had won bigger.

She returned to the counter and was grateful that I had helped her out.

"Since we're closing soon, we do want to give you a hotel room at our very elegant hotel, which is—"

I stuck my nose under the bars and cut her off. "Did you just say you guys are about to close?"

"Yes sir," she said as she shuffled through a folder, eventually pulling out a paper with a free hotel voucher.

She slid it to me, and I asked her again, "Really?"

"Yes, sir, we close at 3 A.M.!"

"What type of casino closes?" I asked again, baffled.

She was blunt with her reply. "This one does, sir!"

And she was done with me. Her shift was ending soon, and so was the entire staff of the casino. Again, I stuck my head into the area that was open and I shouted, "Hey, I'm hypogly-cemic—it's not official, but I'm pretty sure I am, and I really need to eat before I go to my room. Is there anything open?"

She begrudgingly opened the folder next to her again, pulled out another paper, and slid it to me. "Compliments from the casino, sir."

I grabbed the paper, and saw that it was a complimen-tary dining ticket for two people. It also had an advertisement for a 24-hour restaurant in the hotel. This casino knew what they were doing. Free booze, free food, and a free hotel room to stay in while you still had money to give up the next day. The house always wins.

"So, I just take this other voucher you gave me to the hotel, and I get a free room?"

"Yes sir," she responded with a tinge of annoyance, and I left before she kicked me to the curb.

I found Sawyer in the lobby. He was on the phone with Cammie, throwing out what seemed like threats. I grabbed the phone from his hand and hung it up. We were both hungry as hostages, and I knew that once he ate, he would calm down. So, we took the comp tickets to eat and once we were finished, I checked us into our hotel room. It had been described as fabulous, but was really middle of the road—Holiday Inn-ish. I was ready to sleep as soon as my head hit the pillow. I was ex-hausted, as the drugs had finally worn off. It was the first time in my life I had beat the casino, and one of the few times that I didn't even need to buy a hotel room. Funny how winning is. I was up over three Gs, and I slept like I was on leave from the war.

CHAPTER 10

"Finding the Suicide Notes"

And that's how it went for my entire stay in the Lou with Sawyer. It got wild and extreme, but it consisted of all the usual shenanigans slammed around two Cubbie playoff games. Day drinking, thrift store shopping, and wing spots for the Cubs playoff games at night.

During Game Three, the wing spot was full of Cardinal fans who were cheering on the Giants, all hyped to see their rival get beat when their team won the game. The next day, I found a brand new (AKA lightly used) Cubs hat at Goodwill; afterwards, we went back to the same spot for Game 4. I was wearing the hat in a bold statement of our fandom—something that turned out fine when the Cubs won the series. I took credit for it, citing my lucky hat. Wearing a Cubs hat in St. Louis was just my style, too.

The Lou is the heartland of the country. It's right smack in the middle, and it shows. We ate up the diverse cultures of the area, partying like rockstars and trying to avoid the hamster wheel of the election. It was only a two-day break—a much needed one, at that—and I had it planned out for so long that it went by quick as the wind. I wanted a break post-debate to write a great piece on the debate itself. Unfortunately, that wasn't coming to fruition, as I didn't get much writing done.

So, my last night in town, I decided to stay in and write. Sawyer had a bowling match, and I wanted to craft a masterpiece. I had a solid piece ready to go, but in reality, the story itself didn't need to be any good. The video was the news! We had caused enough trouble during our furlough, and I was desperate to be published after missing my chance with the leak.

Procrastination crept on, and I soon found myself renting a spot on the writer's block. I got up from my laptop and walked through the rooms of Sawyer's apartment to stretch my legs, get my blood flowing, and find a spark. I usually don't smoke, but burning one felt like it might help. As I scoured Sawyer's apartment for a pack, I paused as I located a blue three-subject notebook. It was college ruled, with Sawyer's initials drawn in bubble letters on the front and a pen tucked inside the spiral. I flipped it open and searched for an available page to doodle—after all, doodling can inspire. I walked into the living room and flopped onto the couch, but couldn't find an empty page. Near the back, the notebook was full of Sawyer's drawings similar to blueprints of buildings, but sloppier because he drew them. Exits were marked in red ink very largely on each page. I flipped back a few pages, and he had a list that started with the words "Kill Count." That grabbed my attention. It then proceeded to list mass shooters and the number of people they had killed. It went from highest to lowest. The two dufuses from Columbine were listed there, and I thought I recognized a few others, including Ted Bundy's bitch ass.

Circled at the bottom was the date October 31st, and under it was Kurt Cobain's name.

I leafed through the pages toward the middle and finally located an empty space. I started to doodle on one of them; but a mixture of boredom and curiosity gnawing at my thoughts caused me to flip to the very first page of the notebook. It was a formal letter with the date at the top. It even had the word "Dear" as if it was 1982, and people still conversed via letters. It was Sawyer's chicken scratch, addressed to Kurt Cobain.

Dear Kurt Cobain,

Hey Kurt or Mr. Cobain, my name is Sawyer Barnes. I always wanted to meet you. Even though you were dead before I even found out how great you were. Before I even found out WHO you were, you were already dead.

You've always been my favorite musician. I feel like I know you. One of the only books I have read from start to finish was about you way back in 8th grade. And since then, I always wanted to meet you. I think you would like me if we met. I have memorized the Unplugged DVD completely. It's so great that you didn't just go on there and do your hits, you covered the Meat Puppets, and made them into Nirvana classics. Anyways, I just wanted to tell you that so you would know. I am going to write you a letter a day until Halloween!

Talk to you later Kurt, (I think I will just call you Kurt)

Your boy,

Sawyer

It read like a second grader writing a fan letter. It was either a really old notebook, or a really weird one. Either way, I didn't want to bother with it, so I decided not to doodle and not to pry. I flipped it down, switched on the flatscreen, and it was on Faux News—so, I tuned in.

As I tuned into the Fair and Balanced network, I realized why it was the most-watched network. Faux knew what they were doing with the buzzwords. Emails. Criminals. Crooked Hillary. It was a trumpet of bullshit, yet it was perfectly designed. All the talking points stuck with you and hung around like a weird uncle.

The anchors were all great-looking, with the males more caked up in makeup than the females. The men were doing the hard-selling; but overall, it was great theater. I could see how people bought into the nicely-dressed bullshit. The entertainment value was terrific, and it was constantly attacking crazed liberals, the radical democrats, Obama, and Crooked Hillary. I was tuned in and ready to make some popcorn. It wasn't about breaking stories. It was about the agenda. It was anything but fair or balanced, but it was amazing to watch.

The design of cable news was a brilliant creation. Americans went to work to put supper on the table, and after they ate supper, they turned on the news. They would salute the flag, say a prayer, go to bed, wake up, and do it all over again. But working-class Americans don't have time to decipher the news. The working man might not know the difference if Walter Cronkite and Peter Jennings stopped delivering the facts and began spitting out propaganda. And this was the best propaganda in history, delivered straight into living rooms across the United States and the world. It was so good. I knew that what they were pitching was all make-believe, and yet I still started to question Hillary's emails.

On the subject, I shot Morgan a text just to let her know I was thinking about her. Ladies love that shit, and a chick with an ego the size of Morgan's would be delighted. She hit me back pretty swiftly, and said she had been thinking about me. She didn't address how, so I didn't know her angle: whether she was thinking about what I could do for her career, or because she was interested in me.

We exchanged texts, and I started to feel like maybe it could be something more. She wanted to link with me when I got back to the District.

I sat back and watched the talking heads go on and on about how Trump would prosecute Hillary his first week in office, but it was hard to digest because I was tired of the dog and pony show. So, I didn't take it in; the drone of their propaganda became white noise as I fell asleep.

My body was enjoying the phases of REM and other stages of sleep—which included drooling—when I had one of the most chilling awakenings in my entire life. I heard a clicking sound, but my dream-state mind justified the sound as something else. Something that was not life-threatening.

Slowly and instinctually, my eyes flickered open as I felt the cold metal against my face. I was still asleep even when my eyes did open, and I couldn't make out what was in front of me. It was long, round, and metallic. My mind didn't initially comprehend the object, so I brushed it off before connecting the dots. In that moment, I realized it was the barrel of a gun aimed at my head.

My heart stopped, and I almost shit myself. I jumped my whole body back hard against the couch. That's when I saw Sawyer at the end of the gun with a shit-eating grin on his face. I relaxed a bit as he cut up laughing.

Sinister and scary.

I pushed the barrel away with my left hand and yelled, "Get that fucking gun out of my face!"

"The gun isn't in your face; it's in my hand!"

He laughed hard, and when he finally stopped cackling enough to get the words out, he added, "You jumped back like —"

He started cracking up again and mocking how I jumped back on the couch.

"You're a dumbass who shouldn't even own a gun," I said, moving to the other side of the couch.

"Jesus Chrysler, calm down, bro. It ain't even loaded!" he said back to me as he put the gun over his right shoulder.

I moved my head back, rubbed my eyes, and groggily asked him, "Why do you even have all these guns?"

"It's my constitutional right," he replied simply, shaking his head like I was the idiot in this situation.

"It's not your right to accidentally blow my head off!"

He stopped laughing but continued to smile. He moved the gun up off his shoulder, and it fired.

The shot rang out loud; I froze and then ducked. Sawyer watched me dip, and then he did. It was such a delayed reaction that our families would have been making funeral arrangements if the gun had been aimed at either one of us.

I crouched up, still in shock, and my ears were ringing.

"You're an idiot!"

The room smelt like fireworks, and we both walked cautiously into the kitchen as if someone else was going to shoot at us. The damage was pretty bad. His end cabinet had taken most of the buckshot. Luckily, behind it was the brick foundation wall rather than a paper-thin apartment wall that fed into another apartment.

Sawyer flipped open the top part of the cabinet, revealing a box of cookies and a bag of goldfish that were blackened. A few canned goods took the brunt of the impact on the top. Rather than cleaning up, he just shut the door. I could smell the booze on him. The ringing in my ears was fading.

"It's not loaded, huh?"

"You want a beer?" he responded. I needed more than a few.

I reached over and grabbed the notebook as it had slid partially into the cushion, and I threw it onto the coffee table right as Sawyer walked back into the room.

"That's some weird shit in there, dude. And perhaps let's stop playing with guns. It's my constitutional right, my constitutional right!" I said mockingly.

"What were you doing?" he asked me, and he was looking right at the notebook. His gaze flickered toward me, then back to his notebook.

"Oh, I was going to doodle for a bit. And yeah, I saw your letters to Kurt Cobain or whatever. What's that all about?" I asked him. When I glanced up, he looked at me like I had just run over his puppy. He scrunched up his face, real ugly, and I could tell he was about to start crying. His face started to turn red as a stop sign, and he looked like he had just stubbed his toe and seen a werewolf.

Then his eyes burst open, and he was crying hard in front of me. He was intoxicated enough to almost blow my head off with a loaded gun, and now he was crying about who knows what.

"Man, what are you on right now?" I threw my hands up at him.

He had to be super high or drunk, so I stood up to move toward him. He quickly slammed the beers on the coffee table, grabbed the notebook, and ran off like a kid from a bully.

I was trying to process what had just happened. The gun. The notebook. What?

So, I sat with my thoughts, and I didn't get up for what

felt like an hour. It was probably only fifteen minutes, though. I got to my feet again and went to find the drunk knucklehead.

He was in his room, but the door was cracked open. I didn't know if I should knock or just enter since the door was slightly open, but I didn't do either. I could see him, but he had his back to me. He was sitting at his wife's vanity, writing into the notebook. I stood there and watched as he stopped writing, picked up a black handgun next to him, and aimed it right at his temple.

"What the fuck, dude!" I didn't scream it, but I gradually got louder with each word. I wanted him to hear me, but not accidentally pull the trigger now. Luckily, he didn't paint the wall red.

He turned to me, his complexion resembling a vampire. He uttered "Oh man," in a tone that didn't match the situation's intensity.

"What are you doing?" I asked as I slowly approached him.

"I was joking." The color rushed back to his face. "I saw you standing there. It's loaded. This one is loaded; I loaded it."

He was shaking his head, trying to diffuse the situation. I didn't know what to say, but I just slowly took the gun away from him.

"It was a joke," he stated in a new voice. One that meant something. Everything was awkward.

"Well, let's just stop playing jokes with guns!"

"Yeah, no doubt, it was a joke. And now I gotta deal with a fucking hole in the kitchen. I'm just going to get some sleep. My head hurts."

"Yeah, well, my ears still hurt from that blast."

He started taking his shoes off, and he said he was ready for bed. He was tired, that was all. I left the room, taking the loaded pistol with me. I didn't have a clue as to what to do. I was confident I couldn't fly to Vegas; I couldn't just leave him here alone surrounded by his thoughts and guns.

CHAPTER 11

"Conspiracy Drive"

I was stuck in the middle of two fires. I couldn't just tell my best buddy from high school, "See ya! I gotta catch my flight to Sin City."

Not after I had just watched him write a suicide note and follow it up by placing a gun to his temple to paint the wall red, Sawyer was mentally unstable, unemployed, and his wife was gone with another man. I didn't know what to do, but I knew I couldn't leave him alone. I didn't want to call the cops, and Baker Act him or fifty-one fifty or whatever they do in Show Me State for locking someone up who needs an evaluation. The pigs would probably show up and take me to jail, or worse, hear some rap music and pull their guns out. Sawyer would slam the door and grab his armory. It would turn into a Ruby Ridge type of standoff.

His wife, Cammie, not being in the house at all was a big problem. Half of me wanted to call his parents, but I didn't know how to get in contact with them. They also didn't like me, and that's understandable considering I set Sawyer's mom's garage on fire with roman candles. So I scratched that off the list.

I was kicking myself for not prying more.

I was in dire straits, so I canceled my flight west, and trust me, I wanted to go back to Sin City more than anything.

My stop there earlier in the summer was a legendary, two-day trip that is a book of its own. I'm not a complete asshole, though, and I knew Sawyer was in need. There were red flags everywhere, but I wasn't picking up on them at all.

I emailed Terry my piece on the debate. It was 510 words to the number, and I edited it and rewrote it three times. It was shit, though. Far from what I wanted, I wasn't a very good writer yet since I didn't have any guidelines for what *Rolling Stone* wanted. I did tell her that I was having some family issues in the Lou, and I wouldn't be able to make it out west. I would get back up with my flights in Cleveland since she did make it pretty clear that she did want me to meet somebody from the Green Party while in Cleveland. I wasn't excited about it because it wasn't even a real party. They were baffling to me because it was as if they went through the process of finding a suitable candidate and picking someone they were confident would lose and generate the least interest.

Terry quickly contacted me on WhatsApp, saying it was fine, but she was adamant that I get to Cleveland. She also mentioned that Olga would be there for the meeting too. She, Olga, and Dirk were always up to some cloak and dagger stuff, and I knew they weren't, they were just businessmen in a corporate world, but it sure felt like it at times. This Green Party meeting was essential and stressed to me numerous times. Lastly, she said the email server might go down since it had been going in and out all week and that she put my weekly payment in the nightstand, and I could pick it up and the other weeks pay once I was back in the mansion. And that was that. I had the best boss and job in America.

Sawyer was up before me watching propaganda. I could hear it as I did a checklist of all the red flags I might have seen. He had his arsenal. He had bought some powder to party with, his wife was gone, cheating on him, and he did seem more stressed than usual. He was also jobless, so maybe the issue was financial.

After ten minutes of contemplating the issue, I went with the easiest solution. Instead of facing the problem head-on, I would lie to him. I would tell him my flight to Vegas had been canceled and that we should take a road trip to Cleveland. And since he was laid off from work, he might go for it. We had been having a great time, it would be an epic road trip, and once on the road, I could chat with him, I would get confirmation that everything was fine with him. Then I could meet with the Green Party, Sawyer could fly home, and it would all work out in the end. I walked out confident in my plan.

"Yo, broski, I just spoke with my boss from *Rolling Stone*, and she said she wants me to take a photographer with me to the events in Cleveland. Since you're laid off right now, I figured you could come. I told her I had the guy for the job; what do you think?"

Damn, I couldn't even keep up the original lie, and now he was working with me. It just slipped out that way.

He hit mute on the remote and then said with a puzzled look, "but I forgot the camera last time?"

And he was right, but I wanted to keep an eye on him, maybe even try to read his notebook, which probably held all the answers, and I could get a hold of his parents or perhaps his wife. Anything, but I knew I couldn't leave him here alone and call myself his friend.

So I lied to him again, "No, no, it's all to the good; remember when we went to the red room with the ladies before the event? Well, I got some photos in there on my phone, and I did a short video too. I sent it to Terry, and she loved it. They didn't have anyone in there. That was my connection, remember?"

It was enough to convince Sawyer to come with me. He

had never been to Northern Ohio, and that was good because if he had, he wouldn't have wanted to go again. After agreeing to travel, he started to ask a million questions.

"How much am I getting paid?"

"Paid? If they use the picture you take in the magazine? A lot. A HUGE amount!" And I said huge, just like Trump was known for doing with his lips altogether, and the sound of the "YU" really stretched out.

"Are they gonna buy me a plane ticket too?"

"I figured we could dr-ive," I stuttered in the last part.

'Drive?" He had a puzzled look on his face as if he smelt sulfur.

"Yeah, we can rent something fresh."

"Not an El Camino!" He informed me.

"Yeah, I doubt you can rent a badass car like that, bro; come on!"
Since
"Road trip!" he yelled, and he went to get a bag ready while singing the El Camino song.

That was easy. Sawyer was excited to come to Cleveland with me, he had been laid off, and his wife wasn't around, so it was a perfect chance for him to get away.

Since I worked so hard with *Rolling Stone*, I wasn't afraid to use the company credit card anymore. Terry had not said one word about any purchases, and I had been using it left and right. It was like having free money in my pocket, so I got online and ordered a 2014 Mustang Convertible. Blue with tint and chrome.

After booking the rental, I started to rummage around looking for the notebook again. It held the answers, and it was the only way to get into his head. It crossed my mind to call the suicide hotline and ask them for advice, but I wasn't the one suicidal. I didn't know exactly how that worked, and I might answer a question wrong and end up getting committed to a mental ward; and good luck getting out of one of those places once you're inside. Everyone inside is saying, "I'm sane. Let me out!" The best bet once inside is to act nuts, have them put you on some meds, then act normal so you can get released. I didn't want to spend the next few months doing that shit, so I passed on calling anyone.

The only real person I felt I could call was Sawyer's old man, but Mr. Barnes wasn't too fond of me. Sawyer's parents were divorced, he split time between them in high school, and both sides equally hated me. His mom hated me for the Fourth of July incident, which had at least five other people involved that I didn't snitch on. (Cough Brian, Kevin, Enders, Kermit, and Anthony cough.) Sawyer's old man hated me because I burst his waterbed. Accidently. Hopefully, he was over that, and I could get in touch with him.

Sawyer came outside with two suitcases. There was no plan to get Sawyer back to the Lou, but that wasn't the issue at hand. I just needed to get a hold of his old man while we drove. I asked him for his old man's number, and I said I needed legal advice.

"Man, you gotta call his office if you want legal advice. Free or not. He hates, and I mean fucking hates it when me and my brother have people call him, and he's at the track and gets a call or sees someone asking about legal advice. It's that whole work-box thing, you know? He has a heart issue. His doctor said he had to calm down at work, so that's his theory, and he doesn't talk chop at all. He doesn't much pro-bono either. Dude is a capitalist, ya know, like us good Americans." He said the last part with airs about him.

A middle-aged white dude was driving the rental car when it pulled up, and Sawyer flipped out. I will admit, it was a badass car, and it felt as if a movie score should be playing. It wasn't a GTO 5.0, but she was a beauty. We mutually felt like studs as we hit i64 east and left the Arch in our dust.

As we drove through Southern Illinois, it didn't take long to figure out our mistake. Convertibles are suitable for driving on the beach, not the highway. When the top is down, it's too windy even to think and too loud to talk. Then when the top was up, the AC didn't work, so it got humid and sticky pretty fast. And what's the point of getting a convertible if you can't put the top down and show off? You might as well have a regular car. Then we found out someone put a CD into the radio and got it stuck. The CD wouldn't eject or play. It just spun and spun. Rental cars are always driven by everyone else as rental cars, and it was showing.

Southern Illinois is a desolate place, barren like the start of a horror movie about hitchhikers and zombies. We didn't see much because there wasn't much to see. Trucks on the highways and farmland, and more Trump signs than I had seen all year. Truckers for Trump. Illinois for Trump. The county name for Trump. Trump flags. Trump signs. Trump posters. Trump graffiti. Trump spelled out over barns. It really was Trump Country. We didn't stop anywhere, and we were glad we had gas because there didn't seem to even be gas stations in this part of Illinois, just Trump signs.

Sawyer could confabulate with anyone, but his gift to gab came with the curse of me listening. And with the radio not working, he would whistle when he wasn't talking. It's always the oddball, engineer brains that whistle. He filled the dead air with rants, but these rants weren't as innocent as the tangents he would go on back in high school. Back then, he would ask simple questions like where does all the trash go, or why does Bruce Willis always play the same washed-up cop character?

Now Sawyer had new rants that weren't so innocent, and he had become some sort of expert on the second amendment. There were many parroting terms and phrases he had copied from right-wing echo chambers he visited online. Forums and conspiracy subreddits, but who knows where he got some of his information. It was backwoods, backwater, backward bullshit that's older than the Southern Strategy. It's just more visible now, boosted on social media, and people see it and think they are 'thinking for themselves' about issues even though they are being told what to think. Parroting ideologies wouldn't be so bad if the ideas didn't lead to deadly outcomes. Most were beyond logic, but logic didn't seem to apply. His favorite was that Obama was coming for the guns. It was a conspiracy level of thinking. He thought Obama was some sort of reverse Santa Claus who was going door to door to take back all the guns. That was one of the reasons he loved the 2nd Amendment.

And this wasn't even the tip of the iceberg for Sawyer. His other theories were just as foolish. Slightly more enriched with bullshit, but they were all along those lines. It was enough for me to consider the legalities of him being able to own a gun and not even to consider the arsenal Sawyer had. He took me down a rabbit hole with no drugs as we drove through the southern part of the state where Lincoln once lived.

As we were merging north towards Terre Haute, Sawyer was filling me in on the actual big government conspiracy with guns. He loved the sound of his voice, and it blew my mind.

"In a bit can you stop so I can drain the main vein? Anyway, listen, so all those guns I got at my crib ain't nothing, yeah, shit, this dude Brett, that I bowl with, he has a bazooka. I kid you not, Gun. He got it off some drug dealer from Mexico or Panama City or something. It doesn't have a missile, or whatever it is, but he has the bazooka part, ya know, I think he can order them on eBay, but you know what YOU...CAN'T..order on eBay?"

He hung out the last two words to emphasize them. Then he stared at me like I should have known the answer to his riddle of bullshit.

"You can't order guns on eBay?" I said, and it was like I had guessed it, but I hadn't. I had merely said another thing that couldn't be bought on eBay.

He nodded that I was correct, but that wasn't the answer he was looking for.

"Well, guns, yes, you can't buy guns, but you also can't buy high-powered squirt guns!"

He was dipping because I wouldn't let him smoke in the rental. He was spit into an empty cup before he answered.

"Well, guns, yes, you can't buy guns, but you also can't buy high-powered, squirt guns!"

"I think you can buy super soakers on eBay, dude. What are you talking about?"

"Not a super soaker, a super soaker? That's not high-powered. That's like comparing a paintball gun to a Beebee gun or whatever, like a pellet gun without the CO2. You can't get a water gun like that. You can't even buy them. It's illegal. It is coming, but you can't buy them, nope!"

He was passionate about this one.

"Why can't you buy a high-powered squirt gun? I don't understand," I asked him, and I didn't have a clue.

When he didn't answer right away because of his tobacco, I asked him again, "Why would I even want to own a high-powered water gun? So I could pressure wash something? And isn't a pressure washer a high-powered squirt gun?"

"It is kind of yes, but it usually has to be plugged in," he said without answering the first part of my question.

"I made one, and I am going to give it to you, Gun."

He was smiling ear to ear, and I just nodded.

"Why will I need a high-powered water pistol?"

"It's not a pistol. Use it as if it is a high-powered assault rifle. It's made out of PVC, well, some of it. I want you to have it."

He turned to look out the window and asked me, "Man, can I smoke one square if I hang my head out the window? It already smells like smoke in here."

"No, dude, no, but why will I need a high-powered water shotgun?"

"For the military, duh!" he said, and his voice was excited and erratic, and he looked at me like Elvis would an impersonator.

"Duh, duh what? You can't say duh if I don't know what you are saying when you say the military."

It felt like I was trying to bathe a cat. I wanted him just to tell me, and it was like he was saying the meaning of life was forty-two.

Finally, he broke his silence, "Right, the military! They don't want the general public to have high-powered water guns, so when it pops off. They move into control us with the robots, we can't fight back," He said, and his voice was steady and deep now, and he went on, "the military robots, the super troops, stormtroopers from the New World Order, they are going to have only one weakness. Water!"

He was like a seven-year-old talking about Jedi in Star Wars.

"So the super soldiers, the future terminators, Universal Soldiers, or whatever, the most powerful soldiers ever made, but not if you get them wet?" I asked him as we passed a sign stating we were entering Indiana. when

"Exactly. Now you get it. When they do finally attack, boom, you will be ready to take them down. All those guns I have won't do anything against the super soldiers, and the water weapons will!"

"What if the super soldiers just use a drone and blow up your house?"

"Huh?" He asked me back as if he didn't understand my question.

"What if the government, the super soldiers use a drone, a robot drone, and blow up your house?"

He paused to think, but this was his theory, and he wasn't going to let me destroy his end of the world fetish with logic.

"If they blow up my house with a drone, well, that's why I won't be home!"

He turned the smile on that the ladies loved and turned to me, pointing at his brain. He had it all figured out. I just nodded and shook my head. It felt like I didn't even know the guy anymore, and this was one of his sane theories. Some of them were so wild that I didn't know if he read them on an internet fuck site or just made them up.

I had to squeeze in a question or two about Cammie, so

when he finally paused from his tinfoil hat talk, I straight up asked him.

"So, what's up with you and Cammie?"

"Ah man, she's cheating me on with some fuck, or we aren't even together right now. I ain't worried about all that, ya feel me? So can I tell you how I got Mitch McConnell back?"

He told me the story of how he handed Mitch a bag of turtle food at the Galt House. He got in using his old man's Republican pass or sumshit. He told Mitch he wanted a picture and held up the bag while his wife took the photo. Then when she was done, he handed it to Mitch and grabbed his phone back. No clue why Mitch's wife didn't say anything about a man holding a bag of turtle food up for a picture. The ball was now back in my court, and we decided that the other person would only have 30 days to strike next. Finding ways to hand turtle food to Mitch McConnell was the sane part of our friendship.

Sawyer was upset that I had left the turtle food at Mitch's office for my prank since he had handed it and taken pictures. It was decided that I had to hand Mitch turtle food within 30 days or lose the bet.

We veered off the main highway looking for a rest stop or gas station and ended up on some bunker dink highway 41 that had stoplights on it when the front driver's side tire blew. It didn't make a loud noise like a gunshot, and it didn't even jolt the car. It was like all the air slowly went out of the tire in about a minute instead of instantly. Either way, it was flat. Up ahead of us was a place called Boot City.

There was a parking lot that we pulled into just off of this one-lane highway in front of a peddlers mall or flea market. The type of place that is only open on weekends and sells bullshit for people who buy bullshit. Phone cases that break in a month, fake leather belts that also break in a month, bootlegs among other knick-knacks like cannabis pipes, butterfly knives, brass knuckles, and custom spray paint shirts with a shelf life of 27 days. The items drive the middle class into poverty when they aren't careful.

Sawyer had to put the Mickey Mouse tire on, and he got pissed at me because I didn't know how to do it. I'd never learned and never really wanted to learn. It was only the second time I had ever had a flat in my life. He ruffled my feathers over it, but I didn't care. I called the rental place to see the options since we couldn't drive to Cleveland on a Mickey Mouse.

We were hungry as hostages, but the only place around was the flea market. We headed inside. Sawyer ordered a hot dog and informed me he would find us a new tire. The rental company said I could exchange the car on Monday or buy a tire, and they would reimburse me. That was the best option, even though it would take eight years to get the reimbursement. I could just charge it to the game.

The Hoosiers state was an interesting place.

This flea market was a prime example as the loser flag was visible all over, and in my book flying the loser flag is the same as flying a nazi flag. At one time, Indiana had been a northern state that fought with the Union, but it had somehow turned into the middle finger of the south. America already won that war. The damn traitors should have been hanged as soon as the war was over, not memorialized, and if that happened, we wouldn't see much of the loser flag today. This flea market even had a whole booth of nothing but loser flag items. It was despicable.

Sawyer stuffed his face with the mystery meat in the bun, and I decided to go on being hungry. I hit the can, and Sawyer had found us a tire by the time I was done. He met some old head named Stan, who said his son owned a shop.

We left shortly after following Stan through the city of Terre Haute. It wasn't much to look at, and it wasn't until I saw signs for ISU that I could understand why it even existed in the first place.

Traveling through the city was like traveling through time back to 1959. Even apparent attempts by the city to modernize were obvious failures. The shop was off the downtown area, and we followed Stan inside. He introduced us to Stan Jr., and I noticed the place was empty for a Saturday. Stan Sr. was excited to bring his son some business, and they looked like twins minus or plus 25 years.

While I was picking out a tire, Sawyer and Stan Sr. talked. Sawyer told him how he was working as a photographer for *Rolling Stone* magazine and how I was a writer. Sr. said something like, "That's how y'all can afford that sweet ride!"

Sawyer didn't tell him it was a rental. I didn't shop around for the tire, just asked for whatever tire would get us back on the highway and handed over the company credit card. When I walked back into the waiting room area, Sawyer and Stan Sr. were shooting the shit. Sawyer told about getting locked out of the debates, and then the conversation rolled into politics.

Even the most logical person I know can get behind things, such as Edith Wilson being the first official, unofficial female president as she Weekend-at-Bernie'd her husband around for six months, or how the grassy knoll and the Zapruder are off a bit. There's a long list of maybe's throughout history, and they are great conversational pieces. It's fun to drink some Old Fashion's and discuss what we think happens at the Bilderberg meetings or what is really at Area 51, but it's all speculation and all fun. The best theory I've ever heard was from Sawyer's old man. It was a theory backed up by a video that Connally shot JFK, who was riding shotgun, and Connally shot the President through his arm. It was stretching the bounds of reality, but it wasn't even close to the bullshit that Sawyer and Stan Sr. were knee-deep in when I walked over. These were absurd theories way beyond advanced water pistols for the robot wars. And it didn't matter that these two had just met either. They were informed, and they wanted to share. They had been getting their hogwash from the same pig station. They both agreed that the school shooting in Sandy Hook was a false flag.

Sawyer had already informed me that a false flag was when the government faked a significant event to fool the bourgeois into thinking something had happened. A real-life example would be something similar to the Gulf of Tonkin, only more advanced. Only now, instead of lying to go to war in Vietnam, other agendas are sought after.

And their proof was so evident that both of them thought I should be ashamed of myself for missing it. They explained to me that a picture of a survivor, a teacher, was also used in photos for the Boston Bombing. She wasn't a victim but rather a crisis actor who worked for the government, and she was acting out the false flag.

These delusional dimwits also believed that the government used pictures of the same children for both massacres. I watched the rental get put up on a lift through the window in the waiting room, and then I turned to Sawyer and asked him, "So it's a government-run operation to take the guns back, so why would the government use the same kid's picture?"

"It was probably a funding issue," Stan Sr. said after pondering it for a second. It was the best that either one could do.

"The government had a funding issue?" I asked back,

louder because the answer threw me off. I could see the mice spinning the wheels now.

"Government cutbacks, maybe?" Sawyer added, and Stan Sr. nodded.

"That doesn't even make sense. The government has billions of dollars, and why the Boston Bombing? Look, I hate running as much as the next American, but I'm not dropping bombs off at the finish line to get out of doing laps. What was the point or motive behind bombing a marathon?"

I waited for an answer as the rental was pulled down and then backed out into a parking spot with a brand new tire on it. Neither one of them spoke, and I was starting to leave to go pay when Stan Sr. reached into his ass and pulled out, "The Boston Bombing was an attempt by Vice President Biden to get a war started in Syria."

Sawyer nodded in agreement before chiming in, "Yeah, I haven't heard that one, but it sounds confirmed."

"It sounds confirmed? What does that even mean?" I asked, stopping dead in my tracks to look at him.

"It seems logical, right? Why else would they have staged it?" Sawyer answered me with a question.

"So Obama and Biden set up these false flags by using what, I guess the -"

"The deep state," Stan cut me off sharply to let me in on the big secret. It wasn't Obama and Biden, but the deep state. Goalposts move the boogeyman changes.

"Yeah, so Biden and Obama are doing these massive false flags so they can start a war that never happened, or repel some gun law that still hasn't been repealed, and they couldn't even find different actors? That doesn't make sense."

I was trying to use logic to prove the truth, but in a way, these two tweedle dumbs could understand it.

"Gun, you've said it yourself. The more people you have in on the conspiracy, the more people can tell all the secrets. People would talk, and the word would get out, so they kept the circle small. The lady in both pictures is probably Obama's top agent like she is probably a female James Bond, or like a Charlie's Angel type of chick who can just kick ass. They would keep real small groups like Obama and Biden and this chick."

"Jamie Bond," Stan said, proud of his wordplay, which was quick considering.

"Nice! Obama's Angels!' Sawyer added. They were like two stoners minus the smoke.

"You are right, Sawyer. Two people can keep a secret if one of them is dead!" Stan chimed in, and then he went over the edge with his comments from his ass.

"Just think, Obama probably played a direct part in these things, like he dressed up as a cop or a first responder."

Sawyer nodded but didn't say anything. Stan's comments were just that, comments made by some crazy old man, but Sawyer's, on the other hand, were disturbing. Sawyer had changed, and for him to believe outrageous, unreal, impossible shit was laughable if it didn't mean anything else, but it did. It meant a lot. I needed to dig more, though, because these weren't suicidal thoughts.

Sawyer never really cared about politics before either. We both had a distaste and distrust for authority, just like all teenagers should. All children should have that along with a side of rebellion, or else the whole country would be as dull as whatever in the hell Richard Nixon thought a utopia was. I am all for having an open mind. I am all in on finding out the truth about Roswell and such things, but just believing shit on the spot or just because it fits a narrative a person wants to subscribe to is certifiable and usually leads to a bed in the looney bin or a spot in the Koolaid line.

Stan Jr. opened the door and told us we were ready to go. I followed him into another room to pay while Sawyer and Stan kept talking. They thought they were right, and if I just saw one more piece from their angle, I would grasp the whole picture and understand.

As Stan Jr. was ringing me up, I asked him what in the hell Terre Haute meant. And he told me, "Terre Haute is the French Highlands or just the Highlands, I think. I know all the other cities in Indiana say Terre Haute means Ugly Women in Greek because there aren't any good-looking women in this city, which is actually partially true. The sign leading into the city should read, "Terre Haute Home of the Ugliest Women in the USA!"

"You guys have a University here, though, right? They can't all be ugly at the school, though, can they?"

"ISU is here, but nope they are all ugly. It's illegal to be a prom queen or anything like that in high school and commit to becoming a Sycamore." He said, laughing hard afterward, but I still wasn't sure if his joke didn't have a little bit of truth to it.

I paid and walked outside. Sawyer followed me and headed out. He had a lead on something, and he wanted to get some food, so he asked if I could stop by the Dairy Queen. He had directions, and his diet consisted mainly of chicken fingers and ice cream. While we were eating, Sawyer started talking to all the workers, and finally, the 16-year-old chick working the front and the other bratty kid cleaning the dining area broke. They were huffing on the tanks in the back and coming back out high as fuck. Sawyer had heard in the tire spot that this was an excellent place to score chronic, and it didn't take him long. He could sniff out water in a desert. He just had a knack for it. And I told him I didn't even want to see it. Not one hit of the devil's lettuce for me. So, of course, he showed it to me as soon as he got into the car, and it didn't even look like something I wanted to smoke. It was crunched, but it popped open when he pulled it out of the bag. It was loud as fuck. Like a skunk had just sprayed into the car.

"It's pure fire, Indiana creeper weed," Sawyer said as he wrapped it back up.

"That shit stinks. Put it in the trunk," I ordered him.

He zipped it up, sealed the bag tight.

"Smell it now? Do you?"

I didn't. The goddamn ziplock had changed the game, and he shoved it into his tighty whities.

"I can't smell it, but put it into the trunk. They hang people in Indiana for chronic!"

He did, and I took off.

And as we made our way through the middle finger of the south, we saw miles and miles of cornfields and Trump signs. So many Trump signs to suggest there might have even been a mandate from the Governor. Naturally, our conversation gravitated towards politics. I had been avoiding a subject, but Sawyer was now a political specialist, and it was his newfound love inspired by Mr. Trump.

"Look, you hate Mitch McConnell, and so does Trump."

"Trump doesn't even know who Mitch McConnell is," I informed Sawyer.

"No, he does. Trump is talking about him when he says he will drain the swamp. That's probably where the "drain the swamp" came from because he looks like a turtle, but that's not why they call it the swamp. Trump is going to drain the swamp; it's a fact."

He wasn't a Republican like his old man. We both hated Republicans. And that hate started with Addison Mitch McConnell. Sawyer was a Trumpie on board the train, but I felt after a few days with me that would end, and he would see the light and understand that Trump wasn't who Sawyer thought he was.

"I ain't seen one Hillary sign," Sawyer said, and he was right.

"Makes you think Trump might win," I told him as we drove into a light rainstorm.

"Might? Trump is going to win an easy, landslide victory. Why don't you write that in your *Rolling Stone*."

And he hadn't been right about much, but he was right about that. The media was saying Hillary, but the people across the forgotten parts of this country were picking another president. The road got wet, and I slowed down.

"Don't slow down. You can speed now!"

"The road is slicker. All the oil that was on the road mixes with water. It will be harder to break. I am not going to speed in a fucking thunderstorm!"

"Think about it. A cop isn't going to pull you over in the rain. And what, stand in the rain? Cops have computers with wifi in their cars, and they will just watch a movie or google photos of donuts to masturbate to. They don't want to get out in the rain and give you a ticket for going ten over. Push it."

He sat back as if I was just going to push the gas. It didn't matter, though, because the storm was gone as quick as it came.

"Man, you missed your chance, Gun!"

He was upset at me just as I was upset with him. We were on two ends of the political spectrum, and it finally led to some peace and quiet on our journey.

We merged east and went under Indianapolis. The sun was finally gone behind us as we got closer to the border of Indiana and Ohio, and once we did cross the state line, I pulled off on the first exit. It was a rest stop, a place to stretch and pee. Sawyer rolled up a J, and as soon as we hit the highway, he put it in the air. I didn't want to toke with him since we still had a long stretch ahead, so I pulled into exit two for some coffee at a truck stop. I needed coffee more than I needed Canibus.

I was too tired to argue about smoking in the rental, so I didn't say anything. I was just hoping Sawyer wouldn't fire it up inside the ride, and he would walk over behind the place into the woods.

He didn't, and by the time I came back, he was hotboxing like we were in a legal state. I came back holding my hot coffee, and a donut in a wrapper opened the door and smoked rolled out like it was a chimney. A younger white lady was at the pump across from me, and she was eyeing out my car, and then she said with a nasty attitude, "It smells like you hit a skunk."

She was pilled out or something. The epidemic had hit Ohio harder than Ken Riley hit, and that's why the youth weren't getting out the vote in the buckeye state. They were all addicted to that shit.

I brushed the smoke away with my hand before I sat down in the car.

"He has glaucoma, and he is dealing with it in his own way."

I lied, and I didn't want to say it. It felt like a bad lie, I cringed when I said it, but I didn't want to get the law called on us either.

"Shi--ii--t, I don't have n-o glaw-coma but, but, I need sum med-i-son!"

She was a zombie. Her whole world was moving in slow motion, so her words sounded normal in her head. She was gone, addicted to the harshest shit in the entire known Universe.

"Smells like Snoop Doggy Dogg pulled up in this mug."

I thanked her for some odd reason and slammed the door shut.

"You know she got them percs! And who doesn't want them percs, right? Have you done them!" Sawyer yelled, and he was laughing like a kid who farted in church

"You gotta start being more covert about shit. That shit stinks."

He was so high he didn't know what I said.

"Yo-gurt, comb-hurt, co-vert!' He was mimicking whatever I said. His eyes were squinty, and his face was funny-looking.

"It's fucking fine, dude; it's med-use-in all, that old lady didn't care, who does? Take a chill pill, shit ask your girlfriend there she can probably get you one!"

"The fucking cops will care if they smell this shit!"

I backed up, pulled out, and took us back to the highway northeast towards Columbus. Sawyer was zooted. His political conspiracy theories he had been sharing so far were low level; he wanted to inform me of the real secret info he had collected from totally legit sources.

"We are living in a simulation." He said, and he held it out there, so I took it from him.

When in Rome. It tasted as good as it smelt.

"Yeah, and what is your proof that we are living in a simulation?" I asked after I coughed a bit.

"Because of the middle ages...." He hung out the sentence like it needed to dry.

"Dude, what?"

I was lost.

"Tell me, how or why did they call those the Middle Ages?" He made air quotes as he said, "Middle Ages."

I was still catching my breath, so he continued, "this one is my own theory, well not that we are living in a simulation, that's probably confirmed, but I found the evidence and put it together."

Based on his delusions and nothing else, Sawyer believed that this world was a part of a simulation. We were all, in fact, sims. This life wasn't real, and we were inside a Nintendo or computer game or something similar, being run by some god, or kid, or both so that they could watch trends on our simulation stock market went with specific scenarios that were happening in the real world.

It was impressive for a guy like Sawyer to develop such an elaborate theory even if it was outside any realm of reality. Then he informed me that it wasn't his original idea, and he started to explain how he read it on a forum and believed it, so he started researching it. There wasn't a lot of evidence he could provide, but he did tell me to get on a few of the forums and read the copypasta.

It just drove home that no matter how powerful gods are, they still need to acquire money and do so with a stock market scheme or by letting people tith for spots in their heaven. Which is interesting to hear after the chronic is blazed, but when you break it down, it's a clusterfuck of ideas that made about as much sense as a raccoon molesting a possum.

Sawyer believed it all, though as long as it fits into his agenda, which is precisely how people can believe any propaganda. He did have some morals left, and he was trying to make sure the noise in his head abided by something.

"So yeah, that's my proof."

"What's your proof? The middle ages?"

"Yeah, like how did they know that was going to be in the middle?"

I couldn't even answer; I just shook my head. I shook it even harder when he said the green soda was running through him, and we'd need to stop for the third time in six miles. We were moving at a snail's pace and wouldn't get into Cleveland until after midnight. I pulled off into another gas station and sat in the car while Sawyer ran inside.

I decided to send Morgan a text since she had been hitting me. I wanted to call her, but a quick text to let her know I was on the road would be the next best thing. She hit me right back and told me to be safe. I could feel it building between us, and I hoped it was real. When Sawyer finally got back from draining himself, the Indiana Creeper was in full effect. I was zooted. He plopped down in shotgun, holding another 32 ounces and two bags of Funyuns.

"This is the slowest pace anyone has ever traveled on a road trip in a Mustang. You know that?"

And I didn't even know if I could drive. He could see that

and started laughing as hard as he ever had. I had to go into the gas station myself, use the bathroom, and check out all the oddities that this truck stop had. Sawyer went to the side with the food and got me a burger, and I would need to eat to rid myself of this extreme insanity.

The Indiana creeper had crept on me.

We would never get to Cleveland at this pace, but we didn't care.

And when we came back outside, there was an omen. A black cat was sitting, nice and comfortable, on the hood of the mustang. The bad luck had arrived, and the flat tire was just a precursor.

Sawyer screamed at it, "Getfucked!"

And it jumped off the hood and hissed at us as if we invaded its space.

"You smell that?" Sawyer asked, puffing his nose before we got into the car, and I did smell it. It was the foul aroma of the city of Cleveland. It was still hours away, but the smell was lingering here in the middle of Ohio, and it was gross.

He showed me what he had in his bag, he had left while I was eating, and it was two bottles of Mad Dog 2020.

"Dude, I said no drinking in the car!"

"No, you didn't!" He screamed, but he knew I had said it.

"Look, we already smoked a doobie that put me over, and I said no drinking in the rental!"

"No, you said, No drinking any beer in the car! This isn't beer."

"That's because you asked if you could buy beer. Why would I let you buy Mad Dog if I wouldn't let you buy beer?"

And I drove off, heading north towards the smell of Cleveland.

Sawyer drank on his mad dog, and he put another one in the air. We hotboxed again as we drove through Northern Ohio, the last part going by quickly as a mosquito bite. Sawyer had found the energy to rant about politics again, and this, and time he was talking about Dick Milhouse.

"He went to Duke, which a lot of people don't know, but if you know Duke for anything, it's basketball, right? Because why would the school want to glorify the only president to be removed from office, right?"

"Right?" I said back because I didn't know where this was going.

"That's why a lot of people think some of the basketball players are clones of his. They had cloning back before he died, and think about it, JJ Reddick has the same head and ears as Milhouse; Grayson Allen is the spitting image of Nixon. All I am saying is there is a chance Nixon was cloned."

It was still hard to tell if he was pulling shit out of his anus. He had read it online where someone else had found it by their hemorrhoids or if he was punking me.

"Now, Little Rubio, he has chronic bad breath. It's just a fact. Sawyer let me know, and he was on the edge of his seat as we rolled along. That really hurt him, and why the GOP wasn't pushing him so hard, ya know, Low Energy Jeb was one thing, but Rubio having this stank ass breath that killed him."

"Where do you even read that type of information?"

"*Rolling Stone!*"

I had to laugh at that.

"It's all over. I don't just use one source, and if I start

saying my sources, you will just discredit them. It's a ton of different ones, though, youtube.."

"Youtube? That's not a source-"

"No, look, there are channels on Youtube, and there are good ones and bad ones and different ones, I mean all sorts of them, you got kids opening up new toys, and music videos and then CNN has one, but not just youtube. I get info on forums and stuff like Reddit, 9gag, 4chan, Facebook sometimes depending, not Instagram though, whatever that is about ya know?"

"When you say all those websites, don't you just mean Faux News?" I said, looking at him so he would understand I was joking.

"What? No! I mean, I watch Fox News; who doesn't? It's the most-watched station in the entire world, and it doesn't have an agenda behind it like the other ones!"

I couldn't believe he was saying this. Sawyer had some perverted and misaligned thoughts running around in his brainwashed head. It was like I was in a Dunning-Krueger experiment. A new version of the study that makes patient one learn his best friend, patient two, is a moron who believes Faux News doesn't have an agenda. I still knew deep down I could change his mind on the whole deal. I just needed a few days to get the hogwash out of his brain. I still didn't know if he was a real threat, and he was starting to get annoying. Maybe he wouldn't blow his brains out, and it was all a joke. I couldn't babysit him forever, and the way this was going, I didn't want to.

I let him ramble on with his rants, though, because I had to focus on the road. He got me up to date on some of the new theories he was studying, such as why Dave Chappelle left $30 million on the table with Comedy Central because Oprah didn't

SUICIDE NOTES TO KURT COBAIN

like his show. She had sent assassins to his house in Ohio, right near us on the highway. That was bananas, but it was small potatoes compared to the new theory that was breaking right under everyone's nose. Sawyer had the lead on it, though.

Pizzagate was about to be the biggest scandal in the history of the world, he informed me. It involved a ring of child perverts bigger than the Catholic Church had, and Bill and Hillary Clinton led them. The New York police had opened a case, but it had been closed down by the deep state. And now, only Donald J. Trump could stop it. He was stopping it, but if he weren't elected president, the pedophiles would win.

And it is how Trump was going to save America. I finally had my answer.

When Trump talked about the elites, it wasn't those with money and power. Well, it was, but these people were also pedophiles who not only did terrible things with kids, they also drank their blood. It was why George Soros funded Planned Parenthood so the embryos could be taken by the Clintons or sumshit.

I lost track of his story by that point.

My mind was tired from all the driving that his words didn't resonate, and I was also lifted by the doobies. Sawyer was sure of this one. It wasn't some half-ass theory. None of the lamestream media confirmed it, but it was about to break and become the biggest story in history. It was the reason Trump was running for president, and it was how he would save America and the world. Sawyer was astonished; I hadn't heard of it yet.

"Trump is fighting the chesters, the Clintons, the Obama's, the radical left, and he will save America!"

He was sure of it. I just nodded at him, and I started to understand how Jim Jones got so many to drink the kool-aid. I was at a loss for words.

And finally, without a fanfare but an increased odor of nastiness, we arrived at the Mistake on the Lake, Cleveland, Ohio.

We checked into the hotel smelling of stinky feet and burnt leaves. Our eyes were bloodshot, and our faces were tired.

A balding 30-year-old checked us in, but he didn't even notice or smell us. His own nose was probably immune from smelling anything at all since he lived in Northern Ohio. We fit right in with the locals who only see the sun shining bright for two months in some years, as they spent most of their time under acid rain spewed from pollution clouds.

We had to get into our car and then drive to our room, and the rain was falling as we did. We ran up the stairs and into our room before it started falling. Lightning hit nearby, we made it inside, but as the door took a draft of wind and slammed shut, it knocked a mirror hanging on the wall to the ground, and it shattered into a thousand pieces.

"Holy shit!" Sawyer yelled when it did. I almost stained my pants.

The room was dark, and neither one of us knew what had happened.

"Shit, that scared the shit out of me, and that's bad fuck-ing luck too," Sawyer said as he flipped on the light. And he was right.

"The black cat and now a broken mirror, shit!" He said as I checked out the bathroom to make sure Freddie or Jason wasn't in there.

It was after 2 am, and we both decided it was time to hit

the sack, and we didn't even turn on the flatscreen.

It had been a long, strange trip north.

CHAPTER 12

"Mistake on the Lake, Ohio October 22nd 2016"

A tenth woman had now come forward accusing Donald J. Trump of sexual assault or misconduct. This account was a woman accusing Trump of grabbing her breasts at a US Open event back in the late 90s. In a published statement, this lady said Trump was "leering" at her, and for most of the flyover states, that's a dictionary word, and dictionaries were hard to come by. It's essentially staring, and that's not a crime on either side of the alley.

The groping was another issue, but Trumpies just chalked it into the category of another person trying to defame the Trumpster and perhaps get a payday from him. Some even thought it was a political plot by the Liberal Media and the Clintons. Dude D and Sawyer both firmly believed this, and while they might suggest Trump is a womanizer, they would quickly mention one of Bill's accusations and say he did it and was a two termer! The fact that there were now ten allegations against Trump wasn't an issue at all. The rest of the country was starting to realize that "I could shoot someone on Fifth Avenue and get away with it" was based on reality.

Getting up to start the day, the skies were dark with brisk moving gray clouds replaced with more gray clouds as if they were made nearby. Despite the clouds, the city of Cleveland did have its swagger back. The sixth-largest city in the country had just won the NBA Championship back in June, hosted the GOP convention in August(a shit show but significant for the city), and now the Tribe was on their way to win the World Series. What was once a belt full of rust after the fumble and the drive and shot was now Believeland. It wasn't the mistake on the lake anymore. The Land was a Plum©. I was still rocking my Cubs hat, and it was turning into a conversation piece as the Tribe, and the Baby Bears were about to knock heads in the fall classic. The lovable losers had to get by the Dodgers first, though.

The first event I had to cover in Ohio was Hillary at a community college. I didn't let Sawyer pound any booze beforehand because I had learned my lesson. We kissed the rental goodbye, which meant we had to rely on a light rail to get us there. Inside of the rail, it stunk like urine. The smells of The Land never disappoint. Exiting the rail, walking over an overpass, Sawyer lit up his last j. A row of cars exited right near us, and the secret service watched each one.

After we blazed, I texted Morgan to ask if I was still on the press list for this event and all that jazz. I knew I was on the list; I just wanted to chat with her. She might be at this event, and that would be a great excuse to kick it with her afterward, but she messaged me back and said she wasn't in Ohio, luckily for her sense of smell. Something was brewing between us, though.

At the very bottom of the overpass, two bikers were going up, so we had to merge over, and Sawyer stopped walking altogether. He informed me that he wasn't going to go inside with me. He dropped his camera bag slowly to the ground and then opened it. He pulled out the camera, which he had brought, and he said, "I can't go in there with all them fags, queers, and libtards, and I can't see that Crooked Bitch!"

He pulled out a bottle from the bag and took a sip.

"What are you talking about? Queers? And libtards?!"

He didn't respond, so I asked him, "Are you fucking high or what?"

"I won't support that traitor to this country! This crooked, no, this criminal. I won't do it. When she gets arrested, I will be happy, but until then, no, fuck her!"

"What are you even talking about? She won't be arrested! You're changing, man, and I am worried about you. Seriously, you used to stand up for the kids getting picked on, and now you're calling these people fags and queers?"

"Whatever that fucking means, I haven't changed; you have! Look, I can't say all these people are, but they are going into this event to see a future criminal, a traitor to the American people. They have been brainwashed by the liberal media, shit, by the media in general. Cucks and fags, just look at all these old, ugly women going into support a criminal!"

He was delusional, and I wanted to leave him right there in that stinkin city. He was high, drunk, and brainwashed. I didn't say anything as he pulled out the bottle and took another drink, this time not hiding it from the people walking by us.

"Dude, your Uncle Rob is gay, and he was like your older brother. How can you even say that?" I said as he handed me the bottle. I took it. I fucking needed it. It was true, though; his very own favorite uncle was gay. I took a small shot and handed it back to him. It was hot with eyes on us; I didn't want to pour it down my throat.

He took the bottle and then took a long, stiff drink that looked like it hit his spleen, and then he leaned over his bag like an umpire cleaning home plate.

"Gun, you know Robby was born like that. I am not calling Uncle Robby a faggot, or any gay person for that matter. I am saying, those guys there, right there, going in to watch this criminal speak, they are fags. Not the gay lover type, but soft and without onions. They can't change a tire, can't shoot a gun, can't do nothing but dumb shit like hey you, excuse me, sir," and Sawyer started barking at a guy walking by, "you there, hey!"

The man started to stop, and Sawyer kept at him, "yeah, excuse me, we are with Rolling Stone Magazine, and what do you do for a living, sir?"

The man was wearing black dress pants and a button-down with a tie and a blazer over it.

"Uh, okay, well, I'm a neurosurgeon," and then he looked at both of us to see if we were done, noticing the bottle Sawyer was holding. He faked a smile that didn't open his eyes and nodded at us, waiting for something else.

"Yes, and can you change a tire? Honestly." Sawyer said, putting the booze away and standing up.

"Like a car tire, sure," He responded.

"Sure?" Sawyer asked.

"Uh, yes, Rolling Stone Magazine, huh?" he had his doubts.

"It's a survey type of report," I added so the guy wouldn't call the law or hit a button on a rape tower.

"Yeah, it has nothing to do with the fact that Gunner here can't change a tire. So the last time your car got a flat tire, wherever that was, you popped the trunk, got out the spare, and changed it?" Sawyer said, looking at me, and it was a dig at me since I couldn't change one.

"Yeah, I mean I could have; I think we had someone come to change it for us. It was my wife's car and the.."

"No further questions," Sawyer cut him off and even waved his hand at him.

"And you are voting for Mrs. Clinton?" I asked him since Sawyer left him hanging.

"Yeah, I mean, it's the best option at this point," he pushed his glasses up and ran off.

"If that doesn't prove my point, then nothing will," Sawyer said, and he was done talking about it.

"He's a fucking neurosurgeon; I imagine he can change a tire, it's more affordable for him to pay somebody to do it, and then he can focus on his career, his profession of fixing people's brains!"

"And you know that dude can't shoot a gun!"

He didn't understand what I was saying. He put the camera back into the bag and stood up.

"He can learn to shoot a gun. Are you going to learn how to do brain surgery?"

"Who the hell said anything about brain surgery?" He asked me.

"Let's just go in and do our job. That's it, okay?" I said, but he didn't respond. He did follow me, though, and we didn't talk. He thought I didn't see his big vision, but it was him who didn't.

Once we got inside, the place was full of liberal elites or the types that Sawyer thought were such. It was a multiracial event, and it was three to one in favor of the ladies. The rhetoric wasn't any different than any other Hillary event I had been at all summer and fall, and it was the same record, different station.

The battle lines were drawn, and the people had already decided. The men and women around me weren't ever going to vote Republican. These weren't the swing voters, the real people of America that the media should be polling. I had talked to so many Americans in the flyover, and they weren't "swing" voters. They were the silent majority for Trump, and they just didn't want to admit it. They especially didn't want to admit it to the pollsters they didn't trust.

The talking point of the swing voters didn't really exist. If I lied to a voter who said they were undecided and told them I was probably leaning with Trump, ninety-nine percent of the time, they said they were too. People were pretty committed to one side or the other, and most of the folks in the flyover didn't want someone known as Crooked Hillary running the country. It didn't matter if she was crooked or not, it wasn't a good fit, and she was branded.

And that is where Trump knew how to win. He wasn't just muddying up the race but rather throwing it through the wringer and turning it into a WWE match. And just like Americans do when they watch wrestling, we had all picked a side. Trump was the villain wrestler, but he was also here to save the day. He was the bad guy, but he would save us from the real bad guys.

So all the swing voters were Trump voters in the flyover, well, a large majority. The GOP has branding down just as good as Trump, and they've been doing it well before he joined the party. Abortion, Guns, and God. And so many people fell in line.

The Democrats were too big a group of people with too many differences to fall into these three things. Hillary was hard to fall in line for, and I was thinking this as she was about to come out and speak. They don't love her. The people on the other side love Trump. He gives them what they want to hear. A win for Trump is a win for the flyover folks. Hillary provides nothing to anyone if she wins. Trump is going to win.

Trump was going to win! Shit! I felt it in my bones as I was starting to put together what Sawyer had been telling me. Disgustingly, I repeated it to myself; TRUMP IS GOING TO WIN!

It didn't matter if none of it was true. The narrative was out, and folks believed it. Critical thinking wasn't a skill that most Americans had. Trump was going to win the working class using his narrative of saving America. He was going to win, and as much as I didn't like it, I knew it was going to happen.

I turned to Sawyer, who wasn't asleep but very bored, and I told him, "Trump is going to win."

He woke up, and as he did, I noticed how loud I had just said that. A couple in front of me turned to look at us, so I turned to look behind me as if someone else had said it.

"He's not gonna lose to this boring ass shit!" Sawyer said just to let the young couple know it was me that said it. I nodded at them, and they turned around.

Then Hillary came out. The whole place stood up calmly and did a golf clap. Sawyer didn't, though, as if to say, "Screw this lady!"

He was convinced she was a criminal and supported pedophilia and blood drinking. He wasn't happy about being in the same venue as her or all her 'enablers' as he would call them. And the more they cheered, the angrier he got. It was hilarious to me, but I knew we couldn't stay in our seats, or he might get us into a fight or worse. Snitches were all around. We made our way up to the balcony, and I pretended like we needed more photos for the magazine when it didn't matter in reality.

Out of the blue, my phone rang, and it was Sawyer's old man. I ran into the hallway and stood to talk to him, but there was too much going on. I told him I had a legal matter but was busy. I asked if I could text him, and he said I could, which was a relief because people over 50 can go either way with texting. I badly wanted to speak with him, but if I left Sawyer alone in a room full of people he hated, who knows.

When I walked back into the viewing area, Hillary was still going strong, but she was stopping and drinking water a lot which Sawyer would always point out. He was leaning over the balcony, acting like he had a rifle in his hand, aiming it at spectators and pretending to shoot. He didn't put his imaginary gun at Hillary, probably because he had already acted to shoot her, but I told him to stop and said we had enough pictures. I didn't know if we had one, but I didn't want the secret service to tackle us. They were all around us, and they were already upset at us for trying to sneak in a bottle of booze. Why they didn't take it is beyond me, but Sawyer had looked them right into the eyes and said, "I am diabetic; if my insulin levels fall, I could die. Take a shot of that, boom, same thing. Do you know how much insulin costs?"

And it worked. Who knows how or why, but it did.

So here Sawyer was, up on top of this whole place with secret service right next to us, drunk, high and, he was pretending to shoot people with an imaginary finger rifle like he was four. We've both been hitting the bottle, and I didn't realize what was going on until I was eye to eye with a secret service dude holding a machine gun. He'd been there the whole time, but we didn't see him. I told Sawyer it was time to bounce. And he was more than ready, so we did.

We got out in front of the crowd, I ordered an uber since the train stunk and the rental was gone.

History was about to be made, and we had to see it.

CHAPTER 13

"Game Six"

The Uber driver took us to a part of the area that looked like every other part of the country. The newly developed area with Kohls and a wing spot and burger joints blocking the way and tons of SUVs full of cricket eaters. It didn't matter, though, and by the time the Cuban Missile came to the mound, we were both seeing double. Everyone in the entire place was happy it was the Baby Bears moving on to play the Tribe. Believeland had come alive after winning the NBA chip in June, and the citizens of the city all knew the Cubs were a franchise still fighting the jinx of a billy goat. The Cubs would blow it, but for tonight, Sawyer and I and a ton of others in this wing spot were celebrating.

It was the first pennant for the Cubs since World War Two; Sawyer and I both screamed when it finally happened. We hugged and cried. As lifelong fans of a losing franchise, nothing else mattered. All the problems of our life were gone. My future with *Rolling Stone,* Sawyer's wife leaving him, Trump possibly winning the upcoming election, not even Sawyer's conspiracy theories. None of it mattered. We are human creatures who thrive when living in the moment, so that is what we did.

After we embraced, Sawyer called his old man, and I called my grandfather. He had seen nothing but losing by the Cubbies his whole life. I grew up going to his house every day after school, and he would be sitting there watching a Cubs day game. If they won, he would be elated, and if they lost, he would pull out two cherry cokes, and we would get over it while drinking one. My grandpa was a native of Chicago. A northsider from Roger Parks, and he missed the Windy City dearly. I was twelve and a little leaguer when the Cubs blew the 3-1 lead to the Marlins. I wanted to kill Steve Bartman. My grandfather was now living in Louisville in assisted living, and he had told his nurse there was no way he was going to bed before the game was over. We both didn't even know what to say to each other, so we sat on the phone and cried together. And when I hung up, I looked over at Sawyer, and he had tears streaming down his face too. We were both high, not from boozing or chronic but from winning. It felt like I did at the casino, almost like serendipity.

So when we finally found a cab to take us back to our hotel, I came up with an idea. Sawyer was riding in bucket, so I leaned up to the front.

"Trump is going to win. I don't see a clear path for Hillary to win unless, man, and you know, there is nothing I don't regret more in life than not putting all my money on the Cubs to win the pennant this year. I told you," I patted Sawyer on the shoulder, "that the Cubs would 100% win the pennant. I had a feeling about it. I knew it. I told my grandfather; I told my old man and told everyone, but I didn't put a bet down. I will put all my money on Trump to win, and I fucking loathe the man. Sorry, but I do. I hate the man, but he is going to win. He has Faux doing propaganda; he has the new voters and most of the folks in the flyover country, all the swing voters, he will win. I should make that fucking bet!"

The cab driver was looking at me as if I was crazy. And, of course, at that moment in time, I was. Sawyer turned around and nodded at me.

"Hell fucking yeah, you should!"

The cab driver then said the single most brilliant thing I've ever heard while riding in a cab, "If you had a lot of money to bet, you could clean up!"

It was a great night, and I was drunk. The rain waited to start until we got out of the cab. We didn't mind it as we walked up to our room. The glass from the broken mirror was clean, and there wasn't a black cat in sight. The curse felt broken. And we crashed with our hearts full like children on Christmas night who got what they wanted and then ate goose for dinner.

CHAPTER 14

"Believeland, Trump"

We awoke with a newfound love for life, challenging in a shithole city with clouds gray as ashes. The Cubs had cemented their place in history, win or lose the World Series. We made our way walking to I-X Center for the Trump event. It would be a 180 from the Hillary affair that had golf clappers, and we could tell right away. People were already outside tailgating. Tailgating at a fucking presidential campaign event, and the election was just weeks away. We weren't the lone drinkers in the parking lot like we would have been in any other election year. The partying had started by the time we arrived, and it was full throttle once we arrived.

The air coming in off the lake didn't smell so nasty, and the sun was shining for the first time in all my days visiting the place. Sawyer was excited for the event like homecoming, and he was prom queen.

The folks were friendly, but the vibes were similar to what it must have felt like in Jonestown. The red hats were everywhere, and Trump flags flew high next to the loser flag and Old Glory. The passion was at an unprecedented level. It was hard to find a candidate so loved by the people and nearly impossible if looking in recent memory. These folks would have shot their mother for Trump. These people have smirks on their faces like they don't know the kool-aid was coming.

A pack of people who hated politics yesterday, but now it was a passion of a pastime. They didn't want to admit if they did vote before and if they did vote, it was for a third party and definitely not for Dubya! They'd never admit doing that even though the dumbass got two terms! And they didn't vote for McCain! Nope, he was a loser who lost to the black guy. The same with Romney; they didn't own that loss either. Old Mitt couldn't send the black guy back to Chicago, which was devastating to the right-wingers known as the Teabaggers after Barry won. (The fact that the tea was thrown overboard and tea drinkers' asses kicked didn't matter despite the irony.) Now they were reorganized, and more importantly, they had a dog in the fight. A man fighting for them, the working class, and surprisingly it was a man who had never worked in his life.

Trump was the leader now and the new Jesus, and if he wasn't precisely Jesus, then well, the old Jesus was surely endorsing him. He was here to drain the swamp, build the wall, and end the reign of the crooks controlling the system. He was the only one who could liberate them from the Bush family tree and Crooked Clinton Crime Family, and of course, the Muslim black man in power now. He was their superman. And they couldn't see that he was the superman from that shitty Nickelback song and not a real Superman. (I know, I know!)

The hardened people of Northern Ohio were molded tough by the dreadful winters that carried into June, severe pollution, and awful smells. These white folks were like the great people of Wisconsin but without the cheese and good smells. The excitement was off the charts and riveting throughout the city. We could feel the energy as we walked, and we could hear these people talk. They weren't going to let the Buckeye state fall to the evil empire.

It was a carnival of imbeciles, a moving circus freak show that was electric. It was for-profit, and the crowd was white. The perfect environment for a pusher or grifter to slide right in with a bottle of snakeskin oil. The real stuff though none of that knockoff, generic bootleg brand. Grease up the hillbillies with some propaganda to ensure a red buckeye state. The energy was moving, and it scared me a bit. Trump and the company had got all the ducks in a row. Everyone was walking, elated with smiles and so happy like it was the last day of school. The enthusiasm was wild. These people had concerns, and only Trump could fix what was wrong with this country! They didn't just want to believe these lies. They actually did. If Trump won office, their personal lives would change.

The whole gang was here to help ensure the state turned red. They were planning junior high-level speeches and would give them in front of the whitest crowd to gather since segregation ended. It looked like a klan meeting was about to start, or perhaps a rally in 1937 Germany.

The gang was the three amigos. Julie Awning, Pence, and Trump. Three misfits were leading the charge like toddlers with tin soldiers. It was a dream team of white men who couldn't move forward without trying to screw over a working man. They are good at it, though, perhaps the best in the business, and that's why they are here. And best believe they want to continue to screw over the little man some more to enrich themselves. The trio shares a wet dream of screwing over the folks in the flyover. And these folks here, they have all been developed. They didn't just drink the milk from the tit; they were also addicted to it. They needed the hate, and it created the energy. That's why the place is so full of energy. It is hate flowing through the blood of these white folk who act like rabid animals. They want to be enraged and hear how the brown man is coming from Mexico to steal their jobs and rape their women, which is irrational to almost any logical person. And that's why we need a wall. A wall is the only way to stop these savages who want to rape all the women and work 40 hours a week at the factory!

We made our way up to our seats, and it was elbow to elbow the entire way. I was handed a door hanger for an AC tune-up with Mike Pence's face on it near our seats. That's how low these hucksters had gone. They were selling their likeness to local companies. Anything to make a buck!

I grimaced when I saw the picture of Pence; he had a hittable face. The blush he wore was over the top for this photo, and I had to turn it upside down, or I would lose my lunch.

Our seats were gone, it was too crowded, and general admission had taken over. At the start of our row, a large, younger man with a Trump flag draped over his body. Trumpies took on the identity; it became who they were. He was a black-haired man with baby fat despite being around 20 or 25; it's impossible to tell. I would guess his nickname was Bubba. He spoke with a slight accent that was more southern than Ohio.

"These your seats, yeah, mine are 7 or 8 rows down. It's general admission at this point, boys, unless you want to go tell them down there to move."

"No worries, man," I told him. It was more Ozzfest than a political rally. It was a clusterfuck.

"Everyone just wants to see Trump, and shit, we were supposed to be in the press row area, but Gun here doesn't like sitting there," Sawyer said just loud enough for every person within 40 feet to hear. I put my head down. The media was hated, but I guess he felt since he supported Trump, he would be protected.

"Y'all with the me-day-yah?" Bubba asked, and then he

spat into a cup. His brother or friend next to him leaned in to hear the answer, and I could feel eyes upon us as Sawyer was about to answer, so I cut him off.

"Yeah, we are, but we just report the facts; that is why we can't sit in the press area. They hate the facts about Trump; tell 'em," I lied, and I needed Sawyer to bail me out because it would be hard for me to keep up the lies when it came to Trump.

And Sawyer was right on cue, "Yeah, look, we both know Trump is going to win. We don't listen to the lame-stream media!"

Bubba gave him a fist pump. He moved over a bit and slid into a new seating area with Bubba making room. He was yelling, "move down, move over," and it was working.

Bubba was holding the Pence picture, and I grimaced again. Lunch almost came up, and since we were almost on top of each other at this point, he asked me, "You not a fan of Mike Pence?"

I wanted to unload on him a string of facts about Mr. Pence and how terrible he had been to the state of Indiana. The HIV epidemic, the empty gas stations his family left, and so much more. Of course, I didn't, and I didn't because I didn't want to leave in an ambulance. So I just gave him a fake smile and a nod. It wasn't enough, though. Bubba wanted me to answer.

"It's not that I don't like the future Vice President, and it's what he did with the whole name change, you know?" I said to him, nodding, but he didn't understand.

"What's that?" His mother or sister or both leaned in to ask me.

"Yeah, what's that?" Bubba asked me too.

"Well, I mean, and I just found this out, it's a part of my fact-checking, well, back in the day Penis, I mean Pencil, no, Pence was a radio guy, right? And his last name was spelled, P-e-n-u-i-s, which is greek but pronounced, like, uh, well, like the part of the male body," I said, and I tried not to laugh.

"Part of the body?" Bubba asked, but his sister-mom knew.

"Penis?"

"Yeah, so back in the 80s when it was changed, Mike went to an all-boys school, so you know how that can go with a name like, uh, Pee-nus, right? So, of course, he changed it, but the boys at the all-boys school were mean. And let's face it, kids can be mean, and when he changed it the first time, it was to the word Pencil, so his name was Michael Dick Pencil, since his middle name is Richard. So, of course, that's where he gets his nickname from!"

I was lying my pants off but on a roll like butter. Everything I said made sense, and Bubba and his sister-mom were eating it up.

"So I was just thinking about his nickname back in college when I saw that picture, you know?"

"What's the nickname?" Bubba asked me, but I didn't have to say it, and his sister-mom did.

"Michael "Pencil Dick" Pence?"

"Pencil dick?"

I didn't answer; I just smiled and let it fester. I knew not a soul was there to see or hear Pencil Dick. They didn't care about him, and they only wanted to see Trump. Even the Evangelicals weren't there to see a Pencil Dick; Trump used Pence to get the word out that Trump was saved to the church's people.

Whatever in the fuck that meant.

Mike "Pencil Dick" Pence.

It did fester, Bubba told his buddy in front of us, and it spread like a game of telephone. So as Pence was backstage getting ready to come out and pray and give directions on how a ballot box works, the crowd was running through the game of telephone with his name. I could hear it circulating the people around me, and one guy who was wearing a red Budweiser hat instead of the typical slogan said, "Yeah, I've heard that before!"

It was only a matter of time before Faux News was reporting it.

I hated the Pencil more than Sawyer hated Hillary. He joined talk radio and became a part of the "Rightening of America." He was the type of vile trash that used religion to better himself and step on the heads of people, and when they started to drown, he would tell them it was their baptism.

(Anything to get to the top, which might or might not mean a boy toy in an off-beat motel room, while we are starting rumors and all.)

The people would have to wait for the "Pencil Dick," though since Julie Awning was batting leadoff, it was hard to watch.

Goddamn, America's Mayor had sold his soul, and his price was low. Julie Awning was all in for Trump, and he was doing it so he could be attorney general. He was a monkey who would dance, and that's what he did. He stuck to the talking points, but even that was tough for him.

The crowd wanted to erupt, but it also wanted Trump and not the Rudesters. (Yes, he called himself that.) Julie Awning knew the routine, and he knew where to stop his speech and enjoy the applause. He loved it. He might have been jerking his dick under the podium too, and I didn't have the angle to see.

After a more extended break than I needed around rabid Trumpies, the Pencil came out.

Pence was a low-energy guy who wasn't that bright but wanted to appear brilliant, so he just said what the people wanted to hear with a voice suitable for the typewriter.

If the people were hungry, he would get food delivered, and if they were thirsty, he would order beers. He wouldn't do it himself; he would find someone to do these things, but Pencil was a man who talked about action, and it was the story of his life.

Pence was a Christian by his words and not his actions.

His speech was odd, his facial expressions even more so. He would pause in irregular spots in what appeared to be the middle of simple sentences, then his eyes would flicker so his brain could work, and I could see the words come to the front of his head, and then he would continue.

The crowd didn't know how to read him either, and the cheers mainly were confused and offbeat. His face is robotesque or perhaps a puppet which is fitting considering Trump's wrist and Pencil's asshole have been seen together.

Pencil Dick let us know, a vote against Trump was a vote against God. The Christian one, not the Muslim one who was a terrorist. Sawyer and the rest of the crowd ate it up.

Finally, Pence let us all know that God hand-picked Trump to come and save the country from the radical liberal elites. And, of course, the new sexual allegations were merely a smear campaign aligned with fake news.

Then it was time for the headliner. Trump came out,

and the place exploded, and Trump let the people cheer. He had done enough rallies to understand how it worked. He stood and waited, enjoying the cheers for himself. Then he gave a speech filled with anecdotes and lies about how he'd seen Pakistani citizens celebrating the fall of the twin towers. He didn't mind those two great towers falling because now his building was the tallest in the city.

Trump's speeches were always interesting, but now watching him with Sawyer, it was even better. And not that I liked it; I understood it. Trump's phrases and slogans and comebacks were legendary, and if he had been a professional wrestler, he would have been one of the greatest. Instead, he was aiming to be the leader of the free world.

Trump went through his clown routine, and the crowd acted like they were at a rock concert. Beer was drunk like a big football game, hooting and hollering like a rodeo was happening, and Sawyer was all the way turnt up. He was bouncing back and forth on the balls of his toes like he was watching the fourth quarter of the Super Bowl. Trump would say one of his catchphrases, and the whole place would light up, fired up as ever. As if Trump was simply playing the hits of his tour. His build the wall was like Axel and Slash doing the jungle.

I was starting to understand the genius of Trump. The nicknames were one thing, but the way Trump flipped 'fake news' was the greatest trick in his campaign. Maybe in his life. It was genius. And when that word hit it, it hit me. Perhaps Donald Trump isn't an idiot with the gift of gab who could confabulate about anything and snap out disses on cue, but rather a grifter who knew how to pull the wool over the eyes of people. Trump was a New York Minute guy selling himself to Country Mile Folks, and while the rest of the world was saying, don't buy from the snake oil salesman, these country folks were saying hold on, I might want to lose my money!

In some ways, he was the village idiot, and in others, he was a brilliant tactician for his cause. It started to dawn on me that maybe what he was doing was genius. He wasn't a genius by any means, but he was scripting himself a genius plan. A villain-like scheme to take over the world, but he had a real shot at winning.

The caped hero Hillary, hoping to save the day, seemed flat in her high heels, and Trump appeared to be able to jump over a speeding train if needed. Yet, I am not calling him a genius, merely his plan. It was *his* plan, though, and was evident when he hired Bannon, his third campaign leader.

It's hard to know if it is pure genius or pure ignorance built on false confidence.

The dumb luck confidence that grew from being born rich, and still somehow thinking he did something to end up in the position. It was scary AF, but I was starting to believe that he just might win, based on energy alone.

The pure raw cocaine level of energy was mind-boggling compared to Hillary or any other candidate in recent history outside of Howard Dean. So when it hit me, it hit like a ton of bricks falling on top of me. We were exiting the arena, and I knew it was true. I had to say it out loud, and it was the second time I told it, Sawyer. The first time was drunk Gunner talking; this was real.

"Trump is going to win the election."

The grab 'em by the pussy tape had come out eleven days ago, but it felt like eleven years. And that's when the video was made. The world didn't care anymore, and well, a large majority didn't.

Sawyer didn't answer me until we finally hailed a cab.

"Of course, he is going to win, and he is saving America." And then he jumped into the shotgun.

Trump was going to win. He was selling dreams to the disenfranchised who didn't buy dreams anymore. These were hurt people who needed to buy some hope, and Obama didn't offer any to them. The flyover tribe that doesn't have any identity in life had one. They could be called Trumpies and be proud of it. It wasn't a mockery to them. They all loved it, and if the media and experts said not to pick Trump, they wanted him to win even more. For spite, because Trump will show the experts!

These middle American folks were the losers that had been stepped over and stepped on. The builders of the country and the ones who made it all run together—the people supplying the supply lines.

These flyover folks didn't just sit back and watch Obama fix Bush's economic mess; no, they asked the critical questions like what country he was born in?

Did he even have a birth certificate? And they wanted answers to those questions, and these questions were coming from the very man who was going to save America. They didn't care about the banks and the economy or anything that Obama did, and it was all tied into gay marriage anyways.

No, what many of these people cared about was God and Guns and a white man being president and not a woman and especially not a black man! A God of Guns would have been perfect for these people to worship, but that wasn't available in their bible, so instead, they were investing in Trump and loving the blue-eyed JC, of course, but voting for Trump and Pencil. Trump was the next best thing to the God of Guns who hated Mexicans and other brown people.

As we hit the rush hour of 5 o'clock traffic in Believeland, I started to believe it myself. It was all making sense to me now, the propaganda was coming together, and while I knew it was all hogwash, most Americans didn't. Trump was a bad guy, but a bad guy coming to save the country from bad guys. He was a bad guy in the same sense that Freddie or Jason or Michael Meyers is the bad guy, and these people in the arena with me today, they rooted for the serial killers in those movies.

They all loved the bad guy too.

The white trash across America loved the bad guy. Madison Avenue had been marketing bad guys inside franchise mega-blockbuster movies for years: Freddie, Jason, and Michael Meyers, and, of course, Clint Eastwood and the black hat riders. It created a love for the bad guys, a sentiment created by folks in the flyover who felt for a guy like Jason Voorhees; Maybe if those teenagers stopped coming back to his lake, they wouldn't get murdered.

Trump was the bad guy, and he was fighting the corrupt system for them.

Trump wasn't just their pick for president; they felt he was their type of guy in general. They didn't see him as a silver spoon-fed brat who was born into money but rather a good old boy who would be funny to drink a beer with and who had worked for all his loot. He didn't pay taxes because he was brilliant, and if they were smart, they would all collectively hold their taxes back, but they weren't. He exploited them in every way he could. Trump was like a toddler in a candy store with a blind and deaf owner. He was double-dipping in the candy and lying to the owner. He was doing it really well too. It was like he had found the cheat codes, and somehow it gathered all these people who never really cared about politics into his base. They were now ride or die for Trump, and they would vote for Trump no matter what. He had tapped into the same silent majority that Dick Milhouse had and found more supporters than Jesus. Trump was going to win the election.

Donald Trump was going to be the next president. It was crystal clear and scary.

PART II THE OCTOBER SURPRISE

"Let the Lord judge the criminals."
-   Tupac

CHAPTER 15

"Sanford, Florida October 12th, 2016."

It was high noon, and I was standing in the hot box hell that is the unmerciful, Central Florida heat, waiting with 10,000 mouth breathers who were all gathered to hear this doofus who can't speak, speak. And I was contemplating doing something even more imbecilic than that. I wasn't sure if I would go through with the ordeal, but I was on the verge.

The Trump rally moved inside since the blazing heat was the type Tennesee Williams wrote about, so the massive people-of-Walmart sea ushered into a shaded hanger. The movement of all cricket eaters created pure pandemonium. These white folks wanted their Trump as bad as they wished to get diabetes.

The South might begin at the Mason-Dixon line, but it ends just north of Orlando. And we were standing near that point in Sanford, Florida. Sanford is a flea market town which is an excellent representation of the proverb about the Gunshine State: the more north you travel, the more south it gets. Southern Florida is paradise, Northern Florida is closer to Alabama, not just on a map, but Central Florida can be a mixed bag.

Sanford is the first real Dixie town when traveling south to north.

As we moved out of the hangar, a fuzzy-looking Asian journalist turned to her cameraman and said, "It looks like all the Trump supporters in the entire state came out today."

I wanted to cut her off and inform her this wasn't even a dent in the base of Trumpies in Florida. Not all the Trumpies were nutjobs, but all the nutjobs were in Trump's base. And a Sanford-Trump rally was the perfect place to find what is known online as Florida Man!

Weirdos came out of the woodwork for Trump, and even as a weirdo myself, I was tired of them all. Sick and tired of all things Trumpapalooza. Seeing the circus once is why you buy the ticket, but once you've seen it twice, and with a behind-the-stage pass, you know the freaks. It was putting a real question into humanity.

The median age of this crowd was impossible to tell, and not just because I am terrible with guessing a person's age. I saw all ages, but the MAGA army did have one sharing quality, and that's that they were all caucasian. I can't lie and say it was all the types that compare to carnies; there was everything, weirdos, screwballs, losers, tin knockers, union members, law dogs, bikers, farmers, and both collars, blue and white on hand, plus a mix of boozers, losers, cricket eaters, dog walkers, and more.

The words from the fuzzy-faced Asian were similar to what many Americans were thinking. Most didn't believe it could happen, and most would have guessed this was all the Trumpies in the entire world. But it wasn't. They were all over the place, and that's not even bringing to the table the real Good Old Boys, who consistently voted R no matter what. And none of them were admitting to pollsters that they were voting for Trump. They couldn't admit that they were voting for a man who the media claimed was vile, racist, and sick, and not good for the country. They didn't want to be lumped in with these ignoramus folk.

And that's precisely why the polls were skewed. It wasn't about the stops or amount of events in the swing states; these people wanted Trump to be king. If they got to pick, the crown was his, and they would pick in November.

The Good Old Boy lifers stayed home, and they didn't want to get mixed up in this mess.

See, these were new voters, virgins to the political landscape, and they were here because they had finally found a man that would fight for them. Trump was their leader; despite being everything, they railed against before Trump. Usually, they hated the Richie Rich, aristocrats, city slickers, but now, he was here to save them. He was an admitted bad guy, here to lead the fight of good versus evil, ironically.

It was poetic, as if Alford. E. Neuman had put it together for the cover of his magazine.

Trump just needed a few swing voters to swing to the right, and he would be in the White House. He had the silent majority. He was the Jesus of the Walmart people, the savior of value meals and Christmas, the deliverer of extra large big gulps, and a rock star with no talent. He was everything to the flyover folks. They all loved him, and so did Sawyer.

I'd spotted the trends and knew the polls were wrong, but having Sawyer with me made me understand the madness. And understanding it was why I was about to make the stupid decision of my entire life.

Sawyer was excited like a drunk on steroids. This was his second Trump concert in as many days, and he was swaying back and forth with excitement.

And look, I was going to let the knucklehead go back to the Lou after our stop at the top of Ohio in StinkLand, but

I could only imagine him killing himself. He needed a friend, and it is always better to travel with someone, and I wanted a friend to tag along. So since he was laid off, I convinced him to make the journey south.

"Buy the ticket, take the ride," I told him, which he did, but he was convinced when he found out it was to attend Trump Rallies. He couldn't say no, and he wouldn't come to any more Hillary events. He also made it adamant that he had to be home before Halloween. He wouldn't tell me why, and when I pressed, he told me it was so he could early vote for Trump. It was a lie; I could feel it in my gut.

No more Hillary events, though, he said that several times.

It was a mixed bag; I was thrilled he was coming and not thrilled he was coming. I couldn't gauge his mental illness at all. He had some skewed ideology, but it didn't mean he was suicidal. I wanted to get my hands on his notebook. It was the only way to get into his head, and I saw him pack it. I didn't want to go through his stuff, but it might be life or death if I didn't. I had to make sure there wasn't a suicide note or date, especially on how firm he was about being home before the 31st.

He was as happy as a kid about to see Santa. The whole place was bananas. And I was fucking done with it. I didn't want to hear the carnival barker. I had a hangover or maybe was still drunk, and I was trying to figure out how to put my dumb decision into action.

We landed in a very clean, small airport in Sanford, which is just another airport to fly tourists into the mousetrap in Orlando, and then we hitched a ride to a place called Dixie Girls in a redneck stop on the map called Deland. It was nice and trashy with cheap booze. So we drank a few, bought a few dances, and then made our way back to Sanford.

I was pushing back through the crowd when Trump's plane landed, and the place went nuts like it was the Beatles back in '64. I turned, and Trump appeared fatter and sloppier than usual from my vantage point. His Windsor knot was crooked; his tie was hanging longer; it was as if a clown had tied it like that on purpose.

I could see Sawyer too. He was bouncing around like he was at a DMX concert, and Trump went through his hits, "Build the Wall." "Lock her up."

I stopped walking, and I watched. That's right when it hit me. I knew in my gut that Trump was going to pull it off. He had enough moxie, and the whole energy of the country was behind him just like it had been Barry back in 2008. It was a different energy, but it was from the people. The country's pulse was here, and even though it was vile, scary, and uneducated, so was the country, and it was going to vote for Trump.

I left the madness and went to the back of the hangar, I found a big electric fan to stand by, and I started to play with an interactive map of the electoral college on my phone. I am sure Trump had a path mapped, but I wanted to see if it was doable. He'd have to steal Michigan, but Florida and Ohio were in the bag. He might even steal the Cheesehead state, and if he kept all the other ducks in a row red, he had a path to 270. He'd keep all the red states, and Hillary was wasting her time even attempting to steal Arizona. To win Michigan, he would need to keep the voter turnout low, and that's why he was dissing the whole system. Make all appear like a fraud, so people don't even come out to vote. Both sides suck, don't vote for either one. He could even lose Michigan if he won Pennsylvania and Wisconsin. The more I played with the states, the harder I saw Hillary. There was so much red across the map.

Hillary already blew her load with the Access Hollywood tape, and she didn't have anything left to move the needle. Julie Awning had been hyping up the biggest October Surprise of all time, and if it were true, it would be enough to change the game enough for Trump. Again voter turnout would need to be low, and apathy would play a role, but I needed to know the full extent of what was up the sleeve of the madman because if it was just Bill having an affair, it wasn't close to enough. But if it was Hillary being terminal, it might be.

I needed to find out what it was. Trump would pull this off, but I wanted to make sure Julie Awning had something up his sleeve besides hot smoke and bad breath, so I called Dude D. He was out in Arizona getting ready for another Trump rally.

"Did they not let you use the press pass I sent?" he said as soon as he picked up without even a hello.

"Hello?" I said, but he was cutting in and out, so I ran outside the hangar in search of a better signal and asked him, "Can you hear me now?"

"Uh, yeah," he said, and I could tell he was busy, but I was glad he answered.

"Okay, so tell me just for my own peace of mind, this guy here wants to be me a thousand right now that Julie Awning is lying about the October Surprise and another rack that Trump loses. I mean, so - ?"

I stopped talking to get a gauge on things.

"Are you asking me if I think Trump is gonna win the election?" he said, and I wasn't, but I was. I really wanted to know if Julie Awning had a game-changer and what it might be.

"I know that look, Dude, I won't print it in *Rolling Stone* or even tell anybody, but you gotta tell me, does Julie Awning have an ace up his sleeve?"

A few cops walked by me wondering what I was doing since I wasn't worshipping Trump as if he was handing out money. I just nodded at them and said into the phone, "Give me something here, man."

"Look, on the low, and I mean the low, low, because I am one of the only ones who know, and it's gonna be a talking point for our phone bankers, but seriously, on the low, low, low, low, you can't publish it!"

"I won't, never would I even think of that! I don't get published in the magazine anyways; look, this guy who wants to bet me; he is an elitist, inherited a construction company, and is just a bad guy. He wants to bet me, he's like Trump won't win, Julie Awning doesn't have shit up his sleeve, so tell me, please, so I can bet this asshole, take his money when Trump wins, and we can both go hang out at the White House, capisce?"

"Okay," he replied but nothing else.

"Is that a yes or a no?"

"Is the Pope Catholic?"

"Yeah?"

"Look, Gunner, Rudy is the one who always delivers. When the planes hit, who was fucking there?"

"The firefighters?"

"No, Rudy was. When shit hits the fan, Rudy is there. Why else do you think he is still on board? Rudy and Trump go way back; you can look it up. There is a video online from 2002; Rudy dressed up as a woman, hitting on The Donald. He loves him. They have a thing for each other, and Rudy always, always, always fucking delivers."

"Julie Awning is dressed up as a woman? How is that the

trick up his sleeve?"

"Don't worry about that. Here is how big this is; it's so big that Rudy will be named AG. It's major league and on another level."

"What is it? Is Billy boy dogging around on her? Hillary has cancer or what?"

"Nope, it's," and his voice lowered to a whisper, "the bureau is opening up the case again."

"What? What case?" I didn't know what he meant, and I was still trying to process the Julie Awning in a dress video.

"Her emails. Look, the head of the FBI already said it; Rudy knows it. This will change the minds of not just the swing voters but any middle-of-the-roaders, and let's be honest; most people are in the middle of the road. She's crooked as hell; the FBI is going to lock her up. She might not even make it to election day."

Mother of God!

And when I hung up, I felt a bit of power. It was insider information and confirmation that Trump was going to win! If it was true. Now, let me toot my own horn because I was a great fucking journalist despite Terry being blind to this fact.

I began to write a piece on my phone that instant. Terry would have to publish this; any major outlet would. It was five hundred times bigger than the Hollywood Access Tape. Then I remembered I couldn't break the story; I didn't call Dude D for that reason. I called him to get confirmation, and I got it. I needed to move forward with my plan, and then I could write something for Terry and Rolling Stone.

I dashed to find Sawyer, but the mob was now turning towards me because the Tweedle D's finished riling. The mass exiting made it impossible to find Sawyer, but finally, I did. It was as if he was baptized into some weird cult. I guess he had been, but this was different. He was sweating like a fat chick in gym class and overheated. I thought about taking him to an ambulance when he fell, but we both know ambulances are fucking expensive, so I just got him some water. He got back up, and we had to walk through the parking lot with the other idiots who didn't remember where they parked until we got to the Uber driver that we had booked.

We took the Uber west towards Trampa. Sawyer sat in the bucket. He was soaked from sweat, amped, hyper, but happy as a puppy on a car ride.

I sat in the backseat, wondering what it all meant.

If the future held a Presidency of Donald Trump, that genuinely meant anyone could be president. Anything was possible. Trump wasn't the guy we wanted if shit hit the fan. He didn't understand how things worked, and he didn't even understand the government, laws, or anything. He did understand people, and he was winning on just that. He could read people like a paperback, and he had inherited a ton of loot and company from his old man. He was selling snake oil while telling some folks it cures AIDS and others that it will grow their dick and doing so simultaneously. He just told people what they wanted to hear. It was a pretty simple thing, and a man with no morals can do it all day, every day, no problem.

So I sat in the back of the Uber while Sawyer jumped around as we drove by the tourist trap with the mouse on the logo. We hit a standstill, and I watched all the cars and the people, and it all dawned on me. I had the same type of insider play for which people pay the big bucks. I had the plug just like James at the roulette table. I needed to follow through on this, and if I did, I could change my life. I needed to do the most American thing ever and win some fucking money because of this advantage. I needed to bet all I could on Donald Trump to win the Presidential Election.

CHAPTER 16

"The Witch"

The sun was setting, creating a dancing mix of colors that we drove into, including bright orange and pink. We arrived at our hotel-casino that I will just call Hard Cock Rasino to avoid any legal trouble because it's one thing to call these politicians descriptive words like motherfucker and cocksucker, hard to be liable when it's true, but bringing in lawsuits from the multi-billion dollar corporations that sponsor most politicians is another. Corporations have more rights than citizens in America.

Sawyer was up so high he crashed. He was sawing logs when we arrived—and starting to stink too. At that point, he realized he had left his bag in Sanford or Cleveland, or who knows where. All his clothes for the trip, and he had left them at the rally likely. He still searched the car 17 times like he was looking for a contact lens and not a duffel bag. I had been hauling mine around so much; I didn't even freaking notice it. He was pissed, but he had his wallet, phone, and a backpack with who knows what in it.

"We will get you a few shirts, and the hotel will give you a toothbrush, not that you use it, but I can start calling my people with the Trump campaign, and they will locate it."

He was pissed, but we couldn't do much more, so we headed into the place to check-in.

The entire car ride west, I researched the odds on Trump to win the election. Trump was a twenty-one-point underdog, and some casinos in Europe had him a 23 point dog. I had to cash in now before the odds changed. He would win, but the odds would change after the news broke that the FBI was again investigating the emails.

I would have to go to an offshore betting place, though, since it was illegal to bet on elections in America. I asked the lady checking us in, who was already mad because we were changing our room from a single to a double if she could suggest a nearby casino boat that traveled out to international waters.

"The best gambling in the world is right here at Hard Cock Rasino, sir." She told me with a piercing voice.

"Yeah, right, I get that, but I need a place where I can bet on the presidential election, and you can't do that here. Who knows why right? I mean, bring the kids' college tuition and blow it on the slots while wearing a diaper, or lose your four, oh one K playing blackjack! But betting on the presidential election? Not allowed!"

I was joking, but she didn't laugh. Her voice went monotone, which was more pleasing, and she said, "You can actually bet that on a boat, but be careful it's not as safe as our casino."

"Well, I know, but, " I said, but she cut me off with a hand on the side of her face and a whisper.

"It's okay; my husband worked there for years. You will have to hurry. The last boat leaves the dock in about 35 minutes."

She smiled and slid me the room key.

Sawyer had gone looking for a place to buy some clothes even though I told him we could find a Wallyword later. I called his phone as I ran looking for him, and I would have to rush, and as I got to the elevators, he was sitting on a chair answering his phone.

And he stood up slowly, so I told him, "Look, I gotta go, I want to make it out to the casino boat to place a bet."

"Place the bet here.".

"They don't bet on the elections here. I gotta go offshore."

"You're going to bet on the election, aren't you? Let me come, I got like four grand in our joint account, and I would bet it all. Trump is a 20 point dog!"

"Exactly!"

"Man, imagine if we had real money to lay down, I got four thousand, but imagine if you had like say 20gs or something. Shit, even more than that, but at 20 to 1, you bet 25k, and you'd get back almost half a milly!"

But he was wrong. I had all my money with me. That's the real reason I kept my duffel bag so close. I trusted myself to watch my money, nobody else. I didn't trust banks. It was an innate trait handed down from both my great-grandfathers, who lost it all in twenty-nine. That's a family lineage destined to marry. My mom still won't use a bank unless she has to. They are scams, charging me to take money out of an atm, charging me a fee if I don't have enough in my account, five dollars here, three dollars here, and it all adds up. Too Big to fail my ass!

"We got a room on the 14th floor; I think it's fourteen oh seven, I think," I said, trying to hand him the key, but he just rubbed his stomach. The elevator dinged, and there was only one single lady on it, and she stepped off in a hurry like her money was going to leave her pocket before she got to a slot machine.

I got on, but Sawyer didn't, and he said, "I don't wanna stay on that floor. That's bad luck."

He walked on slowly, stopping the doors from shutting, and I asked, "How is that bad luck?"

"Look," he said as he turned to the buttons, and he pointed, saying, "there is no thirteenth floor, look, it goes from twelve to fourteen. It skips the number thirteen and goes straight to fourteen because thirteen is bad luck, but in reality, we stay on the bad luck floor, but it's renamed the fourteenth floor."

"It doesn't work like that," I told him, but I didn't know how it worked. He was correct, and there was no 13th floor listed.

"Why doesn't it work like that because if they call it the fourteenth, the bad luck doesn't know it's really the other -" Sawyer stopped talking as two young women got on the lift with us. They were lesbians, holding hands, and wanted every-one to know it, so I smiled at them.

And then Sawyer says, "It's a fucking omen!"

I looked at the two lesbians who were now trying to fig-ure out if they were the omen, so I filled them in, "There is not a thirteenth floor at all. The floors are listed 12 then 14."

"Oh, I know, I won't stay on the fourteenth because it's bad luck."

The shorter lady confirmed Sawyer's suspicion. He looked right at me and shook his head. An old couple who wanted to blow their four oh one K got on, and we had to slide back, and then one more old lady got on, and the doors closed.

I had to order an uber stat, so I got on my phone.

"I don't like it," Sawyer said to me, and I just nodded at the couple as the lesbos started holding hands again so the newly arrived people could see they were queer and in love too. Not that I cared, do what you want in life!

The old couple got off on the fourth floor, and before the doors even shut, Sawyer yelled, "You're a witch!"

It startled me and the couple that was walking off. They turned back, and the lesbos were both taken aback too.

Sawyer was staring at this tiny, old, black lady. A hood hid her head like the wolf in a little red riding hood.

And as I turned to her, she slowly pulled it down and moved her mouth to form a smile even slower. The two lesbos turned around to stare at Sawyer, and I had to do the same. I wanted to say something, but I was shocked and couldn't speak.

The little lady then spoke, breaking the awkward silence, and said, "Yes, Mr. Barnes, I am."

Her voice was creepy, like a Halloween doll.

I nearly dropped my jaw back down to the first floor. The two lesbos got off on the tenth floor, but they didn't know what was going on, but they didn't intervene either.

"It WAS an omen!" Sawyer said to me as he had just figured out a piece of a puzzle.

He turned to her, put his finger up again, and said, "How do you know my name?"

And it was a great question. I was confused, but I think I had the answer, so I told Sawyer, "She probably got our name at the front desk lady or something, and it's some sort of con."

"I know she is a witch. I saw, and I said she was a witch before she said anything to me!"

"Come on, let's go," I said, stepping off the elevator on the 13th/14th floor.

I stopped and stared down the hallway to my right and then straight ahead into a mirror so I could see Sawyer. He wanted an answer, and he wasn't moving until he got one. He put his hand in front of the door, so it wouldn't close and looked right at me.

"Did you even put my name on anything at the front desk?"

He was right, and I told him, "No," so how did this old woman know his name?

She tilted her head and said, "I was sent to find you, and I knew you would be with Mr. Bush."

"How do you know my name?" I asked, turning all the way around, and Sawyer stepped off the lift.

"I had dreams about Sawyer, and I am here to grant him a wish. I don't think I am supposed to do anything with you, Mr. Bush," She said as she too stepped off the lift. She got close to Sawyer and touched his arm, and she was staring at him and only him.

"What kind of wish?" Sawyer was intrigued, but it felt the con was just landing.

"Any wish you want. I can't say if it will come true, but I am here to send your wish to the other side. And if it is the right wish, it will come true." She said in a dark voice that wasn't as wildly creepy as before.

"She's not a witch!" I roared. She wasn't. She was a con working a con, and I was in a hurry.

"You don't believe in witches?" She turned to me and said with a mean look on her face. A seriousness as if I had told her that she didn't exist.

"Oh, I believe in witches, do you see my hat? I am wearing a hat of a team that a Billy Goat curses! A freaking Billy Goat! If I believe that shit, don't you think I know about witchcraft!"

"That's not how witches work. I met a witch at Waverly; you remember that Gun? Senior year we went up." Sawyer said, and of course, I remembered going to Waverly and the old TB hospital. And I vaguely remembered him encountering a witch, but this lady wasn't a witch, and she was a con.

"She's a con. A hustler, probably working with attractive exotic dancers too. She is going to drug us, and rape us, and then rob us blind!" I said as I walked down the long, scary hallway looking for our room.

Sawyer wasn't listening to me, though; he wanted to know who the witch was.

"Like I was saying, I was sent here to find you, Mister Barnes, it is the wish of something, someone, well, a not living thing has wished that I find you, and I grant you a wish. It will cost you five hundred dollars, but that is only for my time, my travels, and whatnot."

"Bingo! There it is, there it is! She wants five hundred buckaroos!" I said louder now, not screaming but close, and I knew this witch was a fraud. A counterfeit con-witch!

"You need money for your travels! You need money to gamble with! Where did you travel from? Huh, what part of Trampa did you travel from?" I asked her as I found the room, 1408.

"I came here from St. Augustine," She told me in a voice

that said she was distraught that I had figured out her con.

"St. Augustine is full of witches, Gun," Sawyer told me, and he was right. The oldest city in America was also full of fake witches and real ones, maybe, who knows.

"She is a fraud! She got our names from the freckle face bitch at the front desk. She is not allowed in my hotel room," I said firmly, looking right at Sawyer, and then I told the con-witch, "Goodbye and goodnight!"

And I entered the room and shut the door.

I stood staring at the hotel room with my back to the door when it knocked. I opened it, and Sawyer told me, "Let this witch, " he turned to ask her, "What's your name?"

"It is Nadia," She said in a Haitian accent, and she sounded like a witch when she said it. The dark voice was now replaced with a scary one—the one she had first used in the elevator.

"Let this, Nadia, come inside for a second. I gotta talk to her," Sawyer told me as he passed me and entered the room.

Nadia walked by me slowly, and as she crept by me, goosebumps developed on my arm. I brushed my forearms with my hands as she moved her head around like a black widow spider, eyeing out the room of her mate.

"Don't give this witch a cent!" I said as I shut the door again.

"Mis-ter Barnes knows that the five hundred dollars isn't for his wish and that his wish cannot be guaranteed, only that I was sent here from the other side to give his wish to the other side. It will come true if it is meant to be and what the other side wants to hear. I make no guarantees! The money is for my travels, I was waiting all day for you gentlemen, and it is for my supplies, " She said like she was reading the instruction manual to the wish.

"The afterlife," Sawyer looked at me and said as if I didn't know what the other side was. He continued, "it's gotta be my Uncle Ray. Has to be. I never met him, and he died the evening before I was born," he put his suitcase on the bed and sat down on it, looking away from us and thinking.

"You do remember going up to Waverly, right?" He turned and asked me, and I put my duffel bag down on the other bed. He was asking me about the Waverly Hills Sanatorium back in the Ville.

"Of course, I remember. We thought we were badasses. We had Colt forty-fives at Kermit's dad's house in Valley Station. I remember when we finally got to the top of the first hill, and that security guard put his spotlight on us. We all needed new panties!"

"Yeah, he was waiting on us, and that was right before Halloween, right?" Sawyer asked me.

"I think so because we went to the high school and shot around for a bit, played twenty-one, and those dudes dressed up as two fat dudes beat Kermit and me in basketball. It was freezing, and I climbed the fence to the pool area and cut my arm," I said to him, remembering the fun we had.

"Remember that car pulled up, right when you were climbing back over the fence, and you got cut," He said, but I cut him off.

"Yeah, I just said that; I still got the scar on my arm," I said, now looking for it on my arm.

"So that car it was like an old Pontiac or Camaro, it's not a convertible but has the t tops, well this lady was in it, she was hot, older though, but hot for an older lady, black hair, a white lady with a skull and bones hanging from her rearview mirror, and she stopped her car and said, 'Your name is Sawyer Barnes isn't it?' And I just stared at her, and then she laughed. She was a witch. I knew it right then; I got goosebumps down my arms and spine, and neck. She laughed, and she said, 'I knew your Uncle Ray,' and then she said, Happy Halloween, and drove off," Sawyer said, and he was scared.

"So, what does that have to do with this?" I asked him, and I picked my bag back up and started to go into the bathroom.

"She was a witch. Did she know my uncle? How did she even know that was my uncle? He had been dead my entire life, and we were way out in Valley Station. If it would have been the Highlands or Jeffersonville, sure, some lady knows my old man and one of my uncles, but way out there, and on Halloween," Sawyer turned to her and asked, "Was it my Uncle Ray that sent you here?"

"That's a fucked story, but you can't connect the dots from that one incident to this cuckoo bird here; seriously, just tell her to leave. Here, do you want me to tell her, ma'am, can you please leave our hotel room?" I said, making arrows with my fingers towards the doors. She was running some sort of con, but I didn't have time for it. I had to get an Uber and get to the dock to make it to the boat to place my bet.

"Look, Sawyer, I gotta go," I said, and I went into the bathroom and set my bag on the sink.

Sawyer walked back to the door area, but he didn't come in. He didn't have a change of underwear, but he had booze. He pulled a small flask from his backpack and took a big swig. I reached out, took it from him, and took a big hit.

"Yeah, I will meet you down there. I hope I get good luck this time," He said, taking back his flask.

"Yo, why don't you wish for it. I am not going to the

casino downstairs, though. I told you, I have to go offshore. So look, tell this lady to leave, and come with me. We will get free drinks and be out in the middle of the ocean. It will be cool; you want to?"

I asked, but he wasn't hearing me, so I shut the door and locked it.

"You know what, I think I am going to hear this out," Sawyer yelled through the door.

I checked my phone and confirmed my uber was arriving soon, and I started to pull out my money. I had saved almost every cent I'd made since starting at Rolling Stone. I had nearly 30 racks with me. And that might seem like it would be the whole bag, but 30k is only 300 sheets of small paper. I had carved out a spot in a hard copy of Motorcycle Zen, and the rest was in socks rolled up. I took it all out and threw it in the sink. It wasn't that much money, but it was the most I had ever had.

I was about to do something insane, but it could change my life.

I had to hurry and figure out how much it was, so I counted the rolled-up hundred dollar bills. In total, there were twenty-nine stacks, with one remaining stack with seven. Two hundred and ninety-seven hundred dollar bills. $29,700.00. And I was going to put it all on the line. I hurried out of the bathroom, and the lights were now all off in the hotel room. Incense or sage was burning on the table, and Sawyer was sitting on the bed while the witch was standing over the table making clicking noises with her mouth.

"You and Bedazzled here are going to get us kicked out of this room! You can't smoke in here!" I said, but neither one listened, so I just said, "I'm leaving!"

Sawyer wasn't even looking at me, "Hello?" I asked him, but he didn't turn his head. Perhaps she had already hypnotized him.

The witch made more noises, and I could see five hundred dollars on the nightstand.

He was paying this con-witch! I texted the Uber driver back, and I left.

I arrived out of breath at his car. The Uber driver turned around and asked me, "You're going to the casino boat, right?"

He was staring at the big green hardcover book in my hand.

I lifted it and said, "Yeah, I just gotta deliver this, and of course, inside here is the summons for the captain of the boat to appear in court. I work for the IRS." I told him, and he stopped smiling. I was pleased I didn't stutter. He did a double at me in the rearview, and I could sense his fear. I was with the one organization that all uber drivers feared. He didn't talk the rest of the way, and I was as nervous as could be.

When we arrived, I didn't back out like I thought I would. I got in the line and waited to board the boat. Once I got on the board, I followed a few people to a buffet, but I didn't want to eat. I was nervous, anxious, and getting sick. I was Second-guessing myself so badly that I had to find a stiff drink.

"Do you know where I can book a bet at? Like sports and things?" I asked the waitress.

She replied to me, "You will have to wait until we get out to international waters first, okay, honey, can I get you a drink while you wait, sweetheart?"

"How long does that take?" I asked her, not knowing the rules.

"It takes about 45 minutes, maybe an hour depending. You will hear a loud bell, and you will notice the gambling has started," She replied.

"An hour, you better bring me a double and a beer, a light beer; I'm not a drunk," I told her, and she left.

So I drank, which helped the thought process because I wasn't Titanic Thompson with betting. I didn't play fantasy sports or bet on games with much success. I bet the ponies more than I should and was under even for my lifetime. Better than most, but this was different. This was me throwing away almost thirty grand on heresy and my gut instinct—minor insider info and my educated hunch from traveling across the country following the two campaigns. Well, maybe the insider info wasn't so little, but I didn't even know if it was true. It was a gamble.

It was still a dangerous bet even with the info I had. An idiotic man to win the most powerful job on the planet, but deep down, I knew it was about to happen. And maybe I was the idiotic man as I was about to put $29,650.00 big bucks on Donald J. Trump to win the election. He was a twenty-four to one shot, and if Dude D was correct and Julie Awning had the ace up his sleeve, the odds would lower the second that card was played. It was a risk and probably a dumb one. That's why the booze helped.

As I drank and walked around the boat, I kept repeating what my grandfather would say after he placed a fiver on a 99-1 pony, "No risk it, no biscuit."

I made my way outside the boat's top, where a few people were enjoying the fresh ocean air.

I didn't talk to anyone. I was nervous and working on my buzz. And by the time I had drunk enough to kill a small man, the alarm went off—a loud buzzing across the whole ship. I didn't rush to a slot machine or gaming table, but instead, I went to the bar inside and ordered two more doubles.

The whole ship was alive now. It didn't even feel like

more than 15 people were on the boat until that buzzer went off. All the workers had painted smiles on their faces, and the ones behind the tables were grinning so hard they appeared plastic. Fake, almost like wolves who had been sharpening their teeth all day, and the sheep were running straight into them.

A white dude with dreads and a fake Jamaican accent fired up a white boy and proclaimed to no one and everyone, "Welcome to international waters!"

I double fisted and made my way to the booth that made the gaming bets. I sat down on a big comfortable, oversized leather chair and tried to play it out in my head while I sipped on my drinks. I must have looked like a non-compos-mentis as I sat there contemplating and boozing.

"The media is wrong. The pollsters are wrong." I repeated repeatedly, and after every sip of liquor, I would add, "no risk it, no biscuit."

And I knew why. Unless a person was one specific type, they didn't admit they liked Trump. It was taboo to admit you were going to vote for the guy. The media was telling people how to vote, and so were the elites and aristocrats, and the folks in the flyover hated that. And even more importantly, they loved this idiot. And they hated the crooked Clintons. All of that wasn't enough, though. It came down to me trusting my gut.

As soon as I got to the window, my voice cracked, and my knees hit each other on the inside as I said, "I would like to bet on Dona-ld T-t-t-rump to win the election?"

The lady didn't answer until I repeated myself. She had long, brownish hair with a streak of red dye through it and lipstick on her teeth.

She said in a calming voice that makes you want just to

donate the money, "I see, sir, so how much would you like to wager?"

"Uhm, yeah, okay, so all of this," I said as I pulled out the wads of hundreds I had stashed.

And that's when I did question my sanity for a moment, or perhaps I am insane and should have questioned it more. The teller did too, and her eyes were on me like I stole her swatch.

She nodded, and I had to inform her I had already counted the money, "It should be twenty-nine thousand, six hundred, and fifty dollars."

"Yes, sir, I will be right back. I need the head manager on duty for a bet this large."

She left, and I started to look behind me and see if anyone was around. Nobody was, though. Everyone was trying to win their own game. So I stood there with my life savings in front of me and just drank more booze, figuring I wouldn't regret this decision if I got drunk enough. The story of my life so far.

I uttered it one last time, "no risk it, no biscuit."

Finally, she came back with a bald ex-soldier-looking dude, and he asked me again how much, and I told him. I had some strength in my voice this time, and he didn't hesitate to take my money. He left and came back with a small rectangular piece of paper, and he didn't say anything.

The lady said, "Please don't lose your ticket, sir!"

And if it weren't for the drinks, I wouldn't have made the bet.

Twenty-four to one is what I got on my life savings. It would pay back $711,600.00, and I would be rich. Well, what rich was to me anyway.

When I stepped away from the window, I felt regret sink in like fingernail cuts in the neck of a man who hung himself. I wanted out, but I didn't take it back. I could have, and I should have, but I didn't. Instead, I headed towards the bar.

I still had over two thousand saved, which is more than I had when I started the job five months ago. And if I could write a good piece that Terry might publish, Rolling Stone might pick me up, plus the payday for one article had to be outrageous. They were already paying for so much, plus I lived in a Mansion, and I didn't even have a singular word published yet —all the hotels, the flights, the rental cars, the company credit card. I needed to find the right angle, and Terry would publish me.

So I sat at the bar for four hours and pounded wells and cheap brew while folks gambled around me. I didn't even play the nickel slots. I just boozed and ate stale pretzels. It was uneventful. I tried to envision what I would buy with the money —a few cars, a few trips, and other dumb shit I wouldn't need. I headed to the top of the boat, and I sat by myself, enjoying the ocean breeze and the night sky. I was alone at the top, but slowly, people would lose what they had brought inside and come outside to join me.

The sky was clear, and the stars were the brightest I had ever seen. I looked up and prayed that they were aligning for me. It was self-righteous and dumb, and I know what that might mean for the country, but America is a capitalistic society, so it's all about the money.

After my prayer, I realized that the people joining me to stargaze were the losers of the night, and I couldn't risk having any bad luck rub off of them and on to me and my golden ticket. As soon as I got back inside, the alarm sounded again, and a collective sigh rang through the whole boat. The gambling fun was over, and the ship was now back in American waters.

I found a seat inside and sat down. I was tired of the boat and just plain tired. I was drunk, hungry, and ready to sleep. I had come onto the ship with close to 30 thousand, one year's salary, and I was coming off with a tiny ticket receipt. Every thought through my head was trying to reassure myself that I wouldn't try to get a refund, and once that horn blasted, I knew I didn't have a choice.

If Trump didn't win, this would be the biggest regret of my life, but if he did…

"No risk it, no biscuit."

CHAPTER 17

A light mist was anesthetizing as the boat docked. My mind was racing, and finding a cab impossible. I did, and all I was thinking about the whole time was how much I hated Trump. I had gone from not caring about him at all to an all-out disdain for him. It would be hard for me to vote for him and vote against my financial interest. Not that it mattered; Trump was going to win.

Trump or Bannon or perhaps Satan himself had unleashed enough propaganda to the Wheel of Fortune watching folks in the flyover to convince them that Hillary Clinton was as badass as El Chapo. They'd mucked the waters up so much; the whole country was under the mud.

I had been following the Hillary email story as hard as any journalist, and I still didn't know what was what. And now, if the FBI reopened the case, it would sink her. She was close to falling without it because the GOP had run her through the wringer for decades. And Trump was perfect for the world of Americans. He was greedy, just like they were. He stiffed people on bills just like they would if they could get away with it. He spoke his mind just like they wanted to, and he pointed out the hypocrisy they had been pointing out. Trump was only acting as they wanted to. And now, they were using all the tricks to crush anyone. And it was easy to see how they did it too. The multi-billion dollar industries always used Madison Avenue to sell products. Since forever. They knew all the tricks, algorithms, stats, data, and more to sell any product to anyone at any time. Those elitists who created Madison Avenue have known for years things like what color makes people hungry (it's yellow and orange, and red is associated with emotion, so companies use red with yellow and orange to make people passionately hungry) or how music works on the brain which is similar to smells. A smell and a song can both take your memory back in time. That's why it wasn't just illegal to sell cigarettes to minors, but also illegal to market smokes to teens.

Marketing experts know what they are doing. And the ones with a moral compass following capitalism will figure these things out and use them for an advantage. So naturally, these are the types that the Good Old Boys hired, which meant they had all these weapons at their disposal.

It was a blueprint on how to market to and manipulate the masses. And with the propaganda piano known as Faux playing out the tunes, the masses fell in line, and all they had to market was that Hillary Clinton was a terrible person. It was the fabrication and manipulation of propaganda, and it was the best the world had ever seen.

Trump openly said, "I love the poorly educated," because he did. And so did the GOP. These folks in the flyover didn't understand anything outside of their own cognitive dissonance, and they were a prime example of the Dunning Krueger effect. The masses were spoon-fed what to say and think as long as they tuned into Faux News every night and went to their Facebook feed every break. Echo chambers were the new safe space.

The whole cab trip back to the hotel, I told myself this. Trying to make it come true, and the only way to do that was to think about it over and over and over again. Self-rumination or sumshit.

Sawyer hadn't called or texted me, so I was a little worried about what I might walk into back at the hotel. A sacrificed animal on my bed or perhaps Sawyer dead on the floor. Maybe the con-witch ate him, who knows, but my mind was jumping to every bad conclusion it could. I shouldn't have left him, and I shouldn't have made the bet. But Sawyer was a grown-ass man, though, and I was too. I could do what I liked with my money.

When I got back to the hotel room, I opened the door slowly, not knowing what might jump out and bite me. Perhaps the con-witch had summoned the dead or worse. All the lights were now on, and the room didn't smell like anything had been burning in it. It was empty, and not just empty but almost like they hadn't even been there at all. Sawyer's phone was on the nightstand, and none of the con-witch stuff was in the room at all.

I ordered room service and plugged my phone into charge. I put the end of game one on and saw that the Cubs were about to lose badly. I couldn't call Sawyer with his phone being here, so I just waited.

The food came, and the game ended. The Indians won six to nothing, which was it for my Cubs in game one. I had purposely not watched, thinking I might be able to fix the curse if I just didn't tune in. I didn't even want to turn it on when I did. Since they were down so much when I flipped it on, I knew that was a bad idea. Maybe I needed to watch. It was difficult to understand my role in the jinx, but I knew I didn't want to mess with the mojo. Losing big in game one is never a good precursor. This wasn't going to be the year the billy goat curse ended, and all of us fans knew this. We would still be the lovable losers, and Believeland would celebrate its second championship of the year. I also didn't want to waste my luck on the Cubs winning it all when I needed all the luck to help my Trump bet. So I figured it might all be for the best that the Cubbies lost.

I flicked off the screen and the light and wanted to sleep, but I couldn't. My body was tired, but my mind was racing around like it was wearing jogging shoes. I tried to figure out what Sawyer had wished for with the con-witch. Maybe a personal wish to grow his penis, or perhaps to win big at the casino, and that's why he was down there blowing the rest of his loot. Then it hit me. He probably wished for Trump to win the election!

I started to laugh. Of course, that is what he wished for, and shit, maybe she was a witch. And once I started laughing, I couldn't sleep, so I sat up and reached for the remaining food from room service. I would eat myself tired.

As I sat there mauling on a cold hamburger, I noticed Sawyer's notebook was on top of his backpack. It wasn't inside, and I didn't go through his stuff, and it was on top, so I stood up, went to the door, bolted it, and returned to read it.

It started as a slow and dull read; mostly, Sawyer wrote about his ennui. It felt intrusive to me to read it since it was his personal journal. Each page dated like a diary, and then it would start as a letter to Kurt Cobain. Three pages in, and I almost put it down. It was just a chicken scratch of his dull, married life and how much he loved Nirvana. He wrote how they shared the same birthday, but 30 years apart. It was mainly three pages of overly redundant shit about how Kurt was Nirvana, and a part of the world died when he died. It was hogwash, barely legible garbage, unreadable, and didn't make sense.

On the fourth page, however, the topic of conversation got very dark. Sinister. It was the same format, date, Dear Kurt Cobain, but the first line wasn't about Nirvana or how he hated doing the dishes.

"I have always wanted to shoot someone. I think about

killing people all the time, and I would like to kill 100 people before I die. I like watching movies about the DC Sniper."

And it went on to praise the two doofuses from Columbine, and it had a long spiel about the Unabomber and his manifesto. Then it segued right into his same rhetoric about Nirvana. The last line before he signed it, he wrote, Later Kurt!

I flipped to the next page, and it got even worse. Not more sinister, but details about his wife cheating on him. He wanted to kill her and the guy named Charlie, who he only called "N-word Charlie."

Charlie and Cammie worked together, and he found out about their affair by tapping her phone or something I couldn't understand.

Then it went back to Nirvana and Kurt Cobain. Bizarre.

I kept reading, though. I had to at this point, and if anything, I had figured out why his wife wasn't around. It was alarming.

I read the whole thing, and here is the breakdown besides all the Nirvana fan mail.

Charlie was screwing Sawyer's wife, and he stalked both of them. He planned to murder them both one night, but didn't because he said, it wasn't "big enough." He wanted their affair to end as an affair to remember.

So he came up with a plan to kill them both and more. He was going to shoot up where they worked. He had applied there at one point, and they didn't hire him, so he had a bone to pick for that too. And he was going to pick it. He laid out all the plans in this notebook.

Not just the plans, he had names of people he wanted to shoot in the order listed by who he wanted to kill first to last. Charley and then Cammie were first, with Charley going first so Cammie could watch. Sick stuff. He also talked about a few of her co-workers. One was a Mexican guy, and he mentioned how he would go after him next. And more racist shit I won't go into. Then the other co-workers who didn't run or he could see. He would just start blasting after that. His direct quote was, 'kill anything moving.'

He would dress up as a hunter and attend the company's annual Halloween party. It was at a reception hall in St. Louis. Somehow he had the blueprints to the building, and that is where he drew his map at the back of the notebook. He wrote down when and where he was going to do this. He had been to this party the two previous years as Cammie's husband, so he knew the place. It was meticulously broken down, step by step. He had his exit plan and his backup exit plan. He had locations of where people sat last year, and each one of them numbered. He would block the two fire exits from the outside and park his car behind the building.

Then he would exit through the back doors, drive home listening to *In Utero*, go inside his house, take a bath while listening to Bleach, and blow his head off on Cammie's side of the bed while blaring Heart-Shaped Box. The last song Kurt Cobain ever sang.

The notebook finished with a few pages about mass shooters he adored in some sick fashion. He had the names and then a number next to it, and each number represented the kill count, and Sawyer hoped to get his number over 50.

Jesus Fucking Chrysler!

It was a demented and wild read- detailed with gore and graphic AF. It felt real too. His anger. His plan. He wanted to execute this down to the grand finale bullet in his head. It wasn't just a diary or psycho fiction. It was real. He was going to murder and then commit suicide, and by reading it, I did get into his head. This was his way, and he didn't see anything else happening. He had his whole life planned around Cammie, and she took a big nasty on those plans. He was going to repay her and this guy, as well as several other innocent people. The party was going to take place on Halloween, which was the upcoming Monday.

And Sawyer had been adamant that he was flying back to St. Louis on the 30th. He had written in his notebook that if he did this atrocity on Halloween, which he called the Devil's eve, then he would somehow get to spend the afterlife with Kurt. As if Kurt was just living up in some weird heaven waiting for Sawyer to shoot up the place on Halloween so they could spend the afterlife together. It was deranged.

So after finishing it, I didn't know what to do. If I should call the law, confront him about it, or what. He had already been acting very irrational but so had I, and I wasn't going to shoot anything anytime soon. Then I grew fearful I might confront him about it, and he would snap and shoot me. Since we had been on a plane, I knew he didn't have a gun here, so at least nothing could happen now. I didn't want to call the cops, though. They might lock me up for disturbing them or worse. So I didn't do anything. I put the notebook back, unbolted the door, and I went to sleep. It was closing in at 6 am, and Sawyer still wasn't back.

When Sawyer stormed in about a quarter past nine am, I was in total REM, dream disturbed when I did hear him, so I jumped up and looked at him, not knowing what was going on. I was still asleep, and I just didn't realize it and thought I was dreaming until I looked at him and saw he didn't have a shirt on.

He saw my eyes open fully and looked at him, so he said, "I lost my fucking shirt!"

"How did you lose your-" I started to ask him, but I stopped, and I was too tired to care.

"Where the fuck did you go? I was downstairs waiting, sitting in some big chair waiting on you, and I fell asleep. Security tried to kick me out."

He flipped off the light and got under his covers.

"Huh?" I couldn't respond since I didn't know what was going on.

"Nevermind, Gun, hey, I just hope you bet on the Cubs to win the World Series," he said as I started to wake up.

"The Cubs lost last night. Six to nada. I never bet on them, as is my family tradition, and I won't start with them down a game now. I wish I would have bet on them. I would have bet on them to win the pennant, but I told you that. Where is your shirt?"

"Well, I mean, I'm not as big a Cubs fan like you, but I just went and bet on them. That's when I met this lady, Amber, and we ended up at the pool area, and it was empty, and then security came, and her husband was calling looking for her, so we had to leave, but my shirt was missing. So now I don't have a shirt, but look, I bet on the Cubbies, and I hope you did too; please tell me you did!"

He flipped the switch on the light by the bed, opened his wallet, and pulled out a ticket much like the one I had with Trump's name on it. His was for the Cubs and terrible odds.

"That's everything me and Cammie had in the bank on the Cubbies to win," He said, and he showed me the ticket, and it was for four thousand dollars for the Cubs to win the World Series.

"Damn, four thousand? Wait until I tell you what I bet on-" I paused and then asked him, "What did you wish with the witch?"

"I wished for the Cubs to win the World Series!'

I shook my head.

"Why would you waste your wish on the freaking Cubs! Why did you waste your money in the first place!" I yelled at him, and he looked at me like he knew the answer to a riddle I didn't.

"First of all, I didn't waste my money. Nadia was a witch. My Uncle sent her here, and I didn't waste my wish. Guess what Nadia has at her house? She has goats. She has three freaking billy goats, and tomorrow morning she is going to wake up, go outside, and slit the throat of one of those billy goats and perform a ritual, so the billy goat curse will be reversed!"

"What?"

"By this time tomorrow, the billy goat curse is over. It's OVER!"

"Dude? She came up with that idea, or you did?" I asked.

"It was both our plan. I had to give her some extra funds since she is killing one of her billy goats, but trust me, it will all come true. She was doing hexes and curses and speaking in tongues."

"Dude, are you serious? How much did you give her after the five hundred?"

"I only gave her another grand, another fifteen hundred, but I still put all of the rest of our $5,500, which was this four on the Cubs to win, so after she does what she is supposed to do with the goat, that money is needed to get her there, but if Cammie wants a divorce fuck her. She can take the money in her account that she won't let me see, the five fucking grand we had saved for a house, it's gone. And look, this is for you. I've been thinking about it; this bet is for you. I would write on it, but I didn't want to invalidate the ticket. So I want you to have this."

He was holding out the ticket.

And I could tell he was going to make me take it. I didn't, though, so he pulled open my wallet and stuck it in there next to the Trump ticket. He didn't look at the Trump ticket though, he just flipped off the light, flipped over on his bed, and then asked me again, "Where'd the fuck did you go?"

"Why didn't you just ask the witch to make Trump win the election!" I asked.

"Why would I waste the wish?" He said back with a tone as if I was the idiot paying witches for wishes.

"Why would you want the Cubs to win the World Series? Don't you love Trump more?"

"Trump is already going to win the election. You said that yourself, Gun. Part of my wish for the Cubs to win was so I could hide this money from Cammie. It is one last fuck you to her and her sister, who will get all of my shit if things happen. This wish wasn't for me. And it wasn't 100% for you either, Gunner! I mean, sure, you will get the winnings from the bet, but this is for my old man too. He loves the Cubs, and I might not be around, so I wanted to give him something. A Cubs World Series would put him over the moon. Don't doubt that witch, man. She is dedicated to her job, right? How did she even find me? She said it was a dream, and I just couldn't handle it. And look, even if she just slaughters the billy goat with the right curse on it, that should break the jinx right there! She knew because she got what she called phone calls from the dead. She had to answer the calls, and if she didn't they could kill her or worse. And when she was a little girl a ghost called and she didn't answer she said it dragged her to the toilet and gave her a swirly, or at least I think that's what she said, I couldn't understand some parts of her story like I said she was talking in tongues and doing hexes..."

He was ranting, and I wanted to go back to sleep. He said a few more things and maybe asked me a question that pissed me off, so I sat up and flipped on the light and said, "wait until you hear what I bet on."

I grabbed my wallet, but he didn't hear me. He was asleep, snoring—the ones who snored the loudest always fell asleep first.

I looked in my wallet—two tickets with losers' names to win. Trump and the Cubs, and I didn't even want them to touch. I could see the sun creeping in between the closed curtains, and I knew it was time to get up and start my day. I had to check my emails and try to contact Terry.

And as Sawyer snored, I knew I needed to devise a plan to stop him before he went back to the Lou and committed a mass shooting.

CHAPTER 18

"Evaluation"

The situation had gone from bad to worse, and it had nothing to do with Sawyer. He didn't flip out like a horny rhino in a henhouse, but only because I avoided bringing up his notebook like it was Pandora's box. My ability to avoid any confrontation had me tiptoeing around the issue like a ballerina dancing on hot coals. Sawyer needed a mental evaluation by professionals with physical restraints nearby and maybe a lobotomy, but I avoided the whole ordeal hoping it might just disappear. Mentally, Sawyer was a different person. After reading his notebook, I could see the blatant red flags I had missed. They were flying right in front of my face, but when I wasn't looking for them, I didn't notice them.

The notebook was terrifying, but it wasn't the only thing wrong. He was chock-full of conspiracy theories and anti-democrat propaganda, but that was only part of his delusional mindstate. He also didn't have a freaking shirt, so I had to let him borrow the only one of mine that would fit him, an oversized shirt that read Germantown-Schnitzelburg. If he stretched his arms up, his belly would pop out. It was all we had, though, and I was dealing with enough stress with my job, which was personally the more significant issue.

I couldn't log into my work email, and Terry's WHATS-APP was gone. It wasn't even a username when I searched for it. It was almost as if she was ghosting me. I emailed her from my regular email, and it bounced back, saying error immediately. And none of our old messages were in the queue. There was nothing I could do to reach her. I didn't have her actual phone number. She had disappeared like a Stephen King fart in the wind. My best assumption was that they terminated me. And it would have been justified. I had been running amok across the country acting like the class clown of the rat pack. It wasn't just justified; I should have been canned long ago. I had missed 7 of the last 12 events I was supposed to cover by my calculations.

Honestly, I should have been fired and fined.

So I rationalized with a grain of salt and came up with the idea that maybe she had a family emergency back in the motherland and had to leave the country. Internet service would have been spotty, and perhaps she had to delete her WHATSAPP for some other reason. They had just bought me a brand new iPhone; I couldn't be getting fired now. I turned it into my justification; *Rolling Stone* wouldn't fire me! I was doing everything they asked of me. They didn't care about the rallies if I went or not, and Terry barely ever said anything about any writing I turned in to be published. All she wanted me to do was contact people, and I had done that part of the job effectively, and if I was having trouble logging into my email, maybe she did too. It turned into logic. I would continue to do my job. Travel to North Carolina and then back to the District as planned. Olga or Dirk would know where Terry was, and I still had money paid to me in the nightstand and a few possessions. With that problem solved in my head, I needed to figure out what to do with Sawyer, and just like everything else in my life, I decided not to face that issue yet. So instead of being a grown-up about things and talking to Sawyer about his sinister notebook. I ignored it.

I did convince him to ride with me north to the District by hyping the mansion I lived in and telling him we could hit a club or two with VIP access, thanks to my boy Eddie. I conveniently left out any mention of the stop for the Hillary event on Tobacco Road. It was on the way regardless. We could chew the cud in the car, and if I could bring it up, maybe we could solve it like that. Pushing the problems back, it had worked so far in my life. Nobody likes traveling alone, and I told him he'd be helping me out. He was still unemployed with nothing to lose. Again he was adamant that he had to fly back before the 31st. He didn't say much more about it when I asked him why, and I didn't pry too hard. So, of course, nothing was solved. Status quo.

We headed east and north for the short road trip up the coast as two bumbling idiots driving through the southeast as if we knew the roads like the back of our hands. We didn't, and what we did was turn a two-hour flight into an 11-hour car drive. I booked a rental car because flying would have been easier, and of course, I couldn't do that. And if my thoughts were wrong about the directions, well, Sawyer's thoughts were wrong about everything. He was a man on the edge, quixotic, with a strange ideology, and he most definitely wanted to turn his letters to Kurt Cobain into reality.

It's impossible to hide on a long car ride, and so as we drove north, he started to debrief me on his wackadany conspiracy theories. His new knowledge came from an online source that sold vitamins and supplements and gave info about wars. He also read forums and had information that the average Joe couldn't attain. Sawyer had obtained a map, a blueprint of how the Democrats were working everything, and it involved a pizza place in the District called Comet Ping Pong. He was eager to investigate. This news all broke to me not even

25 minutes into our ride, and had it started even half an hour earlier; I might have left him to hitchhike.

He told me he was "woke," which is the word he used. My word would have been radicalized. Delusional is another, mixed with his guns back in the Lou; he was a dangerous man.

Now Florida is longer than gay porn, and the whole trip would take over 12 hours. It felt longer than that before we even got to Gainesville. The rental wasn't a brand new Mustang; instead, it was a squarish, blue Scion that resembled the first car a child ever draws, a box with wheels. It was another rental that had a bad AC, too, this one worked half of the time, it was a freon issue Sawyer assumed, but it was old faithful as far as getting us up the coast.

We stopped in Jacksonville to stretch and pee and fill up the tank. Sawyer bought a double disc in the gas station, it was the greatest hits from the band that Ronnie Van Zant led, and it was more than music to ears. It was just what I needed, a chance to hear some tunes and not Sawyer. It was too much to ask, however, as all the music playing did was make Sawyer talk louder. He had the hot knowledge, and he couldn't let it just burn up inside his soul! If Dick Milhouse and Hunter S. had to ride in a car together and not discuss football, it still would have been a better conversation.

If only I could see the light, Sawyer assured me. There were pedophiles, child molesters, and blood-sucking perverts all over the place, primarily in positions of power, and once I saw the lines connecting the dots, I would, too, become enlightened. And that is what Donald J. Trump was fighting against.

"Trump doesn't want the presidency for himself; he has everything, billions of dollars, any woman he wants, buildings all over the world, he already has all the power, he is doing this to stop the perverts, the corrupt people in power. It's like the

Catholic Church stuff was just the tip of the iceberg!"

The man was a loose cannon! His notebook wasn't fiction, he was demented, insane, and anti-everyone that wasn't as woke as him. He wanted me to see the light and be saved too.

HE FINALLY JUMPED INTO ANOTHER SUBJECT when I didn't bite on his Trump remarks. SSRIs and how the government created them during the MKUltra experiments at Harvard. The same experiments made the Unabomber and caused Sirhan Sirhan to shoot RFJ.

He admitted he agreed with parts of the Unabomber's manifesto. His brain was full of this type of shit. He started to explain to me how he was supposed to be taking SSRIs, but he had been off of them since he found out his wife was cheating on him.

"I don't need to take them anymore; my doctor said I was doing better while on them, like I was cured, probably; either way, I stopped taking them once Cammie left. She was cheating on me, though, so I kicked her to the curb."

"Wow? I was going to ask you about Cammie."

He smiled a sinister one at me.

"Yeah, the fucking cunt. Do you know what the biggest side effect is of antidepressants?" He asked me.

"No, I don't, but judging by the commercials I have seen on other shit, I am just going to take a guess and say explosive diarrhea?"

"No, but I think that is one. It's actually erectile dysfunction."

"Really? I didn't know that," I said.

I started to figure it out and asked him, "Wait, is that why Cammie was cheating on you?"

Maybe I had just figured out a big clue, and it wasn't that his wife was cheating on him, and it was the medication he wasn't taking. I also should have kept my mouth shut about personal stuff, and I would be depressed and on antidepressants if that happened to me.

"No, I didn't have that side effect. Mine was explosive diarrhea."

He laughed hard and loud like a cartoon pig, and then he opened up his big gulp and poured it all into his mouth.

"I gotta be honest with you, though."

And I could feel a moment of clarity had hit him, and he was about to spill the beans and tell me something or everything.

"Yeah," I leaned in closer to him.

"So, I went into that gas station, and I started chugging Mad Dog 2020, right? So I chugged like half of it, but I didn't want to chug the rest, so I didn't."

"Okay?"

"I still wanted to drink, though, so I went and bought another one and got this cup, and I poured it into here in the bathroom. I've been drinking this whole time!"

He started laughing.

It wasn't the beans I had hoped he would spill.

I hit the cruise control through the Florida-Georgia line, and we saw no less than 1240 police cruisers. It must be a requirement. We would need a Delorean fueled by plutonium to make the Hillary event on Tobacco Road. It was hopeless, but I did have plans to make it to the hotel in time to see Game Two. The Cubs needed me to watch. Sawyer was still babbling about how the world was and how he understood it.

And most importantly, how I didn't. I was just listening now because if I tried to explain that his crazy theories about Obama and Hillary Clinton were asinine, it would turn into a fight. So I let him maunder on, and he was explaining now.

"You aren't a flat earther, are you?"

He was checking all the boxes, so I had to ask.

"No, I am not," he informed me, and I felt like maybe the Jefferson County Public School System hadn't failed us completely.

"I didn't know because there are flat earthers all around the globe." Sawyer didn't get the joke. He dismissed it and went back into explaining the pedophile ring run by degenerates in the District. I had tuned him out and tuned back in at the wrong time.

"Obama is gay, and Michelle Obama is actually a man."

"What?"

"Yep, Obama is gay, Michelle is a man, and look that one is pretty known there are pictures to confirm it and whatnot."

"That's the dumbest thing you've said, and you have said a plethora of dumb shit!"

"Look, whatever Gun, Michelle ain't a man, Hillary ain't a criminal, Barack ain't gay!"

"Exactly!"

"Exactly!"

"She had two fucking kids! It's not a conspiracy!"

We were both heated.

"You are gonna see it one day," he let me know.

"I am going to see what? The middle ages? What?"

"You will fucking see that Bill Gates and Tom Hanks and other elites, you will see that they are going to this pizza place, they have a pedo ring, they are drinking blood, you will see, goddamn it!"

"Oh really? That's what I will see? What else, huh?"

"Hillary is a fucking criminal!"

"Because of her emails?"

"Fucking right because of her goddamn emails!"

He was passionate, but I was pissed. I pulled into a rest stop, and I was finally serious about leaving him. I wouldn't do that to anyone, but it crossed my mind. After we stretched again, we piled back in and hit the road. He was still firm on making sure I knew what was at stake, and I just went with it. Slowly, I started to pry into his personal life to gauge what else was going on and see if his ideas in his notebook would come to fruition. I didn't doubt it as much anymore.

As we drove north through Georgia and finally into South Carolina, he put the second disc in, I turned it up, and we both shut up as Tuesday's Gone started to play. We were on pace to be late and not even make the Hillary campaign stop at all. Par for the course and I got comfortable in the driver's seat as we drove towards Georgia. It felt like Tuesday was gone. The world was changing, and Sawyer had already changed. Everything was different; normalcy was gone with the wind.

CHAPTER 19

"South of the Border"

"Oh shit, South of the Border, my folks took me there when I was a kid. We gotta stop!"

I didn't respond until I could feel him staring at me.

"Yeah, we can stop because I gotta pee again."

And we drove by a big red barn covered in the letters T-R-U-M-P, and it was just continuing the trend of what we had seen so far on our trip. Throughout our travels, we had seen nothing but Trump signs in abundance. Flyover country was in the middle of Trump mania. I was confident in my bet, but it would be terrible for the country. As we pulled off the exit, there was a stop sign, and under it, someone had written, Obama. It was disgusting, but I wasn't second-guessing it anymore.

"Stop Obama, now that is a good one," Sawyer said laughing when he saw it.

We were at the South of the Border, the halfway point from Florida, and the Big Apple, south of North Carolina in South Carolina. And playing into the theme of the south of the border, there was a giant statue of a Mexican man with a colossal sombrero welcoming us from the highway. It was a truck stop and a sad sight for sore eyes, and it should have been razed anytime after March 1989.

SUICIDE NOTES TO KURT COBAIN

We had blown our chance at making it to Tobacco Road for the Hillary event; another pit stop wouldn't matter. There were advertisements for all sorts of tourist trap adventures like a carousel and feeding live gators. I knew it would take a lot to make this stop worth it, and buying fireworks in October wasn't going to satisfy my desires. I parked at a pump and went inside. Sawyer stayed outside to burn one and then pump the petro, and when I came out, he had already found the whole scoop of the place. He was eager to inform me, and I could only shake my head as soon as I saw his face. Sawyer could find a Thanksgiving dinner during the apocalypse.

"We can go up to the top of the sombrero," He told me while pointing at the big hat on top of the giant colorful statue of a Mexican man.

I bent my head back and looked up.

"I am not walking all the way up there just to what? To do what? Spit off of it?"

"Naw, we can get a ticket and take an elevator."

"I always wanted to die at a tourist trap. And this isn't even a good tourist trap like Gatlinburg."

It was a once-in-a-lifetime opportunity. However, it was too late as we were already going to head up.

By the time we bought our tickets and headed towards the elevator to the top of this empty brain, Sawyer had leads on a bag to put in the air and on some chick named Molly. I knew to stay away from myself; the boozing and little bit of THC were bad enough; if I got involved in harder stuff, there might not be any turning back. He had me try one white girl already, and that was enough. Sawyer's skill to find drug intel quicker than water finds a hole wasn't a good trait.

He was buying drugs at a truck stop. If that ain't rock

bottom.

There was no line to get up to the top of the decrepit hat, and I felt it move with the win while we stood under it. I hit a steel rod and questioned why the whole decrepitude statue didn't fall over. Its collapse was imminent. Inside the bottom of the man, it was an abandoned building.

The clerk said vintage, but all he did was push a button to open the doors to the death trap. He reminded us to send the elevator back down once we got up to the top. We entered the matchbox size elevator, and it stunk like rust and urine. And it felt like it might not even go up at all. There was a big glass window on the back to see our way up, and somehow we made it up to the top without even a tiny hitch. It was dilapidated but functioning enough for the state to allow it to be in use. Those tests must only require the bare minimum anymore.

South of the Border wasn't much to look at from the ground; a higher vantage point didn't make it any better. Sawyer spotted some lot lizards working the truckers, and he spit off to mark his territory. Other than that, it was just the roofs of buildings that could have been liquor stores or schools. And ahead of us, trucks and cars flying north and south on I95.

One walk around the top of the hat was enough for me, and as I walked towards the elevator, it dinged and opened. A tall ugly white dude stepped off, and he looked both ways like he was about to cross a busy street, and then walked straight towards me. As he got closer, I could see how ugly he was. His face looked like a Picasso mistake with a nose long and pointing down, and his cheek skin was stretched tight across the bones in his front. He had a thin mustache as if he drew it on, but no other facial hair and dark eyes, and he was wearing a Nascar jacket with a Jellyroll Bad Apple shirt on under it with black jeans and a pair of old jeans Vans.

"What's good with you guys?" he said.

"Nothing," I said, but Sawyer cut me off to say, "It's all good in the hood like Tiger Woods."

And I was embarrassed to know him, and he just shrugged back at me. The ugly dude did a laugh that felt like a salesman, and that's when I realized this was the drug guy.

Fucking Sawyer was going to get arrested, which was a safer place for him, but if the cops take him, then they will likely take me down too. These debunked counties in the south love arresting out-of-towners and taking them to the cleaners with fees and penalties that add more costs. Some of the poorer counties even put it into their local budget, and they plan on arresting so many out-of-towners each year.

Sawyer did a big nod at the guy and told him, "Step into my office."

They walked off towards the far part of the hat.

"You that guy that Sarah or whatever called," Sawyer asked him before they got out of my hearing range, and he nodded yes back at Sawyer.

Sawyer came back a minute later, grinning so hard it looked as if his face was stuck like that. He hit the button to go back down the bottom, and it popped open because the ugly drug dealer dude didn't send it back down, and we stepped onto the stink box, turned around, and I could see the ugly dude give us a nod and then turn around.

I turned to Sawyer as soon as the doors were shut, "What in the hell did you just buy?"

"Chronic and..." but he doesn't say; he just shows me a bag of powder, opens it up, and starts to pull some of it out with his house key.

I start looking around the lift and scream at him, "You

can't sniff that shit right here; what if there are cameras!"

"You don't sniff Molly, idiot. You eat it!"

He pulled out a chunk and put it on his tongue.

We walked around the shithole for a bit. It was a carnie purgatory of a place. It was lot lizards and real carnies tired of the road, or other similar types, and tons of Trump merchandise for sale. If I didn't know MAGA hats came from Chinese slave labor, I would have thought MAGA hats were grown right here at South of the Border. Sawyer decided he would buy a few t-shirts considering he only had one, but I let him know I wouldn't ride anywhere with him if he bought and wore a red hat. I was finally going to draw the line, but it wasn't needed. He didn't want a hat, but he needed a shirt. I agreed as he was stretching mine out.

He wanted to buy every shirt in the place, he had a champagne taste, but he was on a beer budget. All his savings was on a ticket for a team to win the World Series that hadn't done so in 107 years. Finally, he decided on a shirt from the clearance rack that a 12-year-old fan of Trump would wear. Trump's head photoshopped onto Rambo's body holding Rambo's gun. It was classy.

The old man behind the counter, who had the face of a meth addict, let us know, "That one is the best seller."

Trump wasn't even real to these people anymore. He wasn't Donald J. Trump, the guy from the TV show; now he was bigger than that person; he was a cartoon depiction of who they wanted him to be. Trump wasn't just one guy anymore; he was myths and folklore now. This entire store of tourist trap bullshit was 70% full of Trump merch. Rows and rows of Trump shirts, each row topped with hats for Trump, Towels for Trump on the back wall, keychains, action figures, bobbleheads; Trump was the new Star Wars. And who knew if Trump was even getting a cut on all this. It was amazing to see, and I started to wonder if a narcissist could make a good president. I didn't like it, and I was ready to leave this new reality.

"Trump's gonna win easy!" Sawyer told the old meth head checking him out while flicking a bobblehead Trump on the counter.

"Hell yeah, he is, brother!"

He handed Sawyer back his change. His knuckles had tattoo letters, but I couldn't make out what it spelled.

"Hillary might be in prison; the FBI reopened the case against her."

"No, are you serious?" I had to chime in, and as I did, I flicked the Trump bobblehead myself.

"Yep, they announced it on Faux earlier; I turned it off when y'all came in. She's going back to prison!" He said, and he flicked the remote and turned it back on. The news wasn't on, though; it was a commercial.

"That's wild as shit, man. Gun, you hear that shit, ain't no way that crooked ass bitch is gonna win now!" Sawyer yelled at me, and he was right.

"Trump's gonna save the world, man!" Sawyer said, and the man agreed.

I shook my head and picked up my phone. Dude D texted me, and it was just a smiley face. The news came back on the flat screen, and it was true. Sawyer and the man started dancing around like wild pigmen dancing in a pool of mud, and my heart rushed to my feet.

Sawyer pumped his chest out, and he was walking around like a lion about to get laid. He felt assured that a big piece of his conspiracy was coming true; Hillary was a crook.

"We are going to win. We are going to win!" Sawyer and this man yelled out as if it was a team sport, and they were somehow now on the winning team.

Trump wasn't this savior they thought he was, but that didn't matter. What mattered now was that my insider information was accurate, and I had put money down when I did. I just shook my head while they danced. It was all true, and it was the end of the road for Hillary.

I was ready to leave before Sawyer and this guy started kissing over the news. And it wasn't just the bad news/good news about Hillary going to prison; I didn't want Sawyer to find something else to ingest that might kill him. I left, and Sawyer followed me. He was flying, ear to ear shit grin on his face until we got close to the rental. It was completely gone by the time I got into the car, but he didn't enter the vehicle. He just stood outside, so I stepped back out.

"That shit was bunk!"

He banged the pinky side of his hand like a karate chop onto the top of the car.

"Maybe it just hasn't hit you yet, I can speak from experience and say that edible marijuana takes longer to kick in, but when they do kick, boom, you're fucking moonwalking!"

"Well, this shit was supposed to be moon rocks, and it wasn't. It tasted like crushed aspirin mixed with drywall."

It wouldn't take much to make him fly off the handle, so I wanted to avoid going back to see the ugly guy in the Nascar jacket. He turned to walk.

"I'm just going to give him the rest of this shit back and get my money back."

He was walking fast and serious, but that's not how it

worked. And he knew how it worked. He couldn't show up with the goods and return them, so I yelled at him, "What are you doing? You don't have a receipt; look, if you eat one bite out of one slice of pizza, you can't return the rest of the pie!"

He wasn't listening, so we trotted back over to the bottom of the hat again, Sawyer leading the way, and it was like Custer riding to Little BigHorn. The clerk was still at the bottom, and he had a slight resemblance to the kid who had sold Sawyer the bunk drugs. Ugly and whatnot with the same crooked nose.

"I know I saw you two, and you were up, but you can't go up again. You needa have anotha ticket," He said in a drawn-out accent with some nerves behind it.

"Fine. We will just wait right here until he comes down," Sawyer said and folded his arms like he was 7 in a temper tantrum at the supermarket because his mom wouldn't buy him a Snickers.

"Ain't nobody up there, so who in the hell are you waiting on Christ?" The clerk told us without the drawn-out accent this time.

"No, not JC. That little mothercunter named Eric or Derrick or whatever. He sold me some bunk shit, and I want my money back. $75. He can hand it back to me, or I can take my hands to him."

Sawyer was pissed.

"Are you talking about the guy in the Junior Jacket?" The clerk asked us.

Sawyer didn't answer, so I did.

"He had a NASCAR jacket on. I don't know what number it was, though; I think maybe it was eight or maybe nine. I can't remember; it was Nascar, though."

The clerk sat up off his stool a bit, and he was mad now.

"What do you mean, you think it was eight?" He said, putting the top of his head down and turning it a bit.

"What?" I said, and I was right. He looked like the ugly guy with his bootleg Picasso nose; they were probably related.

He put his head up and asked me, "What? There was only one person through here with a NASCAR jacket all day, and it was a Junior jacket. It wasn't a nine; it was an eight. He came down and left right after y'all did."

This ugly dude was pissed that I didn't know my NAS-CAR numbers and drivers, and NASCAR wasn't my thing.

Sawyer was still mad and feeling frisky, ready for a fight, so he chimed in, "NASCAR, National Association of Stupid Cars and Rednecks."

He laughed and I laughed too. I'd never heard that, and I was also trying to diffuse a bomb.

The long-nose ugly dude laughed too and said, "That's funny, I ain't never heard that one."

Sawyer cut the laughter though and said, "So the guy in the jacket, where did he go?"

"He had a car pick him up," he motioned towards the area behind us, and I could tell he was lying.

He knew the guy, they looked like freaking brothers, but maybe that's how racist white folk look in backcountry South Cak. Ugly.

He looked at me and then Sawyer, and then he lowered his head and his voice and asked, "What was y'all trying to get anyhow?"

And it felt like a sting to me. Maybe not the cops, but he

was trying to rob us or something. The hair on the back of my neck stood up, so I told him, "It doesn't matter-"

Sawyer cut me off, though, "Molly, and he gave us some bunk ass shit. It was drywall and aspirin, I bet."

And he pulled the baggie out of his pocket and held it up so the guy could see what was left. He was holding it up like it was a regular, everyday product one could get at Walmart and not a highly felonious narcotic. This was extremely hot, so I shouted, "put that shit up."

He put it away slowly, and he knew better. We'd end up in the county holding cell looking at life if he kept this up, so I told him, "let's bounce."

"Man, I know how it is; I got some of them pills, ya know the ones that them ravers be doing called beans?"

I turned around to see him swiveling on his stool. Sawyer was as interested as a long-fingered child staring into a moving fan.

"Ecstasy?" Sawyer asks him, and this is when I know that this guy was preparing a sting or was already in on it. Sawyer didn't budge, though, because he had the taste to get high.

"Yeah, that's it. A kid got caught with them by his mom a few weeks back, and I happened to be on top of the hat, emptying the trash and doing inspections and whatnot, and I had to say something, so I says, 'ma'am, I do have to confiscate and will need to give them to the local police department.' And she handed them to me and left running as she didn't want her only begotten son to end up in a Carolina chain gang, ya feel lat though?"

"How do you know that's what it is?" I asked him as I was now curious.

"Oh, cause me and my old lady, we ate a few and felt

beautiful. It was like being on a trampoline on a boat in heaven if ya feel me," he said, and he was looking around like he was watching a fly. He was lying.

"You gotta tell me if you're a cop," Sawyer says to this guy to whom he had just incriminated himself.

"I ain't gotta tell you if I am a cop. Where did you hear that shit? No, I ain't no cop, but seriously, you think an under-cover cop is just gonna answer that as, yep, you caught me if he's infiltrated the mob. Guess they shoulda asked Donnie Brasco, hey, you a cop boy?"

He started laughing.

"Naw, I mean, I had to ask, you know?" Sawyer said back in a stumble.

"Yay, you gotta learn, so I got five of them thangs left, and I can do a hundred for all of 'em," He said, and again his eyes were rolling around in his head like he saw ghosts.

"Let's do it," Sawyer said without seeing these things at all, but to my surprise, the guy had 5 of them right there.

Sawyer gave him the five twenties, and within minutes we were back in the car headed north. Thank the lord, baby Jesus in a diaper!

So we drove north, and as soon as we hit the Tar Heel State, it started to drizzle. Our wipers needed to be changed, so I had to focus. I turned on the flashers and slowed down. Saw-yer was bouncy, so I turned up the stereo as Ronnie sang out, "Gimme Two Steps."

Sawyer swallowed one bean, waited 5 minutes, and took another. Less than two minutes later, he ate a third. Fi-nally, he popped number five like it was a Tic-Tac. Then he went on and on about how he knew the beans were good and said he probably wouldn't sleep for a day or two since beans did that to him. And how they " would keep him up all day and night feeling great and horny."

I just nodded because I didn't know what to say about him getting hot and horny on what was probably a truck-stop amphetamine. He went on to confirm my suspicions.

"It might be the meth that they cut it with; shit, these could be cut with anything. It doesn't matter, though. I will be rolling in the deep like Adele before too long."

He carried on, and on so much, it was a broken record or a frontal lobe loop that needed a mute button. He was yapping away as we finally left I95 on route to Tobacco Road. And then, out of nowhere, he was out like a switch.

He was laid back in his seat, snoring like a walrus without a care in the world, which I could only assume wasn't a normal reaction to meth, so I grew fearful. The truck stop meds could be anything, and I started to panic. It was also beginning to rain again, and this rental was equipped with two used toothbrushes instead of wipers, so I had to pull into a rest stop. I googled the number for poison control and then rummaged through his pockets to find the remaining pill. Sawyer still didn't wake up, and I found the pill.

A slow-speaking lady answered the phone. I was frantic, but I didn't let it come out in my voice.

"Yes, ma'am, I am here at my brother-in-law's house, and he is in rehab right now. He was addicted to pixie sticks by way of the nasal passage if not the anus, and we are here cleaning the place out, and my sister, bless her little heart, is telling me that this medication is from her old gonorrhea outbreak, but is there any way you can tell me what this pill is?"

"Yes, sir, I do need a little more information," She said, and she continued, "What is your name and date of birth?"

"Ah yes, I am," And I looked around to find something to make up a fake name with, and since the snoring was getting louder, I just said, "Sawyer Barnes. My birthdate is December 9th, 1941, uh, I mean, 1991."

"Okay, Mr. Barnes, now can you tell me about this medication?"

A car pulled into the rest stop, and it had lights on top. I couldn't make it out, but I was trying while also trying to keep the pill low to read it. It was a state pig.

"Yeah, one second, please."

I was prepared to eat this pill if needed, but Sawyer turned out to be right about at least one thing: cops don't want to get out in the rain. It was cats and dogs outside, so I watched in my rearview as the cop pulled into a spot on the other side to eat donuts and watch a movie.

"What does the pill look like, sir?" The lady asked me again in the voice of a librarian with a cold. She was mad I wasn't responding and probably thought I was a drug addict trying to figure out if I just scored.

"Right, so it's white with blue specs or blue with white specs; it's tough to tell," I told her while holding the pill down to make sure the law dog didn't see it.

"Does the pill have any words, numbers, or markings?" She said again with a painful voice.

I had to squint, and I turned on the light to try to see anything at all, but I could see a word significantly faded, almost like it had been scrubbed off.

"I can see a word and numbers, I think the last two numbers or letters say, T and maybe M, but it could be a three, oh no, it says, T-nol PM," I said into the phone, and it took me a minute

SUICIDE NOTES TO KURT COBAIN

to process what I had just read and said. I filled in the rest of the letters like any loser watching Wheel of Fortune would, but she beat me to it.

"Sir, those are Tylenol PMs," the lady said, but I hung up.

This dumbass had just bought 5 Tylenol PMs for a hundred dollars, popped four of them, and he was now enjoying one of his best periods of sleep in years. I threw the pill to the back seat and backed out as the rain slowed. The copper would be eager to grab someone soon. I pulled off doing the speed limit.

It was after midnight before we even pulled into the hotel in Winston Salem. Sawyer was drooling and snoring like a St. Bernard on tranquilizers. I laughed to myself the whole time, and it was all I had left. I had called the hotel to let them know I would be running late, and I needed a double instead of a single. It was fine on the phone, talking to someone across the world, but when I showed up, Barb acted as if I asked her to change the damn floorplan of the lobby at the front desk.

She thought Sawyer and I were possible on drugs or homosexuals, which her North Carolina upbringing had brainwashed her into thinking was Satan's sin. She only thought this because Sawyer tried to kiss me. He didn't know it was me, of course, but Barbaria at the front desk didn't know that. And for all she knew, we were a couple from San Francisco on our honeymoon. And she didn't know if I wanted one bed or two. I had also rolled Sawyer's lifeless body into the hotel on the luggage cart since he wouldn't wake up, and the valet kid said it was illegal to let him sleep in the rental. He also wouldn't help me roll Sawyer inside as it was against some unwritten rule of some policy. I never understood that; either write the rules down, or they aren't rules. He didn't even move him off the cart. He looked comfy and was sleeping fine.

Once we got into our room, I didn't even move him; I

241

just took my bags off and then sat on the bed as he slept. I tried to log into my email with *Rolling Stone* but couldn't. The whole network was messed up or something. I tried to check my email, but I couldn't log in. I tried to message Terry again on WHATSAPP, but it wouldn't go through. I even typed in her name again, and it said the user didn't exist.

I was happy the room was still booked, and the company credit card worked.

I was doing better than Mary and Joseph. I didn't move Sawyer, and he didn't budge as I turned on the Cubs game. It was about to be the 7th inning, and the Cubs were up 5-1 in Game two. I had to wheel Sawyer back towards the door since his snoring was so loud I couldn't hear the commentators. I ordered room service and sat on the edge of the bed, watching the rest of the game. I ordered Sawyer a burger too, but by the time it came, they were both cold, and to top it off, the beer was hot.

I had missed the Hillary event, but my real goal while driving was to catch the game. I'd caught some of it on the radio, and I was keeping up with the score, but it felt great to sit and watch. Drinking a hot beer and eating an undercooked, cold burger didn't even matter. By the time the Cuban Missile came to the mound, I was five beers into my six-pack, and I knew the Cubs were going to tie it up.

I started to wonder if I should be happy or not. Of course, I was delighted, elated rather, but I didn't want to use up all my luck on the Cubs. I didn't know if that's how it worked, and Sawyer did have his life savings on the line despite him giving it to me. However, I had more than that on the line, so I picked up the cold burger again, and I started to really think about my job at *Rolling Stone*.

I was still coming out ahead, and if I won the Trump bet, I'd make out like a bank robber. I couldn't complain; besides, all that money I had made and put down was made without me even getting published at all yet!. I loved my job; it was the lord's work if Jesus had to get a job. I wouldn't be against begging for my position when I did get to talk to Terry.

The Sawyer problem hadn't worked itself out like I thought it would. I would have to again dig through his corpse and find his cell phone. I had to get in touch with his mom, dad, siblings, or perhaps all of them. Drastic measures, but it was all I could do. There was no way I could let him fly back to the Lou and do what he said he would do in the notebook.

I was between a bad place and a conundrum, and I didn't even know which way was up. The only certainty in my life was that somehow, Trump would be the next leader of the free world. And despite how scary that was, it was the least of my problems. Besides, I was going to make money on it.

CHAPTER 20

SHTF. Yep, and if you don't understand that acronym let me spell it out for you, shit hit the fan. On all levels, except maybe Sawyer, which is the big surprise here. It might be that he will explode, or maybe Sawyer just needed a friend for a bit since he was away from everyone he knew living in another city with a wife who was cheating on him. However, we weren't talking about any of it, not the notebook or anything related. I didn't know how to face it.

The conversation was status quo the entire six hours north from Tobacco Road, but Sawyer was looping about the Comet Pizza Place with his lizard brain. Heated about getting beat for 200 bucks at the truck stop, he was far from fun to be around anymore. None of it mattered to me. I was in a bigger hole, and I didn't even know what it was. It was potentially worse than a potential mass shooting which was on the line here. Mine wasn't "potentially," though.

When we arrived at the mansion, it was empty. Not just empty but deserted. And I don't mean that just Olga and Dirk were gone. No, the whole place deserted like an embassy in Libya. The once stellar mansion now resembled a pigpen. That's the shit that hit the fan. It looked like it had been raided and ransacked by pirates. We parked in the back, and there had been a controlled fire on the back patio.

All around the area were the remains of brown folders and documents and other papers that mostly burned. However, there was still evidence that was still slightly visible in different places around the yard, as if someone had created a fire and then started emptying filing cabinets on top of it.

I'm almost 100% certain that is what happened.

Sawyer noticed it first, but we both couldn't figure it out, and he didn't even have a reason to try to. The back door was still open, slightly, but it also wouldn't close because the frame was bent as if someone had tried to remove it from the wall.

We entered that door and onto the screened-in back porch and saw more fire remains. Cabinets had been emptied, and the contents burned. It was also full of what looked like the burnt filing cabinets contents. It was almost like whoever made the fire realized they couldn't burn everything on the porch, so they moved the fire to the patio.

"This place is a dump," Sawyer said as soon as we entered the back kitchen door.

And it was.

"Russians, huh? I guess they don't know how to clean in the motherland!" I didn't say anything, so he added, "It fucking stinks in here!"

And it did.

The lights were on, which gave me the initial impression that Olga or Dirk was home, but I realized the place was abandoned once we were inside. Almost all the lights were on, even some closet lights, the pantry light, the bathroom lights. And it smelt like something rancid as soon as we stepped in from the porch. I was afraid it was a dead body. It wasn't, thankfully. The fridge had been left open, and all the food expired. I was relieved. The rotten food showed us that it wasn't recent.

Sawyer went to the bathroom, and I started to throw the food out into the trash can. I noticed a ton of plastic shit at the bottom, so I shut the fridge trapping the odor in it, and dumped the trash can over. It was a collection of cut-up credit cards. They weren't wet, but they smelled like gasoline as if they were next in line to get tossed on the fire. I moved them a bit and saw my name, GUNNER A., so I picked it up. It was a Mastercard. I flipped through more of them, and I found a Discover card that had ner A. Bush, and then I found another one that read Gun, and yet another that read Bush. These weren't the company credit cards I'd been using either. These were different cards. It was a mixture of Mastercards and Visas and American Express and Discovery. A few of them had other names, but at least 7 in my name.

Sawyer came back in holding a bunch of the mail. The mansion had an old school mailbox where the mail just fell into the house. Sawyer must have seen it and picked it up because a few pieces were addressed to me.

"You think you should call the cops?" he said, looking around the dining room a bit.

"Yeah, probably, but look at this," I pointed to the credit cards.

"These two fit together, look," he said, matching two ripped pieces together.

I grabbed one of the envelopes addressed to me, tore it open slowly from the corner, and pulled out the paper on the inside. It was a credit card bill for $17,502. I flipped through the statement, and it had hotels, rental cars, and almost everything else I had used the company card for. Yet all this time, I thought it was a company card that had my name on it, but instead, it was my card, in my name address to me here.

"Holy shit," I said to Sawyer, but he had opened the fridge and slammed it shut, gagging.

"Dude, this place is huge, though, and would be nice without the dead body odor from the fridge and the weird-ass fire pits." He opened the cabinets one by one.

I opened the next piece of mail, and it was another credit card bill in my name for $8,808. There was another statement of purchases, and it was nothing I purchased. It had seven Walmart shopping trips for over $300 each time, and it also had two or three Mcdonalds' purchases a day. I knew Olga and Dirk loved Mick E Dees, but I didn't realize they ate there 2 to 3 times a day with a credit card in my name!

I tossed the paper on the counter. Sawyer started flipping through the drawers, and he pulled out a few of the steak knives. He rubbed them on his finger to see how sharp they were. I sat on the stool and opened another envelope addressed to me. It was from the cable company, and the cable was in my name. Then there was another for the water bill, again in my name. The last was for the electric bill, and it was also in my name. All three were about to be terminated for non-payment.

"How did you get this job at Rolling Stone again?"

"Yeah, I know," I said, but I didn't elaborate, and I didn't need to. It didn't take an idiot to figure things out. I didn't know what to do, though, and I didn't know what the play in playing me. Someone had left in a hurry, burning papers on their way out the door, and that wasn't even the most disturbing part. I tried to figure it out, but I couldn't.

I had been a victim of identity theft, but it was all coming back to where I was living. That would be hard to prove, but I wanted to know the why, not the how. The how was I had willingly given them the info, and they had used my information to hook everything up in my name.

Everything was on when I arrived at the mansion; it couldn't have been in my name yet. It was fraud, but I didn't know what to do.

"I think I am just going to go get my shit, and then maybe we should call your dad. He's a lawyer and might know what to do."

I wanted to talk to his old man regardless, but now I was fearful the FBI was going to kick down the door any minute. So I went upstairs and checked the nightstand by my bedroom door, and it was full of envelopes, and each contained my weekly payment of $1700.

At least Terry had paid me. My bedroom door was shut but not locked as I had left it. The light was off, but the bathroom and closet lights were on. The closet door was open, and I could see my extra pair of DCs on the floor, my two skateboards, and my clothes still hanging up. I was glad the Russians had shitty taste in style and music.

Sawyer didn't follow me into my room, and I didn't notice until I heard him yelling like he had found a dead body. I ran into the hallway, and he stuck his head out of the room I thought was Dirk's but might have been Olgas.

"Look," he said, but he didn't show me anything, and he was back in the room again. I walked into the room; the mattress was half off the bed, no sheets were on it, and the computer chair was on the floor.

"Did you do this?" I asked him.

"No, look," he said again, but this time he was showing me a shoebox, and it was closed, so I couldn't see what he was showing me besides a shoebox. He moved out of the closet and pushed it towards me.

"Open it!"

I did, and it was full of money—all hundred dollar bills. There were four huge rows with about six stacks of 200 bills wrapped with a rubber band and a few piles rolled up with rubber bands on top popping out—all of them Benjamin Franklins.

"Jesus..."

"Should I just remind you of a thing called finder's keepers!"

He was poking around the room, looking for more.

"The back door was kicked in, right? Can't we just say the place was ransacked? I mean, it was ransacked, but whoever tore it up didn't find the box of hundreds which is odd considering they were sitting right there on the edge of that computer desk. Man, we should act like we were never here!"

He was trying to rationalize a way to keep the box of hundreds. He stepped into the closet again and then stepped out of the closet, still looking for another box somewhere, anywhere. I didn't blame him, but I didn't think the Russians were coming back. He walked towards the bathroom and stopped to open another smaller closet.

He started talking to himself, "These Russians will learn to lock their doors, you know?"

"Did you knock all this shit over?"

"No, and whoever did, they messed up. I mean, you can tell they were looking for something, but what, right? Money, probably, but look, this box was right there on that desk. Wide fucking open. Just hundreds rolling out of it, so if it wasn't money, what was it that they were looking for?"

I turned to look at the desk and didn't respond to him.

"What's that black box under the desk?" He was pointing at something hooked up to the computer under the desk. He stuck his head under the desk to look at it; he'd already ransacked the drawers to the desk before I entered. The computer's mouse moved as he went down, bumping the computer out of sleep mode.

"Wonder why they didn't burn this computer?" I asked him, but he wasn't listening.

A computer program was up, and it had the hundred-dollar bill on it. I pulled the chair up, sat down in front of the computer, and a notification flashed on the computer screen that read 'printing.'

"It's plugged into that computer and not full of hundred-dollar bills."

"Why burn the papers outside, but keep this computer on?"

"It turned on; I think it's doing something!" Sawyer said as it started making noises, and then a piece of paper started to roll out.

"Damn, it's just a weird-ass looking printer." He was upset now.

He pulled himself out from under the desk, and as he moved out of the way, I reached down and grabbed the piece of paper that was coming out of it. It had printed three hundred dollar bills. It wasn't standard paper either; it was thick and felt like money. And the hundreds looked pristine. Identical, if not better. Fresh, crisp like this thing wasn't a printer, but an ATM just refilled. Sawyer wasn't searching the closet for another shoebox anymore. He saw what I was holding, and he came closer to examine the paper too.

"Holy mother of counterfeits, Batman!"

"Look, look, and all three have the same serial number!"

"These mother-F-ing Russians were counterfeiting money!"

I moved the mouse down slightly to a button read, print, and hit it. And seven seconds later, a new page shot out of the printer; I handed it to Sawyer.

"This is highly illegal, a federal offense."

He handed it back to me.

"I don't even want my fingerprints on these; we should burn these."

"Burn it? Are you going to burn the shoebox full of counterfeit bills you are holding?" I asked him, and he looked at me like he had peanut butter stuck on the roof of his mouth.

"N-no, these are real," He mustered out, but he realized the truth. The shoebox he was cradling was full of counterfeit hundreds.

"Let's check 'em," I said, and I reached for the shoebox.

"Okay, okay, but those are the best fakes I have ever seen. Remember when them G-town bitches Mindy and Nikki or whatever, had that whole garbage bag full of fake $5 bills. Kids were using those for months, buying everything, mostly zanies and loud. Maybe I bought some school lunches with them, but nobody ever got caught. And those looked terrible. These look as good as the real thing!"

He was right. They looked impeccable. We needed to know, though, so we looked for repeating serial numbers to match the three on the piece of paper, we had to do it one at a time, so it was tedious, and Sawyer started to hope for the best.

"Man, see, we haven't found one match. I bet this is real money, probably what the person was looking for, and they just missed it."

He could be right, though. There was no telling what had happened here.

"You said it was right there, and it was open?" I asked him, and he didn't say anything, but I watched his shoulders fall.

"I found one....shit!"

He sat down on the box springs.

"Shit, these two have the same serial number, but it's different from these 4."

He blew out like a dragon and shook his head as the realization set in that all the money was fake. I pulled out the envelopes and went to compare the serials, and I put them on the bed and started to look at them. He put them all back into the shoebox, and I began to realize that I was probably getting paid in counterfeit bills too.

"Where'd you get this? This place is crawling with money, dude!" He said, but he saw I was trying to look at the serial numbers, so he ventured back to the bathroom. I was relieved, though, quickly, since all the numbers were different. Not one single duplicate. I wasn't looking very hard, though.

"Where did you get those hundreds from?" Sawyer asked me as he came back.

"No, these are from getting paid from *Rolling Stone*. They aren't fake; I just checked all thirty-four of them. Not one repeat, no duplicates."

"Yeah, let me check them with these, though, real quick," he said, holding up the shoebox, and he started to compare my real ones to his fake ones.

"These look identical. Seriously, if I handed you back one from the box, you wouldn't be able to tell the difference. I can't tell, and I am holding them!"

"Yeah, it's uncanny, but at least I know mine are real."

"I bet they aren't, though, try to match them with me," He said, and then he started to mix up the hundreds, so I reached to stop him.

"Here it is, quick as shit too," He said, and he handed me one of my bills, and it matched the number that had just printed.

"Holy Mother of Mary," I said, and then he added, "I bet those are all fake."

He was right. They were all fake as monopoly money. They were terrible fakes, though, as in they didn't look fake at all. They were replications, the printing was exact, and the paper was the same or close to mint quality. So good, I was sure I had been getting paid in fake hundreds all summer, but I had never been caught with one or questioned at all.

"How are they faking the metal in this bill?" Sawyer asked me, and he started to look at the printer. It wasn't like any printer we had ever seen, and it was more like a 3D printer with extra advantages. It was strictly for counterfeiting money.

"I don't think the Russians are coming back," he said, but I already knew.

He hit print on the computer screen and out popped three more hundreds. He printed again, took all three of the pages to a paper cutter on the side desk, and started cutting them as a fourth printed out.

"Why did they leave this computer here and burn all the other shit? That doesn't make sense."

"I'm doing this all night," Sawyer said, not listening. He wanted to stay all night, but I didn't want to stick around.

"How did they change the serial number, though? You are going to have the same serial number on all of them!"

I started to look around the room again, and I was missing something, but I couldn't figure out what it was. I showed Sawyer the electric bill as he messed with the computer, changing the serial numbers.

"Okay, so what the power is going to get shut off on the 30th? You better pay that shit," He said, and he had changed the print number to 99 instead of 1, and he hit print.

"No, it's in my name. I never did that. I never set that up; what should I do?" I asked, but he wasn't listening, so I sat down on the bed.

"I will call my old man; let me do some more of these because I am not working ever again," he said.

"Yeah, call your dad," I said, but he already was.

His old man didn't pick up, and as he was lining up more bills to cut.

"Let's order some food, my treat. I am starving."

"Yeah, I am hungry."

"I need to test these out, and a delivery driver would be perfect!"

We ordered a feast. I went to take a shower while Sawyer stayed at it, printing and cutting. I checked my phone before I got into the shower, and I had a message from Morgan.

"I can't believe it. This is going to change the entire course of the election." A sad face emoji followed it.

I washed off, and right as I got out of the shower, the doorbell rang.

"Can you get that?" I yelled at Sawyer, but he didn't respond. I dried off and walked towards the front door. It was open, and Sawyer was standing there arguing with a young Asian kid who was probably not even 18 yet.

"Sawyer, what are you doing?"

"He said he can't break a hundred," Sawyer told me like he was a little kid, and another kid had taken the game ball.

"How much is it?"

"It's $108.96," the kid said with an attitude to both of us.

It was enough food to feed an army.

"We aren't allowed to carry more than change for a twenty-dollar bill because we are a target for robberies. I got robbed one time, and the guys robbing me had set me up, so a lady had paid $20, I gave her change, and when she closed the door, two guys jumped out. All I had was $6 on me, and they were very upset about it. I didn't even have the $20 they had just given me, and that was puzzling to them, but once I told them I was recently divorced and my ex gets half of everything, well, those two crooks they understood," he continued in a deadpan.

"You aren't divorced; you're like 14 years old, you ain't even never been married, have you?" I was impressed with the chops of this young man.

"We are told to say that during training, and, indeed, I can't break anything larger than a twenty-dollar bill. We were worried about this order since this house is blacked out on google maps, and on Zillow, it says for sale. You guys also ordered over $100 worth of stuff and put cash. I do have the square reader if you would like to use a card."

He was ready to leave with the money or with the food.

"Great, well, Sawyer, give me a hundred, and I will pay the rest," I told him, and I knew we would still be cleaning up getting all that food for only $8.96.

Sawyer was still holding the shoebox like it was a football after kickoff. He didn't open it up, though. He had a few stuck in his pockets, so he pulled out a ball of them and popped one loose.

"Awe man, you know what, I was being a dick, wasn't I? Here are two fresh, crisp hundred dollar bills. You just keep the eighty-two dollars and forty-four cents, okay kid, since you just got divorced and all. We've all been there!"

He flipped up two more hundreds and handed them to the kid.

"Are you serious?" He asked Sawyer with a look of puzzlement and glee on his face like a puppy getting a treat after he got his balls cut off.

"I sure am, and I am also starving, so come on and unload those bags this way. Come on, into the kitchen," Sawyer said as he grabbed a few bags himself. The kid stuffed the two bills into his pocket, thinking of where he would spend that money.

Once he put the food down, I went to get dressed, and I heard Sawyer tell the young man, "I like you, kid, what's your name?"

"Ted." He answered back, now wondering what was going on.

"Here you go, Ted, here is another fresh one hundred dollar bill as a tip. I know divorce is hard, so there you go, run off!" Sawyer told the kid who probably didn't even have a girlfriend. He was showing off with his money, so I just rolled my eyes.

I went to get dressed, and then I remembered I had to see what was up with Morgan. She had likely been handling the bad publicity from the FBI all day.

So I sent her a text. I was interested in seeing how far this counterfeit money could go and if it was the same money I had been getting paid with all summer. It had worked at the offshore casino and anywhere else, but now that I knew they were possibly fake, I started to wonder. Not one person had taken even a second glance at these things.

I picked up my phone to respond to Morgan, picturing Morgan in my head. She was the hottest woman I had seen in the District, and perhaps I had ever seen. And it might have been the money that Sawyer had, or maybe something else, but I was feeling extra confident, so I just texted her, "What are you doing tonight? You wanna hang?"

Sawyer was already knee-deep into the food, so I grabbed a fork to join him. It was enough to keep an army in Russia through the winter, and we ate like kings. The shoebox was full of hundreds sitting on the chair at the dining room table with us. I ate until my stomach bloated.

"Yo, what are you going to do with the money, though? You can't just put it into the bank."

"Somehow, they can fake the magnetic strip inside of it. You can see it's part of the printing on the part of it. I guess it depends if it can stand up to the test of one of those pens."

He had been giving the subject a ton of thought since he

realized the Russians weren't returning. He was holding a hundred in one hand, shoving his face, and then wiping his face clean very delicately with the hundred. He was talking with an air.

"So if it fails one of those many tests, I guess then I have to buy narcotics and learn the drug trade, or perhaps I will invest in the stock market."

"Honestly, I think they have been paying me these the whole time. I think I have been cashing them the entire summer across the country."

Sawyer dropped the aristocrat accent and started to cheese before saying, "We should for sure go to the strip club!"

"Dude, you would blow that whole shoebox in a tittie bar, man."

"Then I would come back and print another one!"

Even I laughed at that.

"I am not leaving this box anywhere. I will sleep with it if I have to. I need to take a shower, but what's going on here? The Ruskies aren't coming home, are they? We should throw a big ass house party," He said, and he headed upstairs to shower.

Morgan had texted me again. "Do you think you can still run the piece on me even if she doesn't win?"

I had forgotten that the FBI was reopening the case against Hillary and how that would affect the piece Morgan thought I could get in the *Rolling Stone*. I shot her a text back.

"I will try my hardest to run something on you for sure."

I wasn't lying. It just wasn't what she thought. Hillary was likely screwed. I still wanted to hang out with her, so I hit up Eddie and asked him where he was spinning later. And I also added that I wanted to buy some bottles.

Eddie texted me back. "You don't ever buy bottles, but if you do want to come out, I am at the rooftop spot where you threw up off the side.

Morgan called me shortly after, and I could tell she was distraught. I wanted to see her, but I knew she was in a bad mood with the new news. Her voice was just a level up from crying.

"It's all over for Hillary, isn't it?"

"Is that a joke? She is up; what is it like 13 or 14 points in the polls? The only thing keeping her from working in the Oval Office in January is if she dies tomorrow. That's it."

I didn't believe that, but I didn't want to tell Morgan the truth. I wanted to hang out with her.

I could hear her spirits start to pick up through the phone as she asked me back, "Do you really think so?"

She sounded like a child asking if Santa Claus was real.

"Yeah, I do. Let's just say F all this Hillary and Trump stuff for one night. My boy Eddie is DJing tonight, I think at this place that is like a rooftop bar-"

"The Rooftop? The big Halloween party?" She chimed in excitedly, like we were talking about her birthday party.

"Yeah, so I got my boy in town just for tonight, and we want to have some fun. I am going to buy bottles and do it real big. Why don't you join us?"

"You are going to buy bottles? I think I need to get a job at Rolling Stone." She said without a hint of sarcasm.

"Just how I roll," I said with as much confidence as I could muster, and then I added, "So bring a friend for my buddy Sawyer, and let's make it a night."

"I will be with my friends, and if you can get me on the list, that would be great. I would love to hang out with you tonight, Gunner. I didn't know you danced or went to clubs or anything. We could have been hanging out," She said, and I didn't know if she was saying that because she liked me, or she liked the idea of sitting in VIP after skipping the line to get inside the club or if she just wanted a piece in Rolling Stone. All three could be true.

"Tonight we can, and you can finally fall in love," I said real smoothly, and I knew it was a winning line. I had confidence in my voice.

"Huh, I couldn't hear you," She replied, and my chest dropped a bit. She added, "so you know that DJ? Do you think you can have him play my song tonight?"

And before she even said the name of the song, I knew it was going to be a terrible choice.

"Absolutely!"

"Okay, it's White Iverson by Post Malone," She said back, and I didn't know it was going to be all the way trash. "Post Malone is so cute!"

That's when I realized I had a chance. Post Malone was the first guy in the world to master the effect of looking poor and rich at the same time, but his shitty pop music was worse than a roach crawling up your crack. It meant she had terrible taste. And that opened up doors for me.

"I will have him play your song on repeat if you like," I told her, and I puffed my shoulders back up a bit, and sure, she couldn't see me, but she could hear the confidence in my voice.

"I can't wait to see you tonight! We will be there at about noon, and I will be dressed as a kitty!" She made a meowing sound before we hung up.

Ten days out from election day, the freaking FBI re-opened the investigation into Hillary Clinton's emails. The same emails Bernie Sanders had told the world to shut up about. Everything Trump had said was coming true. Hillary was crooked. Sawyer was right. Dude D was correct too. Julie Awning wasn't lying. Trump was about to pull it off. Somehow Julie Awning had known the investigation would reopen and kill Hillary's chances. It was bigger than Kissinger's "Peace is at hand" and as big as Reagan keeping the hostages tied up. Julie Awning had an inside scoop inside the FBI. The whole thing felt corrupt, and it was!

The power went out. Sawyer yelled about 20 seconds later, "see, that's why you gotta pay your bills, Gunner! You are just as fucked as Crooked Hillary is. The FBI will lock her up, and then come looking for your white ass next! How long have I been telling you she is a crook!"

"You are the one with a shoebox full of counterfeit money, not me," I said, reminding him that he was implicated at least a little already, and if he cashed any of the money, he was a willing conspirator.

"You think that was the October Surprise?" I asked him, and I noticed he had changed his jeans, finally, and he was wearing a Hawaiian button-up shirt that Dirk had left in his closet. The buttons were about to burst open since it was too small for him, but he didn't care. He was happy to have a new shirt, and I was delighted he wouldn't wear the Rambo Trump shirt. He was still figuring out if he should button the top two buttons or not.

"The real October surprise will be next week when they lock her ass up the day before the election," He said.

"Next week will be November. Are you wearing that shirt that not even the weird Russian guy wanted to take with him?" I said to him. I regretted it immediately. I was fearful he might change into the Trump Rambo shirt.

"November surprise then whatever, and yeah, yeah I am. I love Hawaiin shirts, but I don't have any. Plus, you and I both know the Ruskies aren't coming back. Unless you heard from them?"

"No, I haven't, but I did talk to one of the hottest ladies I have ever seen, and she wants to meet us for drinks tonight, and I know the DJ of a club, this rooftop spot, so he is going to hook us up with some bottles on the low. We get to skip the line, sit in VIP, you know the routine, but we gotta buy a few bottles. I figured we could test out the bills. Plus, it's a Halloween event, so you have an excuse for wearing that ugly ass shirt. What do you think?"

"Sure. Let me go print some more. How much are bottles, and how many are we buying?" He asked me.

"They are like a buck apiece, I think," I said back, but I didn't know. I had never bought a bottle in the club, and I had drunk plenty of bottles in the club, but only after buying them at the liquor store and snuck them into the club.

"I will have to text Eddie and ask him." I did, and he said it depends on the liquor but anywhere from a hundred and twenty to three hundred fifty.

I told Sawyer, and he was in the downstairs bathroom using his phone flashlight, staring at himself in the mirror.

"Tell him we want six bottles, and I will print off five new pages of bills just for the club. That's the total we can spend, though, got it?"

"Shit, I can't print off any; there is no power. You gotta learn how to pay your bills, Gun!"

I didn't say anything. I texted Eddie back and told him,

and he just wrote me back saying I better not be joking. I wasn't kidding. I wasn't going to be like the ordinary peasants at the club tonight. Tonight, I would be drinking in the VIP after skipping the line to get inside. This was my one chance with Morgan. So I was playing the game, and if I played, I wanted to win. My confidence was sky high too. I had questioned whether I had made the correct choice with my bet, but now, I knew. Trump was just handed the White House because of this FBI investigation. Hillary was fucked. This investigation announcement was already more significant than the Access Hollywood tape that had come out earlier this month, but that felt like months ago now.

Trump understood how to play the media, and Julie Awning had inside information. There was no way this October Surprise just fell into Julie Awning's lap like a shoebox full of hundred-dollar bills.

Sawyer came back holding the shoebox like before, and I couldn't brush my hair or straighten up at all. It was pitch black. Sawyer starts putting rolls of hundred-dollar bills all over himself. In his pockets, his socks, his tighty whities, everywhere he could. He was stuffed full of hundred-dollar bills like some sort of Scrooge McDuck piggy bank, but he couldn't fit all the money.

"Maybe I should hide some of this money in the rental car in case the Russians do come in, and we need to order some booze ASAP," he said, turning to me and shining his flashlight right into my eyes.

"Get that out of my fa-"

"I'm going to hide the printer and the computer in the rental too. Where are the keys?"

I tossed him the keys. He went upstairs and returned in about 5 minutes holding the odd, black printer and the tower computer.

"There is only a little bit of that paper left," He told me as he almost tripped and dropped everything. He went outside, and I sat back plotting for the night.

It wasn't just going to be a great night. We had a whole shoebox full of reasons to make it a legendary night. Sawyer came back in a few minutes later, and he had found a handle of Heaven Hill vodka in the garage that the Russians left.

"Looky lookie," He said, holding it, and then added loudly, "Let's do some shots!"

And he went into the kitchen and came out holding two glasses.

This vodka was pure fire. Vodka never tastes good, but this was terrible. We drank it, though, because, after two shots, nothing tastes bad. This was cheap vodka in a plastic gallon, the lowest of the lows, but we didn't mind. We could buy any type of liquor we wanted, top of the line, with counterfeit money, of course, and we were chugging the lowest wells.

CHAPTER 21

We were buzzing like bumblebees by the time our Uber showed up. Sawyer yelled shotgun and jumped into bucket while I slid into the back and texted Morgan. I was anxious but ready to have a great night. I wanted to look good, smell good, and be good towards Morgan so I wouldn't blow my chance of hooking up with her. She was all I thought about, so I texted her; Sawyer pulled out a smoke.

"You cannot smoke in here!" The driver yelled at Sawyer as he lit it up.

And I leaned up and smacked Sawyer on the arm, but he wasn't putting out his smoke. He pulled out a hundred-dollar bill.

"How about my good buddy, Benjamin Franklin? Can he smoke in here?"

The man took the money and replied, "Yes, that is fine, but do not change my radio station!"

And of course, Sawyer turned to stare at the radio station, pulled out another hundred dollar bill.

"What about the guy I was telling you about, Mr. Franklin? Can he hear some metal? Do you have any Flaw? And Bukshot, I want to hear some old-school Ville stuff, Mr. Harlow,

Crash, the fat dude freestyling!"

The whole ride to the club, Sawyer asked the driver to do stupid shit, and then poof like a magician, he would pop out a Franklin. He had the guy hook up his aux to hear obscure songs from Youtube, including Flaw. He even gave the guy a bill just to roll down his freaking window, which I am sure is allowed. I am sure Sawyer knew that, but he gave the guy a wrinkled-up bill regardless.

Sawyer was supposed to be cracking the bills to get change back from real money. Instead, he was handing them out like donation baskets at church.

So finally, I stuck my head up to Sawyer, and I told him, "Look, you've been handing out bills like handkerchiefs in a ground pepper factory. Can you just chill?"

Then he told the guy to stop at the Liquor Store. He wanted to bring something into the club. I had to remind him; we had six bottles of booze waiting on us; he slowed his roll and changed his mind. We were almost at the rooftop spot too. He'd spent $800 for a $17.00 uber ride.

Sawyer was proving the old adage that a fool and his money are soon parted.

We skipped the lines and went straight to the VIPs' access when we got out. Walking by and putting our noses up at the peasants waiting in line was a false sense that we were better than them. We didn't want to do this, but it is required at most well-known clubs.

We looked down at the peasants standing in line as if they were below us, and while we didn't want to do this, it is required at most well-known clubs.

Two beautiful Latina models escorted us to our section in the club. Sawyer's blood left his head and hit his pants soon as he saw them, and I knew he was going to blow tons of loot on these two ladies before we even got seated inside the club. So they walk us into the club, and Eddie comes over to meet us. He looked at Sawyer in his skin-tight Hawaiian shirt, and he didn't say it, but I could see by the way he was looking that he was trying to figure out who Sawyer was. Sawyer was buying six bottles of booze with cash and tipping a hundred to everyone in sight.

"Nice to meet you," Eddie said, smoking a black and mild.

Sawyer put away a roll of hundreds and shook his hand.

"Let's get some drinks going down now!" Sawyer said. He was nervous, but I agreed because it would keep him from dropping hundreds to everyone.

So we all did a shot, and then one of the ladies made us drinks with one of the bottles and the orange juice. Eddie thanked us for the shot, but Sawyer wouldn't let him leave.

"Man, he has to go deejay his set," I informed Sawyer.

"I mean, I can stay; it's not like anybody is here yet," Eddie said, and I looked around. The dance floor was empty.

"Yeah, it's about as dead as the morgue in here; what gives?"

"Dude, it's 10 minutes until 10 pm; nobody is at the club yet. I get that you guys wanted to come in early and drink on your six bottles, but it's still early."

And he was right.

"We walked by a gang of people outside; they were in line," I informed him as Sawyer told one of the Latinas who walked us in to make Eddie a drink too.

"Yeah, there's a line of people outside right now," Sawyer added as he stretched out on the couch across from us.

"I don't even have the speakers fully on yet; that line is people that work here. That entices people to come into the club, and it also entices people to want to buy bottles to come up here to the VIP part of the club. Working it sucks, though, and it's a lottery, man. I've stood out in that line. All those people work here; they are bouncers, shot girls, bartenders, barbacks, hosts like these two beautiful Dominican sisters you have here, Yaya and Jazmin!"

And he stood up to hug the two beautiful ladies as they handed him his drink. I finally checked my phone, and Eddie was right. It wasn't even 10 pm yet, and we were beyond tipsy already. Morgan had texted that she would arrive around noon. Midnight. It was still two hours away, and I would need to drink some water. Sawyer had the two Latina ladies make us all drinks, though, so before I could even think of getting H2O, it was time to destroy my liver even more.

Two hours later, I was annihilated. We both were, and somewhere Eddie was barely standing behind turntables. Our hosts, the beautiful Latinas, were smashed somewhere about to puke, and the two bouncers that came in later were indeed drunk as Sawyer gave them a bottle to split. And who knows if they are supposed to drink on the job, surely they do, but they weren't just drunk tonight. They were hammered. I was split.

By the time Morgan showed up, I was seeing double, and both of her looked good. We were mixing our colors with our drinking, and the plastic vodka we had back at the mansion all started to blend in and create vertigo in my brain.

Morgan and her two friends sat down.

"Did you guys drink all the liquor?" She asked me.

I didn't know if we had or hadn't. But of course, we had. Six empty bottles sat on the table in front of us.

Sawyer didn't want the party to stop, though, so he ordered another round. And he told the two Latinas, but they didn't understand what he was saying.

The taller Latina asked, "You want another six bottles, sir?"

"Yes, I do!" Sawyer said, and he started to pull out a wad from his nasty sock. Morgan grimaced, and that was it. That is the very last thing I remember, I guess. Sawyer was pulling out a wad of bills from his crusty sock. He ordered six more bottles of booze, and neither one of us needed another drop for days. He fiddled with his bills and handed over the $900.

Seconds later, I was in the bathroom, fearful I might puke. Somehow, I didn't. I don't remember exiting the bathroom, and I blacked out at that point.

I was blacked out drunk.

CHAPTER 22

When I woke up, I was in my bed in the mansion; Morgan was next to me, clothed, but not all the way, sleeping with her back to me. I was pretty sure we didn't have sex. I still had my shirt on, but not my pants and one sock. I crept to get off my bed into the bathroom.

"Good morning, sunshine."

She was awake!

"Yeah, so, yeah," I said, scratching my head.

"Well, you got plastered last night, and," she sat up and covered herself with her shirt, and turned to me, "I had to take care of you and stop you from getting beat up."

"What, what happened?"

"Yeah, well, your friend and his cash almost got us kicked out of the club."

"Where is Sawyer?"

"Oh, he is in that other bedroom down the hall with my friends, but-"

I had to cut her off.

"You're other friends? Both of them?" I asked.

"Yes, you don't remember coming back here, and we called the power company, and you had to get on the phone, and Kristen paid for it on her credit card, and your friend gave her the money from his fucking shoebox?"

"Oh no - what did you say about the money?"

"No, he paid her; he probably paid her to sleep with him. Although, she liked him before she knew he had money or that much money."

"No about the money at the club, and the -"

"Oh, you don't remember when that guy hit you, and he said your friend was giving out fake hundreds, and then the DJ came over, and they had to use that pen to mark the money to prove it was real? You were on that couch with me. You didn't even want to hurt that guy after he hit you. That's when all hell broke out, but you were just sitting there on the couch, bleeding and drinking a bottle of vodka asking for water. Sawyer moved that whole table and chair out of the way, and the DJ got that guy kicked out. You plastered when I showed up; that was like ten minutes after we got there!"

"No, I mean, I don't know how many I had. So Sawyer is in that other room with that girl and the other girl?" I asked her, now worried about who was in the mansion.

"Yeah."

She jumped up to run into the bathroom before I did. She didn't shut the door, though, so I peeked my head in a bit. Not to look at anything, but to ask her more questions because I couldn't remember anything. She was staring at herself in the mirror.

"Sawyer is where with who?"

I was still confused.

"He was in one of the bedrooms with Kristen."

I didn't have a clue who Kristen was.

"It's all a blur; I am sorry, who is Kristen?"

She stuck her head back out of the bathroom.

"You don't remember if we had sex or not, do you?"

And I didn't. She was bending over, showing her breasts. I was hoping we did but figured we didn't.

"We didn't, well, at least I don't think we did," I replied, but I was wondering.

"We didn't, but we would have done it if you could hold your liquor! Just joking, or am I?"

She looked serious, but she laughed after saying it, so I will never know.

"Well, we gotta run. I texted Kristen and told her to meet me downstairs in two minutes. Our Uber is here."

She walked back towards me after grabbing her phone. She looked better than amazing, and I can't believe I missed my chance.

She gave me a big hug and whispered in my ear, "I never have sex on the first date, but I was thinking about it with you."

And then she turned around and started to leave.

"Was I all over you when we were back here? I mean, Jesus Chrysler, you look amazing," I told her as she walked away, and she looked great leaving.

"Gunny," she said, turning around, "you were asleep by the time we got back here. Me and the DJ guy had to carry you upstairs."

She spun back around and added, "I've got to get to work!"

"The DJ?"

"Yeah, he's in that other bedroom with those two Spanish ladies."

I was the only one who didn't get any. Eddie got twice the love.

The door to the other room opened, and out walked an attractive young model-looking female.

"Good morning," I said, and she smiled back. It was the first time I had ever seen her, and it wasn't, but I couldn't have picked her out of a pair.

I looked down the hallway, and I could see both doors shut. It was early, perhaps not even 8 am yet, so I went back to bed, and I wasn't even hungover yet; I was still drunk.

When I woke up for the second time, I was met with a hangover and headache from hell. I stumbled into the shower and tried to cure my hangover with a cold shower; reality set in like a bad sunburn. Using my poor math skills, I guesstimated that Terry had paid me around 42 thousand dollars in fake money. That's if all the money she paid me was fake. I was always paid in all hundreds, but I had no way of knowing if they were all counterfeit. If it was, it was only 425 fake bills.

My calculations added up to Terry, Olga and Dirk, and maybe others, making millions by this same formula of speculation. Perhaps billions, but at least millions. The three became millionaires easily overnight; these were Russians working for the Russian government or oligarchs, living in a mansion, and networking in America's capital city. They were attacking something, going after information, stealing, spying; it was espionage.

They had scored big and then disappeared.

Now would come the reason they left so quickly, and I was right in the crosshairs of whatever it was. They had played me like a fiddle, and the fiddling was done.

We probably shouldn't have even spent the night in the mansion; we should have gotten out of Dodge, but I didn't know what to do. There was a reason the Russians always had their nose up at me. They despised me. That's the only thing I ever picked up about them. And now, I have started to learn that my initial instinct was correct. They were Russians, and Russians don't love Americans. Americans are the sworn enemy. They would have killed me if that was the order. And I didn't have a freaking clue. That's the problem with most Americans. We are undereducated on top of being dumb —all of us. Myself included. Collectively not taught enough in school as a whole. Most Americans thought Russians loved us after the fall of the U.S.S.R. It was all a smokescreen of malarkey. These Russians were here stealing our culture so they could get inside of it.

The Berlin Wall and communism fell, but the hatred of Americans by the people of Russia was still standing. There was no love for the Americans after the fall of the great motherland. Vladimir Putin made sure that all Russians remembered December 26th, 1991. And he wanted to make America fall into pieces just like their sickle and hammer had.

They had left in a hurry, burning pounds of paper on their way out of the door, so I assumed they were spies. I didn't know what to do, who to call, or what I would even say if I did call someone. If I contacted the FBI, they might line up the charges against me since ignorance of the law was not an excuse. It was terrifying. And it wasn't even the biggest pickle I was in as I still needed to figure out what to do with Sawyer. I stepped out of the shower without resolving either one. I got dressed and opened my door.

The two lovely ladies from the club were in the hallway, and they said hello.

"Good morning. Are you two lovely ladies leaving?" I asked, and they came and hugged me and then went down the stairs. Eddie came out a second later.

"My brother is on his way to pick us up, man, thanks for letting me crash here. You got a nice ass crib."

He was holding his shirt and wearing a wife-beater shirt, and the belt on his jeans unfastened.

"Man, I am licking my wounds already! You got all that delivery food downstairs, but not a single drop to drink in this whole house."

He pulled his shirt on and started to fasten his belt. The two ladies were giggling about something.

"Yeah, man, this ain't my place. And I ain't been here in a few weeks, so that's why there is nothing to drink," I informed him, and then we both walked down the stairs.

"Well, the place is nice. Wild that the power was out when we got here, though. They thought," he said, pointing to the two ladies, "that you guys were mooches or squatting here. I thought that was pretty funny, but your boy, Gunner! Your boy is a handful in a half. He doesn't trust banks or what?"

"Yeah, he's just old school."

The place was a wreck. All the food boxes we had ordered were all over the living room coffee table, and the plastic vodka bottle was empty and on the floor.

"Man, Eddie, I don't know what I am going to do about this house." I moved a pillow and sat down on the couch.

"What do you mean, youngblood?" he asked me as he lit up a smoke.

There was a pile of old smoke on a plate, so obviously, I had let everyone smoke in the house while I was drunk. I started to explain to him some of my predicament. He sat there smoking and listening. The two ladies had gone to find something to drink in the kitchen and never returned.

I told Eddie the basis of everything dealing with the mansion and how the cable, water, and electricity were in my name. And how I couldn't get a hold of Terry, Dirk, or Olga, and how all the papers had been burned.

"I kinda wished I had known that before I came over here putting my fingerprints on everything. So you never put the gas and stuff in your name?"

"Naw, never. I don't understand it," I told him, and I was looking for some words of advice. He didn't offer any, though. He just stared at the flat screen that wasn't on and smoked.

"I don't know what to do," I said, trying to get a rise out of him. Any help would be helpful, and I needed input besides my own.

"Maybe I should call the cops, it's obviously been some sort of identity theft here, and that feels like the minimum."

"Man, I wouldn't tell the cops a goddamn thing. Don't turn yourself in. Let me tell you about another white friend of mine, Tommy. He's a cool cat, humble, doesn't even smoke, and rarely drinks. Almost a church-going dude without the church, married, couple kids, you feel me? Only way I know him is because he likes to cheat on his wife; well, that's not important. So he was up in the B-dale one night back in the summer, cheating on his wife, like I said, he had a thing for that type of thing. He's out late or early; it's like four am or just after, I think, and he has to get home before his wife gets up in the morning, and if he can do that, she won't know if he came home at midnight or 5 am, ya feel me?"

"So he was out cheating on his wife; why was she a cunt or something," I asked him, not understanding the complexity of marriage yet.

"He don't really like women," he paused for a smoke and then jumped right back into his story.

"So he's leaving this guy's house, it's after four, and he stops to tie his shoe and just sits low for a minute tying his shoe and thinking what to tell his wife. He told me he wasn't paying attention to anything but just thinking. And he hears a gunshot, boom. He looks, and sees two men shot this guy in the back for no reason, didn't rob him or nothing. They just shot him in the back. So Tommy falls to the ground. Tommy says it was like they wanted this guy dead, but I know he just got there late. They was robbing him, and then they shot him. Old school shit, and being in B-dale that early in the morning, I could tell you some stories, and if they wanted him dead, they woulda shot him in the head, not the back. It doesn't matter because Tommy cut out fast as hell. He is figuring two shots to the back; nobody survives that, right? The guy is dead as a doorknob. He was an eyewitness."

"Whoa!"

"Yeah, you can feel that heat, right? So he fucking bounces out of there, and he says just a minute or two later, he hears sirens and everything. He didn't want to tell his wife the truth, right? He gets home fast and then lies to her about being home.

He knows it's a gunshot and not a car backfiring, right. It's close to him too, so he stays low, and he looks up and sees what he thinks is a black man running, and he watches him rummage through his pockets, stealing shit, his phone, his wallet, ya know, right? The guy is dead as a doorknob. So Tommy is watching, and the man runs away. He goes over, slow, ya know because he don't know if this guy might come back and shoot him. He stands over the guy, and there isn't a lot of blood, but the guy ain't moving, like I said, he's dead as a doorknob, right? He checks his vitals or thinks he does, he told me he kinda blacked out and knew the guy was gone. He wasn't struggling to breathe or nothing; he was just dead. So what's he do? He fucking bounces out of there, you hear me? He has just been an eyewitness to murder, but he didn't want to have to lie to his wife, right? He gets home as fast as he can and then lies to his wife about when he got home."

"So he did lie to his wife?"

I was more confused than a dog doing a puzzle.

"You get what I mean, right?"

I nodded back, and he continued.

"So a few days pass, and he starts seeing this shit on the news and whatnot. He comes over to my place and is drinking; like I said, this guy ain't no drinker. He gets the liquor in him, and we are talking, and he tells me what happened. He was drunk and balling the whole nine."

Eddie sat up and ashed his smoke, then put it to his mouth and took a long drag. I was anxiously waiting for a punchline the size of the one Jim Jones served.

I just muttered out, "I don't know," because I didn't.

Eddie jumped back into the story like I hadn't said anything.

"Tommy thinks he can help solve this crime maybe, even though he doesn't remember shit, and I had to tell him. Don't say shit. It ain't even snitching because the cops will pin it on Tommy if anything. I told him that, and they would have to. I mean a white guy who has been lying about being out that night, lying about having gay sex, lying to his wife, cheating on his wife, and he comes out and says he knows who shot this guy; it was a black guy!"

He took another hit on his smoke and then blew it out.

"A black guy did it. I done seen that movie too many times, right? White people done it enough times now, and sure, sometimes it might work, and shit, sometimes it might be truth, but Tommy ain't gonna risk his wife finding out he likes sex with men. Police and prosecutors would pin that shit on Tommy quick as fleas on a dog. Election year, ya feel lat?"

"Uh-huh."

"I told Tommy keep his mouth shut; three people can keep a secret if two is dead. The shooter is gonna keep his mouth shut, for sure! Shit, me knowing is enough, so Tommy shut the fuck up and hasn't told nobody else that I know of anyway. Shit, him telling me is more than enough, you feel lat, youngblood?"

"What's that have to do with me, though?"

"Ain't you been listening?" Eddie said, and then he added, "don't turn yourself in, then they can blame you for the whole crime. Let the dumbass cops try to figure it out and put the pieces together; if they do, cooperate. If they don't, fuck 'em."

He shook his head at me as I had just missed everything he had said. And I had, besides the point about the cops pinning everything on me. He hadn't passed the bar, but Eddie did have a great point. I shouldn't make it easy for the cops to lock me up. I wasn't going to live on the lam like the outlaw Josey Wales, but I wasn't going to rush into the precinct either.

As the ladies came back into the living room, we heard a knock, and Eddie stood up, "that's my brother, thanks for the hospital towel and tea." He said jokingly.

"Hospitality," I said, laughing, and they left.

I had a more significant problem, though, and I couldn't pawn off my next problem by doing nothing. I had to figure out what to do with Sawyer.

CHAPTER 23

I needed to think and clear my head, so I grabbed my longboard and hit the streets. The District is unique with historic buildings and landmarks, but skateboarding is a sin in the city. I didn't care most of the time, and there were still spots that skaters could hit despite the city officials frowning upon the activities. There is no skate park in the District, and it just proves that a city without a skate park becomes a skate park.

I wasn't really in the mood to skate, though. And that's the first time that I felt like an adult in my life. I couldn't run from this problem, and I couldn't drown it out with booze despite my trying. I needed answers, but I didn't even know the questions.

I kicked over to Freedom Plaza.

Winter was coming in with every gust of wind, so it wasn't ideal skating weather. I pulled up before the park and sat down on the stairs by a statue of a Polish General. I opened my phone and scrolled through my contact list, wondering who could ask for advice.

I had Sawyer's parents' numbers, but I didn't know what to tell them or the balls to call them. Sawyer had texted me wondering where I was and telling me that he would buy a flight home with his cash. He was still adamant about getting home before Halloween. And that was the biggest reason I felt he was still on track to follow through with his plans.

I thought about calling my mom, but I didn't want to drag her into this. She had her stuff going on, and my old man was too rational. He would tell me to call the law. Which was probably the right thing to do, but there had to be another way. Plus, they would find me guilty of something, somehow, and lock me up too. The fake hundreds and my name on every bill in the house were scary enough. I didn't want the law involved; they would do what they always do and make it more complicated.

I thought about texting Eddie, stopping by his place, smoking one, and then getting some wisdom from the OG again, but that felt a little invasive even if all OGs love giving out advice. Just because they give out advice doesn't mean it's worth taking. His advice earlier had been golden, but I didn't want to drag him into this too.

So I texted Morgan. My confidence wasn't as high as it had been with her, but I did want to see her again regardless. She was pre-law or in law school at Georgetown before working for Hillary. I had messed up by getting too plastered the night before, and I wanted to make it up to her. I wasn't confident she would text me back, though.

When she did, I didn't get too excited, but I was thrilled she hit me back. I asked her if she wanted to get some coffee, and I added, "I know you just saw me, but I do have some important legal questions I don't know who to talk with about."

She hit me right back and said she could go for some coffee. I told her I was at the plaza, and
she could meet me at a Bucks by the Smithsonian. I skated over, knowing it would take her a minute to get there from her house by the Hill.

I went inside, ordered, and got us a booth in the back and did some people watching while I waited.

After I drank my coffee, she walked in. She was wearing a tan pants suit that set her body off like she could have been cast and molded in the Parthenon. I ordered another coffee and bought her one, and of course, the bench I had been sitting in for 23 minutes was taken as soon as I stood up.

We found a new one and sat down.

I wanted to punch myself in the head for fucking up, but that wouldn't do me any good, so I just tried to play it cool. It was probably as far away from cool as could be, though.

We started to small talk, and it didn't take me long to realize that Morgan was using her looks on me for something. I wondered if she was even interested in me at all when she let me know what she was interested in, and it was an article on all the work she had done for Hillary, and she jumped into it before she even hit her mocha.

"If we can get it dropped before the election, it would help, but the charges are mostly bullshit and not even charges against Hillary. The FBI is up to something with this crock of shit. Hillary is still polling ahead, and she is still likely going to win this election."

I couldn't tell if it was to convince herself or me. I could tell that she wasn't sure that Hillary would win, but if she did, she still wanted to be named press secretary. So naturally, she wanted me to do a piece on her, and a significant feature in *Rolling Stone Magazine* would help her secure the position.

She was ranting and raving, and I abruptly cut through her vanity and said, "I think Sawyer wants to do a mass shooting, and he has it planned out for Halloween."

I said it fast, direct, and right as she caught her breath

and thoughts.

She took a second sip of her mocha, pulled herself up-right, and whispered, "no."

Her forehead wrinkled as she thought; then she asked me, "did he tell you this or what?"

"Not exactly, but I stumbled into his diary, and I read the plans; you see, Sawyer is married. He is actually married, yeah, but his wife is ch-"

"Cheating on him. Yeah, he told us all that last night."

She wiggled in her seat like something was wrong, but she didn't want me to know.

"He told you that he was married and that his wife was cheating on him? He barely even told me!"

I was upset, but I was also trying to process information as it hit me.

"Yeah, he told all of us that. I guess when you were sleeping after you threw up. And then he said --"

She paused and moved her eyes around, thinking. Something was wrong.

"And then he said what?"

"He said he was going to shoot the guy that was screw-ing his wife and then shoot his wife and everyone at her office and then shoot himself."

She stared at me coldly, and I was wondering why she hadn't called the cops or at least mentioned this to me.

"That escalated quickly; how did that not change the mood of the night?"

"Well, after that, he laughed and said he was joking, and

he was going to try to get alimony."

She was thinking as she said it and not even looking at me.

She added, "It felt forced, the end part, like the hair on the back of my neck, it stood straight up, and my bones got cold. It was an odd vibe, and it's happening again now."

She held out her arm showing goosebumps.

"So yeah, now what?"

I watched her shiver her entire body. She sipped her drink.

"I don't know."

I could sense she didn't like the situation any more than I did.

"I can't call the cops. They can't even arrest him; he, and it's hasn't committed a crime."

"What about his parents?"

"I know his parents, um, they are divorced, his old man is an attorney, and his mom is remarried; I don't speak to either one, though."

"Well, let's start there and see what happens."

I was thrilled she was making this a group effort because if I had to call Mr. Barnes and inform him his son might be planning a mass shooting, well, I don't think I could.

"His mom or his dad?" I asked.

"Both, I don't know. This sounds serious. Did you walk here or drive? We can head to my place and call them."

"I rode my board," I held it up.

She stood up, and she was ready to leave, so I did too. It was exactly what I needed, and for all the talk about a strong woman being a bad thing. I was ecstatic that she was taking control and helping me.

Her place was brick colonial in the middle of the block. We walked in, and it was full of Hillary campaign stuff and a few staffers making phone calls in what should be a dining room area. There was a station set up for phone banking in the dining room and part of the kitchen. I saw a wooden box of Cuban cigars; they were preparing for election night.

Her bedroom was in the back. It was a maid's room with the bathroom right in the back. There was a bookshelf in the front, and I flipped through a few books while she moved around some laundry so I could sit. She wasn't used to company. She tossed the clothes onto the small bed and pulled a chair out for me.

"We all have that chair," I said, trying to lighten the mood, but she was already in attorney mode or something.

She sat on the bed and asked me, "Are you going to call him?"

"I don't know what to say."

She was taking notes in her head. She will make a solid attorney one day.

She stood up, reached by me, grabbed a legal pad on the desk behind me, and pulled herself back to her bed. She started to scribble out a map of what in the hell we were going to do. And I was grateful as hell.

Finally, she agreed to call Mr. Barnes, but she wanted me to talk to him too. So, of course, I agreed, but it turned out to be a sham because as soon as she identified herself on the phone, she said, "Gunner Bush wants to talk to you about your son

Sawyer!"

And she handed me the phone.

I took the phone, but I didn't say anything. I could hear Mr. Barnes getting frustrated without him saying a word. Finally, I was able to say, "Mis--te-r Mil-uh, I wanted to tell you 'bout Sawyer."

But he didn't have the patience, and I didn't have the onions.

Morgan snatched the phone and took over. She told him exactly what was going on, smooth as an operator reading a script. It was like she had been rehearsing it all day. I couldn't hear Mr. Barnes' responses, but they were quick. She did most of the talking and wrote out the word "SSRIs" and "Is he not taking his meds?" I nodded yes, and I was timid as I didn't want to get back on the phone with Mr. Barnes. I didn't know what to say.

The conclusion by the lawyer and future lawyer came to agree that an intervention type of ordeal was the best course of action. Since Sawyer was with me, and I was the one driving him back to the Ville, it was decided that the best location to do this would be my apartment in the Ville. I suggested his dad's office at least 20 times, but they informed me that that would be suspicious and Sawyer might not even go with me.

My apartment in the Ville was a dumper in Germantown, and I hadn't been there since June. It was just a place to park the El Camino I'd purchased in August. It was $480 a month with a garage, not an ideal place to have Sawyer's family over for an intervention. If Morgan's room was cluttered, my place was pitiful.

Sawyer's dad offered to buy us two plane tickets back to the Ville for the next day. I was supposed to tell Sawyer that I would drive him to St. Louis from my place, and I agreed, and

Morgan wrote down his contact info. Then he asked to speak to me.

"I'm glad you told me this, Gunner. We all know Sawyer has been on and off depressants for the last few years, and that wife is a good for nothing gold digger, but we will get him straightened out. I will have my secretary buy two plane tickets and then email you the information; what is your email?"

"GunnerBush at Rolling -" I paused. I'd been saying it for five months that it was natural. Now that I couldn't access that email, I had to tell him another one, but I was nervous because Morgan was listening, and she didn't know I didn't work at Rolling Stone anymore or if I ever did.

"Gunner Bush at eye cloud dot com.."

She didn't notice, though. I hung up the phone and immediately told her like a moron with a guilty conscience.

"Yeah, I can't log into my Rolling Stone email."

"Oh yeah? We all know how emails are right now, right?" She said back with a sarcastic smile.

"Well, that was easy," I said like I had done something to help.

"That was intense, huh?" She asked me.

"Yeah, I mean, I've been dealing with him, so it has been tough."

Sawyer had been blowing me up via text, but he called me, and I picked up and let him know I could take him to St. Louis so he could be back by Halloween and that I had just scored plane tickets to the Ville. He wanted to check out the pizza place he had been reading about on his forums, so I told him I would meet him there.

I didn't want to leave, but Morgan had to get back to work; phone banking never ends.

I was about to walk into a headache, and all I wanted to do was chill with Morgan. She was beyond beautiful. I thanked her two or three hundred times before I left, and she said we would get together when I got back from The Ville.

I didn't know if I was coming back from the Ville. I would for her, though. She didn't know about Rolling Stone or Terry or the whole Mansion being empty and all the bills in my name. She didn't know about the counterfeit hundreds, and I wouldn't tell her either. Her helping me with Sawyer was enough. I didn't need to bring all my problems into the relationship now. Those could wait until after our wedding.

I had to face Sawyer and all the problems in my life alone, so I ordered an Uber. She waited outside with me. It was cold with a brisk wind, and I told her five times to go back inside, but she wanted to stay with me. When my Uber showed up, she gave me a big hug, and I didn't want to let her go. She kissed me on the cheek, and I was praying it wasn't the last time I ever saw her.

CHAPTER 24

"Pizzagate"

I met Sawyer to chow at a pizza place, and that's exactly what it was, a pizza place. Sawyer wanted to believe it wasn't with every fiber of his being. It was an average pizza parlor with a friendly staff, above average pizza, and a hipster twist.

Sawyer wasn't seeing the same thing I was though. He was delusional and it felt like he was also psychosis. I saw the Comet logo, he saw a Satanic logo. He swore there was a secret underground lair used to hide children, but when we asked, there was no basement. He knew a ring of pedophiles was using the place for sex trafficking, and he was determined to uncover it. So he went to the bathroom half a dozen times searching for this secret dungeon or hidden doors in the walls. At one point he was certain that a lamp on the wall opened a secret passage. It was hanging above us, and he stood up on the bench and tried to turn it. It didn't turn, and the family across from us thought he was trying to steal the lightbulb or something. He sat back down like nothing happened, and continued to glance around while ignoring the pizza in front of him.

"He's a fire inspector, a similar light burnt down a Chuck E Cheese in Virginia last year. No child was hurt, but the entire band was killed." I yelled across to the family trying to cover for his dumbass as they were still wondering what in the hell was up with Sawyer and the light he was investigating.

"There's a secret staircase around here, I can sense it, and I know that doesn't make sense, but look over at that wall, that wall shouldn't be there. It's a false wall hiding something. John Podesta drinks the blood of children in the basement!"

He said the last part loud enough for Obama to hear it, and the family across from us was asking for their check.

"Dude, are you insane? There isn't a hidden wall, behind that is the kitchen. Did you not see our food come out from there?"

"Gunner, this isn't me, several of my sources online have confirmed all of this!"

He was shaking his head, and I was starting to grow fearful. His lunacy didn't feel innocent. Even if I showed him logic or a fact such as behind the wall was indeed the kitchen, he wouldn't believe it.

"Yeah, the kitchen is back there, but the wall is too thick, I bet that's where the hidden staircase is," he said and then he let me know, "I'm going to check it out!"

He slid to the end of the bench, and he was preparing to dart back into the kitchen.

"I wouldn't eat the pizza, it could be drugged!" He said to me after checking for a waiter, and then he made his move.

Seconds later, I was in the kitchen talking to the head cook with an assistant to the regional manager on his way over.

"I understand this section is closed to the public, but we wanted to throw a party."

"The party room is over...sir, excuse me sir, you can't go back there!" The cook had turned to yell at Sawyer who was still snooping around like he had a warrant.

"Can I help you gentlemen?" The manager asked me.

"He said they were looking for the party ro-"

I cut the cook off.

"We are from Kentucky, and about to start our very own pizza place, and we aren't in any type of competition to your wonderful establishment, or we won't be, and we just wanted to see what type of oven you had back here since you have the best pizza we have ever tasted. It's even better than ours which is saying, well it is saying a lot frankly."

I was lying my dick off, and saving Sawyer's ass from getting a trespassing charge.

"Oh no problem at all, I am the owner!"

"Oh great, I'm Peter Griffin and well my partner in crime here is, Bob Belcher."

I finally got Sawyer's attention, and he started to realize we couldn't be snooping around like Scooby and the Gang. He walked back over, and jumped back into my lie. We spent the next 10 minutes bullshitting about pizza ovens that we didn't know a thing about. We were given names of ovens, companies that sold ovens, websites to buy oven mitts, and a whole bunch of other info we didn't need. We exited the kitchen, I paid for the food, and got Sawyer out of there before he got us arrested.

"Those people were nice, the pizza was solid, I would go back for sure." I said to Sawyer as soon as we were outside.

Sawyer wasn't buying it though.

"I didn't like the manager guy, he seemed fishy, right?"

"Dude, he seemed fishy? How? He was just a guy, a normal freaking guy who is the manager of a pizza place. That's it. He wasn't weird or fishy, he was nice. Overly nice, he didn't have to show us the oven, and where to buy those fire-proof oven mitts. You were illegally trespassing!"

"Overly nice is how kids describe chesters!"

He meant it, but he had pulled it out of his ass. I mean, sure, maybe, but this was just a freaking guy. Reasoning and logic had been thrown out the window though.

"Let's just get back to the mansion and watch the Cubs game, Jesus fucking Chryslar."

I didn't know what to think about Sawyer anymore, I had grown tired of the conspiracy bullshit, but now I was wondering if he wanted to believe this shit. He needed a reason to vote for Trump, or that he wanted it for another reason. He wanted his theories to be true so much that even after seeing proof that they weren't, he still believed there was a slither of hope that just maybe, they were. We all secretly want to be alive during the Armageddon, but Sawyer wanted to be the Sherlock Holmes of conspiracy theories so it had to be true. He was going to keep bringing up 'magical what if' scenarios until it could be true. The wall was extra thick so it had stairs hidden in it, the bathroom had a false wall, the light triggered a hidden area, until he saw it was all bullshit. Then he went with another theory.

"What place do you know built after 1970 doesn't have a basement? Even if it is just a small room with the furnace, a bunker, a crawl space, I mean unless you are really close to the beach, right?"

I didn't have an answer for him. I didn't know a singular fact about basements. I was assured by reason that the pizza place was just that, a pizza parlor. It was a pizza place with workers and people eating pizza, that was it. There was no proof it was hosting a blood drinking parties or it had cells in the basement for sex slaves. We found zero evidence, and we had been there searching for proof.

"Was I right about Crooked Hillary? Seriously, was I? The FBI is about to lock her up, you know that now, I was fucking right about Crooked Hillary, and I am right about this!"

By the time we got back to the mansion after stopping for booze, the Cubs were down big, and I didn't feel like watching it. The Tribe were going to take an insurmountable three games to one lead, and would only need one more win to clinch. The fat lady wasn't officially signing for the Cubs, but the team was pulling up to the opera house.

As the game ended, I was drinking alone upstairs, Sawyer was downstairs. I didn't want to hear it. He needed help, and I was one day away from getting it for him. I didn't feel like skating earlier, and now I didn't feel like watching the Cubs in the freaking World Series!

Something was up.

CHAPTER 25

"Back to the Ville"

Sawyer and I were inseparable and about as far away from each other as two people can be. Our ideologies were just so different, but we were both twisted. We had barely talked all morning. Sawyer mailed a shoebox full of counterfeit money, the black printer, and the computer to my spot in the Ville. It was the only thing we talked about, and he also pocketed a ton of the money and took it with him. I don't know how much, but enough.

He couldn't send it to his spot as his wife still checked the mail, and technically she still lived there. And since we weren't talking, he wanted to change his flight and just fly straight back to the Lou. So I had to lie to him and start acting like I wasn't upset with him. I felt like a shitty friend, though, which began to hit me the hardest. Maybe all Sawyer had needed over the last year was a friend. His wife had left him, he lost his job, he was a man on the ledge close to being pushed over the edge by isolation, and it might have been my fault. I hadn't been there for him at his darkest hour, and now I was setting up an intervention behind his back.

He was still adamant about getting home by Halloween.

"I got this thing on the 31st, so I gotta be home for that."

"It's like 3 hours from the Ville to the Lou; it will be nothing, just ride with me."

He would stay at my house overnight until the mail arrived, and he was in a good mood.

But he told me repeatedly that he didn't want the printer and that I could keep it.

He appeared happy, upbeat, and far from someone who wanted to kill others and then himself. Perhaps I had jumped too quickly to my conclusions about him, and setting up the intervention was a bad idea, and I was a lousy friend.

I didn't know if I could call the intervention off, though. And he was so adamant that I keep the shoebox and printer. He didn't even overnight it; he mailed it regular mail. That made me think that maybe, just maybe, he would go through with his sinister plan.

When we got to the airport, we both needed a stiff drink, and I did because of him, but maybe he did because of me. The booze got into his blood and loosened him up, which meant he went back to tipping like he had money to burn. And with his shoebox, he did.

"Keep the change," he'd say to people after handing them a hundred.

The strong drinks made the flight more bearable, and of course, Sawyer wanted to keep the party going. I did too, but I didn't have my pockets laced with fake money. He bought $300 worth of the small shooters from the stewardess and tipped her a hundred. He walked around the aisle handing out shooters. Most people turned them down, but we were flying to the bourbon capital of the world, so many people took them.

He handed an 11-year-old boy three hundred dollars and told him to invest it in the stock market.

By the time we arrived in the Ville, people wondered who Sawyer was too and why he wasn't sitting in first class.

We didn't have a ride, and booking an Uber was impossible.

I texted Mr. Barnes and informed him we were heading that way. He hit me back and said they were already at my place.

And we found a cab. Sawyer began to play the money game with the cabbie and tipped the guy over five bills, and I guess he knew he couldn't take the money with him.

Things felt hunky-dory until we arrived at my rinky-dink place, and Sawyer's family was waiting outside like a surprise party for his half birthday. And it didn't take long for things to escalate.

Sawyer was clueless but excited to see everyone. His initial reaction was to ask, "Did somebody die?" Since it was such a rarity to see his entire family together: mom, step-dad, dad, and dad's new girlfriend. The only explanation was a funeral.

His old man patted him on the back as we walked into my apartment and said, "Nobody died bub, we are all here to see you!"

"Noone died, Sawyer, don't be ridiculous. We were just in the neighborhood," his mom added.

I invited them in, and I regretted not throwing out my trash before I left months ago. It was terrible, but I've walked into worse. I got chairs, and Sawyer processed what was happening.

"You guys were in the neighborhood and came to Gunner's stinky apartment?" He asked them.

"It smells worse than Cleveland in here, Gunner."

As reality hit him, Sawyer glanced around the room like a raccoon holding the Thanksgiving turkey. When he saw me pull out his notebook with the notes to Kurt Cobain, his face went pale, and his neck vein bulged. Then a red tone of anger waved over his face.

His mom started to cry.

"Why--y," his voice was cracking, but he continued, "why you got that there, Gun. That's my property."

"I-," I couldn't answer him, though.

So he asked me again, and now he was starting to get mad.

"Why you got my shit, Gunner!"

"What's in your notebook, son?" Mr. Barnes asked, and he reached for it.

Sawyer smacked his dad's hand back and then punched me dead in the chest. The wind left my body, but I grabbed the notebook before I fell, and I landed on my recliner.

His mom ran over, trying to comfort him, but he pushed her away.

"THIS IS WHAT Y'ALL ARE HERE FOR?!"

Spit flew out with every other word, and he stared around the room, looking like a fire was coming in from all angles. His walls were closing in, and I thought he might just sit down, tell us that he wanted help; he didn't want to do these things, but he needed help. That didn't happen, though. He didn't sit down, though.

"FUCK YOU, GUNNER!"

I stood up, and he rushed me. His stepdad grabbed him and held him back before he murdered me. He escaped from his stepdad's grip.

"I'm just trying to help you, Sawyer!" I yelled as I braced for impact.

It never came.

He shook his head, and his old man had reached for him, but he let him go.

Sawyer turned from me, opened the door, and walked out while his mom screamed, stop or don't leave. He slammed the door so hard, and it bounced back open.

Mr. Barnes didn't follow him outside, and he was right there by the door. He didn't, so I didn't.

Mr. Barnes just stood there shaking his head, gripping his right fingers in his left hand as they came within an inch of being slammed in the door.

Sawyer's mom was crying, and his dad's girlfriend was crying too.

His stepdad opened the door and ran after Sawyer. He was yelling for Sawyer, and then they all followed.

Mr. Barnes left last, and he turned back to look at me. He didn't say anything though, he just nodded and left.

I sat back down and wondered if I had just betrayed my best friend. I didn't get up, and his family didn't come back inside. I didn't know if I had done the right thing.

I grabbed my phone and called Sawyer, and he didn't answer, so I called Mr. Barnes, but he didn't answer either. I tried him one more time, and then he texted me back, stating Sawyer was with him, and that was about it.

Another text came in a few minutes later, and he thanked me and said he would call me when things calmed down. I wanted to help, but I knew Sawyer being in the hands of his old man was better than anything I could do. It was a family issue now.

The whole intervention made me start to question my problems too.

Sure, I wasn't planning on shooting anything, but my boozing was out of control. I needed to look in the mirror at myself. Sometimes, we all need to see if the reflection matches the person inside all of us.

I wasn't going to start right now, though. Stopping now would fill my life with boredom. So I wasn't going to do that, and as soon as I knew none of the Barnes clan was coming back, I popped open a cold one. Old habits die slowly, and after that ordeal, I needed one.

Drinking a brewski, I popped my feet up and popped in the only DVD in my place that worked, Belly.

And as I watched Nasir Jones and Earl Simmons run amok on my old school tube, I wondered what in the hell was going on in the District. The mansion with bills in my name, the credit cards, the emails now down, the fact that Terry was MIA, Dirk and Olga too, and the fires.

They needed to burn so many papers, but why? I couldn't figure it out though, I didn't even know where to start, and I didn't know what to do. The only attorney I knew just left with my best friend to stop a mass shooting, and I didn't know who else could help me.

I was nervous, but the beer helped. I googled the issue, Terry's name, and a few other things before I tried to log into my email at Rolling Stone, and to my surprise, it worked. I

SUICIDE NOTES TO KURT COBAIN

logged in, and I saw a ton of emails from Terry that didn't say anything meaningful.

There was one email from someone I had never seen before, but there was a complete conversation of emails between us when I opened it. I had agreed to meet this person in Cleveland to make a payment back in September and another for a meeting in November. The communication was between myself and Hank REDACTED at the Green Party.

It was the same person from that party I was supposed to meet Cleveland before but never had. I'd never talked to this person, but Terry had mentioned his name.

Looking over the content of the messages, I saw three different times that I had planned to meet this person, but I never did. I never even saw those messages, and Terry must have had root access to my email. The messages were baffling; I said I would meet this person three times, and I apologized for not making it.

The last message from me was telling Hank that I would be in Cleveland on November 2nd to deliver one more payment. So I wrote back and asked for Hank's phone number, and I waited on a response.

Even more baffling was how I could log into my email now. Perhaps I did have a position at *Rolling Stone Magazine*, and the magazine was having email issues or server issues.

I called Sawyer 3 times, and all my calls went straight to voicemail. Mr. Barnes never hit me back either.

So I prepared to watch Game Five when this Hank person emailed me back with his phone number and asked me for my new number. He said he called my old number with the 202 area code, but it was now off. He listed the whole number, so I googled it, and it was a landline phone that came back as registered to Gunner A. Bush, and the address was the Mansion.

I sent him an email back, telling him I could meet him on the 2nd.

I booked a flight back to the smelly Mistake on the Lake using the company credit card. It worked too. I was amazed, but then I remembered it was my credit card. It still didn't feel like it was mine, though. I needed answers, and flying back to Believeland was my only option to get any.

I ordered grub and opened a bottle of Henny, so I was wasted by the time Game Five came on.

It was probably all over for my boys, though. The Cubbies were down three games to one, and the billy goat curse held the status quo.

Rizzo snagged a pop-up, foul ball that fell out of Ross's glove, and I screamed. It was short-lived happiness, though, as some dude on the Tribe hit a solo dinger. No team in my life had ever come back from down 3-1.

But Heyward continued the roller coaster for me with an incredible catch moments later, so I took another shot. I wanted to be sloshed if I watched the Tribe celebrate winning the whole enchilada at Wrigley.

Bryant tied the game on a solo jack, and I poured two more shots. Rizzo hit a double into the ivy, and I was yelling so loud the cops should have been called. And by the time Eddie Vedder came out to sing Harry Caray's favorite hymn during the stretch, I was seeing double but still seeing.

The Cubs somehow won the game, and I fell asleep with Steve Goodman singing about WGN. I wanted to celebrate, but I was too twisted to do so. I'd been excited to sleep in my own bed, so it is fitting that I fell asleep on the couch.

CHAPTER 26

"Serendipity in Seven"

The best two words in sports were about to take place, Game Seven, and it was my favorite team playing to win the whole goddamn thing. It felt like serendipity.

Sawyer's money and money machine had arrived. I'd love to tell you I burnt the fake cash and threw the money printer into the Ohio River and not indict myself, but I won't lie. Sawyer had spent at least half of the shoebox before it arrived, and he had nothing to show for it. Not that I wanted something to show for it, I wasn't trying to invest this money, but I was interested in attending Game Seven in person.

I was already going to Believeland.

I packed one change of clothes, put on my Cubs hat, and headed into enemy territory.

Believeland, The Mighty Plum©, was alive, so it was impossible to get an Uber from the airport. And the airport was a madhouse. Wearing my Cubs hat wasn't my best move, and I could hear the whistles and shit talking right away.

Hailing a cab downtown, and the cabbie informed me that tickets were outrageous, and bleacher-level seats in the nose bleeds were going for over a thousand. He also told me that my hat was ugly.

Traffic was bumper to asshole, so I was late for my

meeting with Hank, and he was already in the coffee shop, and it was packed.

I called him when I got there since I didn't know what he looked like, and he stood up. Hank was an older white dude with black hair and a touch of gray in his beard. He was over 40 but under 55, was wearing a pair of glasses that didn't match him, and it was like they were fake and used to hide his face. He was wearing an ugly brown Affliction brand shirt, and he said hello into his phone, so I waved at him.

He walked over, shook my hand, and gripped it incredibly hard while saying, "it's great to meet you finally."

I said likewise and nodded.

"Sit, sit," he motioned at his booth. He had a cup of joe in front of his seat, and I sat down across from him.

"So, uh, okay," I said and nothing else.

He was awkward, and I chalked it up to his nerves, but I didn't know why he would be nervous. Thinking of his nerves got mine running, and I had to make myself not fidget around in my seat.

I turned around to glance at the line and saw it wrapped around to the door. I wanted a coffee, but I didn't want to wait.

"It's impossible to tell how long that line is; coffee shop lines are unpredictable. It could be hours, but it could also be three minutes."

"Yeah, I got mine before that happened. I got here right in time, I guess," he informed me.

"We have never met, but how many times did we talk on the phone because I don't remember ever talking to you on the phone?"

He smiled at me and answered, "How many times? Is

that a joke?"

"Let me just say this, a lot of weird shit has been happening to me lately. I came here to get some answers for myself. So if you could tell me, how many times did we talk on the phone?"

"We would talk once or twice a week, or, I guess I should say, I would talk to Gunner Bush, who worked at Rolling Stone Magazine once or twice a week back in the summer. Then you changed your number, but I do have to admit, I thought you were a foreigner because you had a different accent on the phone. I don't mean to sound rude."

"Gotcha, well, that makes about as much sense as everything else that has happened to me over the last few days."

"You have been going through it, huh?" he asked me.

"Yeah, but okay, so tell me, why are we here today? Do I owe you money? I do, don't I. How much, I have lost my memory, obviously, and I don't remember."

He looked at me as if he was staring directly at a light bulb.

"If we are getting technical, it was five hundred, but look, I get it; I mean, I tried to do what I could, right? I got you the photos that I could and set up the meetings I could for your boss about the adoptions, and with all the higher-ups at the Green Party, but I mean, again, technically, you said you'd pay me the five no matter what."

That was why he was so nervous. He wanted to get paid, and he thought he would get paid today. I had promised him, or someone, Terry or Dirk, someone, had promised him five hundred bucks.

"Yeah, I got you, dude. I got it right here."

I rummaged around in my bag until I found the book, and I slid out five bills and handed them to him.

"Oh man, that is freakin sweet! Times have been tough lately."

"Yeah, trust me, I get it. You think you can tell me about me. What have I told you? Like, can you help me out?"

I pulled out my wallet and showed him my ID.

"See, I am Gunner A. Bush from Louisville, Kentucky."

"Right, that's what it says," he replied.

"Yep, that is me, I worked for Rolling Stone, but I do think I have been a victim of identity theft."

He didn't respond, and his face said he didn't have a clue what I was talking about. He was just as lost as I was, but he was now up five hundred buckaroos.

Finally, he spoke, "So who in the hell was I talking to on the phone, and who was that blonde that paid me last time?"

"Blonde, hmm, was she Russian?"

"Yeah, I would say she was Russian, maybe Ukrainian or whatever, but if you say, Russian, I will agree."

He flashed his head as if to look at something on his right. It was quick but very obvious.

"Tell me, Mr. Gunner Bush, those photos I took for you for the December issue, will they be in the magazine?"

"I don't know, man, how would I know, right? It is up to the editor, shit; I have not even gotten one article published in the magazine yet."

"Not even one article?"

I wasn't there to answer his questions, and I was already

down five hundred even if it was play money.

"That's not important," I said as I gathered up my belongings.

"Who did I have you set up meetings with? Like on your end?"

"Besides the folks from the Green Party?"

"Yeah."

"Well, you told me to get any and all Republicans from the state of Ohio, but I don't have that type of pull."

I regretted giving him a cent, and it was counterfeit. He was done with the convo too, and he again glanced to his right. An older chick was sitting there, and he kept nodding at some dude sitting behind her.

Sliding to the end of the bench, I asked him, "How much have I paid you so far?"

"It was always five hundred from Rolling Stone, always in hundred dollar bills too," he said with his chin down as if he had a wire in his shirt. Shit, maybe he did.

I stood up, paranoid. I grabbed my shit.

"You alright there, bud?"

"Are you wearing a wire right now?"

I know he wouldn't answer me truthfully even if he were, but I also know I had to get gone ASAP. If the cops had me, they had me, but I could ghost them with all the traffic and people if I could get outside.

Then I felt a consensus stoppage in the entire place. It was very suspicious, but it was gone as quickly as it happened. Everyone in the whole place put their eyes on me for a split second, and then they all glanced away. It happened, and if it didn't then, I am insane.

"You got something in your pants? Am I wearing a wire? Hell no, man, hell no!"

"Yeah, sorry about that late payment; I have been dealing with a lot right now. I don't know what's going on, but I thought I could get something out of this, but I gotta run."

He stood up, and we shook hands. And then I left, but two customers exited swiftly behind me. It wasn't random, they were from different sections, but they were both watching me. It had to be the police. I turned back to see them. It was two white men about the same age as Hank, and they both smelled like bacon. It was 100% the boys in blue.

I didn't stick around to find out if it was or not. I turned the corner and ran like the wind. Every step I got away, I envisioned an undercover car cutting me off and a gang of cops tackling me. I turned another corner and kept the pace. I was out of shape, carrying my bags, but I wasn't going down easily.

I sprinted into a hotel lobby, briskly walked to the elevators, and joined open doors going up. I got off on the first stop, my heart racing near a heart attack, and I walked to a vending machine area. I bought overpriced water out of a Coke machine and drank it while walking back down the stairs.

Walking back into the lobby, I realized nobody was after me. I needed a strong drink to calm my nerves, so I headed towards the hotel bar.

"Your hat sucks, fuck the Cubs!" I heard a few haters, but I kept it moving.

After my drink, I calmed down and noticed a PYT looking at me. She was in the lobby part of the hotel just before the bar, and she said, "The Cubs are going to lose tonight."

She was dressed provocatively but not over the top like

a hooker.

"Is that right?" I asked her.

"You got tickets?"

"I am still looking," I informed her, and I was, but after what the cabbie had told me, I didn't think I'd be able to get a good price.

"Yeah, I might be able to help. My name is Missy."

"Missy, huh," She was hustling, "I am only looking for a single."

"It's hot in here, but if you follow me, I can hook you up."

She began to walk towards an exit at the other end of the hallway.

"Single, can you get me a single game ticket?" I asked, but she didn't answer. I followed her nonetheless. My suspicion wasn't as high, so I didn't think she was a cop.

She exited the doors into the hotel parking garage. I followed her a second later, and she still had her fingertips on the door holding it for me. Her hands were long and skinny and detailed with neon green fake nails.

"Yeah, I just spoke with a fellow that said he had some mid-level seats, the third baseline for about a rack."

I was lying out of my ass.

"A thousand for mids? Those are probably counterfeit, and there is a lot of those floating around; mids are over three grand, hun."

"Where are you from, not from here, are you?"

"Yeah, well, I am from Akron," She informed me, but she wasn't watching me. Her attention had turned to a car driving through the garage.

"Akron, oh isn't that where, what's his name, the best basketball player in the world was born?"

"Do you mean Lebron James?" She asked as if I was dumb.

"No, Steph Curry, Stephen Curry was born in Akron, Ohio," I winked when I said it.

"You are funny, but the Cavs won in June, remember?"

"So how much are mids, or I should ask, what do you have?"

"Just a single, huh? You don't have a girlfriend with that quick wit?"

"Yeah, but she ain't here, so?"

"I got mid; I can do twenty-eight, it's on the baseline - "

I cut her off, "Twenty-eight!?"

"Listen, this is Game Seven."

"Shit, you know the best place to watch a game? In the comfort of your own home, sitting in your favorite chair. The networks have figured out the perfect camera angles."

I was nervous, but I didn't want to pay twenty-eight for mid-level seats.

"Yeah, but you aren't in Chicago at home, are you?"

"Well, have you got anything closer?"

"Seventh row, right behind the dugout, close to the plate, first baseline, one seat on the aisle. I had four, but this guy overpaid for three; I didn't think I'd be able to move it, and I was contemplating going myself."

"How much?" I was done with the bullshit.

"I can do five-"

She hung out the five, and I couldn't read if she was going higher or lower, and I'm not great at America's game of poker, or bidding so I screamed out, "Fifty-two, wait."

I had started the bidding higher than her asking price.

"Five." She said firmly.

"Forty-eight," I replied.

She was firm at five. It was take it or leave it, and I took it.

"I can't do a check."

"A check? Who the fuck would do a check. I wouldn't take a check if I owned a department store."

Luckily, I had that much on me. I had a lot more, but it was fake money. I dug in my bag and pulled out a wad of hundreds.

"Those aren't counterfeit, are they?"

"Your tickets aren't counterfeit, are they?"

She shook her head to tell me that her tickets were real, and I handed over 50 one hundred dollar bills.

"You are going to see history tonight, no matter who wins!" She informed me as she pulled out a ticket from her purse.

The car she had been watching pulled up close, and she ran to get into it.

"So where should I go pregame?" I yelled as she opened the car door.

"You might try the Thirsty Parrot, but don't wear that ugly hat!"

I prayed my ticket wasn't counterfeit, and even though I gave her fake money, those hundreds could be used anywhere.

I checked into my hotel, which wasn't downtown because everything had been booked, and then made my way to this watering hole for some day drinking. I proceeded to get hammered like a nail, and when game time got close, I made my way to the stadium. Luckily, I could follow everyone else because I was twisted and didn't know where the place was.

The stadium was a madhouse. The lines for anything were outrageous. It took me 22 minutes to get inside the bathroom. I desperately wanted a beer, but those lines were crazy long, too, so I made my way to my seat. I had to talk to three separate ushers before getting down to my seat; usually, I would be sitting so high up the usher was coming around to sneak a smoke.

The aisle seat was a beautiful site for my tired legs, and I plopped down hard and yelled to nobody, "This is a great seat for Game Seven!'

The guy next to me agreed; he leaned towards me and said, "Should be a good one!"

I turned to look at him. He smiled and then turned to the guy next to him.

"Holy fuck," I blurted out on impulse.

I said it so loud people in every row in front of me turned around.

"It's freaking, wow, it's Phil Connors," I said to everyone, but not a soul picked up on what I was saying, so I continued, "Phil, you remember me, Ned, Needle Head Ned, I tried to date your sister back in high school until you told me not to."

Then I laughed, but nobody else had a clue what I was talking about.

Except the man sitting two seats over from me. He flashed his famous sarcastic smile at me, bent over the guy between us, and he said, "nice hat, kid."

Holy shit, it was Bill Fucking Murray! The man, the myth, the legend. This wasn't happenstance; it was a sign, and the Cubs were going to win.

I became as giddy as a young girl seeing her crush. Fidgeting around, I leaned over the man in between us, stuck out my hand, and said, "I am Gunner Bush with Rolling Stone Magazine."

"I'm Bill; nice to meet you."

He said that. It was Bill. Everyone within 2 thousand light years knew he was Bill, and he still said it. I laughed, although I don't think it was a joke. It was just his name.

"Rolling Stone, huh? How is Gavin doing?" He asked me, but it didn't feel like he wanted an answer.

"Popcorn?" He leaned his bucket over, and I took some. I wasn't going to be rude to Bill Freaking Murray.

The salt on the popcorn hit my tongue, and I needed a beer even more. I ate the rest, leaned back over the man in the middle, and said, "Hey Bill," as if we were now best friends, which we weren't, not yet anyway, and I asked him, "you want a cold one? I am going to get one."

"I think we are all good, Gunner Bush with Rolling Stone Magazine."

He nodded, and the man in the middle of us nodded too as if to say, stop leaning over me.

The national anthem was about to be sung, so I stood up and bounced for the concessions. I made my way back through the three ushers and found a beer line. Bill said he didn't want a beer, but I was buying him one anyway.

The line was still backed up to Dayton, Ohio, but it was slowly going down with the anthem being sung. People were finding their seats, and I stood in line to wait. Finally, I got two brews, but as I turned to leave, some knucklehead knocked my hat to the ground. I was holding two cups of beer, so I couldn't just bend down to pick it up. I set one beer down on a ledge and bent down to get it while saying, "Ha ha ha, very funny, knock off the hat because it's a Cubs hat."

Right before I grabbed it, some asshole kicked it, and another one yelled out, "Fuck the Cubs!"

Then beer was poured all over. The beer that I had just put down.

I remained calm.

"First of all, that beer was for the legend Bill Murray, and second of all, that is freaking alcohol abuse. I should fight you on principle alone."

I turned around to see the biggest, ugliest, lumberjack-looking dude in Northern Ohio staring at me.

"Fight me on principle, huh?" He asked me through his dirty beard.

"No, not you; I was speaking about that man there who kicked my hat." I pointed at a smaller man standing next to him.

"I knocked your hat off, and I poured the beer on you," The ginormous lumberjack said to me.

"I understand; I guess you aren't a fan of Bill freaking

Murray, the man who saved New York City from the Ghosts, not once, but twice!"

"I poured the beer on your head," He said again as if I didn't hear him the first time and somehow still wanted to fight him. Mike Tyson wouldn't want to fight this dude.

"I get it. Pour one out for the homies. We have all been there, and look, let me drop some too. Rest in peace," I said as I poured the very tip of my beer to the ground.

He growled at me like a dog to a trespasser, but he didn't say anything.

"Okay, well, I guess I will get going and let you guys get back to playing the banjo or whatever in the hell."

I began to walk by him, but he didn't like my comment or my face or something because he rocked my jaw with the force of Thor's hammer. I was asleep before I hit the ground.

If we are going to be factual, I was inside the stadium during the greatest Game Seven in World Series history. I bought the ticket and sat next to the Ghostbuster, Peter Venkman, who also gave me some of his popcorn. Those are all facts, but I didn't see an ounce of the game until the 10th inning.

I was sleeping like a baby. And I never saw the punch that dislocated my jaw, and I didn't feel it until I woke up either. I merely fell to the ground and went to dreamland. I woke up with a massive migraine, and everything was pitch black, and I could hear a TV. My entire body was sticky.

My eyes adjusted, and slowly, the faint light from the television brightened. The announcers were discussing a rain delay. My brain came back into focus, and I began to understand.

I sat up from the cot I was in and noticed I was in some

sort of concrete, underground bunker. There wasn't a soul anywhere around me, and I couldn't remember what in the hell happened. Yet, the more the announcers talked about the game, I wondered why I wasn't watching the game.

It all came back to me at once.

I stood up and tried to find an exit. The game wasn't over, and I had to see the ending.

I found a door and realized I was under the stadium's seats. I walked down a hallway and saw an open door with a man sitting inside it with a great view of the field. I approached him from behind; he was an older black dude rocking big glasses so he could see the whole field. He had a great view of the diamond, not as good as the seats I had paid for, but still a great view.

The pain in my jaw was terrible, and I put my hand on it as I approached him. The players were returning to the diamond, and he was wearing a security shirt, and he turned to look at me.

"You've been standing there this whole time?" He asked me as if I knew him.

"Huh? No, I was asleep, I think."

He glanced around, concerned. He knew me, but I sure as hell didn't know him.

"You're that boy who got knocked out, right?"

"My jaw hurts like hell."

"Yeah, I bet it does. I saw that guy hit you. You fell asleep pretty quickly, and you are lucky you didn't hit your head on your way down."

"Did you arrest him?"

"Arrest him? Shoot, I'm not a cop, and look, maybe don't wear the hat of the enemy when you go into the Young Tribe section of the stadium."

"I want to press charges," I implied with a stern voice.

"I can't help you there, kid. I thought they took you with the paramedics."

His attention went back to the field, but he did say, "I couldn't have caught him anyway. He ran off after hitting you, and I got a bum knee. Plus, as I said, I am not a cop."

"Yeah, well, I would like to be escorted back to my seat. And I feel like you guys owe me a beer, and that beer that poured on me was for Mr. Bill Murray."

"We owe you a beer? Who owes you a beer?"

"The stadium, the city, I don't know, I paid a lot of money for those two beers, and I only got the one sip."

"Okay, well, you can file a complaint."

"I need to go back to my seat to watch the rest of the game. I should be escorted!"

"Escorted? Listen, kid, the ambulance wouldn't even take you to the hospital because everyone in the city is watching the game. Escorted to your seat; that is hilarious."

He said it as if I was a princess demanding a throne, but he wasn't a prince charming type of man. And I don't blame the dude; it was the 10th inning of game seven.

"You can go find someone else to escort you, but it ain't gonna be me."

He was finished with me. I had been assaulted, knocked out, and then forgotten about and placed in the back of an underground office for hours while the entire city watched the game. Nobody in the stadium cared about an unconscious Cubs fan. And usually, I would agree with this sentiment, but not when it was my jaw on the line.

I didn't have enough time to make it back to my seat, as going through the three ushers now would have taken forever. We were in the middle of the press boxes with a better view than the press, so I just turned to the man and said, "scoot over."

He puffed but moved over. He wasn't mad that he had to slide over; he was upset because the Cubs were one out away from making history. My jaw was swollen, my head aching, but I was about to view it in real time and in person.

Then it happened, and when it did, I cried tears of joy. Mainly from the pain in my body, but some of it was for my team. I glanced down and saw the empty seat that my five thousand dollars had bought. Bill Murray was now sitting in the seat next to mine, and he was balling his eyes out too.

The security guard made another huffing puff sound, and then he stood up and left without even asking me to leave the area. He was pissed, and I don't blame him. I sat there staring at the diamond alone in the security box with my eyes watering, and my jaw felt as if a tank had hit it.

My old man called me, and he had his old man on the line. None of us said a word until my grandfather just sighed softly into the phone and said, "it feels like a dream, and I don't want to wake up."

Nothing was said, and I didn't even tell them I was at the freaking game. What a moment in time.

Billy Murray walked onto the field, and I could have been there with him if not for the lumberjack's fist. My phone went off again, and it was a text from Morgan.

"Yay, your Cubs won!"

Then my phone rang, and it was her.

"Oh my God, Gunner, I know you love the Cubs, and I am not a baseball fan, but we were all here watching the game, and I know you were watching it. What's up? Hello, Gunner?"

"Yeah, I am here," I replied.

"Is Gunner Bush at a loss for words?"

"Yeah, I think I am." I said and wiped the tears away.

"Well, congrats, I guess; it's awesome that they won."

"Thanks, so how are you?"

"Good, and hey, Gunner, I was thinking, why don't you come to New York and join me at the Clinton event on election day. It will be a major event at a hotel in Manhattan, and we can talk, hang out, and whatnot. It is going to be a major news event when Hillary shatters the glass ceiling."

She was inviting me to be her date for this major event. I couldn't say no.

"I'd love to join you."

CHAPTER 27

"Election Day"

On the morning of November 8th, I arrived in the Big Rotten Apple ready to live with whatever happened in the election. The Cubs winning and the serendipity around it hadn't faded yet, so I wasn't capricious yet. I'd spend the six days post-game at Churchill Downs losing money on the ponies but avoiding politics altogether. If I watched politics, I would immediately start to look for flights to cancel my bet. Trump's October Surprise hadn't moved the needle as much as everyone thought it would.

The consensus around the country was that Hillary was still going to win the election. The narrative was thriving in the media and repeated everywhere. The polls still had her winning easily despite the newly open investigation. My doubts in the media kept me in the Ville.

The money I had riding on the election was already gone; I didn't even know if the casino would cancel my bet. Thirty thousand dollars is a lot of money to anyone, but I didn't know what to do. A casino in Ireland was already paying out bets to Hillary so flying to Florida to cancel my bet was the right move.

Morgan and I were putting each other to bed on the phone every night, and during the day were texting each other non-stop. We were building something, a special relationship to say the least, but it felt like a strong bond. It was difficult not to tell her about my bet. I was a nervous wreck and eagerly watched the news for any change. A change didn't appear to be coming, so I had a decision to make.

Would I fly to Florida and try to cancel my bet, or fly to New York and spend time with Morgan?

Flipping a coin felt like the best plan of action. Heads, I would fly to Florida, and tails, I would fly to New York City. I tossed the coin high into the air and left my apartment before it landed. I didn't even look at it, and I went to the airport to book a trip north.

(This was a Judgment of Troy moment where my future self might hate my former self for following my penis instead of my gut, but men had died for less, and to me, Morgan was my personal Helena. Not that I would kidnap her, but I would move across the world to bring her back. I might even build a giant, wooden horse, raid a city, or leave 30 racks on a losing betting slip.)

It was impossible to fly into JFK or La Guardia, so I had to fly into the armpit of America, Newark, New Jersey. And as I got off the plane, there were military men with machine guns, cops with bomb-sniffing dogs, cops, more cops, cops on horses, military, more cops. Newark to Manhattan, that is all I saw.

Ubering into Manhattan was quite the thrill. The city's pulse was lit, and I got excited when I saw the massive New York City skyline. The pace of the city that never sleeps is absurd, and it was palpable.

I was eager as a baby in a delivery room to see Morgan, but I stunk like an airplane. I desperately needed a shower. My body was full of BO and likely full of grotesque airplane and airport germs. I didn't have a room booked and planned to crash in Morgan's hotel room despite her not asking me yet. I didn't know if it would be a problem, but I didn't realize I would smell like death and feet when I arrived.

I didn't want to just hook up with her; I wanted to build on top of what we had going with our nightly calls. I would love to date her and her exclusively. She was still dead set on becoming Hillary's press secretary, and I was also looking into moving to the District.

And that is where I was torn. If Trump won, I would win, bigly, but if Trump won, she would lose. If Hillary won, I would lose, but she would win. I had one foot in both holes, and I was seesawing back and forth. Somehow, I still thought Trump might pull it off.

And if Trump did win, I would step into a new tax bracket. Perhaps, it was wishful thinking, but Trump was still mucking up the waters, and he had run as perfect a campaign as he could, considering he lost three campaign managers.

Dude D was still assuring me that the polls were wrong. The new man in charge of Trump's campaign dressed like a flood survivor, but he was tapping into the crazies. The mainstream media didn't see it, but what did they know anyway.

Morgan met me in the hotel lobby, and she was a sight for sore eyes. She was beyond beautiful and wasn't even dressed up yet. She had on pajama pants, a Georgetown t-shirt, and no makeup, and she looked like a million bucks. She really did wake up like that; she was simultaneously the hottest chick in the room and the most beautiful lady.

She gave me a tight hug, and I had to inform her, "Sorry that I smell, the guy next to me vomited on me."

"Yuck," she said with a pinched face. "A grown man

threw up on you?"

"No, it was a child, a child without parents, he was flying to see one of them, a nasty divorce, and I was watching over him."

It was a white lie, but I was in too deep to pull out now. I stunk so bad I couldn't help it.

"Well, let's go upstairs, and you can use my shower."

"That is pretty cool that your Cubs won the World Series."

"Yeah, I didn't tell you I was at the game, and guess who I sat next to?"

"You were? Who?"

"Bill Murray."

"Stop it! Are you serious?"

"Yes."

I stopped myself from saying anymore because it would be bragging, and it also still didn't feel real. I didn't believe it, and I had just lived it.

We stopped outside her hotel room, and she turned to me and asked, "So did you book a room, or did you just assume I was a slut and you were going to sleep with me?"

"I would never assume you are a slu-,"

She cut me off before I could finish, "Maybe I can be a slut. You will find out, but you can stay here with me."

She flashed her wicked beautiful smile, and her eyes had a twinkle.

Her room wasn't super eloquent, but it was nice. It had a shower which is all I needed.

"Make yourself at home, but I do have to go back downstairs and help set up for tonight."

"Oh really, do you have a lot to do?"

"I do, but it is going to be amazing. There is this giant LCD screen on the ceiling, and it is glass. After Mrs. Clinton wins, the ceiling is going to crack," she exclaimed.

"If she wins," I reminded her. I didn't mean to say it, and it slipped out.

"Well, according to all our data, I think she will win."

"I know."

"Why don't you hop into the shower and clean up. I am going to run back downstairs."

"Okay, I have to get some work done myself."

I was lying again, but I didn't want her to think I didn't have a job. I still hadn't told her about Rolling Stone yet.

"I have a table booked for us when the polls close; it's pretty close to the stage. We get food and drinks."

She quickly slipped on a casual outfit and left.

I took a shower and flipped on the flatscreen to avoid the silence and thoughts in my own head.

The pundits, cynics, critics, talking heads, and experts said the same thing. Hillary was going to win and become number 45. Unless I turned on Faux, they were still holding out hope just as I was.

That's when it dawned on me that I was going to lose. Trump wasn't going to win. I had bought the kool-aid at the tail of the fox, and I was going to be out thousands of dollars. Sure, Trump had energized a new band of Republicans, but he was going to fall short of the White House.

"Fuck me."

My blood pressure went up and anxiety hit. My mood changed with the channel I tuned into, so I decided to just keep it on Faux. I didn't want to give myself a heart attack; thirty thousand dollars was a year's salary for most of my family.

I flipped the channel to CNN, and I was disgusted. It was like they were fake news, and they couldn't see the truth. They thought America had embraced Obama, and we would stay in this cute world where the people sang all the time in harmony, but that wasn't the reality I had seen across the country over the summer and fall.

"Bullshit, bullshit, your idiots and your pollsters are wrong. Trump is going to win, I hope, and our country will go down the shitter with him!"

As the day wore on, Faux began to believe the Hillary hype too. They'd been pushing a narrative for years, but they were changing it ever so slightly, and I was watching it.

"Shit! All my money, gone, gone, gone."

Morgan texted that she couldn't join me for lunch.

I told her I would find something and not to worry about me.

I ordered room service for lunch, but I didn't need the food. What I needed were the beers. I told them to bring a sixer up, and I was going to need it. It wasn't even 1 pm yet, but I needed a drink.

I drank the sixer and ordered another one before three o'clock rolled around. I hid the cans behind the loveseat so Morgan wouldn't trip, and I dozed off a bit with cable news blaring in the background. None of the experts knew what was what.

Morgan woke me up around 3:30. She had to change her clothes again.

"How was your lunch? Sorry, I couldn't join you, and we had lunch for all of our hard work on the campaign."

"It's fine. The food was okay, but all they had to drink was pop, and I gave up pop for lent, so I had to get beer," I pointed to a stack of four unopened brews.

"Yeah, well, save some room for drinks with me later. After we win, I want to celebrate with you. The White House is in sight for Mrs. Clinton."

"Yeah, that is what the pundits are saying on every channel."

"I am sorry we didn't get to hang out, Gunny. I didn't know I would be this busy, but tonight it will be just the two of us, I promise."

"It's not a problem."

"Okay, well, I will see you soon, Gunny."

She left again, but I could feel a bond between us. It was real, and I knew she could feel it too.

I removed the empty beer cans from behind the loveseat and took them to the hallway to throw them away. I'd killed eight brews in the middle of the day, and my nerves were still on fire. Thirty thousand is a lot of money, and it was all about to disappear. I felt nauseous, so I ate the room service burger, but sobering up wasn't good for me mentally.

It was time to hit the hotel bar. I threw on my wrinkled gear, grabbed a pass and room key that Morgan had left, and I headed down to find a watering hole. Finishing beer nine in the elevator, I popped number ten while searching for the bar. The lobby was packed full of Democrats ready to celebrate.

I had to cross through a security line, and they told me to wear the pass Morgan had given me around my neck. Once beyond security, I entered a lobby area as festive as a Jimmy Buffet song. It was Margaritaville. A DJ was setting up to spin the music that drives soccer van mom's wild. The crowd was still filing in, and it was a mixed bag of folks. Everyone was excited and ready to celebrate.

As the first polls closed, the place got jammed. There was a gigantic screen at the far end of the reception hall with a map of the United States on it and several flatscreens all over the place with different news stations airing.

The bar was smug, but I didn't need much. The bartender was a Hispanic female who somehow looked just like Michael Jackson. It was uncanny, but I didn't mention it. She did bring me the best cheese fries I had ever had, and her old fashion was nearly perfect.

The whole building was tense and anxious and ready for a Hillary win as the first numbers came in, but they didn't solve or decide anything, creating more predictions.

I grabbed a chair at the bar, and sitting next to me in the captain's chairs was an older pale dude. He was tall and awkward, and he looked visibly nervous. His hands were shaking and his head nodding, and he was wearing an all-white delegates hat that read, "Hillary 2016."

He turned to me and said, "This is going to be a blowout. Trump is going to have his tail between his legs before nine o'clock."

"I feel lat," I said before motioning for Latina Michael Jackson to come back for another round.

"I'm going to call my brother-in-law before ten tonight and just laugh. That's all I am going to do is laugh," he told me.

He had a pen in his hand and a napkin in front of him, and as the first numbers came in, he jotted on his napkins. Then he said to nobody in particular, but also everyone at the same time, "It's going to be a longer night than we expected if this holds up; The same outcome, though, the same outcome. Trump is going home with his tails between his legs!'

His voice was deep and cutting like a radio host on an after-hours show.

His hands were still shaking, but he turned and stuck out his right paw to me.

"How are you doing tonight? I am Roger Watson."

"I am Gunner. That's a pretty common prediction, it seems. Trump is going home a loser."

"You're damn skippy, Gunner."

His voice was deep but a fake deep that caused a cringe. The beer in front of him was N/A, and as soon as I saw it, I wanted to move. I glanced around the bar, but I had the last seat, and I didn't feel like standing, but I never trusted a man who doesn't drink beer. It's not my philosophy, but I'd heard it enough to know it must be true.

Trump was up early, 24-3 in our archaic system of voting known as the electoral college.

Roger took a swig of his fake beer and then said, "It's early."

"I will drink to that," I said, and I threw Mike Jack behind the bar two fresh hundred dollar bills straight out of Sawyer's shoebox.

"Go ahead, and make as many shots as this will buy, after you tip yourself fifty," I said as she picked up the money.

She was happy to fill my order, and she made up a ton of lemon shots. The barback helped her pass them out along the bar and behind the folks sitting down. Once they were all handed out, everyone put them up in unison and looked at me to say something, so I put up my glass and said, "For Hillary!"

"For Hillary!"

Everyone repeated it before they took their shot. It felt wrong, almost dirty as if we were toasting to Lenin because Stalin was in the room.

After they took the shot, everyone cheered, but not before I added to the toast, "that she loses with dignity tonight."

Mike Jack thanked me as she collected the glasses.

"No problem, can I get water with low ice? I need to surprise my liver."

The chair next to me became free, and a squirrely-looking bespectacled dude who looked like a bookworm sat down. He was white, round, short, and wearing wire-framed glasses. He had white hair and a white beard and a short, fat neck with tree stumps for legs. I couldn't help but stare at his odd proportions, and when he noticed me, he coughed to clear his throat.

"Thank you for buying the shot for all of us. We all need it."

His voice was high-pitched like a cassette tape sped up too fast, and he spoke with an odd demeanor with each word as if it hurt to say certain syllables.

He shoved his stumpy fingers out in front of my face so I would shake his hand, "They call me Bookworm."

He didn't just look like a bookworm; he was the bookworm.

"Bookworm, okay, I am Gunner."

His hand was hot and moist, and it wasn't a good feeling to feel it.

"It's still early," Roger leaned over to tell us both.

"Kentucky and Indiana, two flyover states always voting against their self-interest," Bookworm said as he pointed to the screen with the two states on it.

"Both of them are red."

A man walked up behind Bookworm, "Indiana and Kentucky always go red!"

"Yeah, well, I grew up in Kentucky, and I went to college in Indiana. Indiana is all for Michael Pencil Dick Pence, you know?"

The man behind Bookworm leaned in and told me I was wrong, "It's not Mike Pence that won the state; it was Bobby Fucking Knight. That old man came out of the insane asylum and became an opening act at Trump rallies all over the state."

I leaned back, "Please, don't speak badly about the dead."

His jaw dropped, and he looked at me with puzzlement and awe on his face.

"I am from South Bend, Indiana, and Bob Knight ain't dead."

"He is dead to the family now that he supports Trump."

They both cut up.

I turned to the smooth criminal behind the bar, "let's get a round of beers for my new friends here!"

"My name is Jimbo," he told me.

"Jimbo, Bookworm, and Roger," I said, and I bought three beers and one N/A.

I was turning into Sawyer with the fake money.

"Gunner, where you from?" Jimbo asked.

"Louisville, Kentucky."

"Is the grass really blue in Kentucky?"

"I haven't seen any bluegrass in Louisville, and for all, I know we call it the Blew Grass State because of all the weed we smoke!"

That got another good laugh out of them. We were building on our tribalism.

The numbers rolled in from the Gunshine State, and we all tuned in.

Hillary was up by a few thousand, and the place went crazy like our team had just hit a home run.

The Vermont numbers came in right after that, and the crowd went crazy again.

Roger was grinning ear to ear, and he looked goofy, but he yelled, "We got the lead; it's early, but we got the lead!"

Morgan walked in a few seconds later, and she was grinning so hard her cheeks would hurt later.

She gave me a big hug and whispered into my ear, "We did it."

She slapped a peck on my lips so fast I didn't even respond with my lips. Keeping her arms wrapped around me, she turned her head to see the first numbers from North Carolina. Trump's lead was significant, and it wasn't a swing state, but it was necessary.

Ohio's first numbers came in next, and the entire place turned to crickets. Trump's lead was huge.

"It's only three percent," Bookworm noted.

"It's early," Roger replied, and he was right; 3% is just that 3%.

I motioned for Mike Jack to come back down, and I asked Morgan, "what do you want to drink?"

She whispered in my ear while rubbing my chest with her hand, "No, I have to work, but hey, don't get too drunk. I want to hang out later, okay?"

She kissed me on the cheek and added, "I got to run, I am still working, but we will both meet the president-elect later."

She left as quickly as she had arrived, and I noticed the entire room had eyes on her. She was a sight of beauty. Her lips had the taste of cotton candy, and I puckered mine to taste her again.

The Virginia numbers flashed onto the screen, and Trump was up with just under 4% returned. As soon as I read that Trump was leading, I got a jolt in my ass up my spine to my head, and I had to stand up.

Trump was going to fucking win!

I felt it in my bones.

Roger calmed me though when he said in his deep voice, "Kaine will win Virginia. These are early numbers just to keep the Trump voters around all night for the ratings."

Then he added his slogan, "It's early."

His voice was deep, and it was heard across the bar and into the reception area. I was nervous again, and I grabbed the bowl of popcorn Mike Jack had placed in front of me when I asked for water, and I nibbled away on the stale kernels.

Bookworm repeated the motto, "it is early."

The heat I had felt from thinking Trump might pull it out was gone. I was back to being cold, so I needed to warm the place up.

"Shots, we need some shots to get the mojo back," I handed Mike Jack three crispy Franklins.

"Keep fifty for yourself, and make us 250 bucks worth of shots, please."

It took her longer to make up the shots, but she made at least 35 shots, and she started to hand them out. The barback was running to get more shot glasses, so I helped her distribute them. People were gathering around from all over the tiny bar, and they all looked at me with their cups in the air. I didn't want to do another "For Hitler" type of cheer, so I held up my shot glass and said, "It's early!"

"It's early!" Everyone repeated it.

I slammed my glass down onto the bar and said it a third time, "it's early."

Roger nodded at me, and Bookworm put his arm on my back.

"Hurry up and wait, I guess," I said, and we did.

It was a hotel utterly full of people waiting to explode and celebrate. Hillary was down early, but it was still early. I was the only person in the entire hotel that wanted Trump to pull it off, and I still had a slimmer of a chance.

By the time 8 pm rolled around, and the second wave of numbers flashed on the screen, all of us except Roger were hammered; even Mike Jack was blitzed as I had made sure she was keeping up with us.

The good news hit us first as we saw Hillary was likely the winner of Illinois, New Jersey, Maryland, Massachusetts, Rhode Island, Delaware, and the District. The place lit up like the ball was dropping; everyone was clapping, hollering, hooting, cheering, and pounding on the long oak bar.

Then the bad news hit, and everyone found the shut-up button. Trump was the likely winner of Oklahoma, Tennessee, and Mississippi. The place got as quiet as a high school keg party with the cops at the door. (So yes, it was still noisy, but only from small conversations.)

Roger was still writing on his napkins, keeping score, so I leaned in to read his pigeon scrawl. He yanked the napkins back, "this is all chalk; Florida and Pennsylvania is the real game."

As he finished his sentence, a text hit my phone, and it was from Dude D.

"We are going to take Pennsylvania!"

Shit!

"Shit, Trump might take Pennsylvania," I said softly, but Roger heard me.

I showed him my phone, and Bookworm moved over my shoulder to see it, and Jimbo came on the other side of Roger.

Jimbo questioned, "Who is we?"

I snatched my phone back and put it in my pocket.

"That is a text from a guy in Trump's camp. I am a writer for Rolling Stone Magazine, so naturally, I talk to both camps. He is a - "

Bookworm cut me off, "A writer? Damn it; I was betting on you being a tech guy like Markle Zuckleberry!"

Roger cut him off, "How credible is that?"

"It is difficult to say at this point, but if I had a gun to my head, I would say it is very credible. 90% likely and the ten percent chance that it isn't is because he got fed false information."

Roger pulled his napkin back out, smoothed the wrinkles out, "The key to win is 270. That is it; that is the ballgame. Trump is at forty-eight right now, and Hillary is closing in on seventy."

The top of his napkin read H68 T48.

"It is early. Let's do another round of beers just for us. Roger, you want another N/A?"

If I didn't drink, I would blow it and admit I was for Trump, and these guys were either people who worked on the campaign for Hillary or fanatics. The friction might turn into fisticuffs.

I ordered another round and bought Jacko whatever she was sipping on behind the bar.

"Florida is going to come down to one vote or sumshit," I blurted out before sipping my beer.

The whole place got quiet as new numbers flashed. Hillary was leading Ohio and North Carolina. My stomach fell to my knees, and I chugged my beer.

Shit, Hillary is going to pull this out. The media was right!

I chugged my beer until it was gone. I would need to be wasted to not cause a scene after losing thirty thousand dollars.

More numbers flashed across the screen, but my vision was getting impaired. I bent in to see Roger's numbers, and he had new ones written on a fresh napkin. H68 T66.

A knucklehead yelled from the reception area, "New York is all in for Hillary!"

Roger pumped his fist, "That is 29!"

And I wanted to ask him, "How credible is that?" I held it back since it was some random dude yelling from another room, and he was taking it as gospel.

The voice rang out again, "Nebraska for Trump."

The screen flashed us the news too. Trump was taking Nebraska, Wyoming, and Kansas.

Roger began to jot down the numbers, and that is when I realized Roger knew how much each state was worth in the electoral college.

He did the math, and looked at me, "it's early."

Then he leaned into Mike Jack as she walked by, "can I get a clean, double shot of the best whiskey you got in the house?"

The heat shot up from my butt again. I stood up from my barstool and felt I might win again. It was real. Roger had been drinking N/A all night, and he had been stating "it's early" after every sentence, but now he wanted a shot of the best whiskey in the bar. He knew something, or he had a hunch.

He turned and looked me right in my eyes, "I only drink once a year. I take one shot of bourbon on Christmas Eve, but I guess this year I am drinking twice."

Was he celebrating or nervous? I didn't know, but my gut was telling me he was scared.

The whole place went dark, and the big giant screen in the reception hall lit up. The states that Hillary won were blue, and the state's Trump won were red. We all looked at the screen as both the Dakotas turned red for Trump.

Nobody in the place said a single word.

I broke the silence, "those states are always red."

Mike Jack placed a shot of Old Pappy Van Winkle in front of Roger, and I said, "I need a double of that too."

I didn't offer to buy anyone else one.

Roger took his shot, and pounded it onto the wood of the bar, "she is almost at a hundred."

Then he coughed like an 8th grader drinking Jim Beam.

"What do you think?" I asked Roger.

He shook his head before he answered.

"If it goes Ohio to Trump, Florida Trump, it's trouble. It is early in Virginia, and I think Kaine wins it, but it's not looking good. It is early, though."

"It's early," I repeated, and then Bookworm did too.

I began to pace behind my chair, and I chugged the rest of the expensive whiskey in front of me and then paced again. Two steps left, two steps right. I didn't want to lose my seat, but I couldn't sit down. Then numbers flashed on the screen for the Keystone State.

Roger pumped his fist and said, "You might want to call your friend back and let him know Trump isn't winning Pennsylvania."

His voice was deeper now, and the whiskey flowed in his blood. I wanted to remind him that it was early, but I didn't, and I didn't have time either as the new numbers for the Mile High State flashed.

Hillary was up big.

Shit!

My mind raced to the realization that maybe I was a born loser. Luck wasn't on my side, and it never came my way. Multiple generations in my family had been trying to win the easy money, most of them tossing away tickets betting the ponies at Churchill Downs, and I wasn't any different.

A voice rang out, "Texas for Trump!"

And it was repeated a few times, so I knew it was legit. It was also chalk.

Then another voice, "Trump wins Arkansas."

I picked up my pacing and stopped behind Roger to see how many points that was. Then I asked him, "Arkansas, wasn't Hillary supposed to win her home state?"

Bookworm let me know, "That's not her home state, she was born in Illinois, and she was in the Senate from New York. She won both of those states, and New York is Trump's home state."

I turned around to look at him, and behind his wire-rim glasses, his eyes were bloodshot, and he was sloshed.

Hopium kicked back in, and I began to believe I had a chance.

I pulled out a few more hundreds from my wallet, and I motioned to Mike Jack.

"I need another round of shots!"

"The glasses are all getting washed; you bought us out earlier," She informed me.

"Okay, well, let's get a round of beers for everyone," I

said.

The eyes were on me now as everyone wondered why I was buying a round of beers to celebrate Trump winning a few states. Nobody declined the free beer, though.

Roger's napkin read, H97 T 128.

When he saw me looking, I said, "it's early."

It was repeated down the bar.

"It's early."

"It's early."

"It's early."

I told Roget to guard my seat, and then I told Mike Jack to watch it too.

The bar was crawling with people now. I walked into the hallway and could see the reception area was packed too. The band was about to jam. I walked around searching for Morgan, but I didn't see her, so I called her.

"Hello," she answered, but before I could say anything, she said, "Trump, Trump, Trump might win floor, uh, duh."

"Trump might win Florida?" I asked.

She didn't answer me, because she was crying too hard.

"No, I don't think so," I said with a sad tone, but I wanted to jump up and down.

"It's early. It is still early," I told her as she whimpered on the other line.

"The Dade County numbers are not looking good."

"It's early, babe; it's really early. What about Pennsylvania?"

"I don't know."

She was sobbing like a child who just found out the Easter bunny wasn't real.

"Okay, well, the night is young, and it is early."

"I am in here working on my pitch to Hillary; I am prepping for it, and now she might not even win."

She was balling harder now, and at the point where she couldn't say a word even if she wanted.

"Do you want to meet me at the bar? You need a drink."

"Okay," she spit out somehow.

"It is early; we are all going to celebrate tonight!"

Walking through the crowd back to the bar, the mood was like the passengers on the Titanic after the giant boat hit the iceberg. I didn't see a single smile. The guys were all just as depressed too. I quickly asked Mike Jack if the shot glasses were back, and she said they were.

"Let me get another round for this, and you keep yourself fifty," I handed her three bills.

Roger slammed his fist to the bar and said, "let's fucking do it!"

The glass in front of him was empty. He was drunk, but he did say, "I am sorry about that," at least seven times afterward. Finally, he put his hands up as if he had just been called for his fifth foul. He was embarrassed, but nobody cared. Most of the room wanted to pound their fists too.

"Trump is up in Ohio," Bookworm reminded him.

Roger clenched his fist and told us both, "If Trump holds in Ohio and Florida, I don't see a path for Hillary."

I had to remind them, "it's early."

Holy shit, I might actually win this thing!

Jacko was handing out the shots and yelled out, "We gotta change the mojo up in here!"

Jacko smiled at me like a middle school child in a communistic country getting picked to be an Instagram influencer.

I smiled back because I was about to be rich and not from counterfeit money. She was having a nice night for herself at my expense, and she was also lit.

"Can I still get some food?"

"What do you want, hun?"

"How about a burger and fries?"

"I will put that in for you, hun."

My phone had two messages from Dude D.

"Trump is going to steal Michigan."

I repeated it to Roger, "Trump is going to take Michigan."

Jimbo leaned over to inform me, "He is up right now, but Detroit isn't in it. That is the Democratic area."

Bookworm reminded us both, "It is early!"

"It's early."

It was closing into 10 pm, and the night was all Trump.

Roger was worried about other things, "Kaine better win his home state, or this will be ugly and over."

A voice rang out from the back of the bar, "New Hampshire for Trump!"

The four of us at the front of the bar yelled out in unison, "it's early!"

But it wasn't early anymore. It was after 10 pm, and it was getting late. The tide was turning against Hillary. We all sensed it; Roger was inches away from turning into an angry drunk. He was sipping a beer now and not a N/A.

He pounded the bar again, but this time not as hard, "the conservative meatheads in New Hampshire would still be licking the queen's boots if it wasn't for the rest of the country!"

Another voice rang out, "Connecticut for Hillary!"

Nobody cheered. The mood was dampening towards dark, and the screen flashed with the information that Louisiana was all in for Trump.

Roger quickly added up the numbers.

H104 T136

Shit, it might happen!

Mike Jack handed me a burger, and I dropped her a hundred, telling her to keep the change and asked for a bloody Mary. I wanted something healthy to drink.

Bookworm said, "Montana is red."

He couldn't even say the guy's name.

The nerves in the room could have started a fire.

I asked Bookworm, "Do we have the final results from Florida?"

"Not yet."

Jacko handed me a shot and pointed to a man at the other side of the bar, "that man bought this for you."

I held the shot up high and pointed to the man, "I appreciate it!"

I took the shot, and that was it. That was the shot that destroyed me. It put me over the top and the edge. I didn't lose my cookies right away, but my stomach made a noise, so I knew I would later. That is the type of survival skill I had acquired in my life of drinking.

"I need some fresh air."

My vision was blurry, and the whole room was hazy as I tried to leave the bar. It was as if I was trying to wake up and walk simultaneously. I left the bar and turned down the corridor. The hotel floor was tilted and spinning around like a merry-go-round, and I managed to hold onto the wall and make my way to the lobby.

Once I was in the lobby, the carousel continued to spin, but landmines of hidden trampolines were now positioned all over the place. I had to avoid them at all costs or risk falling in front of these Democratic elites.

I stopped walking dead in my tracks when a tall, green man was before me. He was dark green, and his arms were dangling like an octopus.

"It's an alien!" I said, but I hushed myself with my hand over my mouth. If he was an alien and a part of the new world order, I didn't want to disrespect him.

"I meant to say, good evening, sir!" I pretended to pull off my hat and tip it at the green man like it was 1922. I bowed in front of him and said, "have a wonderful evening."

I kept it moving and overshot the exit doors. I wandered into the front desk area when BOOM! I'd stepped on a trampoline landmine. I slipped while I tripped and lost my balance. I didn't fall entirely and was able to balance my way to a big, comfy chair.

I crossed my legs and acted as if I meant to do it. I glanced around, and when I saw that no one was watching me, I stood up. It was too fast for my body, though, and I lost my balance again. I fell forward and knocked down the velvet rope that forms the line front of the front desk.

"Goddamn it!"

It fell quickly, but it didn't smash or make much noise. I paused, and I pulled on the rope to get back up, but I couldn't, so I did a complete circle and fell back into the chair.

"Gunner!" The voice was carrying throughout the whole lobby.

Shit, it was Morgan. I knew the voice before I even turned to see her.

"Gunner."

I squinted my eyes to see the numbers on the screen behind the counter, and I read them to myself.

"149 to 109."

Then I turned around to look in the direction of my name being called.

"Morgan, my darling, how are you?"

And for some reason, I pretended to tip my hat again.

"Gunner, what are you doing?"

She was wearing an odd outfit, and a young lady was wearing the same type of outfit, so I asked her, "What are you wearing?"

I stood up, but very carefully as I was afraid to hit another landmine.

Morgan walked close to me, and I gave her a hug and said, "Congratulations, my lady. What are you wearing?"

"It's a suffragette outfit," She said, but the lady next to her was making a mean face at me.

"Did you have a little too much to drink?" She asked me.

"A little too much to drink, huh?" The lady with her said.

"No, I mean, I would be able to pass a breathalyzer test, I just had one drink, and it was stronger than I thought it would."

Morgan turned to her friend and then turned back to me and asked me, "So you would pass a breathalyzer?"

"Of course, I would, my dear," I said.

"Okay," she replied.

"Okay, what? Do you think I am lying?"

Her friend did for sure, and she said, "Webreathalyzered you walk down the hallway holding onto the wall so you wouldn't fall, and then you tipped your hat and said hello to a fake plant, then you did fall, but you landed in that chair. When you tried to stand up again, you fell forward this time, and you knocked over all those ropes, and then," I got off.

"That is not what happened!" I assured her.

"Really?"

"Really! I was trying to see the score on that television back there!"

Morgan's friend didn't hold an ounce back, and she shouted, "Did you just say the score? Like a score to a game?"

"Who the fuck is this anyway?" I belted at Morgan while her friend was coming at me.

"Are you wasted?" Her friend asked.

Morgan ignored her friend and wasn't listening to me.

"We won California," Morgan told me, and it came at a great time because I was about to unload on her friend.

The whole place erupted when it was announced that California was going blue.

"Gunny, I told you not to drink too much. Can you please get some water?" Morgan said to me in a motherly voice.

She turned to her friend and said, "Maybe she still has a chance."

I opened my mouth but said nothing; I was too drunk to respond.

Morgan gave me a quick hug and said, "I have to run, Gunny, get yourself some water, and please, don't embarrass us, okay?"

Her friend glared at me, and my sixth sense kicked in to let me know she was a cunt.

Water wasn't going to help me now, and I needed a beer. I headed back into the bar; the talk with Morgan had sobered me up, so my walking was better. I sat back down on the barstool next to Roger.

"We are back up!" Roger said as soon as he saw me, and he picked up his napkin and showed me.

H190 T186.

"Okay, it is early, though."

"Let me get four cold ones," I said to the moonwalker

behind the bar. I handed her a Franklin and told her to keep it. I checked my phone, and I saw Dude D had texted me.

"Michigan and Penn for Trump!"

"Yes," I said a little bit too loud.

Bookworm thought I was happy because Hillary was back in the lead, and he put his fist up so I would bump it.

I knocked his fist with mine, and he said, "we are back in the lead!"

We all took a sip of our beers when the familiar voice rang out, "Wisconsin for Trump!"

"Yes!" I yelled out, and I took another swig.

Bookworm noticed, and he said, "Did he say Trump or Hillary for Wisconsin?"

"Trump," Roger said.

"Oh shit, I thought they said, Clinton. I am drunk," I said to save face.

I motioned to Mike Jack, she walked over, and I asked her, "Do you have any champagne?"

"Yes, sir, we have them in the back, but we cannot open them until it has been announced."

"Until what is announced?"

"Until it is announced that Hillary is the winner."

My phone chimed with another text. It was from Dude D, and it read one word: FLORIDA!

I couldn't help myself when I said, "Those filthy rednecks did it; Florida is going to Trump!"

Bookworm was the first to say anything, but I felt all

eyes on me.

"Whose side are you on, anyway?"

"Huh? No, I know, I am *for* Hillary, and if you want me to root for her to win as if it makes a difference, I can. I rooted for the Cubs to win the World Series for years, and I don't think that's why they won this year. Does it even matter if I cheer and root for Hillary to win? Look, guys, I voted for her, which was against my interest. I could win close to a million dollars if Trump wins, and I put a thirty thousand dollar bet on Trump to win before the odds flipped."

I said it with a long wind. I was hoping they would understand my predicament. They were all quiet, so I figured they understood. I shot Morgan a text since none of them said anything and asked her where we would meet.

Jimbo was the first to say, "You bet on Trump to win?"

It was a short sentence, but it was with a condescending tone as if I was the idiot, and I was the one about to win. They were all about to lose it, and Roger's fists were clenched. I didn't care, though.

"What happens if Trump wins Florida?" I asked, ignoring his question.

Seconds later, the same voice shot out across the bar, "Florida to Trump!"

Roger began to shake. He was trying to speak, but he couldn't get the words out. Finally, he lowered his head and said, "two hundred, and sixty, two hundred and sixty-eight. Trump is two away from victory."

"Let's get that bubbly on ice," I said to Mike Jack, and she was confused.

I turned to see the depression on the faces of my compadres, so I said, "It's early, and it is still early."

"Washington state for Hillary!"

"See, it is early," I added after the voice yelled.

Roger unclenched his fists, pushed his barstool back, and stormed off like an upset child. I flipped through his napkins, and they were full of more data than the NASA notes that had saved astronaut Tom Hanks on Apollo 13.

"I'm going to get some fresh air," Bookworm said, and he left with his head between his knees.

The mood of the whole hotel had transformed from a party to a funeral home. A wake was about to take place for the hopes and dreams of a candidate. A dead body of reality was setting in, and we all looked up when Georgia came across the screen for Trump.

"Can I buy just one of those bottles?" I asked Mike Jack.

Jimbo was quick to let me know, "Hillary still has a path to victory."

The hotel wasn't counting Florida to Hillary yet.

Mike Jack came back and said, "We have to wait until Hillary wins before we can touch the champagne."

"Fine, fine, fine," I said, and I left the bar.

Searching for Morgan among the tired eyes of the lobby, I stopped and stared at the big screen with the states on it. I turned to an older bespectacled man in a suit and asked him, "So Trump has 268, surely he will score two more points, but can Hillary still win?"

The man pushed his glasses up and answered me quickly, "no."

It was over. I was on my way to becoming the richest person in my family, and Donald Trump was headed to the White House. It was time to pop the champagne. I made my way back into the bar and told Jacko, "I just need one bottle."

The bar was empty and a mess and Jacko also knew the game was over. She went to the back and returned with an ice-cold bottle of yellow champagne, and she popped it, and I tossed her three Ben Franklins.

"Here, let me pour you a glass," I told her, and I snatched a cup from behind the bar and poured her some.

I took the entire bottle into the hallway, drinking out of it, and headed off to find Morgan.

It was all over but the shouting, and I was the only one shouting. Sure, Donald Trump would control the free world, but that didn't matter now. I had just won the biggest bet of my entire life, and to quote Dave Chappelle, I was about to be rich, bitch!

CHAPTER 28

"11-9. Remember, remember the 9th of November."

"I was rich!"

"I was rich?"

The words popped into my head as I lay uncomfortable in a dark place. My left arm was tied to something, and my pants were wet.

Why was I rich? I questioned myself before I remembered, Trump had won. Jesus, did he? His shrine of idiotic followers had done it, and they were now going to build that fucking wall. And I was rich!

Trump was freaking President; maybe I should build a freaking bunker.

So as liberals shed tears for the future of our country, I woke up in my urine with my hand trapped to the back of the closet. Somehow, I maneuvered out. The hotel room was empty; Morgan was gone. A pile of hundred-dollar bills was on the desk.

I took off my pants and attempted to dry them with towels, and then I called Morgan.

"Hello," she had a tone that said she was done with me. I was jumping to conclusions, but considering how I had acted, maybe I wasn't.

"Hello, hey, yeah, hi, Morgan, uh, thanks for letting me

spend the night in your hotel room; I hope I wasn't too much trouble!"

"Too much trouble, Gunner? I do have to say it was a nice touch this morning seeing your legs poke out of the closet, one shoe on, one shoe off, and you were probably lying in your urine. We lost the election last night, the glass ceiling wasn't shattered, and the .."

"Lying in my urine? I was getting something, I believe my Cubs hat out of the closet, and I guess I fell asleep!"

I was lying. She knew it, and I knew it. Her silence on the other end said everything.

"So yeah, I guess you left so...."

"I checked out, so you can stay until 11 am," She said to me firmly as if I was renting the room from her.

"Yeah, so, I guess I put all these hundred dollar bills on the table, huh?"

"Oh, the counterfeit ones that you said I could have?"

"Counterfeit? That's a federal offense; I would never touch fake money!"

"The money on the table that you tried to give to me last night. The counterfeit money you stole from the house where you worked for *Rolling Stone,* or you thought you did, but you probably never did because of these Russians who printed this fake money with this printer. You mean that money?"

Fuck, how could she have known! Perhaps she was a cop.

"How did you know that? Are you a cop?"

"A cop? Are you serious? You told me all that this morning when you were going back and forth to the bathroom because you were hurling! You would come back to the bed, kneel and pray, 'God please make that be the last one, and I will slow the hell down on my drinking. Father, Son, Holy Ghost!' Then you would lay on the bed sideways, and tell me more stories, let's see, you told me about a witch that is hexing out a billy goat curse, how the house you stayed in all summer was a fraud using identity theft, and about who knows what else. Listen, some of us have jobs and we can't just print money!"

"Yeah, well, what about the counterfeit money in my bag? And not all of that was fake; some of it was mine from -"

She cut me off, "You got paid in fake bills, Gunner! You told me that too."

"I don't think they are all fake," I was lying.

"You don't even remember last night, do you?"

I didn't remember, though, so I said not a word.

"Well, we went up to the room after Hillary had conceded, I thought to have sex, but all you did was throw up. Then when you came out of the bathroom, I was naked, and you went to your bag of money and gave me money like I was a whore or something. Then, not until then did you remember who I was, and you started to explain, and you said you think you were poisoned at the bar. When I asked who was poisoned by who, you said, by Russians or by a female Michael Jackson if Michael Jackson was Latina or something wild. You were drunk, and you told me everything, everything!"

"I am sure I was just joking!"

"Oh, you were joking, alright! You said you needed cheese fries from Latina Janet Jackson in your stomach so we went down to the lobby again, which was a terrible decision considering how drunk you were. I was babysitting you at this point. We went to the bar, and it was empty but you demanded to see this Latina Michael Jackson. We left, and you started talking to people. People I know, Gunner! You were telling people, 'take this chump change from the guys on the Trump train.' Seriously, Gunner!"

"I was just trying to help out the Democratic party. Trump won; we should all probably be building a bunker, ya know?"

"Helping the Democratic party? You voted for Trump!"

"I did not; I would never vote for that Cheeto looking mo-"

"Gunner, you told me. You told the whole damn lobby, you put thirty thousand dollars on Trump to win!'

"I bet on him, but I didn't vote for him. I voted for the country, not my own personal gain! Now that I think about it, I am a true patriot here."

"These are people in the DNC and other prominent Democrats, Gunner!"

I could see the pile on the table was very small, and I didn't have a buck in my wallet.

"How much did I give away?" I asked.

"A lot of money, Gunner. A ton!"

"Well, why didn't you stop me?"

"We tried me and my sister and mom. We all tried!"

"Your sister, the cunt in the lobby?" I asked, but I tried to pull it back after I said it. I don't think she heard me as she spoke louder, now telling how I had fucked up.

"My parents drove in from Connecticut, and I thought they had already left. They were outside talking with my sister. You tried to hand money to my dad. When I tried to get you to leave, you would ask about Michael Jackson's cheese fries. It was babysitting; worse than that, it was babysitting a 24-year-old toddler!"

She was pissed.

"So you didn't stop me, and it looks like I handed out about well all but this nine hundred here."

"At least you can go cash in your thirty thousand dollar bet, is that true? Tell me, is that true or just another dumb story you made up trying to impress me like the Russian spies and Rolling Stone?"

She didn't believe me. Shit, I didn't believe the story, and I lived it.

"I think so, but I don't know what I told you," I said to her, and I could hear her sigh with frustration.

That was the end.

The end of my beautiful friend.

The end.

At least when she hung up mid-sentence to me asking, "so what time are you coming back to the hotel?" I knew she wasn't coming back. She had already checked out of the hotel room. I had nine hundred bucks left, barely enough to get a cab to the airport. Thank the good lord for the subway. I arrived a sunken man an hour early for my early flight.

As for Morgan, well, you don't get third chances with ladies that are that beautiful. Although I didn't want to admit it then, I knew the reality, and she was gone forever.

It was over.

PART III MUELLER KNOCKS

"Mistakes make masterful teachers."
-Nas

Two Years Later

Certain names have been changed to protect the guilty and innocent and myself from the guilty and innocent.

CHAPTER 29

"4:42 am Sunday, March 18th, 2018. Bardstown Road Louisville Kentucky."

Hindsight isn't always 2020. Perspective is key, and mine was altered after a night of boozing as I walked up to my new apartment building. I'd been out celebrating my Irish heritage by drinking car bombs and green beer. It was closing in on five am, and a misting rain was falling. It was the type of misting rain that you walk in without realizing you're wet until you get into a dry place. I was singing as I stumbled along.

"Raindrop, drop top, Cookie Monster loves to hotbox!"

Shutting my left eye to see out of my right and avoid double vision, my walk had a cattywampus.

It had been a long night, but it had been a long two years for the country. Well, not for the idiots who were happy a demagogue was in the oval. Collectively, the sane folks were suffering from WTF syndrome every single day. Daily we all said, What the Fuck!

I was trying my damnedest to tune it all out. If I never attended another political rally for the rest of my life, I wouldn't be upset. I avoided the topic of Trump and Trumpies if I could; I couldn't, but I steered clear of political conversations, which helped. The dumb had prevailed, and now they were entitled about their man. Trumpies felt entitled because they had predicted the establishment takeover despite being told Trump didn't have a shot at winning. Now, they all had Dunning-Krueger and wanted to inform the rest of the world how smart they were. They had banded together to beat Hillary, and they were in charge.

The election had flipped the entire country on its ass and backward in time. Science didn't matter because the pollsters were wrong. Black lives didn't matter because Trump said so, and he was in charge now. That's how these folks thought, anyway. They loved the Trumpster as if he was king. He was their king, and since he was the sitting president, he was, in a sense, everyone's king.

He was living like one too. The king was running up outstanding bills on taxpayers, giving tax breaks to all his wealthy friends, and the working class, who would be paying these taxes, freaking loved him. It was the death of America. Nero fiddled, Trump golfed.

The man was both ubiquitous and inexorable. And I tuned the F out.

St. Paddy's day arrived, so I ran amuck, wildy. It was over now, and I was eager to saw logs on my new king size.

As I got closer to my new apartment building, I noticed a man with an assault rifle. My mind was so discombobulated, I didn't even stop walking. Fight or flight, and I just kept walking like a drunk moron.

I saw the man, saw the gun, and didn't comprehend.

The lone gun-toting man turned into three, and I walked up on three men; they were packing to the max and dressed in black with LPD printed across their backs. They were about to raid some unlucky fool in my building and pulling on the door as if they just pulled hard enough; it would open.

"The Federales!" I exclaimed, and I began singing another tune.

"The federales want to see me dead; that's why I got two rottweilers by my bed; I feed them lead."

I held up my fob.

"You gotta use a magic fob to get inside."

I put it up to the sensor, and a loud buzzing rang out as the door unlocked. The cop in front, who had been tugging at the door unsuccessfully, now opened it. None of them thanked me as they went inside.

I could only imagine who they were about to arrest, and I hoped it was the cunt on the second floor with the loud rat dogs. I wouldn't be that lucky, though. It was probably the middle-aged guy, Joe, and his girlfriend in 2C. They were drug addicts bringing down the value of the whole place.

The three amigos stopped once inside, and turned to me.

"Which apartment are you going into, sir?"

"I am not going into 2C," I informed them because I knew where they were going.

"2C, okay, you are clear. Please go into your apartment, lock the door, and do not come outside."

I wasn't going to 2C, but these guys had donut crumbs in their ears. Shit, if I didn't help them inside with my fob, they would still be outside pulling on a push door. I headed up the stairs, and watched them hit the elevator button. I had to walk four flights up, but it was better than riding with the bozos. They might smell the chronic on my clothes or accidentally shoot their weapon into my back.

I raced up the stairs, and my adrenaline was hot. There was about to be a major bust, someone was going to get a rude morning awakening, and I could film the whole thing on my new Sony handheld camera. I ran and grabbed it, but I had to make a pit stop since the beer was coming out.

I heard something on my floor and thought, "Maybe it's not the guy in 2C, and it is Bruce up here!"

The closer I got to my door, the louder the voices got, so I knew they were here to arrest Bruce. I put my eye up to the peephole, and the whole door came down on top of me.

CHAPTER 30

"Bobby Three Sticks"

The local boys screwed the pooch. I can only wish I was conscious and heard how it all went down. The three little pigs weren't alone when I came to my senses. My apartment was crawling with LE, and I sat, handcuffed, trying to remember what in the hell happened.

They were scrambling around my place like hobos looking for loot, and Bobby Three Sticks was yet to arrive. He was on his way, though, along with the local fed boys. A few of the local feds were onsite as I woke up, and they were already searching for a person to point the finger at among the local boys.

The three stooges and the rest of the local Louisville boys in blue thought they had jurisdiction and an arrest warrant. They didn't. The FBI did. (I didn't know any of this at the time, and it didn't matter because, according to the F.B.I, I was a wanted man. I'd find out the details later.)

I'd never find out why Bobby himself was in the Ville for the arrest of a peon. I was a tiny guppy amongst the sharks he should be hunting. The speculation ran rampant; he was in town to have his heart looked at, or his wife was playing in a women's league golf tourney, or his brother lived in Kentucky. Nobody knew, and I never found out. It might show that he didn't know what the hell was going on with the entire case; I will leave that up to others to decide. It is funny how nothing came of it all, though.

I sat up and watched the changing of the guard happening in real-time. I didn't know it at the time, but the local boys were running around like chickens trying to exit the scene and find a fall guy. The rooster was coming to roost, and he was the head of the freaking F.B.I. They didn't want to be around when the consequences of their actions came calling.

The big cock stepped out of the elevator, and it was all eyes on him.

Bobby Three Sticks was taller in person, and his presence cooled the room. I felt it, and I didn't even know who he was at the time. The skin on his face stretched over his bones, making him look like a 1950s comic book detective. He was lanky like Abraham Lincoln and carried himself with stoic poise.

Flanking him were two men, one about his size and the other an NFL linebacker-sized black dude, and they were giving him the rundown of the situation.

He stopped walking, so they stopped; his eyes scanned the scene of local boys scrambling. He turned to the linebacker and asked him, "an ambulance; why the hell do we need an ambulance."

"It is from the local situation; I was trying to relay it in, some sort of jurisdiction issue, and sir, I guess the local boys went ahead and did a no-knock," the linebacker-sized man said.

"A no-knock? What kind of hillbilly stuff is going on? A no-knock warrant, has that been legal this century?"

Bobby stared at the linebacker man, cutting him down

to the size of a dwarf. The huge man put his head down to respond, "Yes, sir, it is legal in our commonwealth."

"A no-knock warrant, you might get somebody killed doing that backward -; it isn't the 1800s," Bobby responded without listening.

The linebacker was nervous. He nodded and then said in one breath, "Yessir."

"So, what's the status?"

"We have a local guy; he is, uh," the man was visibly nervous. The eyes were still on them, and he began to yell, "Where is Roberts?"

A voice shot back at him, "Roberts is inside."

"Get him out here, stat!"

Another man approached and handed Bobby a few papers, and he read them while Roberts came out of my apartment.

"I'm Roberts," he said.

The linebacker turned to Bobby and said, "That's Roberts."

"Who the fuck is Roberts?"

Bobby was as frustrated as I was, and I had a squad of cops sniffing my boxers.

"Roberts, sir, this is Roberts. Roberts, this is -"

Roberts cut off the linebacker.

"Robert Mueller, I know who it is. Mr. Mueller, it is an honor!"

He stuck his hand out to shake it and began to act as if he had Bobby's poster on his wall at home.

Bobby didn't have time for it, though.

"So?" Bobby was a man of few words.

"Yes, sir, I wasn't on the scene," Roberts told him.

"So who was?" The linebacker snapped.

"Welchie was here. Officer Chuck Welch."

"Okay," Bobby answered.

"Welchie! Welchie!"

They had their fall man in Welch, and he was moving slower than a peanut butter drip, so Roberts ran inside to find him.

"One minute, sir, Welchie!"

Finally, Welch stopped stealing my belongings and exited my apartment.

He was fat and pale and dripping bullets of sweat. Unbeknownst to me, he was the cop who walked on top of my door while I was under it after they kicked it down while I was looking out the peephole.

Welchie didn't have a clue as to how badly, collectively, the local boys had screwed up, and he didn't know that he was about to take the blame. Messing up an F.B.I investigation is one thing, but messing up an investigation led by Bobby Three Sticks was damn-near career suicide.

Welch stopped and almost saluted Bobby before he straightened up his sloppy uniform. His fat ass was too big to be a cop. He didn't say a word, and Bobby stared at his receding hairline before turning to the other man flanking him and asked, "Who is this?"

"Welch, sir," the man responded.

"I am Welch."

"What is going on? Why do I care?" Bobby asked.

Welch was ready to talk now, "Sir, we broke down the door as soon as we arrived. We were serving the warrant, your warrant, but before we could ID the man, he was under the door. I was the one who walked on top of the door with him under it."

"Why in the hell did you do that?"

Blood was drying on my face, and I vaguely remembered this flat-footed, fat ass on top of the door while I was under it.

"Sir, we didn't know he was behind the door; he was looking out the peephole or right near it when it came down."

As it all flashed back to my memory, I decided it was an excellent time to have my voice heard.

"That dumbass walked on top of the door with me under it. They didn't even knock before they kicked the shit down; there was no warning at all. Officer Numbnuts stood on top of the door with me under it and tell us, how much do you weigh? 300 pounds? Does the LPD not have a weight limit!"

"Shut him up," Welch yelled out, but Bobby put his hand up to tell him to shut up.

"Did you identify yourself?" Bobby asked.

"Yeah, did you identify yourself?" Welch yelled at me, but Bobby was staring at him.

"Not him, you. Did you knock and tell them you were with law enforcement?"

"Me? No sir, we had a warrant, and we were doing a no-knock."

"A no-knock, what type of Wyatt Earp BS are you local boys practicing down here in Kentucky?"

Bobby wasn't looking for an answer, but Welch tried to give him one.

"The good kind, sir, we are practicing the good kind."

Bobby approached me, ignoring Welch and his excuse. He asked me, "Are you Bush, Gunner A. Bush?"

He stuck three fingers up with his ring finger down and asked me, "Is your head hurting? How many fingers do I have?"

The whole hallway was quiet; everyone was suddenly worried about my wellbeing, but five minutes earlier, they didn't give a fuck and wouldn't shut up.

"Gunner A. Bush, no, no, I am Gunner B. Bush, I am heir to Bush Beans. I can show you a finger!" I yelled back.

I was tired of getting pushed around and stepped on, and I also didn't know who in the hell Bobby Three Sticks was at the time. I didn't collect baseball cards of my favorite police officers. I had no clue; he was just another asshole cop in a room full of asshole cops throwing my possessions around while looking for counterfeit money that was long gone. The legal money I had won from my Trump lottery bet was scattered around the city in banks. The tiny amount of cash in my apartment was legally obtained.

My words jolted Bobby, and not because they were superb lines. If I were given a chance again, I would come up with something clever to say at these assholes. No, Bobby was confused because he'd never had anyone talk smack to him before. He wasn't a low-grade mall security cop, he was the top dog in law enforcement, and he likely never did these types of raids. The fact that he was in the Ville meant I was in deep doo-doo.

"He is drunk, sir, really stinking drunk, we had a unit tailing him, Agent Jones, and he was at the bar yesterday morning before anyone else. He might have spent all day and night there."

"I'm Irish; I was celebrating my heritage!"

"You guys should see the amount of liquor we found inside his place. More empty bottles than a dumpster behind a bar," Welchie was quick to add.

"Get this guy to the hospital, and then bring him back over to, where in the hell is the -?"

"Sycamore Street," someone yelled out.

"Yeah, Sycamore Street, and I want to see if the Russians call you Gunner A. Bush or Comrade Bush!"

Bobby was pissed. He stormed into my apartment to see the mounds of liquor bottles, and that was my whole encounter with him. I was taken downstairs and put into an unmarked vehicle with Agent Jones, and Officer Welch rode with us.

They took me to Kindred, I was examined by a sleeping ER doctor working with a spoon, and I got to have a real encounter with the law.

Agent Jones left to get food, and Officer Welch stayed with me to ensure I wouldn't skedaddle.

As soon as the doctor left the room, Officer Jones wanted his revenge, payback for my obese comment. He hadn't forgotten about it, and he reminded me with a punch to my gut. My jaw dropped, and I gasped for air.

"Punk ass kid, you are a traitor to our country," He said it through his teeth, attempting to sound tough.

A nurse entered, and he kept up the stern voice and said, "Hands behind your back, you are going to federal prison, dirtbag!"

"Dirtbag, you're the one with that stank ass breath. Can you get this guy a tic tac?" I asked the nurse.

"Shut up, Bush, or do the comrades call you Russian?" He was butchering Bobby's line.

"Sir, the doctor said he is free to go," the nurse told Welch, and she was talking with a hint of sexiness. It was just luck; she had a fetish for a man in uniform or sumshit.

Welchie flipped me down, cuffed me, and stood me up. He was trying to impress this ugly broad.

"If I end up a suicide with two gunshots to the back of the head, you remember I am not suicidal," I yelled out.

"Shove it up your pie hole," He tightened the cuffs so tight I lost circulation.

"He's a bad guy, huh?" The nurse asked as Welch walked me out of the room.

We stopped before leaving, and Welch said, "I need to recheck him and make sure he didn't steal anything when the doctor looked him over."

He kicked my legs open, slammed my head into the wall so hard the drywall cracked, and began to frisk me.

"Yeah, I stole the stethoscope!"

"Shut your pie hole!"

"This is a big catch for us boys in Jefferson County and Louisville Law Enforcement; he is wanted for serious crimes against the country."

"Oh my goodness," the nurse moaned.

"What the heck, crimes against our country?"

They had the wrong person; from the jump, I figured the cops were arresting me for counterfeiting money and maybe credit card fraud.

"We gotta go, ma'am," Welch said in his macho voice.

"Let's go, Bush Beans."

He marched me out of the room, down a hall, and into a waiting room area that was empty besides an aquarium.

Exiting the ER into the parking lot, rain clouds blocked the sun, and a soft rain fell.

The parking lot was desolate besides an ambulance driver burning a smoke.

Welchie led me with his hand on my back; he shoved me right and then left and then back right and then left. He turned me completely around in a 180, stopped, and moved me in a 180 the other way.

I was dizzy, so I snapped, "Are we dancing here or what?"

"I said to shove it," he said while spinning me around again.

My body was getting whiplash from his movements, and he turned me one more time before stopping right in the middle of the road that was covered.

"Welch here at the hospital, I need to find Agent Jones, Jones left me at the hospital, and I need to contact him, over," he was speaking into the CB on his shoulder.

"Jones, left you at the hospital, over?"

"Uh-huh, we rode down here together, I'm at Kindred, and I was with the no-knock, Bush, he was getting value-ated, but he has been discharged. I need to contact Jones, and he left to get some food, over."

"Value ated? I didn't get E-valuated at all, and you punched me and slammed me into the wall after the doctor left!" I was screaming, but Welch jerked my hands, so I shut up.

"Jones isn't working tonight, over."

"Not Doug Jones, no I need to get in contact with Agent Jones from the F.B.I. over."

"We will get you that information over."

"You guys couldn't go fifteen minutes without a donut run in the middle of the shift, huh?"

"You're pissing me off, Bush."

He was pissed, and I was handcuffed, so I stopped talking.

He was breathing hard and flustered. He wasn't the type of guy who handled challenging situations very well. He wouldn't be high on my list of ideal candidates to make rash decisions while holding a gun, but here he was.

"Well, do you mean Agent Jones with the Mueller stuff?"

"Yes, over."

He loosened my hands to think, and a car approached the hospital. It was coming our way, and since he wasn't holding my back anymore, I moved to the curb nearest me. Being the numbnuts he is, Welch walked away from me towards the hospital.

The car had its lights right on us, but it wasn't slowing down, so I sped up my pace. I glanced back at Welch as he looked at me and realized we were heading in opposite directions.

Wanting to save any grace I could, I yelled out, "I'm not leaving."

But with the car approaching, the rain, and Welch not being able to hear, all he heard was, "I'm leaving."

His cop training kicked in, or sumshit, and he turned to sprint back towards me. The car was slowing down, so I did too, but Welch didn't. He leaped into me, hitting my shoulder first like an awkward fat lineman might, and I didn't even have hands in front of me to brace my fall.

I landed on my fucking face on the blacktop.

All 264 pounds of Welch were on top of me for the second time that morning. The headlights from the car were on both of us, shining brightly into my eyes, and I regained my composure as the driver's side door opened. Agent Jones stepped out of the vehicle with his fingers sticky from Clifton's Donuts and precisely placed on the trigger of his weapon, which was aimed at my noggin.

"What in the hell is going on here? Did he try to run? He was trying to run?" Agent Jones barked looking for an answer.

Welch flipped me over, and I didn't resist one iota.

"He was running?" Agent Jones holstered his weapon.

"No, yeah, no," Welchie finally responded.

My body had been through more than Joe Theisman playing the Giants. I was regaining my thoughts, however.

I snapped, "Are you kidding me? Do you think I couldn't outrun you, you fat fuck?"

"It doesn't matter, get him in the car," Jones yelled at us.

We created a scene, nurses were staring out the window, and the ambulance driver was also alerted.

Welch threw me into the back of the car, and we sped off.

CHAPTER 31

When I arrived at the F.B.I building, my brain hurt, my body ached, and my hangover came. I was searched (again), fingerprinted, and mugshots were taken. I was going to view a judge via a screen. None of it felt real, and even the mugshots felt fake as if I was getting pranked.

I honestly thought I might pass out as I waited for the judge to appear in front of the screen.

The judge read the charges against me, but I couldn't even process a single digit.

Espionage, conspiracy, counterfeiting, fraud, and treason. Fucking Treason!

After he read through the laundry list, he asked me, "with the possibility of treason, at this time, how do you plead?"

"Huh?" It was all I could say.

My follow-up statement wasn't much better.

"What?"

"At this time, would you like to enter a plea?"

"Not guilty. Not guilty at all; look, I was being funny when I told the cops my name wasn't Gunner A. Bush, I am, but I think I was a case of mistaken identity. I was a victim of identity theft. It was probably by these Russians that hired me to work at *Rolling Stone Magazine*."

"Not guilty is the plea, and we will schedule a court date and an arraignment for 30 days. Since you are a flight risk considering your outside-the-country connections, including the just mentioned Russians, and the high value of this case, I am not issuing a bond. Please take the paper with you, and I advise you to speak with our agents. I will see you in thirty days."

The screen went black, and a paper shot out of a printer.

"I want to speak to an attorney; this is bullshit!"

Finally, I remembered my rights.

Agent Jones was behind me, and I turned to him to tell him that too.

"I want my attorney, my rights, shit, my rights to an attorney, and my phone call. Don't I get a phone call?"

"Yes, you get a phone call," he informed me.
"Good, I would like to call my attorney - "

I paused, and then I started to laugh hysterically.

"My attorney, like I have an attorney. I don't have an attorney; what am I, some sort of life-long criminal with an attorney? I'm not Don Juan with the mob, or wait; it isn't Don Juan, it is Mafia Don. I'm not Al Capone here; I don't have an attorney."

I was slap happy and hungover. Delusions would be coming on next.

I was laughing, and Agent Jones was staring at me, likely wondering if I should be committed. I was charged with treason, and I was laughing.

Jones knew the routine, though, and he led me into a side office with a phone.

There was a desk with a blue chair behind it, so I sat down and picked up the phone. Then I put it down. I didn't know who to call.

Staring at the sheet of paper with my charges, they still didn't register.

"You need to dial nine to get out; you got five minutes, kid." He told me.

"Dial nine to get out? I don't know the number of an attorney by heart. I don't even know my mom's number, and I call her every day. All the numbers are on my phone, and I don't have my phone. I don't have an attorney's number on my phone either. I can't pull an attorney's number out of my ass like a magician."

"There is a phone book," he said as he pointed, and then he added, "dial nine to get out; you got five minutes."

If I didn't mention I wanted to call my attorney, the law dogs wouldn't bring it up. They would let me confess to every petty crime, speeding ticket, I'd ever done in my life before they mentioned the word lawyer. They would have taken me to Guantanamo if I hadn't brought up my rights.

I spun around in the chair and picked up the phone book.

I thought about calling my parents, but I only had five minutes, and they weren't attorneys.

"Do I even know an attorney?" I asked myself. I couldn't think of one.

Flipping the phone book open to the A's, the first attorney listed was an advertisement for Sawyer's dad, Wayne Barnes. His mug was smiling right at me with the words, "We Never Stop Until We Win."

"Right, Mr. Barnes!"

I dialed nine and then dialed the listed number.

It rang once, and a female answered, "Barnes and Miller."

"Barnes, I'd like to speak to Barnes, Mr. Barnes. Please."

"Okay, can I ask who is calling?"

"Yeah, sure, this is Gunner Bush; I am a friend of his son, Sawyer."

"Let me check if he is available."

After a minute, Mr. Barnes joined the call.

"Gunner, my man, I have been meaning to call you."

"Oh really, oh yeah, about Sawyer, how is he?"

"He is doing better, we got him some help, therapy, and he is back on his meds. He is doing good."

"Good," I said, but then I paused.

"So, is that why you are calling?"

"No, it isn't. I got in some trouble; I got arrested."

"Oh shoot, did you get a Dewey?"

"A Dewey?"

"A D-U-I."

"A D-U-I, oh no, I got arrested by the F.B.I for some things; hold on, let me read the charges from this paper."

I found the paper on the desk.

"The feds got you? Do you have a bond?" he asked me.

"The judge said no bond, so my charges are treason, fraud, counterfeiting, identity theft, but let me assure you, I was the victim of identity theft. I didn't steal anyone's identity; I don't even know how to steal one. As a young kid, I thought identity theft was like the bad guys on Scooby-Doo, you know, with the masks on that the gang would pull off. I always thought that was what identity theft was as a kid; you know what I mean?"

"Have you been drinking, or are those your real charges?"

"What?"

"Are you joking here or what?"

"No, I wasn't a bright kid, but this is when I was like four or five years old. I would be at home watching Scoob, I liked Scrappy the best, and for some reason, a commercial for identity theft would always come on during the show. They were really missing their target audience, don't you think? So -"

"What are you talking about, Gunner?"

"I was a victim of identity theft, but this list goes on, so it says conspiracy to commit election fraud, interfering with a national election, possessing the identification of another person, which doesn't that kind of sound like identity theft again?"

"Jesus, Mary, and Joseph, what in the hell did you do?"

"I know I didn't do any of this bullshit."

"I thought you were a journalist for the Courier Press or a magazine?"

"Yes, I was, sir, Rolling Stone."

"Yeah, Rolling Stone, so what in the hell is all this?"

"I'm not sure; I worked for Rolling Stone, or I thought I did back in 2016, but I think that's when I was a victim of identity theft, but I never confirmed it. I never really dug into it, though."

"What do you mean, you didn't dig into it?"

"I don't know, I guess; I never looked into a few credit cards opened in my name."

"It sounds like you are in a whole lot of trouble."

"You could have said; it sounds like you are in a whole heap of trouble. I always wanted to use that line in a sentence but never had the chance."

The delusions were alive.

"Are you down in Jefferson County right now?"

"County, no, I am not. They got me at the federal building on Sycamore Street."

"Son, you are in some deep shit. Do your parents know where you are?"

"No, I did get abused by the local police, but -"

He cut me off, "Have you been in front of a judge yet?"

"Yeah, that is where I got this paper, but let me tell you this, I was assaulted by a local police officer, his name is Welch. I don't know his first name, though. He thought I was trying to escape at the hospital, but I was just walking, and this is after he punched me hard in the stomach, which I know is impossible to prove since it was just us two in the room, but let me tell you, we need to sue him for his badge -"

"Why were you at the hospital?"

"I was at the hospital because the local pigs kicked down my door as I was looking out the peephole; they didn't even knock!"

"Really?"

"They didn't knock, and I was the one who let them into the building. They were pushing on a pull door without a FOB, and I let these cruller donut-eating fat asses into the building. They kicked my door down without a knock. It was a no-knock warrant."

"A no-knock warrant! They need to stop those before someone gets murdered," Mr. Barnes yelled.

"Yeah, no shit, like me. I was almost killed."

"What is your folk's number? I want to give them a call, and then I will be right over."

"Maybe we should keep my parents out of this, at least for right now."

"You are an adult now, son. I will be over as soon as I can. Sit tight and don't say a fucking thing. They already know everything. If they got you there, they know fucking everything. Don't utter one complete sentence until I get there!"

CHAPTER 32

"Ignorance of the Law"

The delusions and slap-happy laughter exited, and my hangover turned into a migraine. It was difficult to tell if it was from head trauma from the multiple hits to my cranium or pure exhaustion from a night and day of boozing, but it could have been stress. I was facing life in prison.

It was likely a combination.

I was trying to piece together the pieces, but I couldn't come up with much when Mr. Barnes arrived.

I was also sleep-deprived and hungry.

Mr. Barnes arrived but only saw me briefly. He would have his assistant collect the evidence against me and go through it. It took another hour for us to get a room we could meet inside. I was moved twice, but I met with Mr. Barnes three hours later.

He brought me a cold breakfast sandwich.

"They probably got these rooms all bugged up illegally but using the Patriot Act," Mr. Barnes warned me before he even sat down.

I was eating the McGross when his assistant walked in carrying a long, brown box full of folders.

"This is my assistant, Brian. He is a paralegal."

"That's for my case?"

I didn't get an answer.

The food was nasty, but it made me feel slightly better. Coffee was the real helper, though.

"So you were looking out of your peephole at the exact instant your door was knocked down?"

"Yep, luck of the Irish, my ass," I responded.

"That is when you suffered the head injury?" Brian questioned.

"Yeah, and then after that impact, the fat ass cop named Welch, he walked over the door while I was underneath it."

I moved my head to show them how my head was turned while he walked on top of me. Brian was taking notes.

"And you hit your head again?"

"At the hospital, the same fat pig, I wish I had his badge number, but yeah, he slammed my head into the wall, and he punched me in the stomach. He was mad because I pointed out how he was obese.."

"Then this same officer, he tackled you onto concrete?"

"Yep, he is an idiot, and he thought I was trying to escape, but let me assure you, I am not in shape, but I could outrun this lard ass if I wanted to, but I wasn't trying to at all. I was avoiding a car, and he tackled me. I was in handcuffs, and I couldn't break my fall."

"It's not in the report," Brian informed me.

"Of course, it isn't in the report. Did they mention the F.B.I agent went to get donuts?"

Mr. Barnes was annoyed, and he asked me, "Why were you looking out of your peephole right at that moment? Did they knock?"

"I was the one who let them into my apartment."

"I thought they broke the door down?".

"Not my apartment; I let them into the complex. I didn't know they were there for me; I figured they were there for the dude in 2C. I let them in, and I ran upstairs. I was going to go back and film the raid. I just got this new Sony and -"

"You heard a knock and looked outside, and bam!"

"I didn't hear a knock; I heard them talking and looked out when bam!"

I slammed my hand against the table.

"So they didn't knock?"

"There was no knock!"

Mr. Barnes was over it, "So tell us about the house in Washington D.C.?"

"What house?"

"Your house."

"I don't have a house in Washington D.C. I lived there, but my residence is here in Kentucky."

"A house at this address, REDACTED, REDACTED, Washington D.C?"

"I lived there, I rented a room, or when I worked for the magazine, I lived at that address back in 2016."

"You don't own that house?"

They were getting the wrong information from some-where.

"No."

Brian read from one of the papers, "The house is in your name, the mortgage was paid for almost five years, and closed out, but you didn't pay taxes on the property in the last two years, and the house has been cited four times by the city for high grass."

"It's not my house."

"The deed says it is."

He slid a piece of paper across the table to me.

It was the deed, and it was in my name. Then he slid over a folder with pictures of the Mansion, citations for the yard, and a printed Zillow page stating the house was worth $832,000 and sold in 2016 for $281,700 to Gunner A. Bush. The previous owner was a company listed as Barrikady Factory LLC.

"I told you guys, I was a victim of identity theft."

"Yeah, you said for some credit cards and maybe an electric bill. You didn't say a house worth almost a million."

"Well, I didn't know."

"You didn't know you bought a house?"

"I didn't buy a house! Look, I know this all sounds crazy, it is crazy to me too, but I didn't buy a house!"

"What about the surveillance the feds had you on in Cleveland?" Brian asked.

"What?"

He flipped swiftly through his stack of papers.

"You had a meeting with an undercover agent; he was posing as a member of the Green Party. His name is Hank RE-DACTED, and you owed him a payment. He was in the Green Party at one time, and he helped set up meetings with you and a superior named Terry about adoptions. Does that ring a bell?"

He flipped open another folder and slid it across the table. Inside were photos of me at the coffee shop in Believe-land.

"I know that guy was a cop; I freaking knew it."

I had a feeling of vindication as I flipped through the photos of myself at the coffee shop.

"This undercover agent was involved in another case, he turned state's evidence, and during that trial, he mentioned your name. He stated that you had contacted him wanting meetings with politicians, and you would also pay for photo-graphs of politicians. You met with him a few times; the last was in Cleveland in November 2016. You were under federal surveillance."

"I was?"

Mr. Barnes was finished with the games, and he cut us both off, "Listen, son, the feds were watching you back in Oc-tober of 2016. They have you on film with Morgan REDACTED, trying to obtain illegal evidence stolen from the Hillary Clin-ton campaign house, and they had eyes on you in Cleveland when you met this Hank fellow. Then on two separate oc-casions, they had local feds here in Louisville watching you. The second time led to your arrest. They were watching you for some reason. They stopped watching you back then, but now they got you. These are serious charges against you, so it is time to come clean and tell us what happened. The truth, we need to hear the truth, Gunner. The feds already know it all. They have phone records, cameras, witnesses, emails, the whole nine. You have been caught, and not by some good old boys; the feds have caught you, and let me assure you that you never, ever, ever, lie to the feds. They will fry your ass if you lie about how many times you wiped your ass last shit!"

Mr. Barnes wasn't playing around anymore, "Your ass might fry even if you tell the truth!"

"Don't I get a trial or sumshit? A chance to say my side of the story?"

Brian leaned in, "You are scheduled for a court date in 16 days."

"What do I do for the next 16 days?"

"They are transferring you to Jefferson County Jail; you will wait there."

"There is no bond?" Mr. Barnes asked.

"The order from the judge was no bond considering his out-of-the-country connections."

"Out of the country connections? I've never even left the states!"

"That is steep; he has no priors, we need to get on the phone and figure that out," Mr. Barnes told him.

"So, what do I do?"

"Sit in jail," Brian said.

"No, he has to have a bond," Mr. Barnes said.

"It will be insanely high."

"Can't we put his house up for the bond? That's a huge asset; it's almost a million, probably a million since the last time it was evaluated was over a year ago."

"It's not my house; that house isn't mine!"

"The deed is yours; we have that, the court will take the collateral of the house. The last thing you want to do is sit in county jail. Anything can happen in population."

"That will take some time; you will at the very least spend the night in jail."

It was all news to me, and it was all hitting me fast.

I was the freaking Forrest Gump of the 2016 election cycle, except Forrest was innocent. I was facing charges and about to spend the night in jail. I had played a role in something, even if it was unwillingly, but ignorance of the law is no excuse.

It was going to be complicated even to prove my ignorance.

My life was slipping away. All the surveillance, phone taps, and information gathered on me was scary. The counterfeit cash wasn't mentioned, and that was a crime I was guilty of committing. I knew it was coming, though.

According to the feds, the mansion was my property, and I rented it out to three Russians who the F.B.I now wanted. I was guilty by that association, if not anything else.

I would have never known any of it either, not the surveillance or anything, if it wasn't for the Robert Mueller investigation into the Russian collusion in the election. I would have slipped under the radar and fallen off the map, but now that the world wanted answers, I was in the middle of it.

"Mr. Barnes, you said it yourself; the feds already know everything, so surely they know I was a victim of identity theft. I worked for these Russians, but I didn't know they were bad Russians. I thought I was working for Rolling Stone, that is all. They stole my identity!"

"Working for Rolling Stone doing what? Did you not notice that you weren't in the magazine?" Brian asked me.

"Of course I did; I was a fact-checker, some of the best journalists in the world started as fact-checkers."

"Oh yeah, like who?"

"Uh, Jeff Pearlman," I answered after some thought.

"Who?"

"Jeff Pearlman, a best-selling author, who was a fact-checker for Sports Illustrated."

Mr. Barnes wasn't even listening anymore.

"In this report from the F.B.I. in Ohio, it says you weren't the same Gunner Bush who met this person when you paid him on two other occasions," Mr. Barnes cut through our conversation.

"Yeah, he told me that."

"Then the feds tailed you down here in Louisville for two weeks in November 2016, and you put large amounts of money into different banks."

"What?"

Brian changed the subject, "What is your relationship with Tasha and Terry Kuznetsov?"

(Terry's real first name wasn't Terry. It was Tasha. Terry was her dead husband's name. Terry Kuznetsov was a former KGB agent who worked in East Berlin. Tasha used his name when dealing with anything in *Rolling Stone* Magazine. Rachel Maddow did a segment on her, but it didn't include me.)

"So what did you do for Rolling Stone as a fact-checker?"

"I did different things; I contacted people, I would deliver envelopes to people, make contacts on the Hill, set up meetings about adoptions. It was easy to work, and I was overpaid. I got to follow the campaigns around the country, and I wrote about that. I never got any articles published, and I did always wonder about that part of it, but -"

"Five minutes," a voice from the hallway cut me off.

"You didn't think or figure out that you weren't getting published in the magazine; I mean, what in the hell were you doing?"

"I was making connections in both camps, and writing about different things like the pulse of the country, the people, the campaigns, I was providing a detailed look at our country. I was providing insight into the backroads of America, at the people that live in Flyover Country. I was creating the whole scene, painting a picture; I was creating the profile for the rest of the country."

"You were giving Russians, known spies, intel on our country?"

"Well, when you say it like that," I answered.

I slumped in my chair. My head was pounding, and I was heading to jail for the night.

"What happens now?" I asked nervously.

"You'll be escorted over to the jail, but we will work hard to get you a bond and get you home." Mr. Barnes informed me.

They were packing up, but I wanted them to stay. I didn't want to go to jail, but I didn't have a choice.

It was all starting to make sense too. I wasn't the victim; I was the criminal. I had committed crimes, provided intel, and made connections for spies. I thought I was writing to be published in Rolling Stone Magazine, but I provided intel to the enemy. And who knows what I was delivering to the congressmen and women. It probably wasn't advertising materials like I thought.

"Don't worry, Gunner; we will get you home soon!" Mr. Barnes told me as the cops put me back into cuffs.

I was put into a van and driven to a Jefferson County Jail, where I spent the night in an eight-by-four solitary cell. I slept on a matt the size of a gym towel on top of a steel bunk with my head next to a toilet. The walls were concrete and yellow, the light was on, but it didn't matter. It was almost 3 pm, and the bed looked like a king size at the Holiday Inn. I crashed hard. I'd been up for two days, and I had the world of a fight in front of me.

CHAPTER 33

"November 11th, 2016."

The country was split like a butt crack, and the asshole doing the splitting just became president. The left cheek was full of tears, and the mainstream media ran with it. The silent majority, right butt cheek, swam in the liberal tears as if it brought them zen.

The folks in the flyover had been told for too long what to do, how to act, what to eat, who to like, and who to vote for, but now they had picked a man they were told shouldn't be a leader and wouldn't win, and he won.

Somehow, Trump and company pulled off a miracle on 34th street, and his voters were entitled. They were right; the elites were wrong. The media pundits were wrong. The liberals were wrong. Those fat cats with their college degrees were finally wrong. The factory workers were right.

A country gets a president they deserve, and Trump was exactly that.

The Democrats should have seen it coming; we all know how the pendulum works. BO was too much for many of these folks, and they couldn't get past his skin color. Racism, ignorance, xenophobia, and more were back on the menu.

And I would have been upset, too, if I didn't win so

much goddamn money betting on him.

The fear of the Trump presidency was created in the media, but it wasn't a false causality, and he was proving them correct. Sure, he wasn't politically inclined with legislation or even opening a book, but he had the reins of power now.

Anything was possible, but it wasn't that dire if you didn't tune into cable news. Sure, Trump was an idiot, but we'd survived Dubya. Things would pan out just as they had every other time a dingus was in office. Somehow, someway, it would play out as Trump would serve his four years, the country would see what a dumbass he was, and he would lose his second bid by a landslide. Hopefully. And of course, bearing any major war or unforeseen once in a lifetime event like a global pandemic arising. We would all survive.

I didn't have time for liberal tears or buttcheeks, though. I had to get my butt to the Gunshine State and cash in my winning ticket before the boat casino filed chapter 11. I was low on fake money and kicking myself for messing things up with Morgan.

Morgan was gone, but my future looked bright. I did call her one last time before boarding my flight out of New York City. Straight to voicemail.

I flew home to the Ville, and then on November 11th, as the nation collectively realized it was now, President-elect Donald Trump, I ate with my mom at the birthplace of the cheeseburger, and then she drove me to the airport.

I didn't tell her about my bet or why I was going to Florida. My mom was a converted liberal who loathed Trump, and she tried to campaign against him in Kentucky.

As I got out of the car to head into the airport, she said, "It likely won't even change our lives on a personal level."

I didn't know if it would or wouldn't. Trump's winning had already changed mine.

I walked into baggage claim and bought a one-way ticket south, paying cash. There was no direct flight, so I would have to stop in Alabama for two hours.

I arrived in Trampa close to 8 pm, and the casino boat was gone for the night. I took an Uber to Clearwater Beach, booked a hotel room, and got drunk by myself on the beach.

I woke up early and took a yellow cab to the boat dock. A few fishing boats were departing, but the casino boat wasn't open. I ran into a few fishermen, up late and trying to hurry to work, but I did get the information that the casino had a nearby main office. I headed in that direction on foot.

When I arrived, it was another docking area, and the corporation that owned the casino boat was about to launch another one. There were signs all over, so it was straightforward to find. The whole place smelled like fish getting baked in a microwave, and the sun was right on top of me.

I walked up a wooden staircase and opened the doors to go inside. A tall white dude with a Fryer Tuck hairstyle said hello as soon as I was inside.

"I have a payout, and I would like to cash it."

I pulled the ticket out and put it on the blue counter.

"Uff-da, I will be goddamn, eh, you are the person, eh?"

He was either Canadian or from Minnesota.

"Yes, I am that person."

"We've been wondering when you would turn up, but I have to admit that is pretty quick, eh."

"The early worm gets the bird," I explained, and I wasn't

there for small talk.

"It was almost as if you knew the odds were going to change. You made your bet right before they changed, right before the case was opened against Hillary."

He let the last part hang out to dry, but I wasn't biting, and I kept my mouth shut, and he yelled back into the back office.

"Jeffrey, we got the person who bet on Trump!"

Shit, the last thing I needed was more questions.

"I got some forms you gotta fill out, and then you can get your money."

"I need it in cash, too," I said timidly.

He didn't respond, and the other man came out of the back office.

"Hello, eh, here are the tax forms, so tell me, mate, do you like telling all these crying liberals that Trump is their president and you bet on it?"

"Yes, I do. We are heading into a full-on kakistocracy, so that's all I say, really," I tried to pull the snark out of my comment, but it was evident.

"Jeff, he said he wants the cash option," the first man said.

"Cash, eh, well, we do take a cut out, and that is a lot of cash," Jeff replied.

"I won't take a check. I paid in cash, so what's up?"

"Come to the back; I want to get a picture with you in my MAGA hat."

I grabbed my winning ticket back before we walked towards the back. The whole operation felt shadier than a forest.

I took the picture and then took the cash. They counted it, and then I counted it, and then we weighed it. I wasn't sure how much it should weigh, but I trusted my counting. I wasn't going to take a check. These two would shut down shop before I got to a bank, for all I know. It was the only casino in America that would bet on the Presidential election. Technically, it wasn't in America since all the betting was done in international waters. Still, it was the only place to get the bet down.

The banks would probably rape me on the fees to cash a check.

I left with a briefcase full of $711,600. It wasn't handcuffed to my arm, but if they had offered that option, I would have taken it. I was rich, not wealthy, but it was the first time in my life I could say I had some money.

It was more than enough money for a kid who grew up in the Highlands.

I took a yellow cab to a rental car spot, booked a midsize SUV, buckled the briefcase into shotgun, and drove north. I didn't stop except for gas and food. I took the briefcase inside with me both times. I contemplated leaving it in the car, but I didn't want to risk it.

The drive took me close to fourteen hours, and when I arrived at my apartment in the Ville, I went straight upstairs and locked the door.

The following day I bought a safe. The biggest one I could without drawing attention to myself; it was fireproof and claimed to have never been cracked. I read all about how safe this safe was, but it made me not trust the safe even more.

If anything, someone would break into my place, steal the safe, take it somewhere else, and blow it up, trying to open it. I didn't feel safe keeping all my eggs in one basket, so I put together a plan. I only put about $10,000 into the safe.

I divided it up into seven stacks. Then I drove around the Ville and opened up safety deposit boxes at seven different banks. I was paranoid driving with that much money on me to each bank, though, so I went to my parent's house, hid half the cash in my toy box, went to four banks, and came back for the other three piles before going to the last three banks.

My mom didn't have a clue, and she was home the whole time.

I figured even if two banks burnt down, that would still leave me with a ton of money at five banks. And there was no chance in hell that seven banks all were robbed or burnt.

I was paranoid with that much money. I watched for cars that might be following, and I didn't trust anyone that whole day. I was afraid that someone might carjack me that day, and they wouldn't just get an El Camino.

I guess I wasn't looking too hard because the F.B.I was following me. When I came home, they were at my place and followed me the whole day as I opened safety deposit boxes at seven different hospitals. They were shooting photos of me while I was turning my head to make sure nobody was following me.

And I didn't have a freaking clue. Clueless and dumb, I was Forrest Gump.

I also came up with my second plan. I was going to live cheaply. I grew up cheap; my mom used coupons on ketchup; my dad bought used tires. I was Gunner A. Bush, and the A stood for A-Cheapie. I wouldn't buy anything significant like a car or house. I had the El Camino; it was a new purchase and the car I had wanted since high school.

If I bought a house, that would just be more upkeep, and it would be a yard to mow, rooms to clean, and a hefty heating bill in the winter with an enormous AC bill in the summer.

I didn't need it; I would live cheap.

I wouldn't need to work; I could find a nice apartment, pay for a year and enjoy life. I was going to retire, enjoy some guitar lessons and go to the skate park. I could hit the bars and drink wells. This money would last me forever.

I was a simple man, and I had a simple plan.

And of course, I was going to pay taxes; I wasn't stupid. That is how they caught Al Capone. I didn't know how to pay taxes, and since it was an offshore casino, I felt like the guys had initially kept 25% for taxes.

I didn't know.

CHAPTER 34

With no clocks, time moves as slow as a Christmas eve, so six days in self-isolation inside the concrete cell in Jefferson County Jail was more than enough time for me to go batshit insane. Seriously, half of a day in that cell was enough to break me.

I had daily half-hour meetings with Mr. Barnes. It only took one session to find out he was a full-on Trumpie. I guess Sawyer as an apple didn't fall too far. The meetings turned into migraines because Mr. Barnes wanted to make sure Bobby Three Sticks didn't put a fork in Trump's Presidency.

Mr. Barnes was not an extremist like Sawyer. He wasn't wearing a tinfoil hat, but he was still a fan of the Cheeto in the Oval. He also believed in his fair share of jiggery-pokery. He thought the Clinton "crime family" had magical powers, and they were in cahoots with the liberal media to bring down Trump. He didn't mention that Hillary still lost the election despite these magical powers. Mr. Barnes was adamant that it was a setup; he even believed that the boogeyman, George Soros was in on the attack. And that is where he thought the Bobby Three Sticks investigation was headed, so he wanted to play a unique role in fixing the "Russia Issue" for the president.

The media ran rampant with the Trump/Russia narrative, but most stories didn't make sense. It didn't take a genius to see Trump was a crooked businessman; he would rob from his businesses to pay himself and set up fake charities to do so. Yet the whole Russian asset didn't make sense the way the media broke it down.

Why did the Russians contact his son if Trump was a Russian asset? Why were meetings set up with his son at all? These connections would have already been made.

None of it made any sense, but I had learned logic didn't matter in political discussions. Working the rounds during the election was enough for me to see that I didn't want anything to do with politics. And that is why I was living back in the Ville, and most importantly, that is why I was ignoring cable news and Trump altogether. Trump was a businessman, but his main business was keeping his name in the news. He was a PR mastermind.

Mr. Barnes wasn't tuning things out, and he quickly brought his political bias into my case. It was frustrating, but I couldn't do anything about it. He had signed up for Cult 45, and he was going to make sure Bobby Three Sticks didn't get any proof from me to take down the president.

This was the most significant issue because I was ready to sit down with Bobby and tell him everything. If the feds knew it already anyway, and according to Mr. Barnes, they did, then my logic was simple. Mr. Barnes was flipping his advice, and I was caught in the middle.

He also didn't believe my story, which I can understand because it is hard to fathom the whole ordeal, and I couldn't do so, and I had just lived it. Every time I told anyone a part of my story, it felt made up.

"So why did you go around to seven different banks? Look at these photos of you going to all these banks in one day. You opened safety deposit banks at each one? It was November 11th, just three days after Trump won the election."

Mr. Barnes and his assistant, Brian, were staring at me, waiting for an answer, but I didn't know what they wanted to hear. They were creating their own conspiracy theories in a case they were working on.

Brian leaned into me, "What did you put into these security boxes in the bank?"

Mr. Barnes flipped to a picture of me holding the briefcase.

"What's in the case?"

"It was cash; I told you guys this yesterday. I had money in there, money that I won betting on Trump."

"Winning that you didn't pay taxes on?" Brian chimed in to ask.

"How much money was it?" Mr. Barnes asked.

"It was over seven hundred."

Brian was pissed, "You don't need a briefcase to carry seven hundred dollars!"

"Not seven hundred dollars; I won seven hundred thousand!"

"Yeah, and how much did you bet?"

"I bet twenty-nine thousand and something," I said back sharply.

"Horseshit! Why in the hell did you bet so much on Trump to win? What kind of insider information did you have? You got the info from these Russians?"

Brian yelled at me, but Mr. Barnes was sitting back in his chair. He looked afraid as if my answer might scare him.

"The Russians didn't tell me shit; I figured it out on my

own. I was working for the magazine, traveling around and talking to people -"

"The Russians own the magazine?"

"No, I didn't know if they owned it, but they ran it. They paid me to work for them, so I did."

Mr. Barnes cut us both off.

"They paid you to make deliveries and connections for them?"

"Yes."

"So the money was from the fucking Russians?"

Brian was ready to jump back in, and the whole thing felt like an interrogation from my defense team.

"You worked for the Russians, but all you have is three or four emails, and not one phone call or text message from this Tasha or Terry person directly?

"We always used WhatsApp to contact each other; that is how everyone on the east coast does it. It is untraceable."

I sounded like a criminal. If Mr. Barnes thought Hillary was crooked, I looked like Benedict Arnold.

"So you just happen to know that Trump was going to win the election; the election that the entire world was saying he was going to lose?"

"Yes."

"And you bet thirty grand on this despite all of this?"

"It was a gut instinct."

It didn't make much sense to me now either.

"Then after you win, you hide the money, uh, because you didn't want to pay taxes on it?" Brian asked me, but Mr.

Barnes cut him off again.

"Why not just put the money in the bank, or perhaps in a safe in your house? Why all the deposit boxes? You could invest the money into the stock market with Trump in office. The market is skyrocketing!"

"Invest it? I don't know how to invest it in the stock market, and I am a journalist, not a stockbroker."

Mr. Barnes threw his hands up as if to give up. Brian wasn't done with this cross-examination yet.

"So let me get this straight, you have no article in *Rolling Stone Magazine* or on the website; your name is never mentioned as a fact-checker. The only proof or tie you have to *Rolling Stone* is Gunner Bush's email at Rolling Stone dot com. Still, this same email was used in a DDoS attack on our country which brought down," he flipped through a stack of papers and then continued, "Twitter, the Guardian, Netflix, Reddit, CNN, and of course Rolling fucking Stone's website among a long list of others. This was on October 25th back in 2016, less than two weeks before the election. *Rolling Stone* issues a statement to congress that no one named Gunner Bush ever worked for them, and a hack likely created the email to their server that happened back in 2015."

He was reading the last part for what felt like the first time, but I had read it days ago, and I knew I was in trouble.

"Cut the fucking horseshit, Gunner. Did you work for *Rolling Stone* or not?" Mr. Barnes asked, but I didn't have a new answer for him now.

"I guess not."

"You guess not? Gunner, look, son, you are in trouble, big trouble, and let's be honest here, okay? What were you doing in Washington D.C. in the summer of 2016?"

"I was working for a woman named Terry or Tasha, and I thought I was working for *Rolling Stone* magazine."

"But there is no record of you talking to this woman who you worked with for six months? There is not one single email, not one phone call; there is nothing."

"I have the initial email that she sent me from her email at Rolling Stone, and it also says for me to contact her via her WhatsApp."

"That username, T.RollingStone, could be anybody. We haven't been able to confirm that it was Kuznetsov," Brian added. He was beginning to be a real asshole. Then he said, "Rolling Stone has no record of this Russian lady working for them. How did Mrs. Kuz-nets-whatever pay you?"

"I was paid cash, weekly, $1,700 a week. It was in cash every single time."

"Cash?" Mr. Barnes asked, but it was Brian's turn to harass me.

"You were paid in cash by *Rolling Stone* magazine? And this is while you lived in the mansion house that you own?"

"I don't own it!"

"The thing is, Gunner, that you do own it. That is how your bail is getting made. It is already confirmed that it is your deed, your house. Drop the bullshit routine and tell us the truth so we can help you. *Rolling Stone* didn't pay you in cash because you never worked for them. Tell us the truth about this Russian woman, and don't lie about it."

Mr. Barnes used a sharp voice to say, "tell us the truth, son."

"Look, sir, you said it yourself; the feds already know everything. They know the truth, so why can't I just tell them the truth?"

That isn't what Mr. Barnes wanted to hear, and I was starting to wonder if the feds even knew the truth at all.

Mr. Barnes was off the milk rack, crazy, and his assistant Brian wasn't too far off either. Our daily meetings were all insane, but that wasn't the worst of it. Mr. Barnes wanted the shine; he loved it; he was the type of attorney who ran cheesy commercials and put up corny billboards, so of course, he started discussing my case with right-wing media for the spotlight. My case took a back seat to his philandering with the press. It was a conflict of interest if there ever was one.

Somehow, they managed to put the mansion up for my bond despite all of this. Six days after entering the county jail, I was free.

My parents were outside waiting for me when I was released. My old man didn't say a word; he just gave me that look that said without words that he was disappointed in me. My mom was crying or had just finished, and they were both wondering, "What in the fuck did you get yourself into, Gunner?"

Honestly, I was wondering this too.

Despite their disapproval and disappointment, they took me to my favorite chicken wing spot, Indi's, for lunch. Then they drove me to my apartment since I smelt like a dead skunk.

My door had been reattached to the hinges, and there was a note on it from my landlord. He wanted me to call him ASAP.

My place was a wreck, and the cops had destroyed it, looking for my secret stash of donuts. I cleared off my couch and told my folks to sit down, and then I proceeded to tell them everything.

My parents loved me and wanted to believe me, but it was challenging at first. There had been some reports in the local media, and they had seen some of those, and they had been talking to Mr. Barnes, so they knew the gist of it.

The articles in the local paper were pretty bad. Many local journalists ran my name through the wringer because I didn't pay my just due at the Courier-Journal and jumped straight to *Rolling Stone*. My parents finally settled that I had no reason to lie to them, and they believed me.

They questioned all the empty bottles in my apartment more than anything else, and my apartment looked like a dumpster behind a New Orleans bar after Mardi Gras. When the discussion got heated about my drinking, I asked them to leave and stated, "I need to sleep; I have been sleeping with a gym towel as a cover on a metal bed."

They agreed to leave, but they also said they would help me find new legal representation. We all decided that Mr. Barnes wasn't working out.

I was out on bail with a court date pending. I also had a new piece of jewelry around my ankle to track my every move. I took a shower and got some sleep. My house was a pigpen, more ransacked than the mansion had been after the Russians left.

When I woke up, I had a text from Sawyer. Mr. Barnes had given him my new number. He invited me over to his new place in Clarksville, Indiana. I couldn't leave the state, so I invited him over to my place and told him that nothing would be better than drinking with my best friend on my first day out.

He wrote me back and said he wasn't drinking anymore. It was devastating news, but I was already sipping on something, so I again invited him over. He texted me back and said no thanks.

He wrote me back later and invited me over to his spot again. He said his old man would get it cleared to leave the city, and since Clarksville is visible from the Ville, it wouldn't be a big deal. It was a hop, skip, and a jump away.

I informed him that if his old man got it cleared, I would come to check out his new digs. I poured myself another drink and turned on a cassette tape of Chet Baker. I would get drunk and listen to my tape collection on my first day out of the bing.

CHAPTER 35

Mr. Barnes was able to get me permission to leave the state. I was actively looking to fire him and hire another attorney, though. He didn't know that and got me permission to travel across the Ohio River to see his son.

Sawyer sent me the directions to a park by his spot. My nerves were on edge when I jumped into my El Camino. The ankle bracelet was annoying, and just knowing the feds were watching my every move was terrifying. They were also likely following me in a car. I was staring down the barrel of some hefty charges, and that was weighing in my mindstate too.

As I pulled onto Bardstown Road, an unmarked car began to follow me. It was unmarked but should have had sirens and an F.B.I sticker on it for how close they watched me. I drove slow so they could keep up; I didn't want to think I was trying to flee or sumshit. I kept up the snail's pace until I crossed the Second Street bridge.

As soon as I got into Indiana, I got lost. The roads in Clark County were designed by drunk dyslexics as a joke to confuse Louisvillians when we accidentally crossed the river. Eventually, I found my way to the park. It was a park at a dead end with a basketball court, tennis courts, a walking track area, and a spot for picnics.

Sawyer was there shooting bricks on the basketball goal. He looked different. His belly wasn't hanging over his belt, his face was thinner, and his hair was cut. He flashed his grin at me as I stepped out of my El Camino; then, he dribbled, shot, and missed. The ball hit off into the grass, and he walked towards me as he sang.

"El Camino, El Camino, the front looks like a car; the back looks like a tru-uuck, El Camino, El Camino; The front is where you drive, the back is where you fu-uuck, El Camino, El Camino."

It was apparent that he was jealous of my ride. I assessed the area while walking up towards him.

"Gunner El Camino Bush!"

He smiled, and it was good to see the motherfucker.

A lady was walking towards us while pushing a stroller.

"Gun, this is my wife, Raven, and our beautiful daughter, Blake."

Then he turned to her and told her, "Raven, this is Gunner Bush, the guy who saved my life."

I was stunned. Raven was beautiful. She was tall, thin, with braids and a perfectly dark brown complexion. My gun told me she was a beautiful person inside and out, and first impressions are everything and an innate trait passed down for millions of years.

He stood by her, and they all looked great together. I stuck my head into the stroller and saw a tiny infant, and the baby girl was asleep.

"It is nice to meet you, Gunner. I have heard a lot about you."

"All lies, I can assure you," I answered, followed by, "It is nice to meet you too."

Sawyer said, "She needs to keep the baby moving, or she will wake up. Let's go talk, Gun."

"Sure thing, and again nice to meet you."

"Likewise."

"Let's go over to that shelter house, well, unless you want to get beat in a little one on one, huh, do you?"

He picked up the basketball, pretended to throw it at me, turned and shot it at the goal, and it missed badly, and he ran to grab it.

We headed towards the shelter.

"Don't you love that Trump is *your* president?"

Sawyer hadn't changed at all.

"Your wife, your beautiful wife is black, your beautiful daughter is half black, and you still support the racist president?"

"Shit, Trump isn't racist. How do you know if he is, man? No evidence says he is a racist, and plenty of evidence says he isn't a racist. How many black people support him, huh? All those black celebrities that support him. You don't know him on a personal level, so how do you know if he is racist?"

Sawyer assured me, and he was right. I didn't know if Trump was racist or not, and the right-leaning media had a massive effort to prove that he wasn't. If a racist story about Trump popped up, five more would pop up out of the propaganda machine to shoot it down with proof that he wasn't. It was getting harder and harder to deceive what was real.

Sawyer pulled out a pack of smokes, lit one up, and tossed the box onto the picnic table.

"El Camino Bush, we did some wild shit, huh?" He said before he started laughing.

I picked up the box, pulled one out, and lit it.

He asked me, "How you been?"

"I am good, considering."

"Shit, Gun, I can't thank you enough for everything you did for me. I was in a bad pl-"

I cut him off, "Stop it, man, please. I didn't do anything that you wouldn't have done for me."

"I appreciate it, though, Gunner. I really do. You saved my life."

"It's nothing."

There was an awkward pause, and then he asked me, "This shit with the Russians, is it coming back to bite you in the ass?"

"It's not good."

"You always want to be famous."

"Yeah, but this is infamy."

We both laughed.

"I am sure my old man will get you out of it. It's a bunch of malarkey stirred up by the lamestream media. CNN is leading the charge, and they are upset that Trump won. It's all a hoax; hopefully, you can see that now."

He shook his head and blew out smoke rings while looking away.

"We don't have to talk about my case, dude."

Again, there was a pause in our conversation before he blurted out, "I clean, and it feels good, Gunner."

"I am, too," I lied.

"What? Really, how long?"

"Shit, well, I did six days sober in the clink. I couldn't even get a beer inside, and I don't think I had any withdrawal symptoms, which means I am not addicted. I did ask your old man to sneak a beer into me, but he didn't answer me. I had a few last night, nothing crazy, you know, I was trying to celebrate my release."

I laughed. My whole statement was a sarcastic joke, but he didn't laugh with me.

"Yeah, so, Gunner, that is what we wanted to talk with you about today."

"We, who is we? Your wife? She seems great, and I can't believe you are a father. You of all people -," I stopped talking mid-sentence.

Sawyer wasn't looking at me, and I turned to see what he was looking at; a car was pulling into the parking lot. It was my old man's car, and behind it was my sister's car.

"Well, ain't that some shit, this park is hidden back off in the cut, and my freaking family shows up here the same day I am here. This is a cool park, though."

As I finished my sentence, I realized what was going on. Sawyer had set me up, and this was going to be an intervention for me!

My brother got out of my sister's car, so it was my entire family. My old man walked up, and I said, "Shit."

My mom was behind him; she was crying or had just finished.

Sawyer turned to me, "Look, Gun, we partied pretty hard; we did crazy shit, and you helped me get sober, and well, you helped more than that. You saved my life. Look at me now; I am about to marry my best friend. I have a daughter, and I got a solid job here. I go to meetings every week. It is good, no, it is great."

I didn't want to hear him, I didn't have a problem, and I didn't need to go to meetings. Sure, I had helped Sawyer because he was out of control and threatening to murder people. The worst I was doing was being an asshole in public, and I didn't need an intervention because I didn't need help.

"Hi, Mom, Dad; hello Kayla. Hi Patrick," I said to my family.

My mom started talking, "Gunner, we need to talk. We saw your apartment and all those bottles. It is -"

"Mom, I collected those bottles for my bottle collection."

My sister Kayla cut me off, "Cut the shit, Gunner; the police report stated it was the most amount of booze found during a raid at a residence since prohibition."

My brother Patrick followed her words with his, "Gunner, we think it is time for you to get help. Sawyer is doing great because you helped him."

Patrick could always be a condescending asshole.

"He is doing great? Yeah, Sawyer is doing great from where he was, but I am not in the same place as where he was. I just did a whole week sober!"

Kayle didn't let that slide, "You did a week sober because you were locked up in jail!"

She always cuts through my bullshit.

"Right, well, it's still a fact -"

She cut me off, "It's bad enough that your name is in the paper, and my kids, your niece, and nephew, have to go to school and hear that their uncle is a traitor to our country who worked for the Russians and the -"

I cut her off, and the pace was back to our regular family gatherings.

"A traitor to our country? Nobody has said that. Didn't Mom and Dad tell you guys that I didn't even know I was working for the Russians? I mean, I knew they were Russians but not bad Russians."

"Whatever, Gunner, you always have an excuse. You're the victim here, right?"

We were about two minutes away from getting sent to our rooms by our parents, but she wasn't done.

"Cut the crap, Gunner; you need more than help. You are in a fight for your life, and the last thing you should be doing is fighting us."

"Fuck you, Kayla, a fight for my life, whatever. I didn't do anything wrong, and my boozing isn't as bad as yours. How much wine are you drinking at night, huh? Should we count the bottles in your recycling bin each week? And Patrick, you drink like a fish. I swear to god, you two are both hypocrites, and Sawyer, this is some bullshit!"

I stormed off towards my El Camino.

My mom yelled out, "Gunner Axl Bush, you come back here to talk to us!"

She was using my middle name, so I know she was pissed.

I kept walking, though. I wasn't going to stick around and let them 'Baker Act' me into some facility that I wouldn't be able to leave. I had just been in jail.

I turned around before I got into my car, and I yelled, "Fuck you guys, I don't have a drinking problem just because you have a problem with my drinking!"

I got into my car and punched my steering wheel, saying, "Fuck Sawyer!"

I drove back to Kentucky, went to the liquor store, bought a brown bottle, then went straight home and poured myself a tall glass of bourbon. I needed it like a moth needs light because my family was driving me to drink.

CHAPTER 36

"Dip in the Ohio"

The police report tells a different story than I remember about that night. It was Monday, and Monday's can be dead in my area. I didn't want to spend another night browsing cassettes and drinking alone, so I ventured out of my place. My local area was dead, though, so I would need to venture outside of my normal bar circumference to find some fun. I couldn't walk, and Ubering would take too long, so I hopped into the El Camino and traveled to a house party off Eastern Parkway.

It was dead when I arrived, thanks to an uninvited guest in a blue uniform. I hit a hole in the wall bar did a shot, but I needed more excitement in my life. I called my boy, Ernie, and he informed me that the only place that popped off on Monday was in Indiana. Luckily, I had recently been approved to cross the state lines, so I made my way back to the Hoosier state.

I'd not been eating and boozing pretty hard, but I still figured I was safe to drive. I wasn't drunk yet, but that's not why I got lost in Indiana. The roads are impossible to navigate without GPS. Also, I had a big gulp full of Crown Royal that I was sipping on like it was water.

I also didn't think the boys were behind me anymore. When I came to Indiana to meet Sawyer, they stopped tailing me after crossing the bridge. I figured they would do this again, but they stayed with me since they didn't know where I was going now.

As I got off the highway searching for a bar called Jimmy's on the River, I found my way onto a backstreet where I sideswiped a parked vehicle. The boys behind me didn't try to stop me, though, and the damage was minimal.

My memory is fogging, and it's tough to recall this event. I remember hitting the car, but it felt like a love tap. I turned down another side street and ran the El Camino onto the curb. As I adjusted, I swiped another parked car. This car was parked but out in the middle of the street. It wasn't my fault. The damn Hoosiers need to learn to park in the driveway!

I made another turn, and at this point, the boys should have probably pulled me over before I killed someone and myself, but they didn't. (protect and serve, right?)

I made my way to a long road alongside the river and somehow popped my left tire on a curb. I believe the curb was in the middle of the street, but the police report failed to mention anything about it. Somehow, I kept driving even with a flat tire, and once again, the boys behind me didn't pull me over.

So since they didn't pull me over, it isn't my fault that I swiped another parked car. This time it was a Jeffersonville Town Truck, and I got out to assess the damage to my truck. I got back into my car, drove over a curb, turned down an alley, and lost the boys as I moved through a field.

I managed to drive in a circle and returned to the exact truck I had just hit. I noticed the empty lot and decided to find a place to pee. I got out and saw that someone had hit my El Camino! I was pissed. There was a gray streak down the side of my baby. Then I realized someone had slashed my left front tire with a knife.

I was pissed and called Ernie to tell him, but he didn't answer, so I left a message.

"Yo, somebody hit my El Camino, dude! It must have been at the bar, and I was just in the Ville. Someone sideswiped my car, and then they slit my tire!"

I was pissed, but I didn't want the party to end, so I headed out. Hitting the gas to speed away, I drove over an embankment area, looking for the road. There wasn't a road there, though; it was just water. I drove my car straight off the edge into the Ohio River.

I punched it into reverse, but my car was submerged in water. As the water began to fill up the inside of my El Camino, I began to sober up. The memory of my El Camino going under is something I will take to my grave, and it almost brought me to my grave.

It is advised to stay inside your vehicle while submerging in water because the door won't open. The pressure from the water is too much. And this is a true statement. I couldn't open the door to save my life. Panic set in, and I tried to use my phone to call the cops, but it was soaked. The water was rushing in fast.

The driver's side window doesn't roll down, so I slid over to the passenger's side and rolled it down. Thank heavens for manually opening windows. I pulled myself to the top of my car, as it was sinking and floating west, and I just sat there.

A voice rang out as I was figuring out what to do, "Hey, you okay, partner? Is there anyone else in the car?"

I yelled back, "I am not okay. Does it look like I am okay?"

I wasn't trying to be a smartass, but he asked me a dumb-ass question.

The current was fierce and pulled me west. I weighed my options, but I knew I would have to jump. The Ohio River is full of toxins that will kill you, but I would have to jump or risk drowning once we hit a deeper spot. I said goodbye to my baby, and I jumped into the freezing water.

It was colder than a polar bear's toenail, and I screamed as soon as my head popped up. The current was harsh, and I moved about 100 yards beyond the man who had yelled at me. I saw the unmarked car was now back, and they were now screaming at me.

I managed to float and swim to shore, and I was greeted by two uncovered cops and the man who had been yelling at me. He was a Jeffboat working on his way home from work sick. As I got closer to them and almost to the shore, I fell on rocks and busted my elbow open. Blood rushed out, but I was in shock and drunk, so I didn't even feel it.

Once I completely made it out of the water, the two undercovers waited to arrest me. They had some local boys show up, and that's who put me into cuffs. They didn't even give me a blanket, and I was shivering with blue lips.

My El Camino was gone; it was floating towards the Mississippi River, and I was booked into jail on charges of DUI, Reckless Driving, Hit and Run, Leaving the Scene of an Accident, Destroying City Property, and even a BUI for Boating Under the Influence.

I also had a wet dime bag that the cops found once I was inside the jail, and in Indiana, the possession of the devil's lettuce is a felony. As soon as they pulled it out, I expected to get sentenced into the stocks and pillories for it.

Either way, I was fucked, and not the good kind of fucked either!

CHAPTER 37

"Family Bond"

After my swim in the Ohio, the coppers took me to a shithole county jail in Clark County. I was placed in a cell with about 200 other men; they could have been murderers, rapists, or idiots who drove their El Camino into the Ohio River while drunk.

The cell I was inside was long and concrete with bulletproof glass at the front and showers I would try to avoid in the back. It made my solitary confinement cell across the river in Jefferson County look like the Holiday Inn Express. A television was hanging on the wall in the middle of the cell, but it wouldn't turn on because an inmate had tried to light a smuggled cigarette on the outlet. There were metal bunks, and I was afraid of what the night might hold.

I was offered a smoke, so I took it. I didn't want to disrespect anyone. Shortly after the morning breakfast was delivered, a musty bowl of oatmeal, and I declined to eat it, fearing it might cause scurvy or some other unknown disease. And after breakfast was over, I realized how the cigarette I had just smoked got into the jail. A weekend inmate named Benny smuggled it into the facility using his anal cavity.

I wanted to puke.

I dressed in a new orange outfit, and it came along with

my standing in front of a judge on TV again. This time, I read all my charges and my bond of 100k. The 100k was for my damages and drunk driving; nobody even knew I had on an ankle bracelet or about my other crimes yet.

The high price of 100k meant I wouldn't see daylight anytime soon. I would have to sit in jail for 31 days until my court case. My future was bleak.

Sharing a cell with 200 other inmates and one phone was like having 50 sisters who all needed to use the phone. I put my name on the list to use it, but I didn't make a phone call until 2 pm. I called Mr. Barnes, but his secretary said he wasn't in at the moment. And that was it, my one free phone call.

I thought about calling my parents, but it wouldn't be a free call, and calls from jail are like $29.99 a minute or sumshit. I was once again regretting not memorizing anyone else's phone number. I thought hard about calling Mr. Barnes again and figured his secretary would accept the collect call charges, but I had to put my name back on the list to use the phone. I was back on the list but last.

I found a few good names for lawyer replacements by chatting with the other inmates. Mr. Barnes had to be replaced; I needed someone who wasn't addicted to Qanon leaks. However, finding a good reputable name was challenging, so I chalked it up as a loss. Most of these guys had public defenders that they called public pretenders.

For the most part, everyone was pretty chill. There isn't much room to act like a fool, so I put my head down and minded my business. A guy named Sue, from Louisiana, gave me the rundown of how to get on the phone list, how to eat from the commissary and not the jail cafeteria, and things of that nature.

"You know you can make your bail, right?" Sue asked

me, but I had no idea.

"No," I answered with my head down, slumped in my arms.

"Yeah, if you got the cash or a credit card."

"If only I could get to the bank," I responded, and if I could, I could make bond, but I was stuck in jail, "but I am stuck in here."

"How much is your bond? Maybe we can ask the boys, they made my brother's bond, and he is waiting on Simps and me to get out." Sue stated as he pointed to a gangly-looking man in the corner.

"It's one hundred thousand dollars," I replied.

"Well, shit, we aren't going to find anyone with that type of coin!"

"Yep, I guess I will be sitting in here," I said sadly.

"Simps and I will be here for two more weeks, and then the judge should give us time served."

I was stuck for at least thirty days.

"How much is your bail?"

"Mine is $12, and Simps is $12," he informed me.

"Twelve bucks? And y'all can't m-," I stop my sentence dead. Simps and Sue were hobos and didn't have even a quarter on them.

"We got charged with drinking in public cause we were enjoying a beer for Simps born day. We were watching the falls, and the cops rolled up on us sharing one can of Miller High Life."

"Damn, and he took you guys to jail?"

"Yep."

"Talk about a broken system."

All I could do was hurry up and wait, so that's what I did.

When it was finally time for me to use the phone again, I called Mr. Barnes' office, and his secretary accepted the charges. She also punched me through, and Mr. Barnes answered.

"They are going to try to push you for a flight risk and keep you locked up!" He said before even saying hello.

He already knew I was in jail.

"What? Why? I had permission to come to Indiana!" I screamed.

"Oh, I know, buddy, I got you the permission. They are trying to play hardball, but let me assure you this, Gunner, we won't play that at all. I don't care if we have to have you sit in jail over there for two freaking years; they aren't going to get you if I can help it."

"Two years? What? No, look, Mr. Barnes, I need just to tell them what I can, and -"

He cut me off without listening, "This is a conspiracy the size of Roswell, and I am not going to let this horseshit fly!"

"Sir, so what should I do?"

"Sit tight and let me work my magic!"

And he hung up. Jesus, I needed new representation. The jail was the last place I wanted to sit, and it wasn't because I didn't enjoy the butt cigarettes or waiting for hours to use the phone. I needed to find a way out of this place.

Right before dinner was served, a guard came to the door and yelled, "Bush, Gunner."

I jumped up and ran over to him.

"I am Gunner Bush."

He was holding a clipboard, and he looked at me, then his clipboard, and then back at me.

"You're Bush?" He asked me, confused.

"Yes, sir," I said.

"Well, I don't give a fuck who you are. You made bail; follow me."

Holy shit, Mr. Barnes had pulled off a miracle.

I signed a million papers, was handed my thousand-dollar, waterlogged smartphone, and I was free to go. I walked outside into the darkness because the sun was already down, and I would have to walk home, but at least I was free.

I didn't have a cent on me to book a cab, but the second street bridge wasn't that far, and once I was over it, it would only be a few miles to my apartment. I made my way to the sidewalk, and I saw my sister's van. Kayla was sitting in it, slouched over asleep. I knocked on the window lightly, and it startled her. She motioned for me to get in, so I did.

"Mom and dad went to get some food since we didn't know how long it would take before you got out. We have been here all day."

"Wow, yeah, thanks, was it Mr. Barnes who got me out?"

"Mr. Barnes? Hell no, that crazy man wanted to keep you in here. Dad got some sort of loan with your old boss on 7th Street."

"Holy hell, man, I got to pay dad back," I said, and I cranked up the heat.

She called my parents, and they would meet us at Waffle House for some grub. There was nothing in the world that sounded better.

"You got to pay dad back, yeah, sure thing, Gunner. You just happen to have 10,000 dollars laying around."

"I thought my bond was 100k?"

"It was; we had to pay ten percent."

"Well, I will pay dad back. I don't care if it is a hundred or ten thousand."

"You are going to be ruled a flight risk, or that is what crazy-ass Mr. Barnes told us."

"Yeah, I had permission to go to Indiana," I told her.

"Did you have permission to take your car for a swim in the Ohio River too?"

"Funny, but no, no, I didn't."

"You know your El Camino was on the news, right?"

"On the news? No, why?"

"Why? Because it was floating down the river, that is why Gunner. How do you think I knew you were in jail?"

"Mr. Barnes called you?"

"Hell no, we called him! I saw your dumbass truck car floating down the river on the news and thought you were dead."

"Well, you aren't that lucky; I am not dead."

"You could have been!"

And she was right. I could have killed myself or something else. I was lucky.

"You stink like prison," She told me.

"I wasn't even in prison, and how would you know what prison smells like unless you've been going on conjugal visits with your ex-boyfriend from Lively Shively."

"I don't even talk to Derrick anymore!"

We were right back to conversing like siblings.

When we arrived at the Waffle House, my old man had a look on his face again that told me he was upset. My mom was crying or had just finished, and I felt terrible for putting them through so much. I was starving, though, so they let me eat before they jumped my bones. I ate like a dude who just got out of the clank.

"I am going to pay you back, Dad."

"It's okay, Hunny; it is not about the money. We didn't want you to be sitting in jail," my mom said.

"You can't pay dad back; if you had ten thousand dollars, you wouldn't be living in those shitty ass apartments," Kayla chimed.

"My apartments are nice, and dad, I am going to as soon as the banks open."

"Well, I will get the money back when you have your court date, but you do what you can," my old man said.

My mom yelled at him, "He doesn't need to pay us back; we are his parents!"

"If he has the money," my dad responded, and that was

the end of that.

I was an emotional wreck, and after spending all day in jail, I needed to let it all out. I was at rock bottom. I didn't want to quit boozing, but I HAD to quit boozing, or I would end up in prison or dead. It was that simple.

My eyes were hot in the corners.

My mom comforted me, my dad sat back and said nothing, and Kayla shook her head.

"I need help," I said with tears rolling down my face.

"We will get you help."

After we ate, we did a collective hug in the parking lot. It was much needed and a great family bonding moment over a tragedy that was my life. My old man was still pissed and didn't think I would pay him back, but my mom told him to get over it. I was grateful to have such a loving family, and this was just one day after I shunned them as they tried an intervention.

Kayla offered to drive me home, and as soon as I got into her van, I asked her, "Can you stop back by the jail for me for one second?"

"No, I cannot. Why?"

I knew she would.

"I also need to borrow $24 bucks," I told her as she pulled off.

"I can drive by the jail, but I am not losing you any money," She said.

"You will, Kayla, and I will pay you back $30 when we get to my place."

"Forty, you gotta add in gas for me driving you home,

jailbird!"

"Whatever," I said, and she drove me to the jail, loaned me the money, and I went inside and bailed out Sue and Simps. It was the best 24 dollars I spent all year.

CHAPTER 38

"Q-ack Attack"

"**T**his place is a pigpen; it is messier than your bedroom was when we were kids," Kayla said as soon as we stepped into my place, and she was correct.

"It was in pristine condition before the messy ass law dogs shit all over the place!"

There was another note on my door from my landlord, but it was illegible, so I tossed it. Either my landlord was a Trumpie, or he wanted me gone or both. I didn't care, and I wasn't blaming him; the law had kicked down my door, and my name was circling the local papers for all the wrong reasons. It turns out that the adage, no publicity is bad publicity was false information.

"Why don't you come to stay with us for a bit," Kayla said with her nose up.

"It's fine," I said, and I made my way to my bedroom to get the forty I owed her.

I wasn't going to be intrusive to my family, especially with a good chance that I was going to prison anyway. I would likely be getting evicted soon, and if I weren't in an orange jumpsuit, I would figure it out then.

I paid Kayla, and she offered to stay and help me fight the urge to drink, but I told her I was fine, and she split.

And I took the longest shower of my life, cleaning both my body and soul. The alone time also meant it was an excellent time for a deep contemplation into my life. It was long overdue, and I had been blocking my inner voice with booze for too long. Somehow, I needed to stop boozing even if I went to meetings, and I had to do it even though I didn't want to do it.

Envisioning life without booze was scary, and it appeared dreadful. I couldn't even imagine it, but the reality was, I might be locked up in a cage without the choice. And it could also be possible that boozing got me into that situation.

So I didn't grab a beer or head for the bar; instead, I opened up my laptop and searched for a new attorney. I was desperate for a left-leaning attorney; I would settle for a middle-of-the-roader, and if I could find one that wasn't political at all, even better. The bare minimum was someone who didn't drink the kool-aid.

My google search took two minutes, and I found one that might fit the profile. Her last name was Goldfish. Susan Goldfish was somehow attached to the local Democratic Party; her name was easy to find in repeated google searches since it was Goldfish. My phone was a useless paperweight, so I had to call her from my laptop. I found what appeared to be her cellphone too.

I dialed her number, and it rang twice before a female voice answered with a hello.

"Hello, yes, is this Mrs. Goldfish? Susan Goldfish?"

"Yes, speaking."

Her voice had just enough tone in it to let me know she was pissed I called so late.

"Yes, I am sorry to bother you, ma'am, my name is Gunner Bush, and well, I need new legal representation. I have an attorney, but I need to get a new one as quickly as I can."

"Okay, well, Mr. Bush, what is it that I can help you with?"

"As I said, I am sorry to call so late."

"It's okay; I am on the phone now."

"Yeah, so I was arrested, and uh, I am being charged with something I didn't do," I rushed through the last part.

"Okay, well, you said your name is Bush, correct?"

"Yes, Gunner A. Bush."

"Oh my, Gunner Bush from the news, involved with the Mueller Investigation?"

Her tone completely changed as she figured out who I was. Goddamn it!

If I squinted my ears low, Rachel Maddow was airing on the flatscreen inside Goldfish's living room. She was too liberal, and it was all going to backfire in my face. She was now acting like an ugly schoolgirl getting a call from her crush, who was way out of her league.

"Why yes, I know your case, but I thought you already had a legal team."

"Right, I need a new one," I said.

"Well, Trump, oh my, where can I start when I tell you about Trump and me. I think Trump is a criminal, a fascist using nepotism."

I'd barely told her anything, and she was jumping to conclusions like she had a matt to do so.

A substantial portion of our country had lost their damn minds, and I found the two attorneys in my city who were on the exact opposite spectrums of the political aisle.

"Trump is incompetent, but if he weren't, it would be a lot worse than it is. He is a narcissist, and the country has never seen an incompetent president. It is new ground, but his coverage on the right is that he has been hand-picked by Jesus, and on the left, we know he hasn't."

She was ranting, so I had to cut her off.

"Yeah, I know all about that, and seeing it, or let me say knowing it, doesn't help. I think I need to find a lawyer who isn't partisan," I said, but she wasn't listening.

"Great, so how about tomorrow morning at nine?"

"Uh," I replied.

"Oh, is that too early? I can do 10:30."

"Yeah, great," I said, but I just wanted to get off the phone, and I couldn't find how to hang up the Google voice phone I was calling her from.

"Okay, well, you have our address, correct?"

"Yeah, I do," and as I said it, I hung up.

I slammed my laptop shut.

"What in the hell is wrong with people!" I yelled out to nobody, or perhaps the F.B.I agent listening to the bug in my apartment. I wasn't ever going to meet Susan Goldfish.

The walls were caving in on me, and the last thing I wanted to hear was anything about Trump. I needed fresh air, so I put on my shoes and headed out for a walk. I wanted a beer too, but I was trying to fight the urge.

After nine pm, winter was hanging around like a bad cough, so my hoodie wasn't enough. I put up the hood and headed east away from the noise on Bardstown Road. I wandered back towards the neighborhoods of the Highlands.

The street my apartment was on was dark and full of parked cars marking the sidewalk. As I got towards the middle of the block, lights flashed on, and it startled me.

"Fuck," I shouted as I flopped my arms at the car. I had forgotten I was under surveillance.

The agents following me didn't know what to expect, but I wasn't a fan of them either. I shoved my hands into the pocket on the front of my hoodie and kept moving. The car pulled out to follow me, and I turned around to look at it, and it was an unmarked Ford. I shook my head hard so they would know I wasn't happy being followed.

Then it hit me like a missed hammer; I should talk to these knuckleheads following me. I would tell them that I wanted to confess everything to Bobby Three Sticks, and I had nothing to hide; I would spill the beans and tell everything I knew.

I slowed my roll, turned back to get their attention, and the car stopped. I walked towards it, cutting between two parked cars to get into the street when the driver's side door opened, and I stopped dead in my tracks.

A fat, unhealthy-looking white dude stepped out, and he was anything but an alphabet boy. He was over 50 wore painter's clothes, white pants, a shirt, and an ugly white beard.

"You Bush? Are you Gunner Bush?" He yelled at me.

He knew who I was, and I almost darted away right then. My instincts told me to do so, but I didn't listen.

"I am the one and only, Gunner A. Bush," I responded, but I regretted telling him my name a split second after I did.

His car wasn't nice either, it was a Ford, but it was a

beater. He wasn't a cop, but he knew my name.

"Uh, never mind," I yelled at him, and I turned around to walk away, but he wasn't done, so I stopped and turned towards him.

He reached back into his car and came out holding what appeared to be a baseball bat.

"Hey man, never mind, I don't want any trouble," I said as I checked my khaki pockets to feel for my knife. It wasn't in my pocket and likely at the bottom of the Ohio River.

I stepped back a few paces, but he was now approaching me.

"I said never mind, dude, what is your problem," I said, but I was trying to process how he knew my name.

As he got even closer, he put the bat up. He was wild, and so was his swing, so I threw my left arm up to guard my brain. He was grunting, and the bat didn't hit my head thanks to my arm.

"Donald Trump sends his regards," he yelled after the bat smashed my arm.

The wooden Louisville Slugger cracked me just above my left elbow, but he was aiming for my skull.

I grabbed the bat with my right hand and held onto it.

"Jesus Chrysler, motherfucker, holy shit, what the fuck," I screamed.
My arm stung like hell.

We both began to jerk back and forth with the bat, but his old man's strength was substantial. I was desperate, though, so he wasn't going to get the bat back quickly.

His face was right inside mine now, and he reeked of

liquor. His teeth were yellow, and his beard was dirty. His eyes were insanely wide open; he was rabid. The noises coming out of him were the sounds of a pig fighting for his life at the slaughterhouse; I didn't stand a chance with this crazed maniac in a wrestling match.

Gripping the bat with his left, he swung at my face with his right, and he landed a hard blow to the top of my forehead. I swung back.

We both exchanged pleasantries for a few seconds, and it is hard to accurately describe who was landing what since it was all happening rapidly. I had to break free, or he would kill me.

I pushed my knee into his groin, aiming for the onions because it was life or death. He fell backward, and I fell onto the hood of a parked car, and I rolled off of it, bounced to my feet, and began to run like a bat out of hell.

"Motherfucker," he grunted.

I turned back, and he began to chase me.

The concrete was damp; I could hear his footsteps. He was a lot faster than he looked, but he was rabid. And I was out of shape. I ran like my life depended on it because it did. I tripped over a bump in the pavement, but I remained on my feet. He was gaining on me.

I hit the corner to the first street hard, going left so I could glance back at him. The streetlight hit his face perfectly, and I could see he was foaming at the mouth. He was gaining on me too.

Instant regret of not hitting the gym hit me, and it hit me right in my mid-section. It was a cramp after running one football field. I put my head down and found another gear as I hung a left into an alley. I grabbed a trashcan in hopes of slowing him down, but grabbing it and tossing it down slowed me down.

(Movie scene chases are never accurate; I was learning the hard way, though)

My lungs were on fire, and I couldn't catch a breath. My feet hurt, and my knees were about to give out. The only thing that kept me going was I could hear him panting harder than me. His breathing was loud, but he was only about a foot away from me now.

I faked a right and broke left. He went for my fake, and I gained a few feet on him. His eyes were still wide open, so he was either rabid or on meth.

I was making a circle back to my place, and it was sprint or die time.

I went into full stride as I turned back onto my street. I would have to go all out and not look back if I was going to lose him. I went for it, and as I felt myself pulling away from him, I heard a whooshing sound. Then I was stung in the back by his bat.

He had thrown it at me and nailed me. Somehow, this old hillbilly had a Tom Brady arm. There was a thud sound, and I was knocked off balance, headfirst into a parked car. I was on the ground before I realized what had happened. He couldn't make that throw again if his life depended on it.

My wrist cracked as I broke my fall, and I felt it break. My nose managed to break my fall into the car, and my knees scraped across the concrete. I didn't feel a thing thanks to adrenaline rushing through my veins, and I bounced up, ready to go.

The bat rolled on the street near me, so I pounced on it. I picked it up and turned to face him. I had his bat now, and my confidence increased in this fight.

"Looks like the cards have changed hands; let's fucking go!"

I banged the bat onto the street to let him know I was ready. I wasn't prepared, though; my lungs were depleted, my body was broken, and my heart was pounding.

Choking up on the bat, I smashed it to the ground again so he would know I was ready to hit him.

He stopped running, and he was walking towards me slowly like Michael Meyers, and as the streetlight hit his face, I could see his ugly teeth as he smiled. His face looked like Charles Mansion. He laughed, reached into his pocket, pulled out a butterfly knife, and flipped it open like street fighting was his side hustler.

His eyes were dark with red around the pupils, and he was blood-hungry like a villain from a cheap horror movie.

"Let's fucking go then," He said, and he was still grinning at me.

"Come on," I snapped, and I said it louder and more demanding, trying to sound tough and as if I was a street brawler myself. I wasn't, but I didn't want to appear weak.

I pulled the bat back and danced forward towards him one step.

He danced towards his left, my right, and I prepared to hit him in his left knee. He wouldn't be able to block it like I did his attack with the bat.

He was holding a knife, though, so if we got tied up again, he could have stabbed me. His laughing continued, and fear ran through my whole body. He was maniacal, a drug-infused and deranged psychopath who couldn't be killed with a baseball bat. It would take multiple bullets to put this lunatic down. My only chance was to outrun him, and that chance was very slim.

I ran hard, but he was right with me. He was a hound on a fox, and I was running out of options.

He got closer, and all I could replay in my head as I ran was him screaming, "Donald Trump sends his regards!"

I couldn't figure out what I did to piss off this man or Donald Trump. Shit, maybe he was sent by Trump, and if he was, this old dirty-looking hobo could be a part of whatever the real-life Jason Bourne program is, and if so, I was a goner. He was as fast as lightning with the throwing accuracy of Johnny Unitas.

I did the same circle, down my street, left, then down the alley, and then left back onto my street, and he stayed with me the whole time. Instead of turning for another loop, I ran back towards my apartment.

His car was still in the middle of the street with the lights on. I sprinted past it, and the driver's side door was open. I heard it slam shut two seconds later, so I turned to see if he was in his car. He wasn't; he slammed his door shut and was still after me.

"Jesus, this guy *is* Michael Meyers," I said, and I turned to run again.

I held the bat tightly, and I ran right past a car with two federal agents inside it. They were sitting in an unmarked, black Chevy, twiddling their dicks and eating donuts, and they had missed the whole ordeal.

I tried to stop, but I couldn't with the wet concrete, so I fell right in front of their car. I made eye contact with the guy in the driver's seat as I went down. Blood was gushing down my face from my nose and mouth, my arm was broken, and I held a baseball bat, but this man casually rolled down the window.

"You aight there, bub?"

I was panting so hard I couldn't even respond. He obviously didn't understand the severity of the situation, and he couldn't figure it out. He wasn't Sherlock Holmes.

"Off -, I, sir, I can't breathe, help me. There is a lunatic chasing me with a knife, and he attacked me with a ball bat."

He stepped out of his car with zero urgency.

I pointed the bat down the street and said, "A crazed madman with a bat, he attacked me, he has a knife, please, help me, and go arrest him!"

His partner stepped out of the car now, too; his face and fingers still smothered in glaze.

Shock began to kick into my body.

"What is going on here?" He asked me.

"I think I broke my arm in two places!" I grunted as I fell over to put my hands on my knees. The madman had stopped his pursuit dead in his tracks when he saw the law dogs.

"You broke your arm in two places? How about you don't go to those two places any more than if you broke your arm," He said, and then he pointed at his partner and began to cackle.

His partner turned towards me and said, "You're the only crazed man I see with a bat!"

I pointed again and said, "That asshole attacked me with this bat, then he threw it at me."

They turned to see the lunatic walking away.

The pain in my left arm was crippling, and I moved to the sidewalk. I fell onto the grass just before it.

"Excuse me, sir," I heard one of them say to the man.

"Hey, come here, hey, hold it, hey you, freeze."

The man was sprinting away. His endurance was insane. I was dead.

The agent was faster, and he caught him just as he reached his car. They began to wrestle, and the crazed man would have won if it wasn't for the other agent arriving to provide a taser to this man's neck.

As they walked back towards me, I could hear the man yelling, "Gunner Bush is a traitor to our country, and Donald Trump wants him dead!"

I was suffering from vertigo, and I couldn't see him. They kept him away from me, and he was in handcuffs.

"What in the hell is all that about?"

"I don't know, I don't know," I replied, but I was hurting.

"We better get you an ambulance," The agent said, and he turned to his partner and yelled, "this kid needs an ambulance!"

"No, no ambulance, I don't have that type of money," I said back as loudly as I could.

An ambulance showed up, and so did the local boys. This time Welchie wasn't with them, but they all knew who I was.

The paramedic checked me out and guaranteed my arm was broken, and I didn't take a ride to the hospital with him, though.

An F.B.I agent made his way back towards me, and he filled me in on what they knew about the guy.

"That guy was saying some pretty off-the-wall shit; he said Trump told him to kidnap you, kill you, and then feed you to a hog farm out in Bumble-Fuck-Egypt."

"I just want to talk to Bobby Three Sticks, so this can all be over, please. Can you set that up for me?" I replied.

I didn't need a federal agent to tell me that the dude who had just attacked me was batshit crazy.

"Your arm looks pretty bad there, kid; you going to go to the hospital?" He asked me.

"No, look, can I please just talk to you guys about the case? I can tell you everything."

Another agent approached; he was taller and wearing a long overcoat. He had heard what I said, and he asked me, "you just want to talk to us, but what about your attorney? He says you won't ever talk with us."

"He is fired; I don't have an attorney. Can I please just tell Bobby Three Sticks or whoever?"

"He is pretty banged up, sir," the paramedic informed them both.

"I am fine, I am fine. Please, how about tomorrow? Can you give me a number, and tomorrow I will call you? I just want this to all be over!" I was pleading.

The man reached into his overcoat and pulled out his card. He handed it to me and said, "Call me tomorrow, kid, and we can talk!"

The local boys came over and got my story about the attack, and I had to decline to go to the hospital twenty-four times.

"I would be better off getting a stretch limo for the week for the price of one ride in an ambulance to the hospital," I informed them on the 25th question.

I told them exactly what happened, and the lunatic was on his way to county.

"We did find a rope and a shotgun in his trunk," one of the local boys informed me.

Another one added, "It looks like he was serious about taking you to feed his hogs."

And another one told me, "He said the Q-codes all told him that Trump wanted you dead."

Yikes. I was in big trouble, and the only way I felt I could get out of it was by working with the F.B.I directly.

The local boys didn't even need my side of the story because he had told them exactly how it went down and that he was going to kill me. The man needed a straightjacket.

One of the local boys offered to take me to the hospital free of charge since I was adamant I wouldn't ride in an ambulance. I declined at first, but I had to go. I took him up on the offer and learned even more about the lunatic on my way to the hospital.

"I guess that dude was from Hardin County and drove here after getting a signal to kill you from some web forums. He said you were working with the Russians and Oprah to take down Trump."

"With Oprah?" I asked, but my pain was unbearable.

"That is what he was saying, and that you were a pedophile," he said as he turned into the parking lot of the hospital.

"I am a chester? He attacked me for no reason!" I exclaimed.

"That is what he was saying. You should probably get a restraining order on that guy; he really wants to feed you to his hogs."

"Yeah, well, he is in jail now," I replied.

"He will get out soon."

"Well, maybe don't let him out. How about that?"

"There isn't anything I can do about that," he told me, and he pulled up in front of the ER.

I got out of his cruiser and made my way into the ER.

Four hours later, my mom drove me home with a cast on my arm and the worst headache of my life. My arm was broken, my head was concussed, and my life was dangling by a thread. I was lucky to be alive and not in a cadaver drawer.

CHAPTER 39

"The Truth Shall Set Me Free"

The cast wrapped around my left arm was annoying to sleep with, and my whole body was sore from my big toe to the top of my head. I needed something stronger than aspirin. And to top it all off, I had to use my laptop to call my mom for a ride.

My old man answered, and he didn't ask me about his ten thousand bucks, but I could hear it in his voice. He put my mom on the phone without much fanfare and agreed to come to pick me up and take me to the bank.

My mom had already freaked out about what happened at the hospital, but she did it again when she arrived.

"You look bad, Gunner, your face is blue, and you just look like a train hit you."

I didn't want her to tell me how bad I looked; I could feel it.

My mom brought a pizza over, and I devoured it.

She drove me to the bank, and I returned the money to pay my old man back. He tried not to take the money, so I told him to hang on to it until my court date. If I showed up, he would get the bond back, and I was going to show up. I didn't want him to lose the house. Kayla was there, and she was surprised I had the money.

My mom said she had a new attorney, or at least one to call, but I wasn't dealing with attorneys at all anymore.

My mom also said, "Maybe you should stay here since this Quack has your address; what do you think?"

I was likely getting evicted, and the last thing I wanted to do was stay at their house. I declined.

Kayla drove me to buy a new phone, and then she took me back to my place.

"I am not going to come up because your apartment stinks, and last time I couldn't get the smell off of me," she informed me.

"I am moving out anyway, so at my next place, you can come up for tea," I told her.

"You're moving out because you are getting evicted," she replied.

"I haven't got evicted yet, but I am for sure moving out," I said, and I got out of her van.

"Thanks for the ride," I told her, and I limped to the elevator like a 180-year-old man.

There was another note on my door, and I didn't open it, tossed it on the floor, and went for some ibuprofen. My knees hurt, my back was sore, my arm was in a cast, and my head was pounding. I needed a drink as bad as I needed oxygen, but I fought it off.

My laptop had seven missed calls, and they were all from attorneys—three from Mr. Barnes and four from Mrs. Goldfish. I didn't respond to either one; they were both ridiculously radicalized, and I wasn't going to respond to either of them ever again.

I did call Sawyer once my phone was hooked up, and I informed him I would try to stop boozing. And I told him I was sorry. He said he understood, and he had been in my shoes. He also offered to help. He would find a meeting near my house, and he said he would drive over and attend with me.

The devil's friend named boredom kicked in, and it came with the temptation to drink God's nectar. I fought it off and searched through my phone, and I needed something to do that didn't involve alcohol. I was scraping the bottom and finding out what rock bottom is.

Rock bottom wasn't getting arrested for conspiracy in the Presidential election; it wasn't getting raided and crushed by the LPD; it wasn't having those same cops search and destroy my apartment. It wasn't driving my El Camino into the Ohio River, and it wasn't getting attacked by a cuckoo nutjob.

Rock bottom was not having a soul to call to do anything with unless it was to drink and party. Besides my family, I didn't have one contact to call. I had Sawyer, but none of the people I thought were my friends.

That's when I started to think about Morgan again. I had royally screwed up with her, and I wanted to reach out to her and let her know how sorry I was. I wondered if I still had a chance with her. Even if it were a long-shot chance, I would take the longest odds.

I would give Morgan a call, and if it was meant to be, it would be, and if not, then okay, well, at least I tried.

I rifled through my old emails and found her number. I called her, but the number was disconnected. I did a quick google search, and I found her on Linkedin and the Zuckerbook. She had a new last name, but it was hyphenated. Dammit, she was married!

I picked up the card the agent had given me the night before, and I picked up my phone and dialed the number.

"Hello," a voice said.

"Hello, yes, uh, this is Gunner Bush, and I spoke to you last night about just telling you guys everything. I have fired my attorney, or I am going to fire him, but that doesn't matter; I am ready to talk with you guys and tell you guys everything."

"When can you get over here?"

"I don't have a car until it gets fished out of the Ohio, but I can maybe take a cab or an Uber."

"We will send someone to get you. Are you at your home right now?"

"Yeah."

"We have a car there now; I will tell those guys to bring you over here."

I hung up and walked back down the stairs struggling with each step. I made my way to the unmarked car, and the guy inside rolled down the window.

"Get in," he said, so I did.

"I am ready for this to be all over," I told him as he pulled away from my apartment.

Bobby Three Sticks wasn't at the building, and he likely wasn't even within 800 miles. I wasn't as important as I thought I was, which is, I guess, the moral of my book. The Feds on Sycamore Street were ready to let me speak freely despite his absence.

They were elated that Mr. Barnes wasn't with me. I was ushered into a conference room, and I met two men and one woman. We exchanged pleasantries, and I sat down on a wooden chair placed in front of the table they would be sitting behind. They had a camera aimed at me, and they all had notebooks in front of them.

I signed a form stating I didn't want Mr. Barnes in the room, and then I told them everything from start to finish. The whole kit and caboodle.

The female agent was the only one taking notes, and she was trying to follow my timeline. The male agents would write something down every once in a while. The taller man had his arms crossed for about half of the time, and I sensed he didn't believe me. The other guy was a little more receptive, and he was inquiring more, but not as much as the female.

They were hard to read, but I was telling them the truth.

I'd seen all the evidence against me, and I was under the assumption that Mr. Barnes was wrong. They didn't already have everything. They had some of the pieces, but they couldn't complete the puzzle. The details were hidden in plain sight, but they still assumed I was lying about certain things.

There had been a massive operation to sweep all the information, but they missed significant parts. It wasn't for lack of trying; they had surveillance, phone taps, emails, and they'd even triangulated my locations from my cell phone, yet they were still missing vital information. Most of it was because they didn't understand technology.

The biggest problem that I could see was that they had phone taps, but they didn't have access to phone apps. It was like they didn't understand how phone apps could decrypt information. They didn't understand the decrypting technology of phone apps, and to my surprise, they weren't even looking into how to get the messages from these apps. It was astonishing considering how many people were using this app or something similar.

I gave them this whole book orally. It took close to three hours. They asked me a ton of questions, but many of them were about the technology of phone apps that I knew nothing about. Phone taps aren't any good if the criminals getting tapped are using apps that aren't tapped. It turned into an Abbott and Costello skit for a bit.

"I only spoke with Terry on WhatsApp."

"On which app?"

"WhatsApp."

"Yeah, that is what we are asking you, on what app?"

"On my phone, the app is called WhatsApp."

"Who is on first? What is on second?"

And these were the best and brightest that the bureau had in the Blew Grass State. It was like they were still using Commodores and the Pony Express, which was absurd.

All the messages between Terry and myself were gone, destroyed into the ether. Terry gave me that account, she had the login, and she could have destroyed them herself. They weren't buying that one, though, and I should have changed the password.

Despite this setback, I still tried to give them a blueprint. I wanted them to have an exact road map on how everything went down. If I could fill in all the missing pieces, guide them through every event, maybe they could see I wasn't as guilty as they thought.

I told them everything. I told them about the deliveries I made up the Hill and how at one point even I thought I was delivering money, but Terry showed me the advertising forms. I told her how I would provide intel with reports every Friday to Terry. I believed I was submitting articles that might be published, but it was really an excellent description of America and Americans for Terry to send back to Russia.

I told them how I had access to each camp and used it to my advantage. I also told them about the counterfeit money, and it wasn't in any of the evidence I had seen.

The biggest hiccup was the money I had won betting on Trump. The entire bureau had assumed it was a payment that Terry paid me. They thought I couldn't put the money directly into the bank and had to use safety deposit boxes because it was dirty money. They had the videos of me setting up the boxes, but they didn't have the record of me winning the money betting on Trump.

The casino where I had won the money was out of business. It was transferred names and went through a lot before it went under, so it was hard to prove. They put some people on it and said if it was true, it might clear me. It was a Windex and napkin that could clear my whole case.

After three long hours of drawing this map, they still didn't have it. They were slowly piecing it together, but I had nothing left to give them.

"Do you guys want me to come back for another session?" I asked once we had agreed I had given enough.

"We will be in touch," the female agent said.

And that was it. The ankle bracelet was removed, and I left without another appointment. I walked away with mixed emotions, and still to this day, I glance over my shoulder in fear I am about to be arrested.

I never heard from the F.B.I again.

CHAPTER 40

"That's all, Folks"

As time went by, I didn't know if not hearing from the Bureau was a good thing or a bad one. I always had a feeling I was being watched, and I had nightmares of having my door kicked down again. I would wake up drenched in a cold sweat. I never stopped looking over my shoulder. I was living in a paranoia exile.

They never knocked, never kicked down my door, never called, and I never heard one word from them again. They must have realized I was telling the truth; who knows, maybe I taught them a few things about apps.

The Bureau still hasn't come calling, but I still had my issue with Clark County. The law dogs in Clark County weren't interested in my story; all they wanted was my money. I had to pay fines for court fees, jail fees, arrest fees, and who knows what else.

I hired a low-key attorney, which cost me a boatload of money. I was sentenced to community service, I had to pay more fines, but if I stayed out of trouble, my record would be expunged in a year.

Sawyer and I rekindled our relationship. He got me into meetings, and he really helped me. He wasn't the only catalyst, and neither were the meetings. I used placebos to trick my body into thinking I didn't need booze, and it was water I craved. I drank so much, gallons a day, that I didn't have any room for liquor. I still drink ten glasses of water a day. It helps, but so do the meetings.

Since I didn't have a court date for the federal charges, the Mansion was released back to me. I don't know how it was mine to begin with, but that's what the legal documents stated. And I wanted to follow the law to the letter.

The Russians had managed to steal my identity, and as they tried to cover their tracks, they put the house into my name. They owned the house and paid it off, but they also left the country without a trace. I can speculate that they were planning on living in the house for another four years until another Presidential election, but the water got too hot, and they had to get out of dodge. Either way, the mansion was mine.

After finishing the community service work, I packed up my newly bought El Camino, and I headed east. I moved back into the mansion with plans to fix it up and sell it. It wasn't in great shape after two years of no occupants. A few rodents had moved in, living rent-free; the yard was a jungle, and the house still had an odd odor. Despite these obstacles, fixing it up would give me something to focus on instead of booze.

I also got back into political writing, and I once again built up my net worth on the Hill. I figured I could cover the 2020 Presidential election, and I made a new connection with a Chinese man named San Holo Fisk. He has relationships with a magazine that rhymes with LIME. He is offering me freelance work, which pays even better than my fake gig with Rolling Stone.

Mr. Fisk said he might be able to get me a budget to get me back on the road too. I do miss covering the campaigns, and I am crossing my fingers.

Finding Mr. Fisk wasn't even the most significant break for me once I got back to the District. I ran into Morgan, and she quickly informed me that she was recently divorced, and I took that as single and ready to mingle. She is also back living in the District, and she is possibly going to work for a political campaign with Kanye West. The Yeezus rapper from Chicago might run for president in 2020.

When I told Morgan I was sober, she gave me a big hug, and then she gave me her new phone number. She looked better than ever, and she also said she had a gigantic scoop on Kanye. So maybe, just maybe, a guy like me can get a third chance with a beautiful lady like Morgan. It is too early to tell, but who would have thunk that, right?

And that's pretty much the gist of it.

ABOUT THE AUTHOR

Gunner Bush

Gunner A. Bush was born in his father's truck as his mother's water broke two months early. Gunner was born prematurely, ahead of his time. Gunner grew up in the Highlands area of Louisville, Kentucky.

Gunner's lifelong dream was to be a writer. While his classmates idolized athletes, Gunner's heroes were writers like Hunter S. Thompson, Kurt Vonnegut Jr., and Gary Webb.

Gunner went to community college in Louisville and later transferred to Indiana University, where he worked towards his B.A. in journalism.

Gunner covered the 2016 Presidential election for Rolling Stone and his memoirs, Suicide to Notes to Kurt Cobain. The three-part book is now available and released posthumously.

Gunner worked in the White House covering the transfer of power in January 2021, and he wrote daily online for a covert blog that went viral as people wanted to hear his daily takes on what was happening.

Sadly, Gunner passed away in November 2021.

BOOKS BY THIS AUTHOR

Albert Gum And The Coup D'état To Save Humanity

As climate change wreaks havoc and the water wars end, North America shatters into several new countries in the near-distant future. The eastern coast is a nuclear waste with some rebuilding; the south has reformed around high waters flooding into Georgia: the west is wild, but the old states of Indiana and Michigan areas are running successfully and known as THOD's district.

These areas function with order and are controlled by the self-proclaimed god, THOD. THOD, along with seven senators, including the most beautiful woman in the history of the world, Wren Carter, use propaganda to control the citizens.

Education isn't allowed, and every man, woman, and child must be working. If the hoi polloi is working, they cannot try to overthrow those at the top. Keep the masses dumb and working, feed them propaganda like candy, and keep them fed and entertained when they aren't working.

This bread and circuses routine by THOD and company has worked for over 20 years. The citizens are happy working under the ruse that they are in a socialist society and 'own the means to their production."

Every worker in the district is a millionaire and is trained to be grateful for their work even though money isn't real and most of the jobs are to occupy time only. The dystopian society is called utopian, and the working class believes what they are told.

THOD and his senators live in downtown Indianapolis in the former Circle Center Mall. It is the tallest building left in North America after the water wars, is guarded heavily by military drones and bots, and the seven story building is known as the mall castle.

Albert Gum is a man who doesn't fit into the usual brain-washed crowd. He doesn't love working seven days a week, 50 weeks a year. He doesn't like getting up each morning to work in his pit, and he believes humans should get more than two weeks off in a year. It is dangerous thinking, but his thinking isn't the only danger.

Albert Gum wins a vacation from Wren Carter, but while on his journey to Chicagoland, Albert runs into the father of Beck Lang, outcast senator, and military man, Ryder Lang, and the adventure begins.

Made in the USA
Las Vegas, NV
22 December 2022